A Done With novel

Done
With

WENDY
LINDSTROM

NEW YORK TIMES BESTSELLING AUTHOR

OLIVERHEBERBOOKS

Chapter One

F our blocks from home, I navigated the RV around the same traffic circle three times. I had no idea where to go. Around I went, in the traffic circle ... in my head ... until I felt dizzy with doubt and second thoughts. But I could not stay in this damn traffic circle or continue living the same circular, oppressive life that was killing me. I *had* to go.

I cranked the wheel so hard the RV, affectionately called Big Bart by my twin daughters, rocked like it had been broadsided by a bus as we lumbered onto the busy four-lane out of town. It took five minutes and breaking the speed limit to hit the interstate. I headed north because I would have rolled the RV had I swerved onto the switchback for the southbound ramp. So, north it was.

For twelve miles, I drove with my fingers clamped around the wheel like a parrot on a perch. As I passed the first off-ramp, my stomach did a sickening flip. I was walking away from everything that constituted my life, but I couldn't wait any longer because time doesn't wait for anyone. It marches on wearing steel-toed boots that kick the shit out of your dreams.

For twenty years, my desire for independence has grown wild and untamed in my mind like weeds growing in the rain of my tears. Throughout my marriage, my dreams have shot up like grass only to be trampled beneath the heels of my husband's polished shoes—and my own self-doubt and indecisiveness.

My husband, Dan, calls me Can't-decide-Kate, Come-along-Kate, Caboose-Katie.

I want to change my name to Fuck-you-Francine and take charge of this train wreck I call my life. I know I can't do that from the back of the train, or if I let everyone else's needs and decisions derail me, or if I stop and wait at every crossing. But that's what I've been doing for twenty-three years. I've been waiting while my husband built his church from a couple dozen congregants to several thousand, and for our daughters to grow up and head off to college, and now ... I was done with waiting.

And yet, the reality of what I was doing, and the resulting ramifications with Dan and our daughters, was too overwhelming to consider, especially while trying to keep Big Bart on the road.

No thinking.

Just drive!

Renewing my resolve, I slammed the door shut on my thoughts.

Eyes focused on the road ahead, I drove in a fog, not allowing myself to think of anything other than keeping Bart between the painted lines on the pavement. Another hour passed with me mentally slamming doors on every thought that urged me to turn back. How long before Dan would notice the silent house and the lack of noise coming from the kitchen where I should be cooking his supper?

I glanced at the fuel gauge. Dan had topped off the tank three days ago when we returned home from his cousin's wedding. The girls had flown to Charlotte from Missouri where they were attending college, and we'd picked them up at the airport so they could travel with us to Charleston, where the wedding had taken place. We stayed at an RV park near the ocean where the girls and their cousins walked the beach and worked on their tans. Dan officiated the wedding, talked to his board members, and played golf with his cousins. I stayed at the RV park and waited.

2

Stupid. Pathetic. Depressing.

A shrill ring from inside my purse startled me. I was wound so tight I nearly drove Bart off the pavement. The rumble strips on the side of the road shook Bart's frame and rattled the dishes in the cupboard. Correcting my trajectory, which was taking me toward a ditch the size of Kansas, I pulled Bart back onto the blacktop and blew out a shaky breath. The phone rang. And rang.

I let it go to voicemail without checking to see who was calling. I didn't want to know. I couldn't bear to talk with my daughters. I would *not* talk with Dan. Not after what he'd done. But the phone continued to ring until I shut it off without checking messages.

Let Dan think I got raptured. He would believe that before he'd believe I actually left him.

Only when the gas gauge dropped to a quarter tank did I allow myself to pull into a truck stop for gas. I swiped the debit card for our joint account and filled Bart's bottomless tank to the top. Needing to stretch my legs and find coffee, I went inside the truck stop. I loaded up on chocolate, water, and a thermos full of coffee—special of the day, lucky me. The urge to hurry back home followed me down every aisle. What was I doing? What the *hell* was I doing?

To distract myself, I spun a carousel of magazines while I waited for the clerk to fill the thermos with coffee. There were teen publications with provocative pictures on the cover and articles on sex and romantic relationships, none of which I presently desired. Books filled with gardening and decorating ideas reminded me of the beautiful house I was leaving behind. Hot cars on covers for the mechanic-minded reader, and a semi load of magazines for truck drivers, dominated the selection. Way down at the bottom of the rack *Scientific American* and *National Geographic* stood side-by-side as if defending themselves against the overflow of nonsense above. I bought them both as a small act of defiance. I believed in science, damn it, and I refused to deny reality any longer.

Bart and I continued north, neither of us certain where we would end up. Evening sunshine faded to twilight and then to headlights cutting through a moonless night. It wasn't until dawn, when we crossed the New York State line, that I finally understood. I was going home, back to Dunwith Falls—back to the wreckage and destruction I'd left behind over two decades ago.

I USED TO BE BRAVE. At nineteen years old, I thought I was going to change the world. I'd destroyed my world instead.

At least that's what my family thought. Going back home after that hadn't been an option. Now, it was the only option because it was Grandma Jean's home that had drawn me northward for nine hundred tense miles filled with doubts and second thoughts.

The tall stone pylons on either side of the driveway still stood like sentinels guarding access to the property. My grandfather had intended to hang a gate there but never had. The house number, painted on the metal mailbox by my younger sister and me, was faded and barely legible now, but the box itself was still in reasonably good shape.

As I navigated Big Bart onto the rutted dirt driveway, I got my first look at everything I'd left behind. Grandma Jean and her two-story farmhouse had been my sanctuary. My grandmother had been dead, four years now, but her property was mine according to her will. The will had been mailed to me in a standard white envelope along with a note from Grandma Jean that simply stated, *"It's time to come home, Kate."*

I hadn't gone back. She'd been adamantly opposed to anyone having a memorial service for her, insisting she'd be happily reunited with my late grandfather. How that was supposed to work, I had no idea, and I'd never asked. I'd simply arranged her cremation over the phone and had the crematorium send her ashes to me. When I'd received them, Dan locked her ashes in his safe— for safekeeping, he'd said—and told me to sell her property.

Ashamed of myself for how deeply I'd failed my family, I'd half-heartedly agreed. But despite a couple of decent offers, I hadn't been able to let it go. Grandma Jean and my grandfather, Papa Ray, who'd predeceased her by ten years, had spent their lives there. Their house had been filled with love, ice-cream, chips, and cats. In childhood, I was allergic to one of those things and addicted to the others.

Their land of fields, forests, and streams—a haven for wildlife and one wild girl—had been cared for with gentle hands. My refusal to sell it was the only time during our entire marriage that I'd not submitted to Dan's wishes. I'd daydreamed about bringing my girls here, but coming back, even for a vacation, would have subjected my family to my sister's rage and my father's brokenness —and my girls would have learned I was the cause of both.

Rotating my stiff ankles, I sat in Grandma Jean's driveway hesitant to kill Bart's engine, as if turning the key would be the final act of leaving my current life behind. But my butt was numb, and I was wasting gas.

Without the noise of Bart's idling engine, I could hear my blood pulsing in my ears and the splatter of raindrops hitting the windshield. In the gray morning light, Grandma Jean's house, with its boarded-up windows and broken porch floorboards and hanging shutters, looked as desolate as I felt. Maybe we were both just tired and not at our best this morning. Maybe with some rest and restoration we could both become whole again.

Rolling my neck, I tried to unlock my spine that was compressed by nine hundred miles of bouncing along interstates. When I could stand upright without moaning, I stepped out of the RV.

Icy rain blasted my face like shrapnel. "Holy mother of *gawd!*"
I bolted back inside for a coat.

All I had in the RV was a sweatshirt I'd taken to South Carolina and my daughter's windbreaker. I'd forgotten how cold New York weather was in early spring. It dawned on me that it was

April 1st ... April Fool's Day. Would Dan think my leaving was a joke? Was I being a fool? Was the joke on me?

The temperature, when I dared to step outside again, couldn't have been higher than mid-forties. The coat and sweatshirt helped, but my jean shorts and my mowing shoes, a grass-stained pair of old sneakers I'd bought before Jesus was born, were little protection against the gray chill. Gooseflesh lifted the hair on my unshaved legs like quills on a porcupine.

As I made my way toward Grandma Jean's house, I tried to recall what clothes I'd taken with me to South Carolina that might still be stashed inside. The knowledge that my wardrobe was sparse, that I had very little cash in my purse and no food in the fridge was as chilling as the cold air circling my bare legs.

I should have thought this through—or at least shaved my legs before I left home.

No thinking. No second guessing. No turning back.

That's when I saw the "Condemned" sign tacked to the door.

Condemned? As in officially unfit for use? The house couldn't possibly be that bad. Maybe they'd only condemned it because it had been vacant and the utilities had been turned off for four years.

Striding across the porch, I avoided the gaping holes and loose floorboards. I pulled open the screen door, ready to see for myself just what sort of damage had caused some nameless inspector to condemn my sanctuary. The screen door crashed to the floor, ripping the knob from my hand and landing with a clatter. Dumbfounded, I looked at the door then at the rotted frame where the hinges had pulled free.

I flipped through the keys on my keyring: one large key with a saw blade edge that opened the church office, a chunky, black fob for my Escalade, a sleek silver key for the back door to our house, and one plain gold key I'd meant to use years ago. I slid it into the keyhole, hoping my sister hadn't changed the locks.

The solid oak door to the house swung open without issue. Years ago, I used to step through that door into a kitchen filled with warmth and light and the smell of coffee and fresh baked bread.

Now, the house with its boarded windows and lack of heat was a cold, dark cave hiding things I didn't want to discover.

I pulled my cellphone from the back pocket of my shorts. Using the flashlight app, I panned a slow circle around the empty kitchen. The table where I'd shared so many meals with my grandparents was gone. The long-outdated appliances still hunkered along one wall, looking anemic and scared in the negligible light. A bank of wall cabinets hung open, all of them empty. My sister Sophie had apparently been here to take what she felt was rightfully her half of our grandparents' assets despite their will that clearly stated everything had been left to me.

The break between Sophie and my grandparents was my fault. I owed Sophie more than a few household items.

As I inspected a plain white porcelain mug left in the sink, I recalled how my grandmother would sit at the table drinking coffee, her gray tiger cat, Georgie, I think, curled up on her lap. How many mornings had Grandma Jean sat here alone in her final years with her hands wrapped around the warmth of her cup, perhaps the only warmth she had? What had gone through her mind during those moments of reflection? What unrealized dreams had she mourned? How many one-way conversations had she had with her late husband?

Had she thought about me, too? Had she wondered if I'd ever come back and try to fix what I'd broken? If I'd missed her?

I had. Desperately. Deeply.

She and Papa Ray visited me and my family when the girls were young. Then Papa Ray died. After that, Grandma Jean wrote letters in place of her visits. I was a busy wife and mother of two five-year-old girls with little time for corresponding. I called Grandma Jean when I could, which wasn't often, I'm ashamed to admit. I'd come back briefly when Papa Ray died fourteen years ago now. But I'd left immediately after his memorial service. My sister had made it scathingly clear that I wasn't welcome here. So, I stayed away. And when Grandma Jean had died ... when that call had come from her lawyer telling me she was gone, I regretted all those missed opportunities to connect with the one person in my life who'd loved me despite my mistakes.

I set the cup back in the sink and followed my flashlight beam into the living room. The only furniture that remained was Papa Ray's recliner and the floral sofa that had been shoved against one wall. My sister had obviously gone through the house and taken what she'd wanted. Small gusts of wind and a spattering of rain blew in through a broken windowpane and soaked the sill. It appeared one of the wooden slats covering the window had fallen off or been pried off. The window glass, except for the bottom corner, was intact, but the small opening likely explained the musty smell in the house. How had this place fallen into such disrepair? Grandma Jean had never let on that she couldn't take care of the house, but she was eighty-four years old when she died. She'd lived here alone. Of course she hadn't been able to manage all of this.

Heartbroken over the state of the house and disgusted with myself, I walked into the hallway and angled my light into the downstairs bathroom. Two eyes stared back at me, then a black streak shot past my legs.

I shrieked and slammed my back against the opposite wall.

Cat! It was only a cat.

The flood of relief made me dizzy and encouraged me to come back with a real flashlight and my camping lanterns—and maybe a broom to shoo away unwelcome critters.

Despite the freezing rain, I was glad to be back outside in the fresh air again. I felt road-weary and in need of a hot shower and eight hours of sleep. Things always looked better when one was rested. Tomorrow would be soon enough to check out the rest of the house and property.

Besides, I was hungry.

I considered what bags of chips and boxes of crackers and cereal might remain in the RV cupboards. I wanted to believe it was intuition that had made me leave our leftovers stashed in the cupboards as if I'd known I'd need them, but the truth was I'd just been avoiding a job I despised.

As I headed toward Big Bart, my empty stomach eagerly anticipating breakfast, I slammed to a dead stop.

The cat was sitting on the retractable steps and blocking the RV door.

"Shoo!" I flapped my hand at the ball of fur crouched in front of the door. "Scat!"

The cat didn't move. Didn't blink. Just stared at me with curious green eyes.

Shivering, I clutched my jacket around me. "G-go!" I flapped my hand again. "Scoot."

Twitching its tail as if agitated by my lack of hospitality, it continued to watch me.

Had I not been freezing, I might have backed down and waited for it to move along. But I'm not a nice person when I'm cold or hungry—and I was both. I lowered my head and stalked directly toward the feline standing between me and my breakfast.

The cat leapt off the step, its tail raised like a flag as it shot behind a cluster of leafless magnolia bushes that were just beginning to bud.

From his matted fur and a glimpse beneath his raised tail, it was clear he was a male, and either a long-lost stray or a feral cat. I could see him watching me from behind the bare limbs. A patch of white fur covered his nose and mouth and formed a vee down his neck, making him look as if he were wearing a white shirt under a black tuxedo. His paws were white too. There was a small divot out of his left ear, probably the result of a fight. Was he cold and hungry too?

The last thing I needed was another mouth to feed, but I couldn't ignore the cat any more than I could ignore my growling stomach. Inside, I rooted through the cupboards and found a can of tuna fish. I put half of it in a bowl and took it outside. The cat was still hiding in the bushes. I propped my freezing hands on my hips and sighed. "You aren't part of my plan, you know."

Nothing. Not even a twitch to indicate he heard me.

I set the bowl on the driveway, then went back inside and opened a bag of chips. I thought about eating the other half of the tuna, but I didn't have any bread so I put the can in the refrigerator. After finishing the chips, I ate half a sleeve of mint chocolate Girl Scout cookies and gulped down a cup of instant coffee I heated in the microwave.

Curious, I peeked out the window in the door and saw the cat gobbling the tuna fish. I dropped my forehead against the window-pane with an exhausted sigh. I probably shouldn't have encouraged him to stick around. I didn't even know how long I'd be here. Too fatigued to think, I grabbed my daughter's sleeping bag and dropped onto the sofa. I just needed a couple hours of sleep, and then I'd figure out what I was doing.

Seven hours later I woke to the sound of rain pummeling the RV and a baby crying outside. My mothering instinct sat me straight up on the sofa, heart hammering. My ears had been keenly honed over nineteen years of listening for my girls, and I knew I was hearing a call of distress now. Tossing back the covers, I stumbled to the door and swung it open. Freezing rain swept inside and soaked me head to toe. Gasping, I fumbled to pull the door closed, but the cry cut through the storm. Squinting to see through the pouring rain, I spotted a drenched black blob of fur hunkering down in the magnolia bushes.

The cat was back. And he was soaked. And apparently hungry.

It was clear he knew he'd found an easy mark the minute he'd set eyes on me.

I sighed in defeat. "Come on then," I said, waving him over. He didn't budge, but I knew he would as soon as he smelled his dinner. I closed the door, poured the rest of the tuna fish in a bowl, and then took it outside and tucked the bowl as far under the RV as I could reach. "There's your dinner," I said, standing up, soaked to the skin, my hands and knees now caked with mud. "Tomorrow, you need to find yourself another home, mister." With that, I went inside and looked out the window. After crouching watchfully for a few seconds, the cat bolted across the driveway and disappeared under the RV.

How sad that a cat who was only hanging around for food made me feel less alone.

After cleaning myself up, I ate my supper of dry cereal and a box of cheese crackers, then made a grocery list. Tomorrow, I'd navigate Big Bart into town and fill the cupboards and refrigerator with real food, top off the gas tank, and buy a pair of jeans and a heavier coat.

And a bag of cat food.

I HADN'T PLANNED to listen to my voicemail messages, but I did. I'm a mom. Moms don't have the luxury of tuning out the world because they're having a life crisis. I needed to know my girls were okay, so I listened to the twelve messages Dan had left. Apparently, he hadn't mentioned my disappearance to the girls yet or they would have left a dozen messages of their own.

Dan thought I'd taken Big Bart to the car wash, then thought I'd taken Haley's motorcycle to the shop for repairs to get the brakes adjusted. Then he admitted he had no idea where I'd gone and told me to call him. Then he left several voicemails, each one growing more agitated until finally the last two were genuinely concerned.

I deleted all of them, turned off the phone, and climbed back into bed.

I slept like the dead ...

And then the sound of a baby crying woke me.

Morning light filled the RV. I sat on the edge of the bunk while my groggy brain processed my surroundings, and I slowly realized where I was. I needed coffee, and lots of it.

The cry came again from outside.

I slogged to the door and peered out the window. The little scamp was sitting near the bottom of the steps singing the song of his people. He meowed until I tapped on the window. "Cool it, Sinatra."

He stared at the door. Waiting. Waiting. Waiting.

Meooooow!

I scrounged up a can of shredded chicken which I'd planned to mix with salad dressing and eat for lunch, but it appeared it was now going to be Sinatra's breakfast.

When I opened the door, he shot across the driveway and watched from the safety of the bushes.

"If you're going to wake me up and demand food the least you can do is stop acting like I'm going to kick you."

He stared without blinking. Waiting for his breakfast. Waiting for me to leave.

"Waiting sucks, doesn't it?" All I received in reply was a narrowing of his eyes. Apparently, he wasn't a morning person either.

It was nearly an hour later, after I'd showered, topped off the cat's food dish and moved it away from Big Bart, before I headed for town—a place I dreaded going. Would people remember me, the outspoken, righteous girl who'd broken two families and left a trail of destruction in her path? Would my ball cap be enough of a disguise to allow me to slip in and out of town without being discovered?

The thought of running into my sister or our father nearly made me turn back, and I would have done so if not for the cat. I could exist on chips and cookies and coffee for another few days, but I couldn't feed that junk to Sinatra.

Taking care of others must be hardwired in some people. I'm one of them. I am risking Armageddon for a cat—a *cat*.

After attending my grandfather's funeral, I'd vowed to never return to Dunwith Falls, and I hadn't, not even when my beloved grandmother died ten years later, but here I was heading to town for a cat.

It's not that I haven't thought about returning. Every holiday, every birthday that my sister and father have had without my acknowledgement haunts me. All the apologies I've constructed in my head that never made it to paper or were never expressed in a phone call still circled my brain like vultures after prey.

If only one could go back for a do-over ...

The sudden lurch of Big Bart's front left tire dropping into a pothole, shook the frame, rattled the dishes, and scared the bejesus out of me. I'd nearly missed my turn.

At the corner where the roads intersected sat the home of Chloe Saunders, once my best friend, now a recent widow. Although I've been reading the newspaper here online for years, life in Dunwith Falls has passed me by.

Chloe's two-story home and the large, metal-roofed barn out back had received a fresh coat of paint at some point in the last few years. Fruit trees and heavy equipment populated the fields where crops of corn used to grow. Chloe and I had played in those fields as young girls, and after graduating high school, we both went off to separate colleges. I completed one year, then married Dan, and raised two beautiful girls to adulthood — but I'd lost myself.

I wondered how many other women woke up one day and questioned how they'd gotten to this point in their life, when they began to ponder their decisions and unravel how those choices had led them into living someone else's life.

As I drove by the house, a woman standing by her mailbox lifted her hand and waved. I recognized Chloe's oval face. She was a black-haired, brown-eyed, bronze-skinned beauty, but today she looked ... broken. I slouched down and turned my face away from the window, ashamed and not wanting to be recognized. Of course she was broken. She'd just lost her husband a few months ago—and I hadn't attended the funeral. Or sent a card. Or acknowledged in any way an event that had rocked Chloe's world.

Instead, I'd prayed for her.

I should have been there.

As someone who'd spent decades on her knees praying for myself, my family, and others, I knew praying was often a cop-out, a ruse to avoid actually having to *do* something. That thought felt harsh, but after experiencing religion, Dan's brand anyhow, from the inside, and witnessing what really happened behind the public facade, it was impossible to ignore that his church was a *for-profit* business and that praying was no more powerful than wishing.

The church coffers had always been under Dan's lock and key. Neither I, nor the congregants, nor his god, had access to that money. For years I'd worked nearly full time at our church, and never collected a paycheck. Dan gave me a debit card for our joint bank account to use for groceries and such. I had never worried about establishing my own accounts or getting my own credit cards because Dan, or rather his church, had paid for everything. But now it worried me. Because when it finally dawned on Dan that I'd left him, and that my absence would reflect poorly on him and his position at church, he would try to destroy me.

As I navigated Big Bart the last mile to town, I tried to focus on the passing landscape, rather than my rising panic. I spotted a herd of deer grazing at the far edge of a field where it met vast woodlands that climbed high into the surrounding mountains. As a girl, I'd crossed that field and walked deer paths through the woods so often I'd known them as well as the wildlife that lived there. During my years living in the city, I'd longed for these wide-open spaces where a person could breathe. I knew I needed to be here. But with only four dollars in my purse, I had no idea how I'd manage to make a life here.

If only I'd better prepared before leaving everything behind. I could have at least filled the fridge and packed more clothing. And I would have taken all the Girl Scout cookies. The best I could do now was get what I could before Dan locked me out. Because he would. I knew it as surely as I knew I would never go back.

Chapter Two

I'd made it through the grocery store without being recognized, or at least without being approached. My debit card still worked. Big Bart's fridge and cupboards were filled with groceries and cat food. But I'd forgotten to buy batteries.

I considered popping into the hardware store to purchase flashlight batteries, but my father owned the hardware store. As I walked past the big bay windows displaying rakes, shovels, pruning shears, and other hand-tools for spring gardening, I ducked my head. The last thing I needed was for him to know I was back in town.

The Maple Leaf Café was in the next block and had been one of my favorite places to eat. I was starving, but I continued another two blocks to the bank. The clock was ticking down fast, and I needed to get cash while I still had access to our account. My hands shook as I slipped my debit card into the ATM. Biting my lip, I punched in my pin number, hoping Dan hadn't cut me off during my walk from the grocery store where the card had worked. To my immense relief, the ATM dispensed the daily maximum amount of cash from our joint account. Cash in hand, I headed to the consignment shop in the next block. Every dollar I had needed to be maximized. It wouldn't take Dan long to empty the account and leave me without funds.

The Red Fox Boutique was in an old Victorian house that had been converted into a quaint consignment shop. The downstairs rooms consisted of women's clothing, shoes, bags, and jewelry artfully displayed on metal racks, wooden tables, and bewigged mannequins wearing stylish hats, scarves, and sunglasses. The upstairs rooms were filled with bric-a-brac, kitchen items, small furniture, and household décor, all so invitingly displayed I wanted to move in. Whoever owned the shop had the eye of an interior decorator and the soul of an artist.

While wandering through the bric-a-brac room I spotted a blue pet bed with a thick cushion and high padded sides. I thought of Sinatra sleeping on the cold floor of my grandparents' dilapidated house or on the cold ground under the RV. Neither place was safe for him to hang out, and neither provided warmth. I added the bed to my other items and headed downstairs to cash out.

It turned out that the Red Fox Boutique was owned by Maggie McKensie, my former classmate and another one-time best friend. Maggie, Chloe, and I had gone through high school together. When we'd graduated, Chloe and I had both headed off to different colleges. I met Dan at college and married him at the end of my freshman year. Chloe had returned to Dunwith Falls at the same time and married her high school crush. From what I'd heard from Grandma Jean before she died, Chloe helped her husband run a tree trimming and landscaping business. Maggie had remained single and was now running what appeared to be a successful consignment shop.

Maggie's red hair was swept back in a ponytail, exposing high cheekbones, full lips, and green cat eyes. As she approached the counter, her eyes widened, and she brought her palms to her face. "As I live and breathe! Is that really you, Kate?"

I wanted to crawl under the nearest clothing rack and disappear. Maggie was stunning. She still had the body of a teenager and looked thirty years old. I was dressed in my daughter's clothes and ratty sneakers, and I looked, or at least felt, twice her age.

"I can't wait to tell Chloe you're back!" she said, rounding the counter to give me a hug. "How long are you in town?"

I released a nervous laugh and forced myself not to bolt for the door. I wasn't ready to announce my return, especially to the friends I'd left behind. I'd been an utter shithead to them, and shame burned hot on my cheeks. "I'm not sure," I said lamely.

"Well, you'd better stay long enough for a girl-gab with me and Chloe. We've got a lot to catch up on." Tilting her head, she eyed me from head to toe. "You haven't aged a bit. The only thing that changed about you is your eyes. There's a mystery in them I'm dying to uncover."

I tried to laugh off her intuitive observation, but it sounded more like a sob. "Is this where I pay for my stuff?" I asked, nodding toward the counter.

"Yes, but you can't cash out yet. Stay right there," she said, then shot off into the adjoining room. I heard the scrape of hangers across metal bars, then a whoop from Maggie. A second later she swooped back into the room and held a dress up in front of me. "This little gem has been waiting two months for you. And it will look spectacular with those boots."

I eyed the cotton sundress with its fitted bodice, spaghetti straps, and slightly flared skirt, thinking the style was too young and too revealing for me. But the combination of muted gray vines and sky-blue flowers against a cream background was too pretty to resist. "It's gorgeous," I said, trying to sneak a peek at the price tag.

"It is, and it's perfect for you," she said, pivoting on her heel, dress in hand. "I'll put this in the fitting room, and you can try it on when you try on your shirts and jeans."

I hadn't planned to try on anything, but being around Maggie was like getting caught in a hard current. Best not to fight it. I spent the next ten minutes trying on my used clothing, wondering what Dan would think of me buying second- or third-hand clothing, and then reminding myself that his opinion no longer mattered.

The dress was a perfect fit. It was soft and pretty and sassy. I loved it, but a dress was not on my necessity shopping list. And the consignment shop didn't accept debit cards. I considered putting the dress back, but buying it was as much an act of liberation as it was vanity. Maggie insisted the dress was a gift from her, but I couldn't accept her kindness when I was already writhing with guilt.

Two pairs of jeans, one sweatshirt, two T-shirts, a pair of sneakers, a jean jacket, two long-sleeve shirts, one sundress, a cat bed, and one pair of gently used cowboy boots later, my wallet was one hundred twenty-seven dollars and thirty-two cents lighter. That left me with three hundred seventy-six dollars and sixty-eight cents to live on if Dan locked me out before I could take another withdrawal. How long it would last was the question that created another swirl of panic in my gut.

Maggie handed me a large shopping bag filled with my new wardrobe. "I called Chloe while you were in the fitting room. She'd love to see you. We can get together at her house Saturday night if you're available."

My stomach plummeted. I wished I could roll back time and undo my inconsiderate silence and share all those special moments the two of them must have shared without me: Chloe's wedding, the birth of her son, holidays, birthdays, and parties, heartaches, and funerals, gossiping and girl-gab dates. But I'd knowingly missed it all. I'd broken our number one rule: never ever turn your back on your besties. "Maggie, I'm really not sure—"

"Please." Maggie slipped her hand over my forearm. "Chloe's been lost since her husband died. It would do her good to have some friends over."

Friends ... I hardly qualified as a friend anymore. "I heard about Josh," I said, my heart aching for Chloe. "It's just ... heartbreaking."

"It is. She really loved him."

I knew she had. They were a forever couple.

"You can't say no, Kate." Maggie fluttered her dark lashes at me and gave me a shoulder-roll, her embellished girlie gesture from our old days making me smile. "Seven o'clock Saturday evening at Chloe's house. Same place she lived when you left town."

Another wave of heat blasted my face. "What should I bring?"

Maggie grinned. "The story behind the mystery in your eyes. I want to know everything."

Clutching the shopping bag in front of me as if to shield myself from her probing questions, I forced a laugh. "Nothing to tell. I've just been living an ordinary life."

"Nope!" She threw up a manicured hand to stop my denial. We used to do that in high school when one of us was trying to bullshit the others. "Your leaving sent shockwaves through this town that can still be felt. And whatever brought you back has surely caused the same tremors in whatever part of the world you just left. Get ready to dish, Kate. Inquiring minds want the dirt."

Her prodding was playful, and she was smiling the whole time she pressed me, but I knew she and Chloe were going to ask questions and expect answers. I had two options: cancel a reunion with old friends I'd really like to reconnect with or figure out how to turn the conversation back to them. Because I couldn't bear to talk about my failings or the families I'd broken—or the one I was about to tear apart.

"Here's my phone number," Maggie said, scribbling her number on the back of her business card. "And here's something for your cat to play with." She gave me a long red string that appeared to have come from a hooded sweatshirt.

I opened my mouth to tell her I didn't have a cat but gave up in defeat. After giving her my phone number, I hugged her goodbye and headed back to the sanctuary of my RV.

Once back in Big Bart, I drove the lumbering RV to the gas station at the end of the street and negotiated my way to a pump. Using my debit card, which thankfully still worked, I filled the tank until it wouldn't take another drop. Then Big Bart and I headed back to my grandparents' property and one homeless cat, both of which were now presumably mine.

Sinatra loved his cat food. He crunched his dry kibbles and licked his mouth after eating a full can of food. He couldn't have cared less about his bed. He was suspicious of the red string and gave it a wide berth when I wiggled it. I tossed it onto the grass beside him, then stood, my knees aching from squatting to play with the little scamp. "Since you're done eating and not interested in playing, I have work to do."

Despite the cold day, I took my time walking my grandparents' forty-four-acre property while Sinatra stalked me from behind, ducking out of sight each time I glanced back. At one point, he scooted off to drink from a small stream that cut across the western edge of the property and fed our private lake. The grassy banks and loamy shore of the stream brought back memories of my sister and me playing there. When we couldn't go to the lake, Sophie and I would hang out at the creek, digging up crayfish, splashing through the rock-strewn shallows, and wading in the deeper water holes to cool off on hot summer days. I could still see in my mind's eye my little sister scuttling down the creek bank on her butt, gangly legs and knobby knees leading the way, her blonde hair tied back in a thick braid that fell to her waist, her laughter echoing down the creek.

Turning away from the bittersweet memory, I fought my way through an overgrown path that cut through the woods and led to the three-acre lake where my family had spent the majority of our time during the summer. Sophie and I had played there as girls, but as I'd moved into my teen years, Sophie, who was four years younger, was left behind. Chloe, Maggie, and I spent our days sunbathing on the shore as self-obsessed teenagers, and I'd lost my virginity there one summer night to Maggie's older brother Ashe McKensie.

The boathouse where the incident had occurred still stood straight and tall. My grandfather had built the big gambrel-roofed building to house his workshop and store his canoes and the tools needed to maintain the grassy beach along the shoreline as well as the trail leading from the lake out to the main road where my grandparents' home sat. Thick weeds and briars had overtaken the beach area, which had once been a ninety-foot span of mowed grass. Lake grass and pussy willows now surrounded the fifteen-foot wooden dock we used to dive off.

Dried weeds the height of my shoulders clung to the outer walls of the boathouse, blocking a good portion of the windows and wide double doors that faced the lake. I pulled aside a handful of brush and cobwebs, and scrubbed a corner of the window clean so I could see inside. Two large overhead beams spanned the width of the building, one of them wrapped with a chain that supported a block and tackle. Shovels and rakes leaned against a wheelbarrow that sat beside two wooden canoes. Three partially deflated inner tubes sat atop a workbench. Small hand tools hung on a pegboard behind the bench where an old desk lamp sat. Memories of my grandfather working there, dressed in a button-up shirt and jeans that were a size too big for him, flooded in. Looking in at all he'd left behind and remembering everything he'd done for us, I'd never felt his absence more keenly than I did now.

Turning away, I stood for a long time drinking in the beauty of the lake, the mountain peaks reflecting on its surface, dried reeds standing sentinel along the shore, and the occasional splash of fish rippling the surface. Some of the reeds would have to be cleared out to keep them from consuming the lake. The amount of work needed to bring the property back to its former beauty seemed insurmountable, and yet I felt a spark of excitement at the thought of doing so. In my mind's eye I could envision the property as it had once been, gently groomed and naturally beautiful—a place where family and friends gathered for the simple joy of being together.

The mating call of wood frogs began in earnest, their clacking sounds coming from small pools of water created by thawed snow and spring rains. The frogs would mate and leave their eggs to hatch in those small pools. Birdsong filled the shadowed forests around me, and the rest of the world seemed far away. I didn't know what I was doing with my life, but I knew whatever it was, it had to be done here.

Chapter Three

I'd been working all morning, trying to hack a wider path along the trail that led from my grandparents' driveway out through the woods to the lake, when Dan pulled in. It took me a moment to recognize him in the rental car. His arrival startled me, but it didn't surprise me. I'd expected him to come. I just hadn't thought it would be so soon. He'd obviously tracked the charges I'd made to our account and followed my trail of debits right to my door.

He stepped out of the car, looking perfectly groomed in his crisp white shirt and pressed jeans, which made me think he'd flown in last night and rented a hotel room near the airport.

"What are you doing here?" he asked as he approached me.

I cautioned myself not to react. I was tired and hungry—a perfect recipe for making bad decisions. "I'm clearing the path to the lake."

He frowned. "If you're ready to put the property on the market again, we can hire someone to clean up here."

"I'm not putting it on the market, Dan. I'm going to live here."

He released a derisive snort. "We are never going to live here, Kate. Why didn't you answer my calls?"

"Because I didn't want to."

He smiled then, the same charming smile he'd used for years, to seduce me, to pacify me, to sway me, to convince his congregation, but now I could see it was simply a movement of his mouth and had no emotion behind it. "What did I do this time?" he asked, his voice dripping with condescension.

Every relationship suffers stress fractures over time. I'd believed those tiny lines that marred a relationship gave it character, like the crackle surface on aging ceramic pottery. I hadn't realized that some of those fractures would run deep, that they would eventually undermine the integrity of the structure, that one small vibration could splinter the entire thing. But Dan's constant condescension and rigid beliefs had brought our whole marriage crashing down in a mess of shattered memories and mistakes.

We were broken. Irreparably. And Dan was a lost cause.

"Why did you just take off?" he asked, reaching for my hand.

I stepped away. "You told me to shred my book."

"Oh, good grief, Kate! Stop with the drama. I told you to stop working on that story fifteen years ago."

"Yes, you did, although for the life of me, I can't understand your reasoning."

"It's blasphemous."

"It's a fantasy story!" I laughed at how absurd he was being. "It's make-believe. Like your sermons."

A hard scowl drew his eyebrows down. "Your book is steeped in dark magic. Can you imagine what our congregants would think of it? You have a commitment to them, to our church, and to our girls. You know why I can't support you writing those kinds of stories."

"My book is based on *science*, Dan. Quantum physics to be exact. And for the record, I can't support that disgusting vitriol you've been spewing in your racist, bigoted sermons the last few months."

He reared back as if I'd slapped him. "Vitriol? I'm trying to protect our way of life."

"By shitting all over everyone else's rights?" My heart clanged in my chest so hard I felt lightheaded. In our circle, wives did not talk to their husbands this way.

His mouth snapped shut so hard his teeth clicked. He slipped the fingers of one hand into his cropped brown hair and inhaled slowly as if trying to calm himself. "I don't know what's going on with you, Kate, but it's not your place to question me or my sermons. If you want to write stories, then write something that uplifts rather than undermines the kingdom of God."

"What I write or how I live is no longer your concern. I won't be going back."

With a slow, measured exhale, he surveyed the overgrown property and dilapidated house. "What's really going on with you? This can't just be about your story or book or whatever you call it. I'm honestly at a loss here."

I'd been trying for years to talk to Dan, to express in the most loving way that I couldn't breathe, that I wanted a home in the country where I could live closer to nature, that I wanted to write instead of work as his personal assistant, that I needed love rather than a new car or a bigger house, that I cared more about what we thought of each other than what others thought of us. He never got it. And I'd been kidding myself to think he ever would. Dan was charismatic and persuasive, and he could always lead me right back to the same stall I'd been kicking in for years. He'd get me so turned around, I'd lie down contentedly and wonder what all my fuss had been about. I would convince myself over and over again that I was happy in my stall with my family and my blessed life.

Well, I wasn't having that one-sided conversation again. And I damn sure wasn't going back to that old stall. The sooner he left the less chance he had of persuading me to go back with him. It was senseless talking to him about my reasons for leaving because he wouldn't hear a word I said, and if by some miracle he did, he would twist and spin my words until I was at the center of the problem. It was beyond his ability to see himself as anything but the good guy.

Frustration and impatience, two expressions I'd seen on a daily basis, took up residence on his face. "I've given you everything a woman could want, and yet you want to live in this dump. Why? At least tell me that!"

If there was one thing he could have said to strengthen my resolve it was to condemn the one place in the world where I'd been free, where I'd been loved. "Because I can't live in *your make-believe* world, Dan. I'm bored and exhausted and ... empty."

"You have the kind of life many women would dream of hav—"

My burst of laughter cut him off. I couldn't even begin to explain the complex reasons why I, and many other women, end up in this place of exhaustion and emptiness. "I want a divorce."

If I'd have slapped him across his handsome face, I couldn't have shocked him more. For a moment, he stared at me as if really seeing me for the first time in years. He took a step forward and reached for me, but I moved away. I couldn't let him touch me or hold me and cajole me as he had whenever I'd veered toward something that wasn't part of his plan.

"That's not going to happen," he said with finality. "You're coming home, and we can talk this over."

I gripped the rake in my hand and prepared for battle. "I'm done talking. Our marriage has been over for years, and you know it. I'm done pretending."

Hunching his shoulders against the chilled air, he pushed his hands deep into his trouser pockets and stared at me with beseeching eyes. For some perverse reason, I enjoyed knowing he was physically uncomfortable. My hard work had kept me plenty warm in the cold spring air, but Dan in all his groomed perfection was definitely affected by the cold. "Kate, I've had to focus on providing for you and our girls, and also my mother. You know she's not well. That doesn't leave much time for romance."

"This isn't about romance, Dan. I'm truly sorry your mother's ill." And I was sorry because Dan really loved his mother. He was a good son ... and a good provider, but a terrible husband.

"Then stop this nonsense, Kate. Think about the example your leaving will set for our girls and our congregants."

If he had just said our girls, I might have considered trying to explain why our marriage had fallen apart. But to realize he was as concerned about the people who filled the collection baskets as he was with the impact on our daughters' lives disgusted me. And made me angry. "Maybe our girls and your congregants will see that a woman can choose her own path. That she has a right to nourish her spirit and create a life where she is free to explore her own creativity and passion. That it's okay to walk away from something that is toxic and is slowly killing her."

"You don't mean that." He gazed at me with his puppy dog look. "Come home and we'll work all this out. I promise—"

I raised my hand to stop him. "No, Dan. You've never once kept a promise to me."

He opened his mouth, then snapped it shut because he knew he couldn't debate that truth. His expression turned shrewd, and I knew the negotiations were about to begin. "You have a moral commitment to uphold the values of our church. You pledged to support our mission and serve as an example to our congregants. How am I supposed to stand before them as an example of love and fidelity if my own wife wants a divorce?"

I laughed so I wouldn't cry. His lack of love for me had never been clearer than in that moment. "As usual, your first and only concern is for your business?"

"It's a church, Kate, not a business."

"It's a business, Dan, and I'm beyond caring about your business or how my actions might reflect on you. You're not a man of god. You're an actor. A theater major. A performer who has built his own stage and writes his own script. I get it, Dan. That's a dream job for any actor. And what better place to perform than in front of a captive audience that is shamed, browbeaten, or brainwashed into attending and tithing whether they want to or not. It's the perfect gig. You don't have to share the stage with anyone. The band, the light show, the spectacle is all to support your lead role. Well, I know what goes on backstage, and I don't give a damn if my leaving brings the whole place down on your head. All I care about is getting our girls through what is going to be a difficult transition for them. This is going to hurt them, but it'll teach them something important about life. Do what you must because I'm not going back."

Fury blazed in his eyes, and for a moment I saw him strutting before his congregation, voice booming with righteous indignation, his gestures prepared ahead of time for maximum impact as he whipped his followers into a frenzy. *Jesus is in the house! Be good followers and show your faith with your dollars.* And he would be the first to drop a crisp one-hundred-dollar bill into the collection basket, encouraging or shaming the congregants to follow his lead with their own generous contribution. I was indoctrinated enough to know that's exactly where he planned to go now. But I refused to sit for another one of his ranting performances meant to shame me into returning home.

"Save it, Dan. Whatever you're planning to say to convince me, sway me, or bulldoze me, forget it. I'm done with ... all of it." I exhaled and tossed the rake aside. "I'll come home for my things after I'm settled here."

His lips twisted and his eyes narrowed. "You're not taking a thing, Kate. Everything you have was purchased with my money."

"I worked for your *business* and never received a paycheck. I took care of our home and our girls and *you.* I've earned the things I've gotten."

"It's your *job* to take care of our kids." Glaring at me, he pulled out his phone and punched in a number. A couple seconds later he requested that the rental car company pick up his rented vehicle at my address.

"What are you doing?" I asked, knowing there was no way in hell I'd let him stay here with me.

"I'm driving the RV back home."

"What? You can't do that!"

"Watch me," he said, his voice like ice. "You've got fifteen minutes to clear out your things before I drive away."

The title, like everything we owned, was in Dan's name. He

could take it all, and it appeared that's exactly what he intended to do. "Where am I supposed to live?" I asked, gesturing to the dilapidated house a few yards away.

"I really don't care," he said. "Fourteen minutes before I leave."

Stunned, I stood in a half-panic until the irony of the situation sank in and made me laugh. "You are a self-centered, self-righteous ass, you know that, Dan? All right then," I said, heading toward Big Bart, "I'll clear out so you can take the RV."

"Thirteen minutes," he shouted to my back as I stepped inside.

I opened the ramp door at the back of the RV, then began hauling out what little I had. In an act of defiance, I grabbed everything, including the insurance and registration cards, from the glove box and stuffed them in my purse along with my phone charger. I hoped Dan got pulled over on his way home. I hooked my purse, backpack style, over my shoulders, popped my sunglasses on top of my head, and stuffed my snacks and other small items into my pockets.

I emptied cupboards and drawers into trash bags, then lugged everything out to the driveway. I went back and stripped the bed, then used the bedding to protect the dishes I'd taken from the kitchen cupboard. I filled a laundry basket with towels and my bathroom items, piling my nightgown and a pair of flip-flops on top.

"Seven minutes," I heard him call from outside.

On my way out, I smiled at my ass-of-a-husband, unwilling to give him the satisfaction of seeing me worry. The cooler we'd used at the beach in South Carolina was still in the RV, so I emptied the contents of the fridge into it, knowing I would need to save everything possible if I were going to survive. The top wouldn't close, but I lugged it outside. I'd have to worry about it later.

Arms akimbo, Dan looked on like an abusive boss as he shivered and glared at me. "Four minutes."

Hurrying back inside, I slipped my journal into my leather briefcase then gathered up the last armful of clothes and shoes. I piled Sinatra's bed on top and lugged it all outside where I added it to the mountainous pile.

Rushing back inside, I unplugged Gussie's battery charger, tucked it beneath one arm and pushed her outside with the other.

Dan laughed when he saw me. "You brought the lawn mower? Good grief, Kate, you really have lost your mind."

I'm not sure what had made me load the mower in the RV before I left, but I refused to let Dan take it. "Maybe, but I dare you to try taking her with you."

He gave a sweeping flourish with his arm. "By all means, consider it a housewarming present."

I trembled from the desire to slap the smirk off his face. Instead, I rushed back inside.

"One minute, Kate! Fifty-nine seconds! Fifty-eight ..."

While he stood outside counting like an ass, I unlashed my daughter's motorcycle from the rack. When we'd gone to the wedding in South Carolina, we'd taken Haley's Honda Rebel with us as she'd requested, and it was still strapped to the rack in the back of the RV.

"Fifteen seconds!" Dan called from outside.

Knowing this was going to cause a battle, I pulled on my daughter's helmet, then pointed the motorcycle toward the ramp.

"Six seconds! Five seconds!"

I turned the key and hit the ignition.

"Two sec—what are you doing?" Dan leaned around the back of the RV just as I rolled down the ramp.

I had taken the motorcycle safety course with my daughter, and I had gotten my license, but I'd never ridden after that. I'd just wanted to make sure Haley received a good introduction to riding safely. Now I wish I'd spent some time honing my skills because it was immediately evident I had next to none. The bike shot across the driveway and off into the rutted yard, nearly unseating me.

"Kate! This is not going to happen."

I glanced behind me to see Dan storming after me. I released the clutch too quickly and stalled the bike. He was closing in fast.

Squeezing the clutch lever, I hit the ignition, and the engine kicked on. Dan was nearly upon me, but I eased out the clutch. As I pulled away, legs sticking out like struts to help keep me upright in the rutted yard, I made a wide turn that took me several yards from him. Dan stood in the yard, slashing his hand through the air, calling me a lunatic, and insisting he was taking the bike with him.

"You want it back?" I shouted over the hum of the engine. "Come and get it."

He lowered his head and stalked in like a bull.

I gunned the engine a couple of times, but he kept coming.

"Not funny, Kate. I'm done with your nonsense."

"And I'm done with you!" As he marched in, I eased out the clutch, cranked the throttle, and headed straight at him.

At the last second, he leapt out of the way. "You crazy bitch!"

I nearly fell off the bike. I hadn't heard Dan swear since our college days. I felt a bit insane and nearly giddy with laughter as I raced by. Maybe I *was* crazy. If he hadn't moved, I'd have rammed the front wheel right between his legs. Wobbling my way into another wide turn, I came around to face him again. "Still want the bike?"

He threw up his hands and stalked away shaking his head.

Just then, a car pulled into the driveway and parked behind his rental car. A guy got out of the passenger side with a clipboard in hand. After Dan signed whatever was on the clipboard, the guy got into Dan's rented car. Then the two cars backed out and took off as if the drivers had felt the air crackling with fire and brimstone.

After casting a scathing look at me, Dan disappeared inside the RV, closed the ramp door, and cranked Big Bart to life. For a moment, I thought he would drive over the pile of my belongings in the driveway, wiping out the last of my worldly possessions. But he backed onto the road, then lowered the window and flipped me the bird.

His unsavory gesture spoke to his present level of anger. I'd always been in awe of his ability to control himself, especially when my head was constantly filled with irreverent thoughts.

During services when he would drone on and on, I'd wanted to shout that it was all bullshit and tell him to shut the hell up. When he'd lied each week to the decent people who hung on his every word, I'd wanted to stand up and tell them he was just an actor selling snake oil.

But I didn't return his vulgar gesture. Instead, I raised my fist in the air like a zealot and shouted, "I rebuke you!"

His eyes flashed with rage so hot they were flaming embers. For a moment, I thought he'd spontaneously combust or get out and throttle me for making a mockery of words he believed held power.

But apparently, he thought better of messing with a crazy woman on a motorcycle because he revved the engine and drove away. Big Bart's tires kicked up dust on the dirt road as I watched the last of my old life disappear.

Chapter Four

The first thing I took out to the boathouse was my daughter's motorcycle. I wanted it as far from the road as possible in the event Dan circled back to get it. But getting the bike through the dried weeds and underbrush on the trail to the lake nearly killed me. I dumped the bike three times.

Sinatra watched from a distance as I struggled.

Lifting nearly four hundred pounds of metal wasn't easy, especially when the bike was three times my weight. But I credit stubborn determination more than physical strength for getting the bike to the boathouse. After catching my breath, I pulled the wheelbarrow outside. It wasn't one of the new lightweight plastic ones. It was an old metal kind, heavy as hell, and with a partially deflated tire.

I'd barely pushed the beastly thing onto the congested path before I heaved it off to the side. It took so much effort just to push it, I knew I wouldn't be able to move it at all if I loaded it up with my possessions. There it sat while I stood rubbing my sore back.

"You could help, you know," I said to Sinatra who was several yards away grooming himself in a patch of sunshine.

I pulled my phone out of my back pocket and checked the battery. It was at half charge. I had no place to plug it in. Probably wouldn't matter anyhow. Dan would cut that off too. I wondered if I should call my daughters while I still could, but I didn't want to drag them into this mess until I sorted out my life. I knew Dan would keep this under wraps as long as he could.

Since I had my lawn mower, Gussie—I can't resist naming my lawn mowers—and I tried to clear a bit of the path.

From the beginning of my marriage, I'd mowed our yard because it was the only time I wasn't required to be on call for my family. I claimed those hours as mine—and Rusty's, our old beater lawn mower at the time.

Summer after summer, I would push Rusty across our two-acre lot while the two of us strained and huffed and talked about the strange events that make up a life—and how easily one's life could get hijacked and redirected down a path of discontentment. Rusty kept me company while Dan was working two jobs to keep us fed and build his church. Rusty patiently tolerated my waddling along behind him during my pregnancy. He helped me write my first short story for a continuing ed class at our community college. He listened to me whine about how hard it was to write a book. Like a father, he taught me how to do a good job and to not quit when the mowing, or the writing, got excruciatingly hard. On good days, I would sing songs off-key while Rusty bounced over ruts, the bones of his rust-eaten deck creaking, his motor clanging like a bad drummer trying to play along. On days when my heart ached, he would just walk with me. I spent more time with Rusty during his last summer than I did with my husband.

My final evening with Rusty was etched in my memory like the dates on my mother's tombstone. Sweltering July heat had saturated my tank top with sweat and made my head itch under my Buffalo Bills ball cap. Rusty and I were deep in conversation about the opening scene of my book when we hit the edge of the drainpipe in the ditch. The sound of metal striking metal shot through the neighborhood, echoing off concrete foundations and making my ears ring. The impact knocked us backward as if we'd hit a power line.

I popped Rusty up on two wheels as the sputtering blat of his motor went silent. A dark puddle of motor oil streamed from beneath his crooked deck. His blade shaft had snapped as fatally as a broken neck. I inhaled the sickening smell of burnt oil and knew this was my last moment with Rusty.

He was gone.

Heartbroken, I sat in the grass and cried because I'd lost my best friend—and because it was pathetic that my best friend was a lawn mower.

That should have been a red flag about my marriage, but at the time I couldn't imagine needing anything in my life but my husband and babies. Now, all I wanted was out.

Although Gussie and I tried for several minutes to make a dent in the lake path, the weeds were so high and thick, and the path peppered with so many saplings and scraggly bushes, that the mower kept stalling out. After admitting defeat, I dragged and half-carried Gussie back to the boathouse.

It took three hours of backbreaking, arm-wrenching work to haul the rest of my possessions out to the boathouse. I was filthy, hot, and hungry. All I wanted to do was eat a bag of chips, drink a cold beer, and sleep until tomorrow. But Sinatra was waiting to be fed. And I needed a bath.

I rooted through the meager pile of my belongings until I found Sinatra's bowls and his food. I filled one with kibbles and the other with wet food. "You can drink out of the lake or the creek," I told him, placing the bowls several feet from the boathouse.

While he ate, I inspected the outside shower at the back of the building, then the outhouse forty yards away near the edge of the woods. Both were in bad shape. At least the latrine had a door that provided privacy I probably didn't need out here but definitely wanted. There was no toilet paper, but there were two old phone books stacked beside the single seat. They were massive things that had to have been put there by my grandfather before the internet made the Yellow Pages obsolete. There was also a bucket of lime in the corner, which had hardened into a solid lump. We used to sprinkle the white powder in the latrine hole after we used it to reduce unpleasant odors in the outhouse. The place hadn't been used in years, so it was odor-free now. But I would definitely make use of the lime if I could crush it up enough to use it. I tore a couple of pages out of the phone book, folded them, then slipped them into the back pocket of my jeans.

After gathering an armload of twigs and sticks, I dumped them in a pile on the beach. Kneeling, I crumpled the pages I'd ripped from the phone book, then layered them on kindling and small sticks. Once finished, I searched the boathouse for matches. I found an old flip top lighter in a coffee can on the workbench. Shaking and tapping the lighter as I went back outside, I begged it to work so I wouldn't have to dig through my pile of stuff to find the butane lighter I'd taken from the RV glove box.

It took about a hundred spins of the flint wheel to create a spark, and then another hundred to get a flame to light the paper. After ten minutes, I had a small fire burning—and a sore thumb. I made a mental note to add lighter fluid and flint to my grocery list. Not that I would have any money to buy groceries, or any way to get them home on the back of a motorcycle that I didn't dare to ride on the road. I spent a few more minutes gathering larger sticks and broken limbs from the forest floor, and when my arms couldn't bear any more weight, I carried my load of firewood back to my campsite. I added a few thicker pieces of wood to the fire, and watched as the flames slowly encased them.

The outside shower was useless without running water, but after a day of backbreaking work, I was grimy with sweat and dirt, and my clothes were filthy. The lake water looked so inviting I slipped off my shoes near the small fire and walked barefoot out onto the wooden dock.

Dan had taken everything. He'd intended to leave me powerless. But all he'd done was reveal his true character. Now, it was time for me to see what I was made of. I could either inch my way into a new life or I could dive in headfirst.

I dove.

Pain knifed my body, and I surfaced with a horrified gasp. I'd just submerged myself in ice water! A vicious claw gripped my chest, and I began hyperventilating. My jaw clenched, my muscles contracted, and my heart banged in my chest as I struggled frantically toward the shore. Sloshing my way out on legs already stiffened from the frigid water, I hugged my arms to my trembling body and stumbled onto shore. How stupid of me! This early in the spring the lake had barely thawed from its winter freeze. I'd been living in the South for so long I'd never given a thought to how different the seasons were here. The temperature was already cold and dropping fast! I had no heated shelter.

I stumbled into the boathouse. Shivering, teeth clacking, I willed my frozen hands to work but struggled to pull off my clothes. Finally naked and gripped with pain, I tied a towel around my wet hair, then wrapped myself in the first blanket I could find. Barefoot, I hobbled back outside and tossed more wood on the fire, silently urging it to burn hard and blaze with heat. Sitting as close to the fire as possible, I hunched beneath my blanket, shivering violently and calling myself every kind of fool. I could die out here. Alone. Because of my own stupidity.

Tongues of orange flame licked greedily around the firewood. Watching the fire grow, I opened my blanket slightly to capture whatever warmth the flames offered. I was so cold and my muscles so clenched, I couldn't tell if any heat was penetrating my body. Pulling the blanket over my towel-encased head, I hoped my breath would add some warmth.

I'd never done anything this stupid in my life.

On the heels of that thought, I knew I had. I'd hurt my sister.

Arranging myself so I could capture the most heat possible, I sat for a long time, racked with tremors, begging my body to warm up and promising myself I'd never do anything this idiotic again. As time crept by, warmth seeped through my chilled skin, eased my clenched muscles, and finally sank into my icy bones. I must have drifted off at some point because I caught myself on one elbow before I toppled into the fire. I was determined to do myself in today.

My stomach growled in agony. I needed to eat. And I needed to put some clothes on and get blood pumping through my abused body.

Loathe to leave the fire, I had to force myself to go inside. I rummaged around until I found a pair of jeans and a shirt to layer under my sweatshirt and jean jacket. The instant I dropped my blanket, chilled air accosted me, and I began shivering again. With cold, stiff hands, I pulled on my dry clothes. I couldn't find any socks. All I could dig out of the mess to cover my aching feet was one second-hand sneaker and one of the cowboy boots I'd purchased at Maggie's consignment shop. *Good enough.*

My teeth still chattered intermittently as I towel-dried my hair, then hung the towel over the workbench to dry. My brush was in my purse which was buried somewhere in the mess of bags and baskets, so I settled on finger-combing my hair in the mirror on Haley's bike. I was a sight, but I was too cold and hungry to care. Wet hair exposed to the frigid temperature was not a good idea, especially when my body was still struggling to warm itself, so I fastened a dry towel around my head, dragged the blanket back around my shoulders, and headed outside.

For several minutes I forced myself to gather more firewood, knowing I needed to keep moving to warm my body and that more wood meant a bigger fire which meant more heat. While I was scavenging for firewood, I came across two old bricks on the ground at the back of the building. Carrying them with aching hands was a painful chore, but I needed them. After setting aside the bricks and layering more wood on top of the snapping fire, I hurried back inside to find something to fill my empty stomach.

I found the cooler, pulling out the items that would spoil first—a partial half gallon of milk and the quart of beer I'd bought at the grocery store as a symbol of my independence—and I made my supper. Pouring a good amount of cereal into a mixing bowl, I topped the flakes with milk, and found my cast iron frying pan in the trash can.

Supper in one hand, frying pan in the other, I went outside and sat beside the roaring fire. Before I ate, I put the bricks in the frying pan, then wrangled the pan onto a bed of glowing coals. After that, I unwrapped the towel from my head and shook out my hair, hoping the heat from the fire would dry it quickly. As the reality of my situation settled in, I fought back panic. It was early spring here when daytime temps averaged in the forties and fifties, and the night temps could drop below freezing. I was out here alone, without adequate shelter, and with no one to depend on but myself. I couldn't afford to be a dumb-ass like I'd been when I'd foolishly submerged myself in ice-cold lake water.

I considered calling an Uber to take me to a local inn where I could savor a hot shower and sleep in a soft bed in a heated room, but I had very little cash left. The few dollars in my purse were all I had to keep me going on my own. Plus, I was too damned exhausted to walk out to the road to meet an Uber driver. Returning to Dan would be worse than jumping into an icy lake. I'd be throwing myself into the fires of hell.

With a hard sigh, I stared at the flames, willing them to radiate more heat. I noticed that my dirty mowing sneakers were where I'd left them beside the fire pit. They were probably warm, and I considered putting them on, but my hands hurt too much to try changing shoes. Still, I tucked them beneath my blanket so I wouldn't forget to take them inside.

Tipping the bowl to my mouth, I slurped down the soggy cereal. I was too hungry and miserable to be civilized. Sinatra watched me eat my supper without a spoon, creeping ever closer to the strange lady with wild hair and mismatched shoes. He completely ignored my attempts at conversation, remaining silent and watchful. I suspect he'd witnessed my earlier behavior with Dan and wasn't sure what to make of me.

"Just because I'm feeding you doesn't mean you're my cat."

He ignored me. Not even a blink of his eyes or a twitch of his ears to indicate he'd heard me.

"Just like a teenager," I said, setting aside my empty bowl.

The crackle of wood and the warm glow of firelight made the encroaching nightfall less lonely. Slowly, I was beginning to shake the bone-deep chill that had consumed my body.

I opened my quart of beer and savored the first drink I'd had in twenty years. Still cold and effervescent, the lovely taste of yeast and hops filled my mouth and soothed my parched throat. I'd missed this ... the simple pleasure of drinking a beer.

The night came alive with the loud chorus of thousands of wood frogs. Unknown critters made rustling sounds in the undergrowth as they began settling in for the night. I'd been away so long I'd forgotten the sound of nature ... of home. For the past twenty-three years my world had been filled with the sound of traffic and lawn mowers and Dan's rousing performances backed by the church band and choir and flashing lights and the upraised voices of beguiled congregants. So much noise. So much nonsense. So much wasted time.

I basked in the night-song, remembering how lovely it sounded. From the corner of my eye, I saw Sinatra inching his way closer to the fire, which brought him closer to me. Seeing him crouched just outside my reach made me realize I'd been like that in Dan's world, a wild soul struggling to survive.

"All right, little man. We can do this on your terms," I said softly to Sinatra. "I'll never cage you. There are no strings attached to the food I give you. I do, however, wish you would crawl onto my lap and let me hold you because you seem to be as lost and alone as I am."

His ears twitched, but he remained at a distance.

And so, I sat alone wishing I could have done this differently, that I could have left on better terms, that I could have prepared my girls for the earthquake that was about to shake their world. Would they understand there had been no way for me to reason or negotiate with their father? There never had been. I'd just always given in to keep peace between us and make a loving home for our girls. And for the most part it had been a good home. I'd gotten good at convincing myself that making my family happy made me happy. But I had poured myself out so completely to nourish my family that I'd become a drained and empty vessel.

As the night deepened and the fire burned down, I huddled beneath my blanket and savored the last few swallows of my beer. It tasted divine. I mentally kicked myself for not buying a twelve-pack. I had felt like such a rebel buying a quart of beer that it had never crossed my mind to stock up. With the RV gone, I no longer had running water, or even bottled water to drink—and milk just wasn't going to slake my thirst.

One more problem I'd have to solve tomorrow. I needed water. And power.

Sinatra was curled up about ten feet away, both of us lost in our own thoughts when the sky opened up. Without warning, icy rain came down in buckets. Sinatra shot toward the woods and disappeared. I struggled to my feet, my body so sore I could barely stand upright. I bunched up a corner of the blanket and wrapped it around the handle of the frying pan that was now hissing as rain splattered across it, but it was too heavy to lift with one hand. Plopping my sneakers on top of the hot bricks, I bunched the other side of the blanket and lifted the pan with two hands. The smell of melting rubber filled my nose as I hobbled to the boathouse.

By the time I made it inside, I was drenched to the skin—and freezing! I clumsily set the heavy frying pan on the floor and swept my melting sneakers off the bricks. Jaw quivering, nose running, I turned on the rechargeable camp lantern. I had no idea when I'd be able to charge it again, but I needed light now. I shook my blanket to remove as much rainwater as possible. Then I rooted through my pile of stuff until I found the bag of second-hand clothes I'd purchased at Maggie's shop. I'd planned to wash them first, but all I cared about now was getting dry and warm—*again*. I made use of the towel I'd used earlier, then hung it, along with my sweatshirt and jean jacket, over the workbench. My fingers were so cold I could barely dress myself—or maybe it was the beer I'd drunk that made the task more difficult.

I was tempted to pull on my sneakers with the heated, or rather melted, soles, but they smelled awful. I tossed them aside and searched for the other shoe and cowboy boot that were still dry. I still couldn't find any socks.

It took another five minutes of digging through garbage bags and shifting stuff around before I found my daughter's sleeping bag. Picking up the damp towels I'd used earlier, I fashioned them into potholders to move the hot frying pan to a spot away from the door. Wrapping myself in the blankets and bedspread I'd taken from the bed in the RV, I topped them off with the sleeping bag. Finally, I sat on the floor near the hot pan. Carefully, I wrapped a damp towel around each brick, then tucked them under the edge of my blankets that I'd tented around me. As I'd hoped, heat emanated from the bricks, but it wasn't enough to chase away the chill.

Shivering, I looked around the boathouse in the place where I'd spent so much time with my family. This used to be a happy place, with summer picnics on the beach and canoe rides on the lake, a haven filled with love, laughter, and family. Now it was a cold, vacant building filled with dust and one woman who'd never felt more alone in her life.

Leaving me with nothing was Dan's way of forcing me to go back to him—and it was nearly working. I was cold, hungry, and exhausted. I wanted a hot shower and a warm bed. But I chose to sit on a wood floor in a cold boathouse with a leaking roof rather than live imprisoned in Dan's fucked-up world.

Splat-splat-splat! A puddle was forming near the workbench.

I didn't know how far the puddle would spread, but I couldn't afford to lose any of my possessions or let my remaining clothing get soaked. Shrugging off the blankets, I scrounged up a cooking pot and set it in the center of the puddle. *Plink-plink-plink!*

Outside I heard the steady beat of rain against a metal barrel at the back of the boathouse, sounding like a kettle drum. *Tum-tum-tum …*

I sent up a prayer to the roof god to keep a tight lid on things so I could get some sleep. But I couldn't sleep.

The full force of my dire situation hit me so hard I couldn't breathe. It felt as if I were perched at the edge of my life, tense, watchful, and filled with fear. Suddenly, all I could hear in the shadowed forest outside was a taunting voice telling me I would fail, insisting I wasn't smart enough to survive, warning me to go back to Dan.

But I couldn't go back to that oppressive cage! I would die there. I might die here, too, but it would be on my terms.

Still, I wondered if the inner voice questioning me was right; was I kidding myself to think I could carve out a life here? I began to wonder if that inner voice I'd long considered my nemesis wasn't the enemy at all but rather the only voice brave enough to challenge me to step the hell up and live my authentic life. Friend or foe, I knew if I were to survive here and create any sort of life, I needed to learn to listen to that voice. And right now it was telling me to get my freezing ass back under the blankets.

Aching from the cold, I settled in again with the sleeping bag and my warming bricks, holding my hands over the dying heat from the frying pan.

Thunder rumbled overhead, and lightning shot down in jagged streaks from the dark sky. Rain created a cacophony of sounds outside the windows, *splat-plink-tum-tum-tum* as it pounded down. I missed my girls so much my bones ached. I thought about how they used to rush into my room during thunderstorms. I would take them back to their room, crawl onto their bed with them, and tell them stories. I made up wild adventures with powerful young girls as the heroines of the stories. Their favorite was the one I'd never finished, the one that had been haunting me since they were babies, the one Dan had told me to shred.

As my mind spun inward to my story world, I reached out and

snagged the shoulder strap on my briefcase, dragging it over so I wouldn't have to get up and lose the warmth beneath my blankets. Pulling out my notebook, I clutched the pen in my cold fingers, and I began again, pretending I was telling the story to my girls ...

Chapter Five

I woke up in a canoe.

For a moment, I thought I was dreaming. Then reality streamed in, and I understood I was really here—in a canoe. In a bitterly cold boathouse.

With my body creaking and groaning, I climbed out and stretched. I could hear Sinatra calling for his breakfast. My stomach rumbled in solidarity. We were hungry lost creatures.

Shivering, I stumbled across the floor with my boot-sneaker limp and went to the door. Bright sunshine glinted off a fresh dusting of snow. The rain had stopped during the night, but the temperature had continued to drop. I'd crawled into the canoe to get off the cold floor, and though I remember shivering in misery throughout the night, I must have drifted off for at least a little while.

Squinting, I wondered why the building had remained so dark inside, then realized it was because its few small windows were covered in grime and obscured by weeds. Job number one today would be cleaning the windows.

Sinatra meowed with attitude.

Correction. Cleaning the windows was job number two.

Apparently, feeding this little rat was job number one. Every. Morning.

After rinsing the cat bowls in the lake, I took them inside, filled them with kibbles and canned food, and put them back outside. Sinatra pounced on them as soon as I took my shivering, runny-nosed-self back inside.

I needed water. And I needed to brush my teeth. And I needed to blow my nose.

The only thing I had to quench my thirst was milk. I'd rather drink lake water, but I didn't have to. The mixing bowl I'd left outside last night was filled with rainwater slush and a couple floating cereal flakes. After fishing them out, I gulped down the slushy water, then took the empty bowl inside.

Cold to my bones, I pulled on my old mowing shoes with the partially melted soles. When I tried to tie them, the shoestring broke on my right shoe. The left shoe was so frayed and worn on-one side the canvas was splitting open near my small toe. Still, I refused to wear my consignment store sneakers while working because they were the only decent pair of shoes I had. Plus, one of the shoes was still wet from the downpour last night. Regardless of their appalling condition, I had to make my old sneakers work. I knotted the broken shoestring together and tied my shoe. I'd have to find the duct tape later to fix the tear in my other shoe because I had other more pressing concerns at the moment.

It took me five minutes to find the box of tissues I'd taken out of the RV bathroom, then I blew my nose and headed to the outhouse to relieve my bladder of a quart of beer and half a bowl of rainwater. I really needed to work on my diet.

I MADE my to-do list over a breakfast of milk and a stale piece of bread. Cleaning the windows was moved way down the list in favor of the necessities. Chocolate vied for the number one position, but logic prevailed, and I listed water and power as the two most important items I needed immediately. The power company wasn't likely to give me an account without some form of credit history or a paying job. I could buy a gas generator, but that presented two more problems. If I paid for a generator, assuming I could find one cheap enough, I wouldn't be able to buy groceries. The second problem was how to get the generator from the store to the boathouse. And I would also have to buy gas ... and a gas can.

Although it was bitterly cold at night, I convinced myself that I could manage another night or two without a generator. But I needed water *now*. My growing thirst reminded me of a book I'd read where the hiker had run out of water and nearly died before he'd found a small pond. His thirst was so intense, and the story so gripping, I thought I'd die with him. Using some sort of bottle that pumped up water and filtered it, he was able to screen the slimy pond water and drink it. That story made me think about the backpack strapped to Haley's bike. She was my nature child, my fearless, motorcycle riding, trail hiking, outdoor girl. On her last birthday, she'd wanted a new pair of hiking boots and a straw thingy that would allow her to drink from outdoor water sources. Kara, her beautiful brainy twin sister, had wanted a new laptop.

Going through Haley's things was painful. I'd taken her shopping for her first real outdoor backpack. That backpack had been discarded long ago in favor of the durable, waterproof bag Haley now used. A beat-up canteen was still in her pack, along with a first aid kit, iodine tablets, a fat tube-like drinking straw, a knit cap, and a big hunting knife I'd never seen before. And there were socks! Praise be, there were two glorious pairs of thick, dry socks, and a granola bar that disappeared as quickly as I could tear off the wrapper. I pulled on the hat and socks, then grabbed the straw and raced outside.

My mouth had grown so dry from downing the stale granola bar, I could barely suck hard enough on the straw to draw up lake water. Haley had been so enamored with the fat straw when she got it that she'd had to show me how it worked. I'd humored her at the time because she was so excited. But now, hunkered down on my hands and knees at the edge of the lake sucking up water with her survival straw, I couldn't have been more grateful for her demonstration, because without it I'd be drinking straight out of the lake with Sinatra who was just down the beach doing the same thing.

With my drinking water issue solved for the moment, I headed inside to see what could be done about the mess I'd made. An overflowing cooler, a mounded laundry basket, a trash can packed to the brim, and a large cluster of white and green garbage bags spilled out across the floor. The boathouse was a mess. But before I began cleaning things up, I needed to take stock of everything on the property and figure out a way to survive here ... with next to nothing.

I had no job, no income, and no transportation, other than Haley's motorcycle that I could barely keep upright. I couldn't afford to rent an apartment or buy a camper or even a car. If I went after Dan for half our assets, I would lose more than my lawsuit. I'd lose any chance of a quick and amicable divorce that would spare the girls from seeing the ugly side of their parents. It would have been nice to have access to our joint account a while longer, but that source was surely gone now. I'd have to figure this out on my own because no matter what I had to do to keep my independence, I wasn't going back to Dan's oppressive, claustrophobic, misogynistic world.

Digging through my stuff, I scrounged up a plastic plate and a roll of duct tape and took them outside with me. As I studied the roof, I tried to determine where the rain had gotten in last night. I thought I spied a missing shingle, but I wouldn't know for certain until I could get up on the roof. That presented another problem. I didn't have a ladder. Defeated, I plopped the tape on top of the plate and set them on the ground beside the door.

As I made my way down the path to my grandparents' house, I considered my situation. I hadn't planned on living in a boathouse, or even in the RV. Big Bart had been a temporary place to hang out until I figured out what I was doing. In the back of my mind, I guess I'd hoped to live in my grandparents' house. I hadn't realized the place was uninhabitable, but now, as I walked through their house in full daylight, I could see it was beyond repair.

The house had been built by my grandfather's grandfather in eighteen ninety-three. I was surprised it was still standing. But in those days, everything had been built to last. My grandfather, Papa Ray, had come from a long line of master carpenters. With the exception of the appliances, fixtures, and a few pieces of furniture like the sofa and his recliner that my sister had left behind, everything else had been created by his own two hands. He'd taken great pleasure in teaching me some basic carpentry skills, and I'd soaked up the lessons, enjoying any opportunity to hang out with him. In my young eyes, he was larger than life. He was a tall man with a warm laugh and a big heart. I'd only seen him angry once in my life, and he'd directed that anger like a sledgehammer. My father had been on the receiving end, and the hard hit had driven him out of the family and out of my life.

Whorls of matted fur covered the recliner, and I realized Sinatra must have made it his bed. Not a bad choice. A deep indentation in the seat cushion from years of use created a suitable nest. Papa Ray would have been happy to know his recliner was being put to good use, and I was glad Sinatra had found a place to burrow in out of the rain and snow. I suspect the cat was coming and going through the window with the broken pane of glass. I couldn't determine how the lower corner of the window might have been broken, but that small opening provided access for Sinatra. I'd planned to board it up to keep the weather out, but now I couldn't do that without leaving Sinatra out in the cold. This cat might be a welcome companion, but he was complicating everything.

Nothing remained in my grandparents' bedroom except an old mattress and aged curtains covering dirty windows. The bathroom hadn't been cleaned out, but I wasn't surprised. There would have been nothing in here that Sophie wanted. An old medicine cabinet, still filled with the contents of my grandparents' life, was mounted over the pedestal sink. A partially used tube of toothpaste, two toothbrushes, a box of band-aids, a roll of gauze, a pair of tweezers, a bottle of iodine, and a pair of small mustache scissors filled the top two shelves. Prescription bottles containing blood pressure medication and pain pills took up residence on the bottom shelf beside a bottle of stool softeners and a tube of hemorrhoid cream.

I swung the cabinet door shut. This was far more than I wanted to know about my grandparents, and I really didn't want to think about my own old age or what it might have in store for my body.

The upstairs bedroom was frozen in time. Two twin beds with wrought iron frames sat atop an old carpet that had seen better days. As the only grandchildren, Sophie and I had shared this room. We used to bounce on the beds until the springs threatened to break and our parents would holler for us to knock it off. Sophie would giggle so loudly I was sure our father would come up and give us a whack on the backside. But he never had. Sophie and I roughhoused on the floor and got rug burns from the carpet. One night, she'd spilled a large glass of cola on the carpet, and I'd taken the blame because we weren't supposed to eat or drink in our room. We'd spent so much time here with our grandparents that we had our own dressers filled with clothes that stayed here even when we didn't.

Did Sophie hate me so much that she hadn't wanted any of this stuff, that she couldn't bear any reminder of a time when we'd been happy? It was the only reason I could fathom why she hadn't taken the dressers or pretty dressing table my grandfather had made for us. I remembered Sophie sitting on the padded bench seat while I braided her hair. I'd spent hours as a teen practicing my smile and flirtatious looks in the mirror while Sophie groaned and giggled at my ridiculous expressions. This was our room, our past, and Sophie hadn't wanted any of it.

I sank onto the bed that had once been my little sister's. Losing her was something I would never get over, and I didn't know how to fix what I'd broken.

I don't know how long I sat there lost in thought and

wrenching heartache, but it was long enough for Sinatra to find me. He sat in the doorway, his green eyes studying me, his black and white face so adorable I wanted to kiss him.

"You picked a good place to hang out," I told him softly. "I can see that you're making use of Papa's recliner and Sophie's bed. I bet you come up here when the broken window downstairs lets in too much nasty weather."

He moved a couple of feet into the room.

Encouraged, I patted the mattress. "Come on over. We can keep each other company."

He didn't get any closer, but he didn't run off either.

"Okay, mister, I'm going to take my bed out to the boathouse. You don't need both beds, and I can't continue to sleep in a canoe."

Sinatra turned and stalked from the room.

I laughed and pulled myself together. I had work to do. The mattress on my old bed was thin and beat up and smelled a little musty, but it was critter-free. I'd expected to find a nest of mice burrowed into the thick padding, but apparently Sinatra's daily patrol kept them out. There appeared to be some benefit to having a cat around.

There were a couple of other items left in the house, lamps, and such, but I'd found what I'd come for—a bed. I would come back later and haul it out to the boathouse after I cleaned up out there. For now, I needed to head outside and check around the house.

Waist-high weeds, brown and brittle from winter, made walking difficult. Using my arms, I slashed and kicked my way through the mess as I made my way around the house. There used to be a well with a cast iron hand pump out here. Sophie and I had drunk straight from the faucet on hot summer days. My grandfather had installed an electric pump at one point, but he'd left the hand pump as a backup. If I could find the pump, I might find a source of drinkable water.

I found the camper first.

An avalanche of memories buried me as I opened the camper

door ... summer vacations with Sophie and my grandparents camping at Lake Placid and Saranac Lake and Lake George. We'd hiked Buttermilk Falls at Long Lake and taken boat tours around Blue Mountain Lake and Raquette Lake. We'd explored historical museums on foot and rode outdoor trails on the backs of gentle horses. We'd taken train rides during the fall foliage peak season. Once, we even attended a winter carnival at Saranac Lake where a great ice palace was being built. We'd stayed in a hotel for that trip, but so many of our young adventures had been with our grandparents in this old camper. It wasn't old at that time, though. Papa Ray had bought one of the best on the market.

I remember the day he pulled in with the blue and white beast hooked to the back of his pickup truck. Sophie was so excited she'd bolted into the driveway. I grabbed her braid and hauled her backward to keep her safe. She didn't appreciate my heroic gesture, of course. She'd punched me for pulling her hair. But we were both too excited to bicker. Our grandparents couldn't get us out of the camper for a week. We ate out there. We played out there. And we slept out there. The foldaway bed Sophie and I had shared looked so small now.

The camper smelled musty, but I was surprised it had remained dry inside. Something had chewed on the bench seat cushions, and the place was home to several spiders if the cobwebs were any indication. The camper was no longer habitable, but as I looked around, I realized I might be able to repurpose some of the stuff.

I had no money to speak of, but I had a roof over my head, albeit one that leaked, a few basic carpentry skills, and an imagination steeped in years of watching home improvement shows. Even though I'd lived in a house fit for a celebrity, I'd been obsessed with shows about home renovations, building tiny houses, and home makeovers. I wonder now if my obsession was really a longing for a place of my own.

Could I possibly create my own small home by converting the boathouse? I knew the structure was sound because my grandfather had built it. It had been two decades since I'd used a hammer and saw or worked with my grandfather, but I remembered his lessons. Whether or not I could aptly apply those lessons remained to be seen, but I had no other choice. I had to carve out a life here with my own two hands.

I inspected the small garden shed next, wondering if converting it to a livable shelter might be more manageable than taking on the boathouse conversion, but it was small. I mean tiny, as in the size of my former closet. I could bunk here for a few nights, but it wouldn't be any warmer than the boathouse, and I could not create a home for myself and my girls in this place. Many of my grandmother's gardening tools, rakes, shovels, and hand tools were still here, and empty pots of various sizes were stacked haphazardly in corners and on shelves. Dust and spiderwebs hung from the overhead rafters and covered the windows on either side of the shed. An old rotary blade push mower with a worn wooden handle was tucked into a corner at the back of the shed. I'd never seen my grandfather use anything but a gas mower, and I wondered if the old mower had belonged to his father or even his grandfather. I wished I'd asked more questions and taken more interest in my family history while my grandparents were alive. All that history had died with them, and I was feeling that loss deeply as I stood here looking at remnants of my family's past.

I found the well a few yards from the house. It was overgrown by weeds, and the pump handle had rusted, but it still worked. Without water to prime the pump, however, I couldn't determine if the well had gone dry, or if it would provide the source of water I so desperately needed.

It took me twenty minutes to walk out to the boathouse, retrieve the trash can, fill it half full of lake water, and lug it back to the well. I was so out of breath and dying of thirst by that time I considered drinking right out of the trash can. Priming a well seems simple enough in theory but is excruciatingly difficult when one is trying to pour water from a kitchen-sized trash can held like a sack under one arm while stroking the pump handle with the other hand. I couldn't manage to do both effectively. I had to go back and forth, pouring water into the exit spout of the pump, then pumping the handle. But not a drop of water soaking my shoes was coming from the well. As the water dwindled in the trash can, I was finally able to hold the thing steady and pour the water and work the pump handle simultaneously.

Finally ... after pouring and pumping until my arms were ready to give out, a gush of water shot out the faucet. Dropping the trash can, I used both hands to work the pump, dredging up a fat stream of rusty water from the well. I pumped for several minutes until the water was mostly clear, and then I refilled the trash can with the well water in the event I'd need to prime the pump again. I had no desire to lug another heavy bucket full of lake water out here.

The icy well water that poured over my freezing hands and dirty shoes was a wicked temptation to my parched throat. But I knew not to drink it until I could get the water tested. Plopping down on my backside, I checked my phone, relieved to see it was still activated. I looked up the number for the health department and called them. Because the well had been inactive for such a long time, they needed to send out a technician to inspect it and collect a water sample. The tech visit and water testing would cost three hundred and twenty-five dollars. That number excluded investigating any issues or fixing any problems. That would leave me with fifty-one dollars and sixty-eight cents. I hesitated for a moment, wondering how long I could continue drinking lake water through a straw. The thought of hunkering down on my hands and knees every time I needed a drink convinced me that I needed to schedule an inspection. Their first available opening was in ten days. It looked as if I'd be sucking up lake water for a while longer.

After slogging my way back to the lake in sopping wet shoes, I set to work clearing out the boathouse. I dragged everything outside where the sun was now shining and warming the air. The canoes were too big and heavy for me to move, so they remained inside along with the tools on the peg board above the workbench. I spent a couple minutes gathering up a few nails and screws scat-

tered on the bench and dumped them—along with a big iron spike
—into the coffee can. Unearthing the broom I'd taken from the RV,
I began knocking down spider webs. I didn't want to think about
the bugs and critters that had made the boathouse their residence
and had probably stalked me last night while I slept.

It took an hour to sweep down the walls and windows and the
plank floor before I was ready to start hauling things back inside. I
decided to use one of the canoes for storage. I folded and stacked
my few pieces of clothing at one end and used the middle section
for the cans and packages of food I'd purchased. At the other end, I
stashed a partial box of green trash bags, a roll of toilet paper, two
rolls of paper towels, and my cleaning products that consisted of a
container of bacterial wipes, half a bottle of dish soap, and a full
bottle of window cleaner. I scrubbed down the workbench and
stacked my dishes and bathroom products on it. I tossed my
bedding back into the empty canoe, which would be my bed again
tonight because I was too exhausted to go get my old bed from the
house.

My back ached, my stomach growled, and Sinatra called for his
supper. After cleaning his bowls and washing my face and hands
in the lake, I fed the hungry fur ball. His tuna cat food smelled so
good I was envious of his supper. The only way for me to cook
anything was to build a fire. But I was too exhausted and too
hungry, so I made a peanut butter and jelly sandwich on the new
loaf of wheat bread I had been unable to find in the mess last night.
My mouth watered as I savored every bite. The sandwich was the
first good meal I'd had in three days. I only wished I had a beer and
a gallon of water to wash it down.

I needed a bath, but I couldn't bear the thought of washing up
with frigid water, especially when the evening temperature was
dropping fast. After I finished my sandwich, I leaned against the
door frame of the boathouse, looking up at the sky as dusk set in. It
was going to be another frosty spring night which made me glad I'd
taken all the bedding from the RV, especially Haley's cold weather
sleeping bag.

Sinatra crouched in the grass watching me.

"Want to come in?" I asked, wishing he would, knowing he wouldn't.

His ears twitched, but he remained where he was and continued watching intently as if waiting for something.

"I'm not going to build a fire tonight," I told him. "I'm too tired."

I swear he seemed disappointed.

I squatted down, my knees popping and aching from being on my feet all day. With a soft clap of my hands, I called him. He didn't come, of course. But he didn't run off either, so that was something. We looked at each other for a bit, and I talked to him until I felt my body seizing up. "Go find your warm bed, little man, and I'll see you in the morning." I gripped the doorframe with both hands and hauled myself up in a hand-over-hand motion. At that moment I'd have sold my soul—what was left of it anyway—for a hot shower, a cold beer, and a warm bed. But I settled for a cold drink of lake water and a sleeping bag in a canoe.

Chapter Six

Today was the day I'd promised to go to Chloe's house for a girl-gab with her and Maggie. As much as I was looking forward to seeing my old friends and catching up on their lives, I was dreading the questions they were bound to ask.

My life was in shambles. I had no answers for anyone. I was just putting one foot in front of the other right now. Literally.

Hauling an iron bed frame through a weed-choked path was utter hell. The bed rails had been heavy, but the headboard was a beast. I half-carried and half-dragged it along the path with the wretched thing catching on clumps of weeds, wrenching my arms and hands, and breaking my back. The footboard wasn't much lighter, but I managed to get the whole frame, headboard, footboard, and rails out to the boathouse. The bedsprings were another matter. There was no easy way for me to carry the thing. The mass of coils strung across the metal frame pinched my fingers. I tried spanning the frame with my arms, but it was too bulky and heavy for me to carry that way. Turning it on its side, I slid it down the stairs and dragged it outside. I tried pulling it upright, but it kept getting stuck in the weeds and tipping over, so I began flipping it end over end. Squat-lift-heave. Squat-lift-heave. Squat-lift-heave.

Over and over until my legs burned and my back cramped, and I couldn't bear another moment of the abuse.

Gasping for breath, I dropped the bedspring and collapsed on my back in the weeds, silently refusing to bring another piece of furniture to the boathouse until I'd cleared this weed-congested path. I'd always considered myself strong and fit. I could do thirty plank pushups and a hundred squats, but I was not conditioned for this kind of work. If cleaning out the boathouse and moving a few things had taken this much effort, converting the place into a home was looking like a long and painful process. I wanted to leave the metal springs lying in the weeds, but the thing was blocking the path, and without the bedsprings, I had no bed. I needed the bed frame to keep the mattress off the cold floor—my only hope of surviving the frigid nights that were taking a toll on my health. After a few minutes of catching my breath and resting my back, I rolled to my hands and knees and began the squat-lift-heave routine again, refusing to quit until I'd dropped the thing near the door.

Sinatra was sunning himself on the grass near the fire pit and was startled by my noisy approach.

With a loud groan, I sprawled in the doorway. "Hey mister, you know the story of The Little Red Hen, don't you? If you don't help move the bed, you don't get to sleep in the bed."

Sinatra settled back down and rested his chin on his paws as if suggesting I wouldn't be sleeping on the bed tonight either. At this pace, he was likely right. No way was I going back for the mattress today. I'd rather sleep in the canoe another night than try to schlep that heavy thing all the way out here.

That's when I realized I could use the bedsprings as a ladder. Sort of. It was a stupid idea, and I would probably break my neck, but I was determined to find out where the roof was leaking. I hoisted the bedspring up on end, then leaned it against the boathouse. I tucked my shirt into my jeans, then slipped the plate and tape inside my shirt. "Here goes nothing," I said to Sinatra who was watching me. I paused for a moment, wondering if I should put the bag of kitty kibbles on the floor and leave the boathouse door open for Sinatra in case I killed myself trying to patch the roof. "Looks like we'll both be taking a risk," I said, starting my climb.

Springs do not make a safe ladder, but if one is stupid enough and determined enough to use them as such, they can be repurposed in this way. I placed my foot as high as I could reach, slipped my bare fingers into the coils, and hoisted myself up. The springs groaned, a couple stretched and popped, and the frame shifted and ground against the outside wall. It took a few tries and lots of wobbling before I was able to get high enough to look on the roof. I could see where something, a branch perhaps, had gouged a hole in a shingle and created a crack in the wood underneath. The rest of the roof appeared to be adequately covered with shingles although they looked worn and ready to give way. My bedspring ladder was a foot too short to allow me to climb onto the roof, so I worked my way down.

For several minutes I considered my problem, then I headed to the woods. Within ten minutes I'd found what I needed. Dragging two fallen logs out of the undergrowth was agony. But I was stubborn and determined, so I worked like a mule, sweated like an athlete, and swore like a truck driver as I wrestled the logs over to the boathouse. After catching my breath, I lined up the logs like railroad tracks jutting out from the side of the boathouse, then propped the metal bedsprings atop them, which raised them a few inches off the ground.

Before I began my climb, I went inside and put Sinatra's open bag of kibbles on the floor and left the door open. Why should he suffer if I killed myself because I was stupid enough to use a coiled metal bedspring as a ladder?

The log skids did the trick, and although they made my climb more dangerous, I got myself onto the roof. I pulled the tape and plate from my shirt and began my repair. After taping the crack, I flipped the plastic plate upside down, centered it over the hole, and taped it down with duct tape. After reinforcing the outer seal with another round of tape, I slipped the roll back inside my shirt, then began my precarious descent from the roof. By the time my sore feet hit the ground I was scraped and bruised and utterly exhausted, but I was proud of what I'd accomplished.

Satisfied I'd survive until Sinatra's next meal, I went inside and put the bag of kibbles back on the workbench. Then I patched the frayed hole in my work sneakers with the duct tape.

After that, I put the iron bed frame together, and spent an hour scrubbing it clean with an old rag and a bowl filled with lake water. I placed Haley's sleeping bag on top of the bare bedsprings and covered it with my two blankets and bedspread. The thought of climbing in and sleeping for a couple of hours was tempting, but I needed to get cleaned up and head to Chloe's house.

After a day of hard physical labor, the thought of walking out the weed-choked lake trail, which was almost a quarter mile, and then a mile down the road to Chloe's place was almost enough to make me bail. I considered riding Haley's motorcycle, but immediately dismissed that idea. I hadn't even been able to get the thing down the path to the boathouse without dumping the bike. It looked as if I'd be walking. Both directions. At night. Alone.

At five-thirty, after feeding Sinatra and washing up with freezing water, I slipped on clean clothes and my decent consignment store sneakers, the left one still slightly damp from when I'd gotten caught in the downpour, then pulled on my hooded sweatshirt. I put the chargers for my phone and the rechargeable camp lantern in my purse and slipped the straps over my shoulders. Tying my jean jacket around my waist, I picked up the camp lantern and headed for the door. At the last second, I grabbed an unopened bag of chips, the only thing I had to contribute to our evening gabfest, then headed outside.

MY HAND SHOOK as I knocked on Chloe's door. I had no idea what kind of evening to expect.

A couple seconds later the door opened, and Chloe greeted me with a warm smile. She was dressed in a faded pair of jeans, a light pink sweater, and red socks. Her eyes took me in at a glance, and then swept out to the driveway and the road behind me. "Did you walk here?" she asked, stepping back to welcome me inside.

"Sure did. Remember how we used to run between each other's houses all day long?" I asked, trying for a lightness my tired body didn't feel. "Well, the walk feels much longer now."

"I'm sure it does," she said with a laugh. Closing the door behind us, she looked me over for a second, then leaned in and gave me a hug. "It's really great to see you, Kate."

Emotion clogged my throat as I returned her hug. I wanted to apologize for deserting her, to express my condolences over the loss of her husband, but I couldn't say anything.

"Come on in. Maggie's in the kitchen pouring wine."

I paused to slip off my shoes in her foyer, not wanting to track across her living room floor after walking the dirt road. "Would you mind if I plug in the chargers for my lantern and my phone?" I asked. "I noticed on my way here that both batteries were low, and I'd rather not walk back in the dark."

"Of course," she said, gesturing to an outlet in the foyer. "But I'll be happy to give you a ride home. You can leave your stuff on the bench and charge everything right there if you like."

After plugging in the lantern and my phone, I followed Chloe through her living room, a cozy room decorated in earth tones, overstuffed furniture, and family pictures on the fireplace mantle. I thought about the years she'd spent in this room with her husband, Josh, relaxing in the evenings, celebrating birthdays and holidays here as they watched their son grow up. I could only imagine how empty and lonely this room must feel to her now that her husband was dead and their son was away at college. My problems suddenly seemed small and insignificant.

"You came!" Maggie said, circumventing the kitchen island to give me an exuberant hug. "Just in time for wine."

"Or beer, if you prefer," Chloe added.

My thirst was too great to be satisfied by wine. "Beer sounds great," I said, hoping she would bring a twelve pack. "And a glass of water, if it's not too much to ask."

"Glasses are in the cupboard to the right of the sink," Chloe said as she opened the refrigerator.

I helped myself and downed two large glasses of delicious water. When I finished, I realized both Maggie and Chloe were watching me. "Guess I stirred up some dust on my walk over."

They were sitting on pub chairs around a rectangular kitchen island. "This should help quench your thirst," Chloe said, placing a beer and a mug on the tabletop.

"Thanks." I slid onto the chair, trying to act nonchalant as I poured my beer into the mug.

"Cheers!" Maggie lifted her wine glass. "To the wild winds!"

"To the towering trees," Chloe said, raising her glass.

It took me a moment to remember the toast we'd made up during one of our drunken high school parties. "To the magical moon," I added, lifting my beer mug, the image of three wild girls dancing on the beach beneath a full moon flooding my mind. The three of us clinked glasses. Maggie and Chloe took a sip of their wine. I chugged half my beer.

Chloe raised an eyebrow. Maggie burst out laughing.

Heat blasted my face. "Maybe I should have drunk another glass of water."

They both laughed, but Maggie leaned in on her elbows, her gaze drilling into mine. "Girl, we've missed you. Where the hell have you been?"

"You first," I said, employing my plan to turn the conversation back on them. "Tell me what you've been doing since high school. I want to know everything."

"Ok, Miss Clandestine, I'll go first." Maggie leaned back, took another sip of her wine, then held the glass between her manicured hands as she rested them on the tabletop. Her red hair had been pulled back in a ponytail and covered with a light blue ball cap. She wore an oversized sweatshirt with dark leggings and gray boot socks. She'd obviously dressed for comfort, but she looked gorgeous. "While you and Chloe were off partying at college, I was learning my father's business. A couple years later, I took classes two days a week at SUNY Potsdam until I earned my associate degree. I worked for my father and also for the bank until I grew bored with both jobs. So, I took two years off and traveled. I back-packed through several countries, visited archeological digs and old cities, drank lattes in Italian cafes, sampled wine and sexy men in Southern France, and visited too many tourist destinations. Turns out I was happiest right here in Dunwith Falls, but not while working at a bank or for my father. When I came back, I bought an old Victorian house with a huge carriage house out back. I hit every yard sale in four counties, then opened my consignment shop. Eventually, I started selling vintage clothing online and also began buying and selling antiques. That's when I converted the three-bay carriage house behind my consignment shop into an antique shop. I turned the upstairs into a flat where I've been living for thirteen years." She grinned and flipped one palm up. "It's nothing grand, I know, but I love what I'm doing."

I sat mesmerized by her story, by her life, by her courage. At twenty-something, I couldn't have imagined following my passion as Maggie had done. Of course, I'd gotten pregnant and married at nineteen, so my focus had shifted to my family. Still, I knew Maggie and I were cut from different cloth. She was made from gorgeous, supple leather that grew more beautiful with age. I was made of cotton, a fabric meant to provide warmth and comfort but eventually became worn and frayed.

"What about you?" Maggie asked, prodding me with an arched eyebrow and a playful grin.

"Not yet. Any men in your life?" I asked.

"Two. My father and my brother." She nodded toward my left hand where my wedding ring still encircled my finger. "I see you're still married. Or remarried."

"Married. Once," I said, not wanting to go into a situation I could barely understand much less talk about. Dan had been overbearing and controlling and unsupportive, but he'd been a good provider, and to my knowledge he'd never cheated on me.

"And ...?" Maggie prodded.

"And I have twin daughters. Haley and Kara are nineteen and are both freshmen in college."

"Ah, you're an empty-nester too," Chloe said, her voice sounding as forlorn as I felt.

I nodded, then looked at Maggie. "Then you've never married?"

"Nope. Don't intend to either," she said.

"No great loves in your life then?" I asked.

"A few great passions but no great loves."

We all laughed. "How about you, Chloe? I believe your son is also a freshman in college?"

"He is. Dylan's struggling a bit, but it's been a difficult year for him."

My heart cramped, and I reached across the tabletop to clasp her hand. "I know, and I'm so sorry."

A world of sorrow flooded her eyes. "Thank you."

For a moment, we all sat in silent acknowledgement of the great loss this woman and her son had so recently sustained. I wished there were words to express the depth of my sympathy for her and to ease her pain even a little, but there was nothing one can give in this situation other than their presence and their time. I hadn't been here for Chloe during the worst moment of her life. But I was here now.

"Tell me about your life," I said softly, hoping I was doing the right thing. "I'd really like to know."

She shrugged. "There's not much to tell, really. I left college after my freshman year and married Josh. I got pregnant with Dylan I suspect around the time you were pregnant with your girls." Her eyes met mine. "I wish we could have raised our kids together."

"Me too," I said, meaning it with all my heart.

"Josh took over my dad's farm," she said, "but he hated plowing and planting and harvesting corn. So, we slowly converted our business to tree trimming and landscaping. He also did part time contracting work. As Dylan got older, I was able to help more with our business. In the last five years, I worked full time with Josh." Chloe smiled. "Believe it or not, I loved it. I liked the work and loved spending my days with him." For a long moment, she gazed into her wine glass, gently swirling the red liquid around the goblet. "I'm beginning to accept that he's gone. But I don't know what to do with myself now. Everything I did was with him." She looked up, inhaled, and released a long sigh. "I have a barn full of tools and equipment, and no idea what to do with them. Dylan has no interest in that work. He's all about computers and gaming. I keep thinking I should sell everything, but I can't bring myself to do it. I haven't even cleaned out Josh's things yet," she whispered, a slight quiver crossing her lips.

Maggie tapped her fingernail against Chloe's glass to get her attention. "You'll know when it's time for that. Right now, it's time for you to surround yourself with friends and take care of yourself."

Chloe gave a nod of acknowledgement. "One day at a time."

"That's right," Maggie said. She swung her gaze back to me. "Now dish, girlfriend, and quit stalling. We want the dirt."

Chloe laughed. "You might as well acquiesce," she said, "because Maggie won't relent."

I could see that for myself. "Well, as you probably know, Dan is a pastor and has his own church. I helped out at the church and raised our girls. That's it, really."

"Nope." Maggie shook her head. "My spidey sense is telling me there's so much more. And my spidey spines are never wrong."

I laughed. "You're right. There is more. I also mow the lawn."

Chloe burst out laughing. She reached over and squeezed my hand. "It's so wonderful to have you back, Kate. Please don't leave."

Warmth suffused my entire body. How I'd missed my friends. "I plan to stay a while."

"Speaking of that, where are you staying?" Maggie asked.

"At my grandparents' property."

"In that old house?" Chloe asked, a horrified expression on her face.

"No. I brought our RV." That was true. I had brought it, but I didn't say I was *staying* in it, so I was being evasive rather than lying. Still, the omission made me feel awful, but I just couldn't bring myself to dump all my life's garbage on my friends, especially when I hadn't been there for them.

"So, why are you back?" Chloe asked. "Please don't say you're going to sell the property."

"I'm not selling. I'm just checking on things."

"Have you seen your sister or father yet?" Maggie asked, a slight grimace on her face as if empathizing with me and what was bound to be an awkward moment at best or an explosive interaction at worst.

It was as if she'd punched me in the gut. I felt winded and sick to my stomach. All I could do was shake my head.

"I don't know if you've heard, but Sophie's divorced now," Maggie said. "And she's better off if you ask me."

Chloe cringed. "Jeez, don't be so tactful, Maggie."

Maggie shrugged and didn't seem to care. "She is, and you know it."

"I'm not disagreeing with you," Chloe said. "It's just that Kate might need a minute to get used to your way of presenting things."

I laughed. "It's all right, Chloe. I knew that Sophie had gotten married." I hadn't received an invitation to her wedding, of course, but I'd read about it in the paper. She'd married a guy we'd gone to school with. "I hadn't heard that she'd gotten divorced though. Thanks for telling me, Maggie."

"Turns out Mark, the superstar jock from school, became a chubby, balding bar owner who couldn't leave high school behind," Maggie said. "Guess Sophie outgrew Mark or got tired of hearing him relive his glory days."

That scenario was so familiar, and so sad, I could only shake my head. Poor Sophie. But I was too raw at the moment to talk about my sister or my father, so I spun the conversation back to our high school days. "What happened to Theresa Tight Jeans?" I asked, knowing it would send us down a rabbit hole into the old days of school and classmates and pimples and teenage angst.

Chloe and Maggie filled me in on our former classmates and where they were now. They hadn't kept track of everyone, of course, but the popular kids seemed to leave a trail that was easy to follow. Many of the jocks grew older while their minds remained trapped in the glory days of high school. A couple of cheerleaders still fancied themselves "all that" and thought every guy they met was immediately in love with them. What they'd failed to see is that the bouncy, cute little cheerleader they'd once been had morphed into a chubby, not so cute middle-aged woman. Other kids had gone off to college and earned degrees and gotten big jobs, or started their own businesses, or went directly to work at businesses that could provide a steady paycheck and health insurance for their family.

As we talked and drank in Chloe's pretty kitchen, seated around her pub style island, the night deepened, and our friendship was rekindled over several glasses of wine and too many bottles of beer. I hadn't felt this relaxed or happy in years. I didn't have to watch what I said or pretend to be a perfect wife and mother who'd dedicated every facet of her life to her family and Dan's church. I just drank beer with my friends. I dropped the F-bomb. I laughed until my sides hurt.

We moved our party into Chloe's living room where she built a small fire in her fireplace. All I remember from that point on is the buzz of our conversation. I don't even know who was talking. Maybe it was me, and the buzzing was in my own head. The warmth of the fire wrapped around me, soothing my sore body, and everything just sort of disappeared as I sank deep into the couch cushions.

Chapter Seven

I woke up disoriented only to realize I was on Chloe's couch covered with a patchwork quilt. I was alone in her living room. I presumed Maggie had gone home, or perhaps she'd made use of one of the bedrooms, and Chloe was likely in her own bed. As I sat up, I groaned and hunched forward, elbows braced on my knees with my throbbing head squeezed between my hands. Other than my one quart of beer by the lake, it had been so long since I'd drunk alcohol that I'd forgotten how wretched a hangover could feel.

It took me a good five minutes for the room to stop moving before I could make my way to the foyer and pull on my sneakers. After unplugging my chargers, I slipped outside, closing the door quietly behind me. The frigid pre-dawn air went straight through my clothing. Shivering hard, I pulled the hood of my sweatshirt up and buttoned my jean jacket. It was still dark, so I clicked the lantern switch to provide a halo of light as I staggered down the road. I glanced at my phone, now fully charged. It was just after four in the morning. I'd been worried about making it through one hour with my friends, and here I was sneaking out the morning after like a clandestine lover. Would Chloe be offended that I'd left while she was sleeping, as if it had only been a one-night stand for me? My brain was not functioning. But my stomach was wildly awake. I barely made it to the ditch before I vomited.

If only Dan and his congregants could see me now, on my knees on a dirt road, barfing in a ditch. The thought of their horrified faces made me laugh. And then it made me cry because I'd once considered those people my friends. But now I knew they'd merely been acquaintances living in the same Christian hive as me, all of us serving our queen, or king, in this instance. I'd never had an honest conversation with any of those people. That's why I'd come here alone. There had been no one I could confide in.

At one time I'd believed I was helping Dan build something special, that the church I was serving and supporting was providing a home not only for lost souls but for decent people wanting to create a better world. But now, alone on my knees in the dirt, I had to admit it had all been a lie. Dan's church wasn't a home, or a special place. It was a mind-trap ... a place where Dan, and those who followed him, preyed on other people's heartaches and fears and their need for community to draw them into their cult. Once those poor souls entered, they were conditioned to believe there was only one way to worship, to love, to live, and that everyone else was wrong. In weekly sermons they were taught to be judgmental and small-minded and exclusionist. They were systematically stripped of their freedom to think for themselves, forbidden to explore science and other beliefs and cultures, and threatened to exile should they stray. To know I'd been part of that, to realize I'd supported something so oppressive, broke my heart and shamed me deeply. Especially when I thought of my girls and how Dan and I had indoctrinated them from birth in his oppressive belief system.

Why these thoughts were pouring through my pounding head while I retched in the ditch, I can't say. But it dawned on me that it was Sunday morning—and I was on my knees. Puking, not repenting. At one time, I might have believed I was being punished for my drinking binge and blasphemous thoughts and for succumbing to the temptations of the Devil. Now I knew it was nothing so ominous as that, but rather a simple physical reaction from imbibing too much alcohol. My body was expunging the toxic waste roiling in my stomach ... and letting me know by my violent shivering that it was too damned cold outside to lie down by the ditch, which I desperately wanted to do.

I don't know how long it took me to slog home or stumble along the rutted lake trail, but as soon as I entered the boathouse, I collapsed on the bedsprings.

Trying to sleep on metal springs without a mattress on top is stupid. Even in my half-drunk brain, I understood this was a bad idea. A sleeping bag between my sore body and the bedsprings was not enough. Groaning, I scooped up my bedding, grabbed the metal mixing bowl off the workbench, then crawled into the canoe. I hadn't even covered myself up before I was vomiting again into the bowl. Wrung out, I slid to the bottom of the canoe and begged the damn thing to stop rocking.

It seemed like only minutes had passed before I heard Sinatra's loud tribute to the morning sun ... or rather his call for breakfast.

Slow and tentative, I crawled out of the canoe like a lobster.

Sunlight assaulted my bleary eyes and made them water. With a hard squint, I shuffled my way to the workbench where I kept Sinatra's food. I was too hungover to wash out his food bowls, so I used a plate for his wet food and a cereal bowl for his dry food. To my surprise, he didn't dart away when I opened the door. But when I stepped outside, he crouched down as if preparing to bolt. I probably looked like a zombie with my wild hair and red eyes. I put the plate and bowl on the ground near his other dishes, then headed to the outhouse.

An outhouse is not a pleasant place to begin with, but it is utter hell when one is hungover and nauseated. By the time I finished peeing and vomiting, I was so dizzy and grossed out I nearly fell out the door. I wanted to die.

For the better part of an hour, I sat shivering in the grass with my back against the boathouse and my head in my hands. When everything finally stopped spinning, I went inside to retrieve my drinking straw and a cooking pot. Outside, I filled the pot with lake water, then used my straw to drink from the pot which was much easier than drinking directly from the lake. Icy water slid down my parched throat as I sucked hard and greedily guzzled what seemed to be a half gallon of water. While I sat on the shore with my left arm circling the pot, and my right hand holding the straw, Sinatra made his way over. He lapped at the lake water for a couple of minutes, then sat and looked at me.

"Let this be a lesson to you," I said, wondering if my words were coming out as slurred as they sounded in my head.

Sinatra stretched out in the sunshine and appeared to drift off.

After setting aside the pot, I flopped onto my back and fell asleep ... or passed out. The sound of something crashing along the path startled me awake. Sinatra shot off into the woods while I tried not to pee my pants. I had no idea what animal or beast might be tromping down the path, but whatever it was it was heading toward the lake. Toward *me*. And I had nothing but a pot and a survival straw with which to defend myself.

To my relief—and great horror—Chloe and Maggie stepped out of the weed-congested path and stumbled to a halt when they saw me still half-sprawled on the beach. Their jaws dropped, they glanced at each other, presumably exchanging looks from beneath their sunglasses, and swung their gazes back to me.

Already on one knee, I pushed the rest of the way up and staggered to my feet. My eyes burned and my mouth felt like a garbage can. I began to think this was just an alcohol-induced nightmare until Maggie laughed.

"Girl, you are a hot mess," she said.

"An astute observation and a huge understatement," I said, sounding as gruff as a forty-year smoker. I wanted to walk into the lake and disappear into the weeds by the dock.

"Oh, Kate ...," Chloe said, moving toward me. "I wish you would have stayed until you felt better. It's obvious it hasn't been a good morning for you."

Another understatement.

"So, this is where you've been staying then?" Maggie asked, taking in the boathouse, the cat dishes outside, and the drinking straw and cooking pot lying on the beach near my feet.

"What do you mean?" I asked, a frisson of panic snaking through me. "I told you I was checking on the property."

"That you did." Maggie surveyed the area as she strode toward me, her red hair glowing in the sun as she began to cluck her tongue. "Dear Kate, you also told us that you left Dan and were living in the boathouse."

"What?!" My voice shrieked so loud it raised a ruckus among the birds in the woods.

"We decided to check on you to make sure you were all right." Maggie propped one hand on her slender hip. How she managed to look so stunning the morning after a drinking binge baffled me ... and kind of pissed me off. "Looks like you weren't joking about living here," she said.

For Maggie and Chloe to see me like this was so humiliating I wanted to weep. I was literally shaking with emotion, although I grudgingly attributed some of the shakes to my hangover. Still, to have them see me at my lowest point ever was mortifying. I'd planned to get my life in order first, and then try to repair my friendship with them. All I'd managed to do was drink all of Chloe's beer and look like an idiot.

As Chloe moved in, she asked, "Are you all right?"

"Not really," I said. "The last time I was hungover on this beach was our senior year after the homecoming dance. In the twenty-some years since, I haven't touched alcohol until two nights ago when I drank a quart of beer out here at the lake." I slid my fingers into my hair, wild from a night of hell, and raked it off my sweaty forehead. "I'm sorry I was such an idiot last night."

Maggie burst out laughing. "You were hilarious, Kate. We'd forgotten how irreverent and funny you are. Chloe and I both talked about that this morning. We had a blast last night."

"We really did, Kate. I can't tell you how much I needed a night like that." As Chloe's gaze took in the boathouse, her eyes became assessing. "I think you're right. This could make an awesome little house."

I was glad she could see the potential. "I'm planning to repurpose some of the items from my grandparents' house and their old camper."

"Yes, you shared that with us last night," Chloe said, still evaluating the boathouse.

I groaned and buried my face in my hands. "I'm sorry. I had no idea I was so drunk. I apologize for everything stupid I probably said and did last night."

They both released a soft laugh and put their arms around me. Tears flooded my eyes, and it was nearly impossible to hold back a sob.

"Last night was the first time I've really laughed in months," Chloe said. "And it was because of you. And maybe a little because of Maggie," she added.

"That's right," Maggie said, giving me a gentle squeeze. "Best girl-gab we've had in years. But girl, I gotta tell ya, you need a shower."

Our laughter rolled down the beach. As my friends released me, I wiped my eyes and thanked them for the much-needed night out and the not-so-appreciated hangover. Still, I felt ashamed that I'd overshared last night, dumping my problems on the shoulders of a woman who was already carrying the weight of the world on her own.

"I've got plenty of room at my house, Kate, and I'd love the company," Chloe said. "Come stay with me while you work on your place."

Her generous offer brought another flood of emotion that I valiantly fought back. "Thank you, Chloe. Truly, I appreciate your offer, and I know it would be the sane thing to do, but I need to fight things out right here." I shrugged. "I know I must sound crazy, and I can't explain it, but it's something I have to do."

Empathy filled her eyes as she held my bleary gaze. "I do understand. We have to climb our way out of our own ditches."

Of course she understood. Chloe was working her way out of her own grief-filled trench.

"Do you have running water or power out here?" Maggie asked.

"Not yet. I'm having the well tested in a few days. At some point I'll get a generator and use that until I can get the wiring inspected and the electricity turned on."

"I have a generator," Chloe said, her eyes brightening. "I'll bring it over later today."

"Thank you, but I can't let you do that, especially after drinking all your beer."

"It's literally sitting in my barn collecting dust along with equipment and cabinets full of tools. To see even one of those things get some use again would make me happy." From the look in her eyes, I believed her. "And you can buy the six-pack for our next girl-gab, so no worries there."

Maggie gave me a slight nod as if to silently convey that I should accept Chloe's offer, that this gesture would somehow help Chloe more than it would help me.

"I can give you a hand here too," Chloe added. "If you want one, that is. I'm pretty handy with tools and such."

I glanced at Maggie for guidance. I didn't want to take advantage of Chloe, but if helping me would help her, it was the only way I could possibly offer her support right now.

Maggie raised her hands, palms out. "Count me out on the hammering. My specialty is decorating. When you girls get to that point, I'm in."

I had my answer then. To think they were both standing here willing to help, after I'd literally abandoned them for so many years, made me feel like the slime left on the bottom of Sinatra's wet food bowl. How could I accept their help when I didn't deserve it? I shouldn't. I knew that. But the thought of having them around, of spending time with the two women I'd missed for so many years, was impossible to pass up. Another flood of emotion assailed me, and I blubbered out my thanks and blamed my wobbly emotions on all the alcohol they'd made me drink last night.

"First things first," Maggie said, taking me by the shoulders and pointing me toward the boathouse. "Grab some clean clothes, a toothbrush, and a brush for that hair of yours." She moved to my side, leaned back, and eyed my head. "I have no idea what's going on with that," she said, stirring her finger in the air to encompass my hair. "But we'll get you fixed up. We're taking you to Chloe's house for a shower, coffee, and breakfast."

"Oh god, no breakfast," I said, guarding my roiling stomach with my forearm.

They both laughed and promised they wouldn't force food on me. But they were both insistent on the shower.

Fifteen minutes later, I stood beneath the spray of Chloe's shower, one hand braced against the wall for support. I was still a bit woozy but recovered enough to feel the warm water raining over my throbbing head and aching body. That might have been the best gift I'd ever been given. I lathered my hair and scrubbed my head using both hands, but when I tipped my head back to rinse my hair, the world tilted beneath me. Splaying both arms wide, I caught myself against the wall and the sliding shower door. The resulting bang made me cringe.

A second later, Chloe called from the other side of the bathroom door. "Are you okay, Kate?"

"Yep! Just fine," I said, so embarrassed I was sweating. "Just banged my elbow against the shower door."

"All right. Coffee is ready when you are. No rush though."

"Thanks. I'll be out in a minute." I wanted to spend the day in the shower, but I'd imposed enough already. It took me another few minutes to finish rinsing my hair and wash up, but when I finally opened the shower door, I thought I might just "live to fight another day."

Coffee is a drink of the gods.

It is jet fuel for the weary.

It is an elixir for the hungover.

As I huddled over my cup, sipping myself back to sobriety, Maggie and Chloe discussed my situation and proposed ideas.

"If you use my generator until you get the electricity turned on," Chloe reiterated, "you'll be able to use a heater inside and also an incinerator toilet instead of the outhouse."

"A what?" I asked, lifting my head to look at her.

"An incinerating toilet. It's clean, efficient, and doesn't use water. No waste or chemicals either. Just plug it in and it's ready to go."

"That sounds too good to be true."

"You can order one online," Chloe said, swiping her phone on. After a quick search, she handed me her phone. "They have them in stock."

The toilet was bulky looking compared to traditional toilets, but it was beautifully designed and came in white and stainless steel. This would be perfect for my small home. For the first time all morning, I began to feel a tremor of energy moving through me —until I saw the price. Over two thousand dollars. I gawked at Chloe.

"I know," she said. "It's expensive, but it will be far less expensive than having to plumb a toilet and put in a leach field."

My shoulders sagged beneath the weight of my reality. "I have fifty-one dollars to my name. I literally can't afford anything right now."

"You could sell your ring," Maggie said, giving a nod toward my left hand. "If you're not planning on going back to your husband that is."

I considered her statement while I studied the diamond ring Dan had bought for me on our twentieth anniversary. I'd been happy with the simple and inexpensive gold band he'd purchased for our wedding. It was all he'd been able to afford at the time, but that band had meant much more to me than the flashy diamond ring he'd given me at our twentieth anniversary party. That ring had been for show, to let his friends and peers know he was a success who could afford to spend several thousand dollars on a gift for his wife. There had been no tender words spoken in private between the two of us. He'd given me the ring at the height of the party. While everyone looked on, Dan performed like an actor on stage as he presented his gift to me. He finished with a flourish by dipping me backward on his arm and planting a brief, popping kiss on my mouth, then giving me a playful spin that left me standing an arm's length away from him. Our guests were enchanted with his performance. They clapped, laughed, and exclaimed that it was utterly romantic, that we were the ideal couple. That's exactly what Dan had wanted them to think, and it's what I had let them believe. It's what I'd tried so hard to believe through most of our marriage.

But we weren't that couple, and in hindsight, I don't think we ever were. At one time we'd been attracted to each other. We'd enjoyed sex with each other. And we'd had two children together. But I don't think we'd ever really been in love with one another.

Still, to sell my ring ... No matter how much I wanted that incinerator toilet, I couldn't hock my ring to buy it. I wasn't yet divorced so it felt wrong. Plus, it was the only thing of monetary value I had left. Maybe I was being dumb to hang on to it when my financial situation was so desperate, but I'd always thought to leave it to my girls when I died. This ring, however jaded, represented the union of the two people who had brought our girls into this world, who had loved and raised them, who would go to their graves loving them.

I couldn't sell it. I would have to find another way to carve out a life for myself even if I had to use duct tape and shoelaces to do it.

Chapter Eight

I hadn't accomplished much after my shower at Chloe's yesterday, but I was up early and ready to go today.

Chloe was coming over with her brush hog to clean out the path to the boathouse. The two of us had struggled so much yesterday evening trying to drag the generator out here, Chloe had dropped the F-bomb and vowed to clear the path first thing this morning.

After feeding Sinatra, I used the outhouse. When I came back out, Sinatra's head lifted and his ears twitched. As the sound of a tractor grew louder, he scouted the area, then shot down the beach and veered off into the woods away from the noise.

The clanking buzzing sound of mower blades cutting through thick clumps of weeds and small saplings filled the air. I couldn't see Chloe yet, but the sound of her rotary mower was so sweet, I nearly wept with joy. While Chloe groomed the lake trail that provided access to the boathouse from the road, I sat on the grass and looked over the list we'd made after she'd delivered the generator yesterday. Together, we had talked about the layout for my house and what materials it would take to convert the boathouse to a livable shelter. I would need plumbing and bathroom fixtures and kitchen appliances among scads of other things, none of which I could afford. I'd been too exhausted to haul my old mattress out to the boathouse, so I'd slept in the canoe, again, and spent most of the night wondering what other things I might be able to repurpose from the camper or salvage from my grandparents' house. The appliances and bathroom fixtures in the house were too big to use out here, but the stuff in the camper might work if years of disuse hadn't ruined them.

When Chloe's red tractor poked its nose out of the woods, followed by the beastly yellow brush hog, she greeted me with a smile, and I gave her a wave. She looked different today, her eyes a bit brighter, her countenance less strained as she brought the tractor to a stop. She shut off the brush hog and waved me over. "I'll bring my stump grinder over tomorrow and smooth out the rough spots," she said as I approached. "By tomorrow afternoon you'll see the old lake trail your grandfather had cut through the woods."

I could already see a short distance down the path where the brush hog had done its job clearing weeds, bushes, and small saplings. A wide mowed section opened before me, and I had a sudden urge to skip like Dorothy down the yellow brick road. To think I would no longer have to fight my way through the overgrowth was such a relief I sighed. "I could kiss you, Chloe." I swung my gaze back to where she sat atop the huge tractor, work gloves covering her hands, a ball cap covering her head, and a look of satisfaction on her face. "Thank you for this."

"My pleasure," she said. "And I mean that, Kate. It feels so good to be doing something useful again."

Her comment sounded more like a confession, and I could see she'd needed to do this work as much as I'd needed it done.

"While I've got the mower here, I'll do a few passes to clear your lawn," she said, gesturing with a wide sweep of her arm toward the overgrown area of lawn between the woods and the shoreline. With that, she cranked the tractor to life, and with a grinding start, she drove down the tree line. By the time she'd finished, I saw the place of my youth coming back to life, the mowed yard and grassy beach area where I'd spent so many summers picnicking with my family and my best friends.

After she cut the mower on the brush hog again, she brought the tractor around, stopping it beside me. "Okay, Kate, let's get your house built."

How was it possible she was here, willing to help me, the shithead who'd deserted her, who hadn't even sent a sympathy card when her world had crashed down around her? It didn't feel as if she were forgiving me and we were moving on. Chloe was treating me as if my abandonment had never happened, as if we'd never lost touch, as if I'd been the kind of friend I should have been to her all along. Same for Maggie. Their welcoming acceptance and love were so foreign to the world I'd been living in where every act was judged, and every misstep was noted and held against you. The code of acceptable behavior and belief had been carved in stone and was enforced with public shaming and shunning. There, you were either *in* or you were *out*. But now, with Chloe and Maggie, there was an in-between, a time when paths diverged and friends lost touch ... and when your paths crossed again it was a moment of joy and celebration—not judgment and condemnation.

"Hop on," Chloe said, waving me up onto the tractor. "I'll drive us out front to the big house."

I grabbed hold of her hand and stepped up as she gave me a firm tug. She scooted over and patted the open half of the tractor seat. We each sat with half a butt cheek on the seat and our feet braced on the floorboard as we made our way down the mowed path to my grandparents' dilapidated house. I smiled at the irony of having nothing and yet feeling unfairly rich with my best friend sitting beside me.

Chloe and I did a walk-through of the house and camper, discussing how we would salvage every scrap of wood, and how we could design a temporary kitchen and bathroom using the camper cupboards, sink, and appliances. I had enough money to buy a box or two of nails and screws, and Chloe had all the tools we would need, but I was a long way from being able to start building. Still, I believed Chloe was as excited as I was about the project we were undertaking.

We were in the living room checking out the windows when we heard a shriek coming from the front of the house. Chloe and I both rushed into the kitchen expecting to see a wild critter roaming loose, but we found Maggie inspecting the old stove.

"This is incredible, Kate!" she said, swinging her gaze to me. "You have a pile of cash sitting here." She gestured toward the stove and refrigerator.

"I do?" All I saw were bulky old appliances that had gone out of style decades ago.

"Are you kidding?" Maggie shook her head. "These pieces are a retro lover's dream. If they work, I can sell these pieces in a hot minute."

"Really?" A little bubble of hope rose up in me. "Do you think I could get a hundred bucks for them?" A hundred dollars would be a huge help right now.

Maggie gave my head a little pat. "You are so cute, Kate."

"What?" I asked, genuinely confused. I suspected I was being accused of ignorance, but I wasn't sure why. "Is that too much?"

She must have realized I was clueless and took pity on me. "You can get hundreds of dollars for them."

"Are you serious?"

"Yep. Just take some pics and pop them online."

My heart sank. "I know nothing about these appliances and wouldn't know how to describe them, much less know where to list them."

"Then let me do it for you so you don't get scammed."

"Would you? That would be wonderful, Maggie. We can split the sale fifty-fifty."

"Oh my god, Kate, I'm begging you to stay offline and to not make any deals on your own. You'll lose your shirt," Maggie said. "I'll take my standard ten percent friends and family discounted rate, only so you don't argue with me."

I threw my arms around her and gave her a hug. "Thank you!"

Feeling a little embarrassed over my loss of control, I stepped back and straightened my dirty shirt. "Do you think you could sell a claw-foot bathtub too?"

Her eyes widened. "You have a claw-foot tub?" When she followed me to the bathroom, she gasped. "Kate, if this is what I think it is, you'll have plenty of money for that incinerating toilet."

When all was said and done, Maggie estimated that the kitchen appliances and cast-iron farm sink with a drainboard drop, along with the bathroom fixtures consisting of a cast-iron pedestal sink, a high tank pull chain toilet, and claw-foot cast-iron double slipper bathtub could potentially bring in as much as six or seven thousand dollars. The estimate was so stunning, and the relief of a potential influx of cash so overwhelming, I began to shake. To think that I'd considered giving the items away just to get the stuff out of the house was so stupid of me I didn't dare tell Maggie.

"How long do you think it will take to sell everything?" I asked, so desperate for money I considered selling everything at half price.

Maggie shrugged. "We'll get a ton of interest, but to get the best price we'll need to find the right buyer. That could take a few days or a few weeks. Hard to estimate, but it will take a little time."

Time I didn't have. "Would it help them sell faster if we discounted the price?"

"Yes, but it would be foolish to do. These things are in pristine condition and worth top dollar." She took another quick look around the bathroom where the three of us had crowded in during Maggie's initial inspection. "Let me take some pictures and pop them online tonight to see what kind of response we get. That will give me an idea of how quickly the items will sell."

"All right," I said, mostly because I had no other option. But I sent up a silent prayer asking for a quick sale. Realizing what I'd just done, that I still had my old life ingrained in me, I silently took back my prayer. Not because I thought anyone had been listening but because I was consciously trying to overwrite the coding embedded in my brain. I was done with that life and that way of thinking. A fairytale deity wasn't going to buy my appliances and fixtures. It would be some person on eBay or Facebook or wherever else Maggie posted it.

Satisfied that I'd scrubbed that piece of code from my brain, I took Maggie through the rest of the house. She was extremely interested in the handmade vanity which she claimed was an exceptional piece, but I said it wasn't for sale. It had been lovingly made by my grandfather's gentle hands. In the beveled vanity mirror, I could still see Sophie looking back at me, her eyes full of mischief, her laughter filling the bedroom. The vanity was all I had left of Papa Ray and my little sister.

We took a quick break to eat the subs and chips that Maggie had brought, and to drink the refreshingly cold water and sodas she'd stashed in the cooler. She'd filled the cooler to the brim with beverages and topped the cans and bottles with a bag of ice. I thanked her effusively by chowing down my whole sub and guzzling two bottles of water and a can of soda. The three of us sprawled in the grass outside, kicking around ideas for my little house, and discussing how we were going to salvage the materials I would need from my grandparents' house. One thing that kept tripping us up in our renovation plan was that the wiring needed to be inspected first. I couldn't put up walls until I had the wiring inspected. And I couldn't get the wiring inspected until I could afford to pay for the service call and any needed updates. Chloe and Maggie both offered to loan me the money, but I couldn't allow them to do that. They'd already given me far more than I deserved, and I wouldn't borrow anything I wasn't certain I could pay back.

"All right, you stubborn wench," Maggie said, leaning back on her hands and eyeing me shrewdly. "Let me buy the bathtub for twenty-five hundred dollars. I'll pay you now, so you'll have the money to get started on your place. I think I can get as much as three thousand for it. When I sell it, I'll just pocket the money."

Her proposal would solve my immediate problem, but I was concerned it would put her in a tight spot financially. "Can you afford to do that?"

Maggie laughed. "This is what I do, Kate. I buy and sell things all the time. This is no different. I'm not doing you any favors here."

"Yes, you are," I said, "and I really appreciate it."

"That's settled then," she said, pushing off her hands to sit upright. "And I know someone who can inspect your wiring."

"This day is too good to be true." I shifted my teary gaze between my two friends. "I don't know how to thank you both. Not just for your help, but for being here when I don't deserve it."

They exchanged a perplexed look, as if they couldn't understand my comment or concern. Chloe raised her can of soda and said, "Friends for life, right?"

"Right," Maggie said, raising her own can of soda.

I raised my nearly empty water bottle and said, "Absolutely. From here on out, nothing comes between us." The three of us brought our cans and water bottles together with a soft thud.

We didn't get much done after that. Maggie wiped down the items she was going to post online for sale, took several pictures of each appliance and fixture, then spent an hour listing them online. Chloe and I inspected the appliances in the camper and were pleased to see the wiring hadn't been chewed on by rodents and the pieces didn't appear cosmetically damaged. As long as they worked properly, I could create a small, functional kitchen with them to tide me over until I could afford better appliances. And while digging through cupboards, I stumbled across the small propane gas grill my grandfather had cooked our hamburgers and hotdogs on. If I could get it to work, I could finally heat water and cook on it. To make something other than cereal and peanut butter sandwiches for supper would be a treat.

By the end of the day, we were all tired. Chloe offered me the use of her shower and a ride both directions, but I'd taken far more than I'd given today, and I assured her I could manage here. She had brought over two thick comforters for me to use, insisting I keep them until I got heat in my house or until summer arrived, whichever came first.

After they left, I went back inside the house and got my old mattress from the bedroom. I folded it in half and carried it with both arms like a big sack in front of me. It was bulky and heavy, but I walked unhindered down the wide path Chloe had mowed for me. At that moment, I realized that's what friends did for one another. They cleared paths for each other. They brought food when you were hungry. They hugged you in celebration and held you when you cried. They overlooked your faults and bad choices —and they helped you rebuild your life.

Chapter Nine

C hloe came back on Tuesday with her stump grinder and spent half the day cleaning and smoothing out the path until it somewhat resembled a narrow dirt road. The path, or rather the lake trail as we'd called it, was wide enough now for a vehicle, which would make it much easier for Chloe and me to haul salvaged materials between my grandparents' house, which we referred to as the big house, and my place as the boathouse. She'd also brought over a thick sheet of plywood that we tacked down on the porch of my grandparents' house to cover the rotting floor-boards and provide us safe passage in and out.

Together in the boathouse, we mapped the layout of my little home using a fat white chalk stick to mark where the walls would go to create a utility room and a bathroom. The rest of my house would be open post and beam. Then we marked the designated spot for each kitchen appliance and bathroom fixture. I wished I could share this adventure with my daughters, but they wouldn't see this as an adventure. They would see it as a betrayal. A wave of unease rolled through me as I thought about the hard conversation we would all soon be having. The girls would finish their freshman year at college soon. Then they would be coming home—to a house I no longer occupied.

Dan and I would need to talk first, to figure out the best way to tell our girls that we were getting a divorce, but the thought of seeing him again rattled me.

Despite the deep unrelenting worry over my daughters, my excitement grew with each passing day and each new idea, but my concern grew too. Until Maggie sold all the items she'd posted online for me, presuming she could do so, I had barely enough money to get started with the inspections, much less the renovation. Maggie, who'd had to work during the week, had called once to say she'd sold the kitchen sink and would deliver the money from that sale along with the twenty-five hundred she'd promised for the bathtub on Friday morning.

During the days I kept myself busy, and usually Chloe, and sometimes Maggie, was with me, so I could block out the reality of my precarious situation. But at night when I sat alone in a cold, empty building everything hit me. Wave upon wave of dread would wash over me. During those dark hours I felt scared and overwhelmed by the mountainous task of trying to build a life here. I worried myself sick over my girls, missing them so fiercely I ached. My sleep was so fitful and uncomfortable, even on a mattress with the extra comforters Chloe had loaned to me, it was a relief to get up in the morning to escape the torture. But when I'd wake in the early dawn hours, and realize the day was mine to do with as I wished, I'd experience such a profound sense of relief it would bring tears to my eyes. No church services to attend. No meals to make. No catering to Dan's wishes, requests, or demands. No hiding my true self. No smothering my dreams and desires.

Still, I felt my past life nagging me. No matter what I was working on, I kept feeling as if I should be doing something else. Sundays and Wednesdays, and often other evenings each week, had been filled with church services and events that had claimed the hours of my life. Now my days and nights were my own, but I could feel that old, heavy sense of obligation bearing down on me.

It was just after eight o'clock on Friday morning when Chloe arrived with a thermos of hot coffee and four single gallon jugs of water. I was already at my grandparents' house waiting for her. Maggie pulled in a couple minutes later with a box of blueberry scones, sweet cream, and twenty-nine hundred dollars. I never thought I'd be so excited over an envelope full of money, but the packet of one-hundred-dollar bills represented my freedom. I was so relieved, I gave Maggie a big hug, then jogged out to the boathouse to stash the money safely in my envelope, then hide it in an old coffee can tucked under the workbench. I couldn't afford to lose a single dollar right now.

I hurried back to find Maggie and Chloe sitting on the tailgate of Chloe's pickup truck. They were drinking coffee and eating scones. "Come on up," Chloe said, patting the empty space between them. Once I'd hiked myself up onto the tailgate, which was no easy task, Maggie handed me the cup of coffee they'd already poured for me. I had just taken a bite of my scone when a utility van pulled in the driveway. At first, I thought it was someone just turning around. But Maggie slid off the tailgate and walked over to the van. A minute later, a man exited the vehicle, gave Maggie a hug, then followed her over to where we were sitting.

The guy was tall and cut like an athlete. Dark hair poked out from beneath his Yankees ball cap, and the face under the brim of that cap was tan and handsome—and familiar.

"Kate, do you remember my older brother Ashe?" Maggie asked as the two of them stopped before us.

That face ... that tall, good-looking guy was one I'd never forget. "Sure," I said, trying to maintain a nonchalance I didn't feel. "Good to see you again, Ashe."

"Likewise," he said, a slow grin tilting his mouth as his eyes roamed free range over my tied back hair, dirty clothes, and duct-taped sneakers.

The sudden onslaught of heat rolling through my body was so shocking, I wondered if I was experiencing my first hot flash. I'd heard they were awful and uncontrollable. This felt exactly like that.

"I hear you're in need of an electrician," he said, hooking his thumb in the front pocket of his jeans.

"I am?" My body was so overheated I could barely think.

He arched an eyebrow and looked at Maggie.

She laughed and gave me a nudge. "You said you needed to get your wiring inspected, so I asked Ashe to do it for you. He's a licensed electrician."

"Oh, um, yes, of course. That's great. Thank you," I said, warning myself to get a grip before Maggie wondered why I was being so weird. "Do you want to check out the wiring now?" I asked, looking at Ashe and trying to ignore how handsome he was. My reaction to him was embarrassing—and so alien to how I'd been living my life. As a pastor's wife my eyes had only seen my husband and children, and my senses had been systematically numbed to anything outside our controlled Christian life.

"I'd prefer a cup of coffee first, if that's all right," he said.

"Oh! Of course. I'm sorry. I hadn't meant to be rude," I said, blathering like an idiot. To shut my mouth, I filled it with coffee. *Scalding* coffee! It burned all the way down my throat and made my eyes tear. Oh my god, could I be any more ridiculous?

Maggie poured a cup of coffee for Ashe and also gave him one of the scones. While we ate and drank our coffee, Maggie and Chloe filled Ashe in on my plans for my little house. I sat in silence, wishing I had an ice cube to stick in my hot, stupid mouth.

When we all finished our scones, Maggie refilled her coffee and said she had to get back to her shop. While Ashe moved his van so she could get out of the driveway, Chloe refilled our coffee cups. Then she turned to me with a knowing grin. "Want to tell me what that thing with Ashe was all about?"

My face must have flamed like a torch because my cheeks were on fire. "Yeah, I wish Maggie would have given me a heads up so I wasn't caught off balance. I didn't realize he was here to inspect the wiring."

"Okay," Chloe said, but I knew she didn't believe a word I'd said. Her just-between-us wink made that obvious. "I'm going to head inside and get started."

After Ashe pulled back in, I shoved his coffee cup in his hand and told him to follow me.

Seconds into our walk, he asked, "Are you a waitress?"

As I strode down the path a half step in front of him, I looked over my shoulder but kept walking. "No. Why?"

"Because I'm spilling my coffee trying to keep up with you." He nodded toward my cup. "You haven't spilled a drop."

"Sorry," I said, reeling myself in. Ashe's unexpected appearance had spiraled me back to my teens, and I was acting like an idiot. "I've had a lot of practice carrying things while chasing two kids."

"Maggie said you have twin girls."

I nodded. "They're in college now, so not much chasing these days. How about you?" I asked. "Any kids?"

"A son, just turned twenty-one."

I'd lost track of Ashe long ago, perhaps intentionally as it had made it easier to keep my focus on my husband and girls. But now, I surreptitiously glanced at his left hand, the one holding his coffee cup, and I didn't see a wedding band. But he was a contractor, an electrician who worked with his hands. Wearing a ring was dangerous business in that kind of job. His lack of a ring probably meant nothing.

Not that it mattered. Because it didn't.

But I couldn't deny being curious.

"How big is your boathouse?" he asked.

"Sixteen by thirty according to the measurements that Chloe and I took yesterday."

"Hmm ... four hundred and eighty feet might not be big enough," he said.

"It'll be plenty big enough for me," I replied, and then blathered on about how sturdy the building was because my grandfather had built it, and that the wiring was surely in great shape because my grandfather installed it, and that I was excited about finishing the work on the boathouse my grandfather had started.

For a moment, Ashe said nothing, but as we exited the trail and the boathouse came into view, he gave it a good looking-over. "Is that a plate taped on the roof?"

And I'd thought I couldn't feel more embarrassed. I'd forgotten about my repair job on the roof. "It's a temporary fix to keep the rain out."

His deep chuckle was both sexy and humiliating. "Creative, I'll give you that." Without waiting for an invitation, he opened the door and let himself in. "So, this is your She Shed ..."

Although I'd cleaned things up and had done my best to store my stuff in some sort of orderly fashion, the place was still a mess.

"Definitely potential here," he said, looking around. "And you're right. It's a nice solid structure. Let's see how the wiring looks."

Like a puppy at his heels, I followed him around as he inspected the wiring and outlets and fuse box. "I assume you'll want more outlets," he said.

I readily agreed but had no idea how to go about adding them. I had about a dozen questions, but I kept my mouth shut and let him talk.

"Your grandfather did a nice job on the wiring," he finally said. "And it looks to be in good shape. No bare spots to indicate rodents."

Good grief, I hadn't even considered that.

After a few more minutes of inspecting things, he said, "You'll need to replace your fuse box with a breaker panel."

Silently, I groaned, wondering how much that would cost.

"Hmm, where does this wire go?" he asked as if thinking out loud. His curiosity led him outside behind the boathouse. He stopped and looked at the dilapidated open-air shower stall. "Did you have running water out here?"

"A long time ago."

"Where did the water come from?" he asked.

I had no idea. "The well out front perhaps?"

"Where's that?"

"By my grandparents' place."

"It would take a big-ass pump and a lot of pipe to get water all the way out here." He began kicking his way through a patch of thigh-high weeds directly behind the boathouse where Chloe hadn't been able to navigate the wide brush hog. "There must be a well out here."

Two wells? Two inspections? And a new breaker panel? A mental image of one-hundred-dollar bills flying out of my cash envelope filled my head.

"What's this?" He kicked something hard. He dropped to his knees and started pulling weeds. As I got closer, I could see he was clearing an area around a steel pipe that stuck up out of the ground about eighteen inches. "Here's your well," he said. "That electrical wire I was tracing is for the well pump. This will make plumbing your house much easier."

That was a good thing for sure. But I wondered how much more it would cost me to get it inspected and perhaps treated, and maybe even dug out again.

"Hmm ... these bolts are rusted. Not sure I'll be able to get them off." He pulled a wrench off his utility belt and began working the bolts that held the well cap in place. It took a few minutes of sweating and biting his lip, but he managed to free the bolts and lift off the cover. He aimed his flashlight down in the well. "You've got water out here. I suspect you'll need a new pump and maybe a new well cap, but as long as the water is okay, you should be set."

A pump? I needed a pump? And a well cap?

From that point on, my brain spun as Ashe walked around outside and inside the boathouse, pointing out the things I would need to make it a livable home. There was plumbing and pumps to consider, a septic tank and leach field for the greywater, a source for heating and cooling, how many outlets I needed, where I might add windows, the best type of insulation to use, and a quick overview of why I should consider using metal to replace the roof, and on and on until I begged him to stop. My brain couldn't hold another detail, and the financial cost of all this stuff was hitting me like an avalanche I couldn't outrun. Ashe must have sensed my panic or seen the defeat that was surely written all over my face, because he leaned against the door and looked at me with sympathetic eyes.

"You sure you want to do this?" he asked.

I had no other options. But the truth was I really did want to do this. I loved this place. I loved the time I'd spent here with my family. I loved the idea and challenge of creating a beautiful lakeside house for myself. But it was readily apparent I wasn't going to be able to do all these things at once. I would have to prioritize my needs and work my way through one job at a time.

"Will the wiring pass inspection?" I asked.

"With a new breaker panel and properly installed outlets, yeah, it'll pass."

"Can you install that stuff for me?"

"Yep."

"What am I looking at cost-wise?" I asked, feeling the room begin to heat up with the two of us now focused on one another.

"With a friends-and-family discount, I estimate between two and three thousand for the electrical work."

My knees nearly gave out. I couldn't even find my voice or words to express my shock and dismay. The reality that I was defeated before I'd really even begun flooded my eyes. Horrified, I turned away and walked to the workbench. I disguised my effort to get a grip on my emotions by filling a dish with cat food.

"If you don't mind upgrading your fuse box with a used breaker panel, it'll save you a bundle. And I have a box full of used electrical outlet boxes you can have. You'd be doing me a favor to take them off my hands and get them out of my way. It would be nice to find my tools without shifting that box around. If you go the used route, you'd be looking at twelve hundred dollars or so."

"Really?" I asked, turning to face him. A thousand dollars was still more than I could afford now, but at least it didn't kill every ounce of hope that I might one day be able to have electricity in my house, and to build a home and a new life, even if only one baby step at a time. "I don't think I can get the electricity turned on until I have a paying job, but at least now I know what to plan for financially."

He was quiet for a long moment while his eyes roved the bones of the boathouse. "Show me your blueprint for your house."

"My what ... I don't have a blueprint. I have chalk marks on the floor."

He laughed. "All right, then show me your chalk marks, and take me through the layout of your house. I want to see where you're planning to place your appliances and such."

I walked him through my small home, indicating how Chloe and I had planned out my kitchen and bathroom, and how we'd even left room for a two-in-one washer-dryer combo. I showed him where the walls would go, which would close off the bathroom and utility room from the rest of the house which would remain an open space. I didn't need a bedroom as I planned to sleep in the living room, hopefully on a sofa bed when I could afford one. For now, I'd be sleeping on my old twin bed wherever it ended up at day's end.

"You can't insulate the walls until you have all the wiring run for your outlets and such, and not before your plumbing is installed and your electrical is inspected and approved. And it's a bad idea to seal things up without a good roof overhead. I assume, based on the plate duct taped to the roof, it leaks?"

I gave a nod as another wave of embarrassment rolled through me. "That's the only place that leaks as far as I can tell."

"If that's the same roof your grandfather put on when he built this place it's pretty old. The shingles are in bad shape from what I could see. I strongly suggest having your roof reshingled, or better yet, upgrading to a metal roof before addressing the electrical work. The benefit of metal is you can put it over your existing shingles. I suspect there's only a single layer of shingles, and the pitch of your roof is steep enough to support the added weight without issue. But it's up to you." His gaze roved the inside structure again. "You'll need to add a second exit door, and I'd also suggest replacing those old windows with double pane ones."

"I plan to replace them," I said. I hadn't thought about adding a second exit door, but my obvious oversight could have spelled disaster in the event of a fire. The feeling that I was getting in over my head assailed me, again, and I suspected it wouldn't be the last time I felt this way.

"All right then," he said, opening the door. I followed him outside where he stopped and eyed the roof again. "Frame in your inside walls first so I can run the wiring and install outlets. Then I'd suggest you fix the roof while I finish wiring your house and swapping out the fuse box with a breaker panel. That way I'll know the electrical will pass inspection, which will allow you to start insulating and hanging sheetrock, or whatever you're going to use for your walls once your plumbing is installed. We can work out a payment plan if that helps."

I wasn't sure why Ashe was willing to help me, but it was help I couldn't turn away. However, until I had a regular income, I couldn't agree to any payment plans. I had to use a pay-as-you-go system. I had three thousand two hundred seventy-six dollars and sixty-eight cents in my envelope. Three hundred and twenty-five dollars of that was earmarked for my well inspection, and that was only for one well. That left twenty-nine hundred fifty-one dollars and change for me to put a roof on my house and pay my electrician.

"If you prefer, I can put the things aside for you," he said, kindness thick in his voice. "And you can let me know when you're ready to get the work done."

"How much more to have you install the outlets?" I asked.

"How about a beer?"

His answer stunned me, and for a moment I didn't know what to say. "You're kidding, of course." I worked up a smile. "Go ahead. I can take it. I promise I won't get all emotional on you again."

His laugh was nice, warm, real. "I'm going to see my son this weekend, so I'll work up a quote on the materials and drop off an estimate on Monday."

"Thank you." He'd been nothing but professional and helpful, but despite his kindness, I felt uneasy and awkward around him. "I'll see you on then."

He gave a nod, turned on the heel of his work boot, and headed down the trail.

After he disappeared in the woods, I exhaled a breath I hadn't realized I'd been holding. I couldn't say if my tension had been from the mountain of work ahead, the financial avalanche burying me, or because the man from my past was still able to make me feel like a teenager.

Until I received his quote, I wouldn't know how severely his services would deplete my cash or what would be left for roofing materials. I wondered if I could repurpose the shingles on my grandparents' house but immediately dismissed the idea. I'd seen pieces of broken shingles on the ground around the house, covered with green moss. I could only surmise the rest of the shingles were in bad shape. Plus, I couldn't even imagine climbing onto a second story roof to pull shingles. Nope. Somehow, I'd have to scrape up the money to buy new shingles or metal roofing.

Chapter Ten

A fter a long day of working on my house, Chloe headed home Saturday evening, and I fed Sinatra his supper. I relaxed outside while he ate. When he finished, he wandered over and lay down a few feet from me. It was the first time he'd gotten so close. If I stretched out my arm and leaned in a little, I'd be able to touch him. But I didn't do it. He'd made it clear that our relationship was developing on his terms, and I respected that.

While he watched, I built a fire. Then I spent several minutes gathering firewood from the woods. As gently as possible, I dumped my armload of sticks near my campfire, hoping the noise wouldn't frighten Sinatra away. His head came up and he watched with wary eyes as I brushed bark off my shirt sleeves. But he stayed.

Retrieving the cooking pot from inside, I came back out and filled it with lake water. Then I set the pot on a flat rock as close to the fire as I dared, hoping the rubber coated handles wouldn't melt. I wanted warm water for my nightly sponge bath. I still hadn't purchased a small tank of propane for the grill I'd found in the camper. And although Chloe's generator was here, I had little use for it other than charging my phone and camp lantern batteries, which she was doing for me a few times a week. I had no electric grill or heater or, to my utter disappointment, a coffee maker to plug in, and even if I'd had those things I couldn't afford gasoline for the generator. That meant doing things old school ... or in my case medieval style.

I stank of sweat, and my jeans and sweatshirt were dirty from my workday. I needed a shower, I couldn't tolerate washing up with frigid lake water. The temperature was in the low fifties and would drop into the low forties overnight. I appreciated the cooler temps of mid-April during the workday, but at day's end, I longed for a bathroom of my own with hot water and a massaging shower head to relieve my aching body.

Sinatra's sudden leap to attention startled me. In the next instant, he shot off into the woods as if a rabid dog were on his tail. Curious, I scanned the woods to see what had startled him. What I saw nearly stopped my heart.

Dan was walking down the path with our daughters, the three of them striding toward me like shepherds intent on rescuing a lost sheep. Kara already had tears in her eyes. Haley seemed curious. Dan looked smug.

That son of a bitch was ambushing me. I could only assume he'd flown the girls in earlier today. He'd probably taken them out to dinner where he'd surely given them his best performance, garnering their sympathy and support before bringing them here. God only knows what he'd told the girls, but whatever it was, I could be sure the blame for our situation had been placed entirely on my shoulders.

Rage brought me to my feet. Fury burned so hard in me, I couldn't speak. I stood there shaking and raging, trying to hold myself together in front of my girls.

Kara broke away and rushed forward to hug me. "Mom, what are you doing here?" she asked, obviously shaken by my unprecedented act of independence.

Instead of answering her, I glared at Dan. "How could you?"

He just stood there in silence and all his misogynistic arrogance, and let my nightmare play out.

"Dad said something is going on with you, that you're not yourself right now," Kara said, stepping back to look at me. "What's wrong, Mom?"

"Nothing is wrong with me, honey—"

"Then why are you here?" she asked, cutting me off with her indignant demand. "Dad said you left him for no reason. That maybe you're in menopause or something."

I fought to hold back my laugh of disbelief. "Kara, this situation between your father and me is something the two of us will handle alone. We had planned to work things out then tell you girls together," I said, which wasn't exactly true. *I* had wanted to come up with a plan to make the transition easier for the girls. But Dan had come up with his own plan, and he didn't give a damn who he hurt as long as he achieved his goal.

"Then come home and work things out there," she pleaded.

"That's not what I meant by working things out, honey." I sighed so I wouldn't sob. I was so fucking mad at Dan for not only ambushing me but for bringing our girls into the middle of an already painful situation and making it worse for them.

Kara burst into tears. "Mom, you can't leave us."

I pulled her back into my arms and held on tight. "I'm not leaving you, sweetheart."

"Yes, you are!" she cried. "We're a family, and we're supposed to be together."

I hated my husband at that moment. He just stood there and watched our daughter fall apart in my arms, as if he'd written the script for this heart-wrenching moment. He knew my vulnerabilities, that I would literally die for my girls, that I would do anything to spare them pain. To see Kara so scared and heartbroken, and to witness the confusion in Haley's eyes as she looked on, tore me in half. They were my babies. I was their mother, and I needed to be there for them.

Holding my little girl, I felt myself splintering into fragments of unrealized dreams. I knew I was entitled to my own life, but I was a mom whose children needed her.

As I stroked Kara's back, Haley slipped into my arms for a three-way hug. "Are you okay, Mom?"

I shook my head because I wasn't okay. My old life and my old self came roaring back. Can't-decide-Kate was waffling with indecision. My girls needed me, and I didn't know what to do.

Haley eased away and rubbed her palm down my arm. "Maybe you could come home and work things out there?" she asked softly. "At least give it a try?"

"Please, Mom. Come home." Kara sniffed and stepped out of my embrace. "Please. For us."

I couldn't break their hearts. I just couldn't do it, and so I gave them a nod while everything inside me dropped into a bottomless pit. I felt dead inside.

Kara threw her arms around me. "Thank you."

Haley didn't say anything, just gave my arm a gentle squeeze.

On wooden legs, I walked over to Dan and put my arms around his neck as if I were willing to reconcile with him, but I was just getting close enough to whisper in his ear. "You're going to fucking pay for this." I felt his body stiffen, and I released him. "I need to get a few things from inside." With that, I turned and walked away from all of them. I needed a moment alone to catch my breath, to catch myself before I crumbled.

Inside, I turned on the camp lantern and looked around, wondering what I really needed to take with me. Other than my purse that contained my ID, I had nothing of value. I would need to take Haley's bike, of course, but we'd be flying home, so we would have to send for it later. My old iron bed sat in the middle of the room. Maybe Maggie could sell it. But I wouldn't need the money so what would be the point? The canoes were of no use in the city. The groceries and clothing that filled one of them wasn't worth taking. I considered taking the sundress and the cowboy boots, but I remembered I was returning to the life of a pastor's wife who was expected to dress modestly.

As I scanned the room, my gaze fell on Gussie, her lime green body pushed into a far corner of the room. I remembered the last time Gussie and I mowed our lawn and the conversation I'd had with Dan when he'd cavalierly told me to throw away my dream. And I thought of Rusty and all the years I'd talked with a lawn mower because I couldn't talk with my husband.

I spied Sinatra's bag of cat food, along with several cans of wet food, sitting on the workbench. Tears burned my eyes. Who would take care of him when I left? Would Chloe do it? Thinking of Chloe brought more tears. The white chalk lines on the floor where Chloe and I had marked out my kitchen and bathroom were visible in the lantern light. Those lines represented the resurrection of our friendship and the new life I'd been building here— before Dan ambushed me. The thought of going back to him, to our oppressive misogynistic relationship, and living in a cage again was a death sentence.

I wanted to comfort my girls, to be there for them whenever they needed me, but I needed more to teach them something of value; that following your dream wasn't selfish, it was courageous, and that you never had to ask permission to take control of your life.

My going back would only teach them how to be submissive, how to give away their power, how to let someone else crush their dreams. My leaving was hurting them. But my going back would hurt them more.

Kara and Haley were watching me from the open doorway. "Do you need a hand with anything?" Haley asked.

As I looked into the beautiful faces of my daughters, I knew this life lesson would be one of the hardest they would learn. "Yeah. I need you to trust me when I say I have to stay here."

"What!" Kara gaped at me, anger flashing in her eyes. "I thought you were coming home."

She was such a beautiful girl with her delicate features and blonde hair. She resembled me in my teen years, but she was her father's daughter. She was anxious and high strung and easily offended. I knew this was going to be a long journey for both of us.

"Why would you want to stay in this place?" she asked,

gesturing to the mess around me. "It's just an old barn. And you smell, Mom! You don't even have a bathroom here." That she was appalled was apparent in her expression.

"I know it doesn't look like much right now, but I'm going to make a beautiful home here."

"That's ridiculous." She gave me a scathing look. "You're ruining my life!" With that, she stalked off without another word.

I shifted my gaze to Haley who still stood in the doorway looking the place over ... looking me over. "I'll call you when I get back to school," she said.

My throat ached from suppressing a sob. Forcing myself to inhale and release the clamp on my throat, I whispered, "Thank you, baby."

"Love you," she said, and then she was gone too.

Dan didn't bother sticking his head in the door. He knew he'd lost.

But so had I.

And so had our daughters.

I went outside to see him walking the girls down the path, an arm around each of them, their backs to me. As I watched my family walk away, I collapsed in tears and wept until I couldn't breathe.

I thought of how tiny they'd been when they were born, thought about the earaches and belly aches and nights of walking the floor with them, and how their little mouths would purse in sleep. Nightly bath rituals and years of bedtime stories and birthday parties flipped through my mind like pages in a photo book.

I'd watched my girls change, losing their baby teeth, getting their first bras, discovering the devastating first pimple, crying over bad hair days, experiencing their first innocent crush. Our lives had played out against the backdrop of church life, and Dan and I had raised our girls in the loving arms of their parents and Jesus. I'd thought I was doing the right thing. But I'd gotten it all wrong.

For a long time, I huddled against the boathouse staring at my dwindling campfire and thinking about my girls. How I'd raised them. How I'd failed them.

Sinatra came around and settled near the fire. I became so lost in thought, it took a moment to realize that he was rubbing his head against my leg. That small bit of affection made me sob again because I was so pathetically lonely and utterly heartbroken over hurting my girls. He let me pet him twice before he sidled away to the other side of the campfire. Then he shot off into the woods.

The sound of footsteps walking along the path scared me. No one came here this late at night. It was dark and I couldn't see who or what was making the noise, but it was heading toward me. I hadn't considered how vulnerable I would be out here alone. I didn't know what to do. By the time I thought to run inside, a person emerged from the woods. I could see a shadowy outline in the backlight of what I presumed to be a phone.

"Mom?"

The sound of Haley's voice made me gasp with relief. Utterly surprised by her return, I asked, "What are you doing here, sweetie?"

"I had to come back," she said, rushing into my arms.

We hugged for a long moment, her shaking, me fighting tears. "Oh, sweetie ..."

Releasing me, she stepped away. "Do you have a cat?"

"What? No. Maybe. I don't know," I said, my brain bending from her unexpected question.

"Are you feeding it?" she asked.

"Yeah."

"Then you have a cat," she said, releasing a little laugh.

"Are you here alone?" I asked, hoping it was the case because I didn't have the energy to deal with Kara's heartbreaking pleas or trust myself not to kill their father.

"Yeah. I'd really like to understand what's going on," she said, her voice filled with love and a maturity her twin hadn't yet acquired.

"Well, I'm not in menopause," I said, and we both laughed

which felt really good after the wringer of a weep-fest I'd just had. I tossed a few sticks on the dwindling fire and sat in the grass where I'd spent so many nights alone. To have Haley sitting here with me was heaven.

For a long time, she just listened while I talked, stopping me only briefly to ask a question or make sure she understood something correctly. I told her everything I could without casting her father in a bad light. No matter how pissed I was at Dan or how much of a misogynistic ass I considered him to be, I refused to color Haley's view of her father. I did explain how oppressive life as a pastor's wife could be. I told her that I'd struggled with doubts and outright disbelief during our entire marriage. After a deep discussion about faith, she asked if I believed in God.

I couldn't lie to her and do more damage by saying I believed in something I didn't. But I wanted her to be able to make up her own mind about these things. "I believe in love, peace, and compassion. And empathy," I said. "And I can practice those things with or without a god."

She seemed to mull this over for a long time as our little fire burned to embers and the night grew cold.

"We should go in," I said, beginning to shiver.

"Can I stay the night?" she asked.

"Of course, but I only have a single bed with a lumpy mattress."

"Mom, I've slept in noisy dorm rooms, in cars, buses, and planes, hunched over a library desk, and outside in a sleeping bag in the rain. I think I can handle sharing a twin bed with you."

"I slept in a canoe."

Haley burst out laughing, the sound of her adorable belly-laugh bringing tears to my eyes. "That's actually not a bad idea."

It was just as cold inside as it was outside, but Haley and I climbed onto the bed. We used the rolled up sleeping bag for a pillow, and I covered us with the remaining blankets and the comforters. I pulled my little girl into my arms, her back to my chest, and snuggled her. Her hair smelled like coconut now, but I remembered when it had smelled like baby shampoo.

For a few minutes we lay there quietly, letting the night settle around us as I savored the special moment with my daughter. Dim moonlight seeped through the windows, creating deep shadows in my little house, but my heart was filled with love.

Haley shifted slightly, her voice soft in the night as she spoke over her shoulder. "Hey Mom?"

"Yeah, sweetie?"

"I think this place will make a great house."

Chapter Eleven

E arly the next morning, I walked Haley out to her father's rental car. She confessed that he'd railed at her last night when she'd asked to use the car to come back here, claiming he hadn't put her on the rental agreement as a designated driver. When he refused to bring her back here, she said she'd walk, but he handed over the keys and warned her not to believe a word I said because I wasn't in my right mind. I'd apparently opened my mind to the Devil who was wreaking havoc in there.

My only thought was that I should have invited the mischievous miscreant in years ago, but I kept that thought to myself.

"I'm sorry you and Kara got stuck in the middle of this situation," I said, looping my arms around Haley and holding her tight for a moment.

"You have a right to feel however you feel," she said, stepping away and looking me in the eye. "You're not the only one who has doubts about all that stuff, Mom. Until now, I just felt I couldn't voice them."

My eyebrows raised, but not in surprise. Haley had always been more science-minded and a hardcore nature girl. The hours we'd spent in church or at church functions had been arduous and painful for both of us. For me it was because I hadn't believed and had grown disgusted by Dan's greed. I'd assumed Haley's issue stemmed from being an active girl with interests outside the walls of a church. To learn that she'd been questioning, or perhaps even didn't believe at all, was enlightening. And honestly it was a relief. I didn't want my precious girls to sell their souls, their freedom, or their power to any misogynistic religion, cult, political party, or oppressive regime. I wanted them to live freely and authentically, whatever that meant to them.

"Okay, Mom, I'll call you when I get back to school," Haley said, giving me a peck on the cheek. "Send pics of your house. I want to see what you do with the place."

"You bet." I gave her another hug and asked her to give it to her sister for me.

Haley gave me a thumbs up. "Don't worry, she'll come around."

But as I watched my daughter pull out of the driveway, I did worry. I'd always worried about my girls, even when they'd been sitting safely in our living room. I wanted to protect them from my situation with their self-centered father, but I knew they had to navigate this world on their own now. They needed to manage their lives with their own two hands. They would suffer scrapes and bruises, broken hearts, and shattered dreams, but those painful losses and their hard-earned successes would make them stronger.

Just like this journey was making me stronger.

As Haley drove out of sight, I turned and surveyed the forty-four acres of beautiful Adirondack woodlands my grandparents had left to me. The three-acre lake on the property had been formed in a small basin in the Seward Mountain range, a woodland paradise dotted with lakes and crisscrossed by rivers and streams. To be here in this place was the only heaven I could imagine.

I spied Sinatra at the back of the house, stalking something in the weeds. "Looking for your breakfast?" I asked and was rewarded with his full attention. "Come on then." I headed down the lake trail with Sinatra trotting along behind me.

It appeared Haley was right. I had a cat.

It was early evening when I went inside to feed Sinatra his supper. He'd just begun crunching his kibbles when I heard voices outside. When I opened the door, Maggie and Chloe were already sitting in Adirondack chairs around the small fire I'd built. They had a large cooler parked between them. "We brought chairs, food, and beverages," Chloe said, gesturing toward a large, insulated shopping bag. "Hope you like pesto pasta."

After surviving on peanut butter and jelly sandwiches, just thinking about a meal like that made my stomach twist with hunger. "Am I hallucinating?"

"Nope," Maggie said. "It's our fun-day-Sunday meeting. We're having a girl-gab. Take a seat," she said, handing me a beer. When I held back, she arched an eyebrow. "Would you rather have wine?"

"After last time it's probably safer for me to drink wine. Beer goes down too easy, especially when I'm perpetually thirsty," I said.

While my friends laughed and filled a wine glass for me, I thought of Dan's reaction to me drinking alcohol, especially on a Sunday. I wished we could have had a sincere, mature conversation to figure out an amicable dissolution of our marriage. But he'd made it clear that wasn't possible. Now, I just wanted to sever all ties with him and his church. There was no room in my new life for either of them.

"You seem deep in thought," Chloe said, giving me the side-eye while she dug plates out of her goody bag.

"Just thinking about what Ashe said after he inspected my wiring yesterday evening. My *house* wiring," I clarified. "He told me I need to put a new roof on my place before I do anything else. He suggested using metal roofing rather than shingles, but I need to do whichever costs less. Not that I can afford either. And I haven't a clue how to shingle a roof."

"What do you think about the color blue?" Chloe asked, sitting with plates and silverware balanced on her lap.

My tired brain made a hard U-turn but could make no sense of her comment. "Um, I like blue."

"How would you feel about a blue roof?"

I hadn't thought about any particular color for my roof. Shingles were shingles, gray, brown, or black. And maybe green. Perhaps even blue. "Any particular reason I'd want a blue roof?" I asked, not following Chloe's conversation.

"A blue metal roof wouldn't cost you anything unless I don't have enough underlayment, sealant, or roofing screws in which case it would probably cost you less than two hundred bucks."

"What?" I didn't dare to believe it possible to put a new roof on my house for less than two hundred dollars. "Are you toying with me?"

"Of course not." Chloe set the plates and silverware on the cooler. "Josh and I put a metal roof on our barn a couple of years ago. We'd planned to put a matching roof on our garage, but I changed my mind after we got the barn finished. The blue roof was eye-catching and sort of cute, but a blue garage roof was just too much for me. Plus, the roof on the garage was fine. I think I have enough leftover roofing material to do your roof, if you're not opposed to the color."

"Blue is my favorite color."

She grinned. "Mine, too."

"I'll accept your incredibly generous offer if you'll allow me to pay you for it when I can afford to do so."

She nodded as if she knew it was the only way I'd be able to accept her offer. "It's a deal, my friend. Now can we eat?"

"Yes! Please. I'm famished."

"Me too," Maggie said, lifting a casserole dish out of Chloe's magic bag.

While we ate, I savored every delicious bite of the pasta and each sip of my wine. Chloe talked about fascia and flashing, pancake screws, wood screws, roofing screws, sealant tape and underlayment. She rattled off a list of the tools we'd need to install the roof: ladders and scaffolding, a jigsaw and staple gun, a couple of drills and various drill bits, tape rules and marking pencils, and so many other things my brain wept.

"Chloe," I said, interrupting her masterful dissertation on my metal roof project. "You do realize, don't you, I haven't a clue how to do this sort of work."

"I specifically remember you working out here with your grandfather when he was building this place," she said. "If I recall correctly, you were pretty handy with tools."

"You were," Maggie said, siding with Chloe, the two of them teaming up against me.

"That was pounding nails and sawing lumber, not putting a roof on the place."

Chloe dismissed my concern with a wave of her hand. "It's just a bunch of measuring, cutting, and screwing. Josh and I installed our barn roof, so I'll be able to walk us through the process. You're not afraid of heights, are you?"

"I don't think so."

"Then I say we give it a go, yes?"

I exchanged looks with Maggie, then smiled at my friends. "Why not? Let's do it."

Maggie immediately shook her head. "No way. My work is inside."

Laughing, Chloe told her that we could handle it without her. Then she said to me, "We're going to be doing some heavy lifting, so I hope you've been working out."

I thought of all the backbreaking work I'd already done. "I think I can handle it," I said, confident in my ability to work hard, but not so confident in my skill level.

"Then tomorrow, after we take some measurements on the boathouse, we can inventory the materials in my barn to see what, if anything, we might need to purchase."

"Sounds great, Chloe, but the town is coming to inspect my well tomorrow morning, and Ashe is supposed to stop by with an estimate on installing a breaker panel and some outlets before doing his final inspection. He said I'd need those things before I can add insulation or put up walls. I could come over after that."

Maggie whipped out her phone and started tapping out a text. "I'll tell Ashe to text you tomorrow when he's on his way. I'll have him send you a text now, so you'll have his number too."

"Can't you just give it to me?" I asked.

Maggie laughed. "Too late, already sent. But yes, I could have done that. Wasn't thinking." She angled a sly look my way. "So, what's going on with you and my big brother?"

My cheeks heated, but I did my best to play it cool. "I don't know what you guys are seeing, but nothing's happening. I don't know anything about him other than he has a son."

"Did he tell you he's divorced?"

"He didn't say, and I didn't ask."

Maggie tapped a manicured fingernail against her wine glass. "Chloe, did you sense a temperature change when Kate and Ashe met?"

"I did," she answered. "But if Kate says there's nothing happening ..."

A ding on Maggie's phone spared me more of their too personal observations.

Maggie frowned and looked up. "Ashe says he received a reply that your number is out of service."

"What?" I pulled my phone out of the back pocket of my jeans, then finger-swiped it to life. The screen lit up. But when I tried to call Maggie's phone number, an automated voice said my phone was out-of-service. A sick feeling rolled through me. Dan had finally done it. He'd cut off my phone. He'd wanted things to look normal to our girls, but now that he'd used them to ambush me, and they knew what was going on, he was breaking the line of communication between us so I couldn't sway them or get them on my side. But that was his MO, not mine. Releasing a sigh, I told Maggie and Chloe what he'd done. Then I told them about his ambush yesterday evening, and about my conversation with Haley later that night and this morning.

"Wow, he's a real shithead," Maggie said.

Chloe nodded. "Sounds as if he's scared."

"He should be," I said through clenched teeth. But there was nothing I could do without money to pay an attorney, and he knew it. "Looks as if I'll be buying a burner phone."

Maggie laughed. "A burner phone? You sound like a gangstah." Typing something into her phone, she said, "I'll have Ashe text Chloe tomorrow."

"Thanks." Wanting to get my mind off my vindictive husband, I asked Chloe if she knew how to install French doors.

"Sure. Build a sturdy frame. Install doors. Pretty simple." She glanced at the boathouse. "Where are you thinking of installing them?"

"I want to replace the old double doors on the lake-facing side." The boathouse sat at an angle providing a view of the kidney-shaped lake from the front side and from what would become the living room end of the building. "I want to add a couple of windows in the living room too. And one at each end of the building, at a second-floor level, centered under the peak."

For a couple seconds they both looked at the bones of my home as if imagining the doors and windows in place. Then Maggie said, "Stellar idea."

Chloe nodded. "I agree."

Although the French doors would provide a beautiful entrance door, I knew I needed at least two exit doors, which meant I'd have to buy another door for a back exit into the utility room. "Any idea how much French doors cost?" I asked.

"On average eight hundred to three thousand or more depending on the style," Maggie said.

Chloe leaned back in her chair and stretched out her legs, crossing them at the ankle. "But you can buy secondhand French doors at a fraction of that cost. There's a used material supply house in Potsdam where Josh and I bought a ton of stuff."

"I love that place," Maggie said. "Let's go tomorrow. Oh, wait, you can't tomorrow, but how about Tuesday? I can get Jill to cover the store." She cast a sideways glance at me as if sending a private message, then turned to Chloe. "Let's go Tuesday."

Chloe seemed to hesitate for a moment. "Hmm ... I don't know." Another moment of hesitation ensued, then she released a sigh. "Okay, yeah, let's go. I'll drive us all out in the Dummy."

I nearly choked on my wine. "What the heck is the Dummy?"

"It's my two-ton dump truck. That's what Dylan called it when he was a little guy. The name just sort of stuck."

I laughed. "I like it."

"It's a date, ladies," Maggie said. "I'll pick Kate up at nine Tuesday morning and we'll meet over at your house, Chloe."

From that point on we sipped wine, fed the fire with small sticks, and kept the conversation light, as if we were all enjoying a respite from the stresses of our daily lives.

Then Maggie dropped a bomb. "I saw Sophie today. She knows you're back."

Chapter Twelve

We were one sheet short on the metal panels needed to roof my house. The color had been a special order, which meant I couldn't go pick up an extra panel at a big box store. I'd have to settle for a panel of another color to complete my roof or try to patch together a panel from remnants in Chloe's scrap pile. Not what I'd hoped for. But I couldn't afford to be picky.

"Let me think about this a while," Chloe said.

But when Maggie and I showed up at her house on Tuesday morning, Chloe admitted she still hadn't come up with a good solution for how we could complete the roofing project without another panel.

"Don't fret over this, Kate," Maggie said. "Chloe is a genius when it comes to this sort of thing. She'll figure out a good solution."

Chloe cast a not-so-sure look at Maggie as she climbed into the cab of the Dummy and sat behind the wheel.

"Shotgun!" Maggie called and gave me a nudge to get in ahead of her.

Laughing, I climbed in. "If you guys don't mind, before we leave town, I'd like to stop by the post office to register my change of address," I said, tucking my purse on the floor between my feet.

"And if we have time while we're in Potsdam, I'd like to buy a prepaid phone."

Maggie arched a shapely eyebrow at me. "I liked it better when you called it a burner phone."

"Me too," Chloe said. "Made you sound badass."

"I am a badass," I said, and they laughed.

I felt such an upwelling of joy it made me giddy inside. I was hanging out with my friends—my real friends. And we were having a girls' day. I hadn't felt this free in ... I couldn't remember. But I knew it had been before I'd met Dan. From the minute Dan and I considered ourselves a couple, he'd taken over the management of our lives. Even before that, though, I'd been brokenhearted and floundering over the implosion of my family. The last memory I have of feeling free and genuinely happy was at eighteen years old. Sophie and I had spent the day at the lake swimming and sunbathing. Sophie was bemoaning the fact that summer break was ending, and she'd be heading back to school in three weeks ... and I'd be leaving for college in just a couple of days. She'd given me the biggest hug and said she would miss me. Then she shoved me into the lake. I'd come up sputtering and laughing and set on revenge, which thrust us both into a lighthearted tussling match in the water followed by a heart-to-heart talk as we dried out on the sunny beach. That was the last time Sophie and I laughed together.

"Are you falling asleep?" Maggie asked, nudging my side with her elbow.

"Considering the fact that this seat is more comfortable than my bed, can you blame me?"

"Don't expect us to feel sorry for you," Chloe said. "The offer to stay at my house is always open."

"That's right," Maggie chimed in. "You're your own worst enemy, Kate."

It dawned on me that they were right. I'd been my own worst enemy since I'd turned on my father. Had I been relinquishing my life decisions to Dan since then out of a subconscious need to punish myself for destroying two families? Or perhaps out of fear that I'd continue to make wrong decisions and hurt more people?

Maggie leaned forward a bit and looked at me. "You know we're razzing you, right?"

"Of course!" I said with a laugh. "I was just trying to think of an appropriate comeback."

And so it went with the three of us talking and heckling one another and brainstorming ideas as we drove out Route fifty-six to Potsdam. As a teenager, I'd come out there with Chloe and Maggie and a few of our friends to boat and picnic on Raquette River. My father and mother had brought me out there to check out the college campus at SUNY Potsdam, but I'd been too adventurous then to want to stay so close to home. I'd wanted to see the world. I'd gone nine hundred miles away to North Carolina where I met Dan.

"Holy shit!" Maggie blurted out, startling me. "Did you guys see that?"

"I sure did!" Chloe burst out laughing as I frantically looked around trying to see what I'd missed while daydreaming.

"What happened?" I asked. "What'd I miss?"

Instead of telling me, Chloe stood on the brakes and pulled to the side of the road, kicking up stones and dust. As soon as she'd stopped the big truck, she threw it in reverse and backed up a couple hundred yards.

Laughing her ass off, Maggie pointed to a deep field where a naked man in boots and a cowboy hat was riding a gorgeous black mare. The saddle hid his assets but gave us a full side view of his bronzed, athletic body. Although the days had grown warmer, it was only in the high fifties which didn't seem to bother him at all. He smiled revealing a flash of white teeth as he tipped his hat to us.

"What the—?" I began laughing so hard I couldn't finish my question.

Maggie gave him a thumbs up and shouted, "Good for you, Nature Boy!" as Chloe pulled the truck back onto the road.

"I can't believe that just happened," I said, as we continued our journey. I felt a little embarrassed by the man's nakedness, and a little envious of his lack of inhibition. Not that I wanted to ride naked through a field, but ... well, I hoped I could someday pull on the sundress I'd bought and wear it without feeling overexposed.

Maggie didn't seem fazed at all by Nature Boy, but she did break into laughter a couple of times. "What do you think he was doing out there?" she asked, obviously pondering the issue.

"Escaping from a mental ward?" Chloe suggested.

I laughed. "That gets my vote."

"Nah, he didn't look mental. He looked ... pretty damn sexy, but not mental. I'd sure like to know his story."

"Well, I'm not going back," Chloe said, "so get your mind back in the truck."

Maggie didn't seem at all offended. In fact, she looked wonderfully relaxed with her elbow bent and partially poking out the open window. The wind lifted her long hair and teased it around her shoulders as she serenely surveyed the passing landscape. Her beauty was enviable, but it was her come-what-may attitude I wanted to emulate. If only I could stop judging everything. Where Maggie had seen joy and humor and freedom in Nature Boy's revealing ride, I'd been conditioned by twenty-plus years of indoctrination to see him as an attention-seeker, a callous exhibitionist with no regard for others. But Maggie's view of the world was so much more accepting, loving, and joyful.

"Did everything go okay with your well inspection yesterday?" Maggie asked.

"As far as I can tell. The inspector said I'd need a new pump, which is going to cost over nine hundred dollars, but as long as the water passes, I'll be able to use the well. I couldn't afford to test both wells, so I had the technician pull a water sample from the well by the boathouse." Like a child, I crossed my fingers and wished from the bottom of my empty wallet that it would pass.

Soon we arrived at a huge brick building. The old two-story warehouse boasted two concrete loading docks with large wooden doors, tall windows on both floors, and oversized barn doors on one end that were wide open.

"Fair warning," Maggie said, gripping my hand, her eyes intense. "I get overstimulated in this place. I can no longer be responsible for my actions."

Chloe grinned. "She's really not kidding."

"I consider myself warned," I said, shaking my head in wonder at how two grown women could be so much fun.

They opened their doors, and we piled out and headed toward the open doors. Although the tall windows let in a good amount of daylight, it took a moment for my eyes to adjust to the softer lighting inside the cavernous building.

A few steps into the place, I stopped in surprise. "Am I hearing piano music and smelling popcorn?"

"Yep, it's a player piano," Maggie said. "Can't beat free popcorn and music while you shop."

"You'll see a cat or two around here too," Chloe added. "They're so adorable and sweet you'll want to take them home."

"One cat is plenty, thank you." As I looked around and took in the endless aisles of wooden shelving crammed full of everything one could think of, I felt a sense of panic. "Where would you begin to find anything in here?"

"Ask someone who works here," Chloe said. "Seriously. They know where everything is right down to wing nuts, coyote urine, and grub screws."

"Or ask Chloe," Maggie added. "She knows the place better than she knows her own kitchen."

"Because it's more fun hanging out here than in my kitchen. Come on, Kate, I'll show you where the French doors will be if they have any." Chloe walked me all the way to the back of the store where another set of large double doors opened into another warehouse half the size of a football field. Every item imaginable filled the place. Shelves and racks and piles of materials were stocked from floor to ceiling.

"All of this is part of the supply house?" I asked, standing in the doorway trying to get my jaw off the floor.

"Yes, and this building leads to an outside fenced-in yard filled with cement blocks, pavers, plastic and metal pipe, and other things of that nature."

A sigh of amazement slipped from my mouth. "No wonder Maggie gets overstimulated here."

"That isn't the only reason," Chloe said with a laugh. "Maggie and the owner have a ... thing."

"A thing?" I asked, not understanding.

Chloe tilted her head and eyed me with curiosity. "Sex, Kate. They have sex."

"Oh!" My face burned. "How obtuse of me."

My response made Chloe laugh again, but she took pity on me and led me to the back of the warehouse where towering racks lined the back wall. Doors of every size stood in the racks. There were modern wood doors, old heavy oak doors, metal, and fiberglass doors, and to my absolute delight, two sets of French doors. Chloe and I wrangled them out of the rack to inspect them. The first set in white trim was in the best shape and was what I'd had in mind for my main doors. Chloe pulled out a pad and pen from her purse, scribbled SOLD across the paper, and taped it to the doors.

"You carry painter's tape in your purse?" I asked.

"I do when I come here. If you don't mark something as sold, it's up for grabs, and you could lose it before you even try to buy it."

"Wow, that's brilliant."

"Not my first rodeo," she said, tucking her supplies back in her purse. "Have a look around if you like. I have to use the bathroom."

A second later, she was off down the aisle, leaving me adrift in a sea of building materials. I found a metal exterior door marked forty dollars. It was a bit scuffed up around the handle and kick panel areas, but it would be fine for the back entrance to my house. I had no painter's tape to mark it as mine, so I hoped it would still be there when I finished shopping.

As I wandered through what seemed an endless corridor of

racks and shelves, my imagination soared. I envisioned small homes like mine being created from the used materials around me. Old wood that was repurposed, refinished, and polished until it shone formed gorgeous walls and floors in my imaginary homes. Second-hand decorative fans with a fresh coat of paint hung from cathedral ceilings. I could see in my mind's eye the rustic chic cottage I wanted for myself, and it made me giddy with hope.

Boxes of hardware sparked another wave of excitement. Picking up an old doorknob, I examined the beautiful embossing on the bronze knob. My grandparents' house was full of these kinds of doorknobs. I'd considered using two or three of the old doorknobs as coat hooks once I got my walls up and painted, but it would be a shame to cover something so lovely. As I inspected the knob, I gasped aloud. It was marked forty-nine dollars! Could that be right? Surely, it was an error.

"Are you in need of assistance?" a male voice asked.

I turned to see a tall, rough-cut, and generally good-looking guy with brown hair coming up the aisle toward me. I could only assume by the look on his face he'd heard me gasp. "You might have to pick me up off the floor if the price on this knob is correct."

As he stopped beside me, he glanced at the knob. "That's a cast bronze Victorian doorknob that sells for around fifty dollars. What's it marked?" he asked.

"Forty-nine dollars," I replied.

"Sounds right," he said, emphasizing his statement with an affirmative nod.

"Are you serious? People buy these old things for that much money?"

"Some sell for more."

My mind spun as I mentally counted the doorknobs in my grandparents' house. "Are you interested in buying some door-knobs similar to this one?"

"Sure. You have some for sale?"

"I think I might have several things you'd be interested in." My grandparents' house had been condemned. It needed to come down, but I couldn't afford to hire a demolition crew. Plus, I was scavenging materials from their old house to build my own home. But I didn't need the doorknobs any more than I needed the old appliances.

"What else you got?" he asked.

"I'll have some doors and other building materials available at some point. And some old windows if you buy that sort of thing."

"I buy just about everything," he said. "I do what I can to keep that stuff out of the landfills. People like to know they're repurposing materials and helping our environment."

He was right. There was something deeply satisfying about reusing things and downsizing my footprint. I was living in a four hundred and eighty square foot boathouse, and I felt more at home there than I'd ever felt in the ridiculously large house I'd shared with Dan and our girls. But I knew that huge, sprawling house was the only place big enough to house Dan's ego.

"Can you tell me how much you're charging for the French doors over there?" I gestured toward the racks at the end of the warehouse. "The white ones."

We walked together to where they stood in the racks. As he pulled the doors out to look them over, he spotted Chloe's note and laughed. "I suspect it won't matter what I charge because it appears Chloe has already bought them."

"It matters," I said, feeling my heart rate increase.

"This is a vinyl door that sells new for around twelve hundred dollars. This particular door was installed three years ago. The homeowner pulled it out last month when he put an addition on and no longer needed the door. There's a lot of life left in this piece." He slid it back into the rack. "Eight hundred is a fair price."

My heart sank. I couldn't afford to spend eight hundred dollars on a door. I had so many other things I needed. Like plumbing and electrical. "Thank you. I'll have to think about it," I said, then walked away from the temptation to overspend. Deducting Ashe's estimate of one thousand fifty dollars that he gave me yesterday when he'd dropped off his quote, it would leave me with less than two thousand dollars to keep Sinatra and myself fed for an unknown length of time, and to make my home livable. I couldn't spend eight hundred dollars on a door.

I needed to get a job.

I wandered the supply house listening to beautiful piano music and wishing I had a bag of free popcorn to silence my growling stomach. I'm not sure how long I moseyed and daydreamed but I finally came upon Chloe standing near the rubber boots and outer-wear section. She seemed deep in thought until I got closer to her. Then I could see that her eyes were filled with tears she was strug-gling to hold back.

I slipped my arm around her. "I suspect I shouldn't have asked you to come here."

"You didn't ask," she said softly. For a moment she said noth-ing, then she drew in a trembling breath. "This song was Josh's favorite. We danced right here in this aisle the first time we heard it play." A quivering smile tipped her mouth. "We were dressed in our work boots and coveralls. We sounded like a couple of nervous horses in a tight stall."

Her description made me laugh a little ... and it made my heart ache for what she'd lost and for what I'd never had. I couldn't help it. Her love for Josh was so palpable, I felt bereft for both of us.

"Here you are," Maggie said, striding up the aisle with her confident, long-legged stride. She opened her mouth to say some-thing, but as her gaze fell on Chloe, she released a sigh instead. Taking Chloe by the shoulders, she said, "You know you had to do this eventually, right?"

Chloe nodded and blinked back tears.

"But if it's too much for you, we can leave right now," Maggie said.

For a moment, Chloe seemed to consider Maggie's offer, but then she sniffed, and her head came up. "I've got it, Kate!" She looked at me, her eyes filled with renewed interest. "I saw two skylights out back. If we put those on your roof, we'll have enough metal panels to cover your roof. We can patch in a couple of those longer leftover cuts from my barn job if we need them. How do you feel about having skylights in your house?"

Stunned by her swift emotional shift and overcome by her kindness at a time when she must be breaking apart inside, I said, "I feel like the luckiest person on earth, Chloe."

"Then you're not opposed to skylights?"

"I love the idea of having skylights."

"Then it's settled," Maggie said, slipping her arms around our shoulders and turning us toward the window section. "Let's get the goods and go get some lunch. I'm starving."

Chloe gave her the side-eye. "Working up an appetite, are you?"

Maggie's laugh rang down the aisle.

The skylights Chloe had found were large rectangles that would let in a glorious amount of light. But they were four hundred dollars each. "I love them, Chloe. They would look amazing in my house, but I can't afford them. Eight hundred dollars for the French doors and another eight hundred for these skylights would leave me with very little cash. I still need to buy a phone and eventually more groceries."

Maggie exchanged a look with Chloe, then smiled at me as if she wanted to pet my head. "Little puppy, there is no way you're paying that much for this stuff. Watch and learn."

For nearly fifteen minutes, I watched as Maggie and Chloe haggled with the owner, Jeff, until he agreed to sell the French doors, the single exterior door, and the skylights to me for eight hundred dollars. That was half of what I'd expected to pay. Knowing the skylights would solve my roofing issue, I agreed to purchase them and the doors.

Chloe told Jeff she was ready to deal on windows, but I stopped her and said I couldn't afford to buy them right now. She insisted that windows should be installed now before finishing the wiring or putting up walls, warning that it would be a major headache to install them later on. Assuring me that she could get them at a great price, we followed Jeff who walked us to a roped off section in the back corner of the warehouse. Once there, he pulled out four thirty-inch double paned windows that would work in my main living area and kitchen. He pulled out another smaller window that would work in my bathroom. Way back in the corner sat two, thirty-two-inch round windows, both egress windows that opened like portholes on a ship. They were ornate and beautiful, and I could already see them in my house. Too in love with them to walk away, I told Jeff I'd take them. The windows, which my friends negotiated an unbelievable deal on, added another two hundred and fifty dollars to my bill, but both Chloe and Maggie assured me installing them now was the smartest thing to do and that it would be foolish not to buy all the windows while we could find them.

After I'd handed over eleven hundred and thirty-four dollars, the total with tax, I stood back and let Chloe and Jeff work out the logistics of loading my materials onto Chloe's truck. Once the Dummy was loaded, and my items were protected and secured with straps, Chloe tarped everything to keep it protected from weather and flying road debris.

"I am about to swoon from hunger," Maggie said, pretending to faint against the truck fender.

The three of us piled into the cab and immediately began discussing where we were going to eat. We found a place and, while we ate, we verbally installed my doors and windows. Chloe and Maggie seemed as excited about my purchase as I was. Chloe talked about the installation process and how they would lower my heating and cooling bills. Maggie talked about the cosmetic appeal of the skylights and French doors. And I talked about the layout of my house and how I wanted to decorate it. We lingered over our coffee, talking, dreaming, and laughing.

After lunch, we stopped by a drug store so I could buy a prepaid phone. While Maggie and Chloe were wandering the store, I picked up a bottle of pain reliever too. But as I was cashing out, I realized how thin my money envelope felt. A crushing weight settled on my chest and my heart began racing. Heat prickled my forehead, and I began to sweat and feel faint. Buyer's remorse flooded every cell in my body. I shouldn't have let Maggie and Chloe talk me into spending so much on windows and doors. But how could I tell them I'd made a horrible mistake? After all the time they'd spent helping and guiding me, I couldn't ask to return everything. But I had so little money left in my envelope! As I slipped a hundred-dollar bill from my purse and handed it to the cashier, my hands trembled.

I needed a plan. And a job. Maybe Jeff from the supply house would buy the doorknobs in my grandparents' house. Even a couple hundred dollars right now would ease the vicious claw gripping my gut. I would get his number from Maggie and call him. And first thing in the morning, as soon as daylight hit my windows, I was going to start writing so I could finally finish, and hopefully sell, my book.

Having a strategy, however remote, kept me from hyperventilating and completely losing it. But as I left the store with my friends, I knew my plan was built on shifting sand and naive wishes.

Once we were back in the truck, I opened my phone and sent a text to my daughters to give them my new phone number. Haley texted right back saying she would call me this weekend and ended with *Love ya*. I wasn't sure what to expect from Kara until she texted back a thumbs up emoji, and nothing else. I didn't want to give Dan my number, but I had to. He might need to reach me in the event of an emergency with our girls. I gave Maggie and Chloe my number and wondered who else might need it. After a few seconds, I realized there wasn't anyone else. Despite my contact with innumerable congregants each week, my life had grown so small and solitary I'd had no one in my life but Dan and our girls.

I was finally beginning to understand my attachment to our lawn mowers.

Chapter Thirteen

At sixteen minutes after five in the morning, I sat on my bed with my blankets wrapped around me poncho style, then began to work on my story. I sank so deep into my story world that I didn't realize the time until Chloe knocked on my door. When I saw that she'd brought hot coffee and bagels, I nearly kissed her. I packed away my journal, fed Sinatra, then ate a bagel.

Sipping our coffee, Chloe and I walked around the boathouse discussing our plan of attack. We decided to frame in the walls for my bathroom and utility room, then install the windows and French doors before tackling the roofing job. But since Ashe was coming by this morning, we planned to have him reroute some wiring to make room for the eventual placement of my new windows. And since he would be here, we also decided it would make sense to install the heavy picture window in my living room. Chloe and I could handle framing walls on our own, but we needed Ashe and his manly muscles to help with the heavy window.

He showed up an hour after Chloe and I began setting up sawhorses and running extension cords from the generator. Most of Chloe's tools, drills, saws, and such, used rechargeable batteries, but the batteries would need to be recharged throughout the day while we worked.

We broke away from prepping our outside workstation to do a walk-through with Ashe. While he and Chloe discussed the layout of outlets that would provide power for my kitchen appliances and lights and the washer-dryer unit I hoped to someday install in the utility room, I took mental notes. Ashe showed me how to wire an outlet, and I did one myself. I was immersed in work and details up to my neck, overwhelmed almost constantly, but I loved it. I hadn't realized until coming back here how claustrophobic and sedentary my life with Dan had become. We were always on the go but had never gone anywhere. We'd lived in a closed community that ran on a small circular track that led nowhere.

"How are you going to heat and cool the place?" Ashe asked as he installed an electric outlet in my kitchen. He was wearing his ball cap backward and his tool belt slung low across his hips. I tried not to stare at him but was mesmerized with the flexing of his muscled forearms as he worked a screwdriver to install the outlet.

"I don't know." I tried to ignore Chloe who was watching me watch Ashe.

He said, "You might consider a small propane fireplace. They use them on boats and for small areas. One of the wall mount units could heat your whole house. If you wanted more heat in the bathroom, you could get a small wall-mounted radiant heater or even an electric baseboard heater for that room."

"Where would I find these things, and what would they cost?" I asked, dreading the answer.

"You can probably get them used," Chloe said, crossing the room with her clipboard in hand. "Talk to Jeff when he comes by this weekend. See if he can find a used heater for you."

"While you're looking at heating options," Ashe said, "you'll need to figure out what you're going to do for hot water."

"I completely forgot about needing a hot water tank." I squeezed my throbbing forehead with one hand. "Any chance the one from my grandparents' house would work?"

Chloe laughed and stopped by the door. "No way are you putting that dinosaur in here even if by some miracle it still works."

Ashe lowered the screwdriver and stood up. "It would take up your whole utility room, Kate. You can get a tankless water heater that would be far more efficient than a standard hot water tank and cost half as much. They're small units that would be perfect for a home like yours."

Releasing a tired sigh, I began to wonder if I wouldn't have been better off renting a cheap efficiency apartment. Then I remembered why I'd moved into the boathouse in the first place. My vindictive, selfish husband had taken our RV and left me with no money and no credit. That meant no options which had forced me to camp out here.

I silently accepted that I'd be taking cold showers for a long time to come because I couldn't fathom how I'd be able to purchase all those things. I had called Jeff at the supply house just before Chloe had shown up this morning, and he'd promised to come out over the weekend to look at the doorknobs in my grandparents' house. Maybe, when I could come up with the money, he could also locate the used items I would need to heat my water and my house. I was keeping my fingers crossed he'd want the doorknobs and would give me a fair price for them. But until I had cash in hand, I wasn't spending another penny of my minuscule reserve.

"Either of you know where I can get a job?" I asked, accepting that I needed one.

Without looking away from his work, Ashe suggested doing an online search for our area. I'd already considered that, but I had so little data on my prepaid phone, I preferred to wait until I could use the internet at Chloe's house, which I would do the next time I showered there. I'd been alternating hot shower days with frigid lake water sponge baths to spare Chloe the extra running back and forth. By the end of our workdays, I was so exhausted I couldn't manage a roundtrip walk which meant Chloe had to drive me both ways.

"I'll give this some thought," Chloe said, promising to let me know if she heard of any openings.

"While you're mulling, will you help me carry out one of these canoes?" I asked. "All this stuff is getting in the way now that we're all in here working." Both Ashe and Chloe helped me carry out one of the canoes and flip it bottom side up to keep the rain out. Next, I pushed the lawn mower outside and parked Gussie beside the canoe, then tossed one of Chloe's small tarps over it. I needed to keep Haley's bike inside for now, but having one less canoe and lawn mower to work around inside would certainly make things easier.

Ashe spent the rest of the morning rerouting the wiring and installing outlets while Chloe and I framed out the bathroom and utility room walls. After a quick lunch break, and five hours of hard work, we had also installed the picture window and the double-paned windows, mounting one on each side of the big window.

Sunlight streamed through the glass, casting a buttery yellow glow in my little home, and suddenly it didn't seem to matter that my money envelope was nearly empty. My house was full of sunshine.

Chloe and I enlisted Ashe's assistance again as we framed and installed one of the round windows a few feet above my new picture window. It was a complicated, difficult job to install a second-floor window without a second floor. Ashe had to haul a ladder off his truck, and Chloe and I used two of her ladders. After an hour of meticulous framing, not an easy task for a round window, the three of us wrestled the window up our ladders. With hammers and drills, insulation, and caulk, we seated the window and secured it in place. Then we did it all again at the other end of the boathouse.

The expression that one small change can net a huge result was vividly evident when I could finally stand back and look at my new windows. All that lovely light streaming inside filled me with ... hope. In my mind, I'd imagined what my little home would eventually look like, but to see the change that just a few windows made thrilled me. I could create something uniquely beautiful right here with secondhand materials and first-rate friends.

We'd had enough hauling, hammering, and sweating for one day. Outside in the evening air, I thanked Ashe for all the work he'd done in addition to the job he'd come here to do, then said I wished I could offer him a cold beer.

He winked at me. "I'll take a raincheck."

I hadn't intended to give him a raincheck, but what was one to say in this situation?

"A cold beer sounds great," Chloe said. "I have some in the cooler."

I wasn't opposed to quenching my thirst, or to having a beer with Chloe, but the last time I drank a beer on this beach with Ashe I'd lost my virginity. And I hadn't been drunk. I'd been alive with life and raging hormones and completely enamored with Maggie's sexy older brother. The humor in Ashe's eyes suggested he was thinking about that night too.

A wave of heat rolled through me, and I tried to avoid his eyes. I chugged my cold beer to cool off, but there was no remaining cool while around this man. He acted nonchalant and talked with Chloe while he drank his beer like a gentleman.

I could see that Chloe knew something was going on, but she was kind enough to wait until Ashe left to ask me about it. My lame response was that I'd had a crush on him in high school.

Chloe burst out laughing. "Um, I hate to break it to you, Kate, but that's old news."

"Well, I feel awkward around him." I shrugged and got us both another beer from the cooler before settling in the chair beside her. "Thanks for everything you're doing for me, Chloe. You can't possibly know what all of this means to me." I gestured to the cooler, my yard full of equipment and tools, and to my little house with the beautiful new windows. "I don't know what I'd do without you and Maggie."

"I feel the same about you, too, Kate. If I couldn't be here helping you or spend my days with you and Maggie, I think I'd ..."

She shook her head. "I don't think I could function or face another day."

I reached over and gave her forearm a squeeze. "We're both a mess with our broken hearts and chipped fingernails, but these are the hands and hearts of strong women, Chloe. We'll get through this together."

Her eyes misted and she nodded in agreement. "To strong women."

I tapped my bottle against hers. "To real friends."

"Hey, you two!" Maggie sang out as she emerged from the trail, her ponytail swinging from the back of her ball cap. "You guys better not be drinking without me."

I exchanged a smile with Chloe as she slipped a beer from the cooler. She handed it to Maggie, who looked ridiculously gorgeous in a navy hoody and distressed jeans with holes in the knees.

"What'd I miss today?" she asked, sinking into one of the Adirondack chairs.

"We installed some of my windows," I said, excitement bubbling up inside me. I couldn't wait to show her how nice they looked, but Chloe began to laugh.

"That's not all that happened," she said, giving me the side eye. "Kate was ogling your brother, and he was asking her for a raincheck on a beer."

I gasped like an embarrassed teenager, which embarrassed me even more. "I was not ogling him, and—"

"Yeah, you were," Chloe insisted, wiggling her eyebrows at Maggie.

"Well, well, well," Maggie said, stretching her long legs out, her stylish work boots resting on the stones around my campfire. "'Fess up, Kate. What's up with you and my brother? Inquiring minds want to know."

"There is nothing going on between us," I protested. "I'm still married, like it or not. And when I finally break that shackle, I won't be slipping on another one. Not interested."

Maggie laughed. "Just so you know, Kate, sex doesn't require being shackled to your partner."

I opened my mouth to say I knew that, but it dawned on me I didn't. Sex without marriage was vigorously disapproved of in my former world. To even think such a thing was a sin. But I was no longer living in that world. I was carving out a new life in a land of freedom where a person could think for themselves and live a life based on their own conscience and values. To realize I could now make my own decisions free from the dictates of an oppressive faith was such a moment of liberation it made my eyes tear. It wasn't that I wanted to have unmarried sex without guilt. It was the simple fact that I could think for myself. That I could explore the amazing world around me without fear of retribution from Dan's vindictive god or his judgmental followers. That I could just sit with my friends and enjoy our conversation without trying to convert them.

Maggie stood in one graceful motion and stuck out her hand. "Come on, girl. Show me those windows." She grabbed my hand and pulled me to my feet. "I'm taking tomorrow off so I can deliver your stove and fridge to their new owner. I sold them for thirty-four hundred dollars. That's three thousand sixty dollars for you."

I threw my arms around her and gave her a hug. "You guys are the best friends ever."

Maggie laughed. "Girl, you need a shower."

Stepping away, I tugged my sweat-stained T-shirt back in place. "Correction. I meant you guys are the most *honest* friends ever."

"Glad we got that straightened out." Maggie nudged me toward the boathouse, and Chloe followed. The instant we stepped inside, Maggie let out a low whistle. "Those windows are spectacular."

"I agree," I said, admiring our handiwork. "Thank you both for pushing me to buy all of them. Even when I thought that meant living on peanut butter sandwiches indefinitely."

"Well, you won't be eating them tonight because I brought pizza."

"This day just keeps getting better." I hugged Maggie again. "Thank you for handling all this stuff for me. I'm afraid to admit this to you, but I'd planned on hauling those appliances to the dump at some point. I thought it was junk."

She clutched her head between her hands and stared at me. "You cannot tell me things like this and expect us to stay friends."

I laughed. "Then consider it a bad joke on my part."

Maggie sauntered over to the kitchen area. "It appears Ashe got some work done today despite your ogling him."

"Yes, he put on quite a show," I said, deciding to play along. "It's impossible to resist a man wearing a tool belt."

"Ooh! Look who's being cheeky," she said.

Chloe propped a hand on her hip and gave me the mama stare. "I see that. She's becoming a sarcastic little chick, isn't she?"

"I'm just a hungry old pigeon who's getting peckish." I hooked my arms around each of them and nudged them toward the door. "Come on you old hens, let's eat that pizza!"

Chapter Fourteen

It took two weeks for Chloe and me to finish installing the rest of the windows and cover half the boathouse roof with sheet metal. We had to wait for Ashe and Maggie to help us install the skylight windows before we could finish the roof. The skylights were big and heavy, and they were a bear to install, but after we'd gotten them in, I struggled to hold back tears. Like the new windows that were letting light into my home, each day with my friends, and every step forward, was bringing light back into my life. I'd learned how to wire an outlet, how to install windows, and how to roof a house. The transformation of my home was becoming a reflection of the transformation in my life.

Being able to be myself, to dare to think for myself, and live an honest, vibrant life, was so beautiful and rewarding it far outweighed the hard work and daily struggles. And I was writing each morning with my pen on fire.

"Are you daydreaming again, Kate?" Maggie asked, straining to hold her side of the French doors in place while Chloe worked on securing the frame. "Cause you're wobbling, and this damn thing is heavy."

Chloe and I had broken away from the roofing job, again, so we could install the doors while we had Maggie's help.

"I am not wobbling," I said. "I was just shifting my grip."

Maggie arched one of her shapely brows and smirked. "You were woolgathering. I could see the haze in your eyes."

"Well, before you accuse me of ogling your brother in my daydreams, I'll come clean and tell you I was thinking about the book I'm writing."

Chloe's drill went silent, and she and Maggie looked at me in surprise.

"I told you I was working on a book."

"You did not," Chloe said. "What are you writing?"

"It's an epic fantasy I'd started when my girls were young." I told them how Dan had reacted to it and that I'd stalled out and had mostly given up on it. "Maybe it's the Adirondack air that's clearing my head. I don't know, but it feels great to be writing again. Oh, and guess what came in the mail this morning?"

"Your vibrator?" Maggie suggested, cracking us up.

"Better than that. My well water passed inspection."

"That's awesome," Chloe said. "But get back to your book. I'm truly curious."

While we talked about hobbies and the possibility of me someday finishing and selling my book, we became so lost in our conversation and with installing the door that we didn't see or hear our visitor until he was standing a few feet away.

"Are one of you ladies Kate Weston?" a man asked. He was a short, thin-haired guy wearing khaki pants, a short-sleeved white shirt, and had a clipboard tucked under his arm.

Something about that clipboard sent a shiver down my back. "I'm Kate," I said as several wild guesses about why he was here streamed through my head.

"I'm Gordon Skives, code inspector for the town of Dunwith Falls. It appears you're building a house here?"

"Yes. Well, not exactly. I'm converting a boathouse that was already here."

"Then you're converting it to a residence?"

The feeling of ice water trickled through my belly. "Just a small cottage is all."

With hawk eyes, he surveyed the boathouse. "You know you need a building permit for this?"

I shook my head. "I didn't know."

"Well, you do." He pulled out some papers and handed them to me. "Residential buildings must be built to code, and everything must be inspected to confirm it meets code. I'll leave this information for you to review. But until you get a building permit, you need to stop working here."

I looked at Chloe and Maggie. They were standing beside the half-installed French doors saying nothing but letting me know I wasn't alone. "Where do I get a building permit?"

"They're issued at the Town Clerk's office. But I'm not sure you'll be able to get one." He eyed the boathouse again. "How big is your building?"

"Sixteen by thirty."

"Hmm ... that's only four hundred and eighty square feet," he said, calculating out loud. "That won't meet code. You need at least six hundred square feet for a residence."

"Why?" I asked. "I don't need six hundred square feet. I'll be perfectly happy in my little house."

"That may be," he said, looking uncomfortable. "But it's not about your comfort, I'm afraid. It's about maintaining a standard for our community to keep the town from being populated by tents and shanties. Some people consider a cardboard box a suitable home."

He had a valid point. "I understand, but a four-hundred-eighty-square-foot home is a little different than a cardboard box. Why should someone else get to decide what size home I need?" I asked, immediately irritated with the man and his ludicrous rules.

He held up a hand to stop me. "That was just an example. Once you submit a plan, we'll review it and schedule a pre-application meeting, then after reviewing your application we can hopefully issue the permit or recommend changes." Tucking his clipboard under his arm, mister whatever-his-name-was repeated that I must stop working until I actually had a building permit, then he pivoted on the heels of his dress shoes and left me standing with my gut churning.

"Did either of you know I needed a permit?" I asked.

"Sure," Chloe said, "but I assumed you'd gotten one when you first mentioned getting the well inspected."

"Same here," Maggie said.

"Well, I had no idea about permits and blueprints or any of that stuff," I said, feeling foolish. "I don't even know what constitutes the plan the inspector is asking for."

"Probably a blueprint of some sort," Chloe said. "Those papers should tell you what you'll need."

I glanced at the papers in my hand and wanted to toss them into my fire pit. That wouldn't solve anything though, so I dropped them onto a chair and looked at my friends. "Blueprint or not, permit or not, we're going to finish installing that door."

"Agreed," Chloe said, spinning her drill back to life and holding it in the air like a war hatchet. "Let him try to stop me."

Her rebellious action made me laugh, but I also felt like crying. I couldn't put on an addition to make up the square footage I lacked. That would require floors and walls and a roof and wiring and windows and ... I thought I might vomit.

"Come on, Kate. Let's get this door in and we'll figure out a way around this problem." Chloe waved me over with the drill, then set to work.

When we'd finished with the door, we all stepped back to admire our work. The door changed the whole look of the boathouse. The white grid style doors contrasted with the slate blue roof that covered half my house and gave me a glimpse of what my beautiful lakeside cottage would look like when it was finished. I couldn't stop working on my home any more than I could stop breathing. Because to lose this place would kill me.

Pulling out my crappy prepaid phone, I took a picture of my

house and sent it to Haley in a text message with a note saying I loved and missed her and Kara.

While I drank a glass of water, compliments of Chloe's daily delivery of four single-gallon jugs, I racked my brain for an answer. Chloe and Maggie poured over the building code for several minutes. I spied Sinatra sunning himself just down the beach. He'd grown used to Maggie and Chloe and our daily ruckus and was now more curious than afraid.

"Hey, big fella," I said, approaching him slowly. "Mind if I sit with you?"

He lifted his head and looked at me with sleepy eyes.

"I'll take that as a yes." I sank onto the grass and sat beside him. Moving slowly, I reached out and touched him. His fur was warm from the sun. For a moment, I felt envious that he was able to spend his days sleeping in the sunshine while I struggled to build us a home. Sinatra had finally started coming inside with me at night, but he didn't sleep with me. To my surprise and utter delight, he'd finally made use of the cat bed I'd bought for him. I'd stashed the bed on a back corner of the workbench to get it out of my way. But apparently it provided the perfect private perch for Sinatra, so I'd left it there for him. I was also leaving a window partially open at night so he could come and go. Without a litter box inside, I wanted him to have outside access should he need it. Plus, I didn't want him to feel trapped. I knew how awful that felt.

But soon I would have to get him in a carrier and take him to the vet. I'd removed a couple of ticks from behind his ears without much fuss from him, but he was completely intolerant of my attempts to brush him. His fur was matted in several places and his skin in that area appeared tender to the touch. "Poor baby," I said, gently stroking his back. "I'll get you cleaned up as soon as you allow me to do so. I'm saving my doorknob money just for you."

Chloe's shout startled both of us. Sinatra leapt to his paws and shot down the beach. I scrambled to my feet and headed toward Chloe who was waving the papers left by the code enforcer.

"I've got it!" she said. "Follow me."

Bewildered, I trailed Chloe and Maggie inside where Chloe immediately began eyeing the ceiling. "What are you looking for?" I asked.

"I'm calculating your overhead space." After another couple of seconds, she grinned like she'd just solved the code of the Kryptos sculpture. "With this high ceiling, you could add a loft over your kitchen and bathroom area that would add another one hundred ninety-two feet, which means you'll have a total of six hundred and seventy-two feet of *living* space. That meets code, Kate. And you're already going to have a ceiling over your bathroom and utility room, so if we just extend that over your kitchen, you'll be able to create a loft." She swept one hand out to encompass the rest of the house. "And you'll still have your cathedral ceiling over your living room area that will show off these beautiful beams."

I imagined the loft Chloe was suggesting and could envision my girls sleeping there when they came to visit. It was not only the answer to my square footage issue but also to my worry that my girls would think I no longer had room for them. "That would be amazing, Chloe, but adding a loft will add cost that I can't afford which is why I hadn't considered it."

"No, it won't, Kate. We can repurpose everything from the big house. It won't cost you anything but your time and labor."

This wonderful, wounded woman standing beside me every step of the way amazed me. "You just made my day, Chloe. Even if I didn't need the extra footage to meet code, I really want the loft for my girls."

"Then guess what we're going to be doing for the next couple of weeks?" she asked.

Maggie shook her head. "That's all you and Chloe."

"We've got this," I said, and it was the first time I genuinely believed it. Chloe and I were more than capable of taking this project home. "Apparently, I need a plan and a building permit first. Any idea how to create a blueprint?"

"I think we can get away with a hand drawn sketch if it's thorough enough," Chloe said.

"Then we're sunk," I said. "You've seen my artistic abilities."

Chloe laughed, but Maggie frowned. "How did that guy know you were building out here?" she asked. "You can't see your place from the road. I certainly haven't told anyone about this place."

"Nor have I," Chloe said.

"I don't know." I shrugged. "I have no idea how this works, so I didn't think to ask the code enforcer how he knew I was converting the boathouse. You don't think the well inspector would have said anything, do you?"

"I doubt it. Who else knows you're out here?" Maggie asked.

"Ashe and probably Sophie. And my girls ... and Dan." The minute I said his name, we all looked at each other with the same disgusted look. "Do you think he called the code enforcer on me?"

"Ashe wouldn't have said anything. He'd have told you about getting a permit if he'd thought you didn't have one. Your husband gets my vote. If that shithead's track record is any indication, he would do something like this," Maggie said.

I growled aloud. "Why couldn't he have just texted that I needed a building permit?"

Chloe gave me a sympathetic look. "Kate, he didn't want to give you a head's up. Dan wants to cause trouble for you."

As the truth sank in, I felt more sad than mad. I hadn't asked him for anything other than a divorce. Yet he was acting as if I were trying to take everything he loved when in fact it was the other way around. I loved my girls. And I loved my new life. He was determined to strip me of both, but I would fight tooth and claw for my girls and my freedom.

Chapter Fifteen

I rode into town with Maggie, and we drove straight to the town clerk's office. We entered the brick building together and waited while a gentleman in front of us finished his business. When he left, I placed my hand-drawn blueprint, compliments of Chloe's artistic hand, on the counter.

"I need to get a building permit," I told the woman at the counter who'd probably reached retirement age a decade ago.

"Sure, honey," she said, picking up my blueprint sketch. "I'll give this to Mr. Skives and he'll get back to you to set up a pre-application meeting and let you know the costs involved."

"Costs? I thought it was one fee."

"No, dear," she said with a light laugh. "There's a one-hundred-dollar application fee plus an A-R-B fee of one hundred dollars, both of which have an additional cost that's calculated based on the amount of work to be done, and there is a one-hundred-dollar property search fee, and a reinspection fee of one hundred and twenty dollars."

"Good grief! Is all that necessary? I just want a building permit, and I need the permit today."

"Well, that's not possible, dear. It usually takes a couple of weeks or more for this sort of thing."

"Two weeks?" I exchanged a look with Maggie who shrugged as if this was normal. "Isn't there any way we can avoid some of those fees and push this through today?"

"I'm sorry, but that's just not possible," she said, and she really did look apologetic. "You'll need to meet with Mr. Skives first, then submit a building permit application. Mr. Skives will review the application to make sure your plans and building materials all meet code. Then he'll walk you through the rest of the process and explain the fees involved."

"Is Mr. Skives in today?" I asked, hoping to circumvent what seemed to be an antiquated and ridiculously slow process.

"Oh no, he's usually out doing inspections this time of day."

Knowing I was beat, I sighed and slid my blueprint across the counter. "If there's anything you can do to speed things up, I'd really appreciate it."

"Well, I can make sure you have a clear deed to the property and pass that information along to Mr. Skives. That'll save him from having to check with me before approving your permit."

"My grandparents owned the property," I said. "They paid it off long ago."

"Wonderful," she said, "but I still need to check and validate everything before a permit can be issued."

"How long does that take?" I asked, worrying it would take another two weeks.

"I can check on that right now, dear." She smiled as if genuinely pleased to be able to give me some sense of progress today. Then with an energetic stride that belied her age, she zipped over to her desk and sent her fingers flying over the keyboard.

Maggie and I exchanged an *oh-my-god* look. I grimaced and felt ashamed for making an assumption, that definitely made an ass of me, about the woman. She might look as if she were past retirement age, but she was a wiz on the keyboard.

As I watched the clerk work on the computer like an IT tech, her smile melted away and deepened into a frown. "Oh dear," she whispered.

Her soft whisper of dismay made my gut twist with dread.

After a moment of holding my breath, she returned to the counter. "Honey, I'm sorry to have to tell you this, but because you haven't paid your taxes for the past two years, it will be impossible for you to get a building permit because the property is listed in an upcoming tax sale.

I stumbled away from the counter as if she'd punched me in the gut. My mouth was open, but I couldn't force any words from my throat.

"You'd need to pay these taxes by the fourteenth to keep the property."

I just shook my head. This couldn't be true. But I knew in my bones it was, and that this had been Dan's underhanded way of trying to wrest this property from me. He'd been paying the taxes on my grandparents' property since my grandmother had left it to me four years ago, but he'd continually pressured me to sell it. I'd finally agreed to list the property to avoid more arguments, but apparently after I refused three good offers, Dan figured the only way to get rid of the property was to stop paying the taxes so it would be sold out from under me. That underhanded bastard.

In two weeks, my property and my little home would be sold off in a tax sale.

"How much do I owe?" I asked, trying to choke back the rage consuming me.

The clerk scanned the printout in her hands. "Your delinquent county and town taxes, including interest and penalties total nine thousand one hundred and thirty-eight dollars."

My knees turned to water.

"School taxes are noted here at ... oh, let's see now ..."—She adjusted her glasses and tilted her head back to look through her bifocals—"one thousand nine hundred and ninety-four dollars with the interest and penalties included."

I gripped the counter with both hands. Maggie put her arm around me as if she knew I was considering murder.

"That brings your total to eleven thousand one hundred and

thirty-two dollars." She gently placed the printout on the counter in front of me. "I'm sorry, dear, but these will need to be paid before Mr. Skives can meet with you."

Numb, I could only nod. I thought about the millions Dan's church took in each year and that he didn't pay one tax dollar on that income. Dan loved that advantage. But the infiltration of religion in government and politics and in our schools was criminal. And it all pissed me off.

Even if I paid the school taxes, which I couldn't possibly cover, it wouldn't stop the sale. I had no way to set up a payment plan without a steady income. And even if I could set up a plan it didn't mean I'd be allowed to build on the property. My thoughts swirled, clouding and obscuring my ability to see past imminent disaster ... or my raging desire to throttle my underhanded husband.

Maggie scooped up the papers from the counter. "Thank you for your help," she said to the clerk, then bodily turned me toward the door. "We're going to get a cup of coffee and figure out how to make that asshole husband of yours pay for this. I could kill that man right now."

"Me, too, but I'm not going to give him the satisfaction of knowing he's hurt me. I'll figure a way out of this," I said, but I couldn't imagine how. All I could think of was my desperate desire to be free of Dan and his vindictive attacks.

In the end, I went for coffee alone while Maggie took care of a few things at her shop. I needed time alone to mull over my dire situation.

The Maple Leaf Café had been converted from a greasy spoon diner to a hip café with overstuffed furniture and walls decorated with colorful murals. Delicious looking pastries filled a long glass and wood counter. Behind it, along the wall, a counter full of latte machines, blenders, and coffee brewing stations created a rich bouquet in the air. Farther down on the same wall was a cleaning station with two deep sinks, four plastic bussing pans, and a stack of serving trays. Above it, a shelving unit full of fat coffee mugs, teacups, and glasses added a colorful display. A glass fronted refrigerator stood at the end of the counter, filled with sodas and a variety of soy, nut milk, and creamers.

As I surveyed my sister's beautiful café, I felt immensely proud of her. She'd created such a warm and welcoming place it was easy to understand why it was busy even during off hours. Small groups of people reclined on overstuffed furniture, talking and laughing over their beverages. College-aged kids sat at pub style tables, earbuds crammed in their ears as they hovered over laptops and tablets, studying, I presumed.

The pungent aroma of coffee beans and spicy scent of chai lattes mingled with the sweet smell of baked goods as I made my way to the counter. I studied the menu board posted high upon the wall behind the counters. My stomach was in knots, so I passed on the deli sandwiches and daily specials and opted for a cup of parsnip soup with toasted hazelnuts, and a cup of dark roast coffee. A teenaged girl pushed through a pivoting door which, from the quick view I'd gotten inside, led to a kitchen. She greeted me with a smile that seemed familiar, took my order, then gave me a number and told me she'd bring my coffee and soup to my table.

Making my way to a small table along the far wall, I collapsed onto the padded chair. I felt numb. Defeated. Betrayed. And so angry I was still trembling. For *two years* he'd been conniving and waiting for my property to be forced into a tax sale. He'd known I would never part with the one place, the *only* place that had ever felt like home to me. So, he'd found a way to have it taken from me —and I had no idea how to prevent it from happening.

Bracing my elbows on the decorative ceramic tabletop, I rested my forehead in one hand. I had to find a way out of this mess. I couldn't lose my home.

"You look like you're holding the weight of the world with that hand," a woman's voice said.

I looked up to see my sister holding a bowl of soup and a cup of coffee. We both gasped simultaneously, which told me she hadn't known it was me sitting at the table. I'd known it was possible she'd be here, but I had nothing left to lose today so I'd come in for a desperately-needed cup of coffee.

I wasn't only surprised to see Sophie but also to see her looking so good. Last time I'd seen her was at my grandfather's funeral, and she'd looked tired and unhappy, and had been too thin. Now she looked radiant and healthy, although not happy to see me, if her frown was any indication.

"Hey, Sophie," I whispered, too filled with emotion to say more.

"I heard you were back," she said, no warmth in her voice.

I nodded. "I suppose I'm not welcome here?" I expected her to tell me to get the hell out, but she placed my soup and coffee on the table.

"I have no problem taking your money. From the looks of it, you can afford whatever you like here," she said, glancing at the diamond ring Dan had given me on our twentieth anniversary. "Nice rock. You need anything else? Creamer? Sugar?"

"I ... no, thank you." Before I could continue, Sophie pivoted on her heel and disappeared behind the counter where she busied herself making coffee and preparing lattes for a steady stream of customers.

As I sat there alone, memories of my little sister slayed me. I cried in my soup, trying to hide my tears by dabbing my eyes with my napkin as I wiped my mouth. I shouldn't have come here while at my most vulnerable. It was a stupid move on my part. But I hadn't been thinking clearly ... and I still wasn't. My world was a spinning top that was wobbling beneath me. Because of Dan. Because I hadn't prepared better. Because I'd been running for my life.

I read somewhere that there's no time to plan or to dream when one is just trying to survive. I could see that now. But not having a plan made things more difficult. And having a vindictive, lying husband cutting off all avenues of escape had me bolting through the forest like a frightened rabbit.

I wanted to be a cougar and tear him apart, but I hadn't found my claws yet. I was too busy trying to survive. And that was my problem. I had to find a way to get my feet under me. But how? *How?* I didn't have any more doorknobs to sell.

When Jeff had come by to check out the doorknobs, he'd said he was interested in deconstructing my grandparents' house. He'd claimed that nearly everything could be repurposed. But I was already repurposing some of the materials for my little house, and until I turned the place over to Jeff to take it down, there would be no income from the place. Even when Jeff took possession, the payments would be stretched out over six months. I didn't even have six weeks. I had ten days to come up with eleven thousand one hundred and thirty-two dollars to keep my property. And that didn't include the cost of the building permit, property search, A-R-B fees, reinspection fee, or the many things I still needed to purchase in order to complete my house. I was sunk!

Parsnip soup churned in my stomach. I swallowed hard and took slow, deep breaths.

How naïve I'd been to have thought I could convert the boathouse into a small home for next to nothing. My face heated at how ignorant I'd been.

While inwardly berating myself for my ignorance, I watched Sophie behind the counter. Her blonde hair was loosely drawn up in a clip at the back of her head, a few tendrils dangling by her ears. Her crisp white blouse was rolled up her forearms and tucked into her jeans. I'd noticed the same white blouse and jeans on the young girl who'd taken my order. It was a fresh, clean look that echoed the cleanliness of the café. Every surface gleamed as if freshly washed and dusted. This was Sophie's world, and she conveyed confidence and a relaxed style as she interacted with patrons. I envied their connection with my little sister.

Observing the people around me, I recognized a couple of faces but couldn't remember names. Slowly it began to sink in that some of the furniture looked familiar. My grandparents' beautiful table was positioned near a front window where five women were drinking coffee and examining a quilt spread out in front of them on the table. My grandmother's hutch stood in the opposite corner. Sophie had used it to display tins of specialty teas, colorful tea kettles, milk frothers, tea infusers, and designer tea mugs with cute quotes on them. The wrought iron chairs and loveseat that had once resided on my grandparents' porch now sported new blue cushions and sat prominently in the middle of the café, girded by low bookcases that created an adorable reading nook.

It dawned on me then that Sophie might not have taken those things to spite me but rather as a way to remember and honor our grandparents. Her creative display and use of the furniture made me glad she'd given those things a good home, and that she hadn't left them to rot as I had done.

No wonder she hated me.

I left a tip on the table and my phone number written on a scrap of paper I'd dug out of my purse. At the last second, I wrote "*I'm sorry*" on the paper and placed it on top of the dollar bills. The likelihood of Sophie calling me was about as likely as Dan paying my back taxes, but I held out hope that one day she would forgive me, another unlikely event, but I had nothing left to lose.

As I stepped outside, people sat around several round tables with red umbrellas opened above them. Waist-high urns of flowering plants were positioned among the tables to create a garden-like feel for the guests. Window boxes filled with yellow pansies and pink and purple petunias decorated the front windows. To think Sophie had created this artsy garden-like café from a greasy spoon diner was unimaginable and utterly amazing.

I wished I could tell her this, but the bridge between us had burned long ago. What she didn't know is that I planned to rebuild that bridge, even if I had to do it alone.

Needing to clear my head before going to Maggie's consignment store, I scooted across the bricked street in front of the café and entered the park. It felt as if the whole town had gotten a facelift in my absence.

The community park had once been a plain green space between South Park Avenue and North Spruce Street, both one-way brick streets that led in and out of town. Now the green space stretched the length of town and boasted a small amphitheater, a farmer's market pavilion, a water fountain, several benches and bike racks, and an outside shuffleboard area where a group of adults were playing and laughing. Peak tourist season was just beginning here. It seemed the average number of people in town had already more than doubled. Cyclists rode paved bike paths that ran the length of the park on both sides. Pedestrians roved walking paths that crisscrossed through the park between flowering bushes and beneath towering trees sprouting spring leaves.

This small town was alive with life.

It baffled me how I'd missed so much of this on my first trip to town, but then I remembered how shaken and distracted I'd been in the days following my escape from Dan's world. I'd slipped into town with my head down, hiding under a ball cap to grab groceries, cash, and gas, then scurried out hoping no one would recognize me. I'd met Maggie on that trip, of course, and I couldn't imagine where I'd be had our paths not crossed that day.

After a few minutes of listening to the splashing fountain, I headed to The Red Fox where Maggie was finishing paperwork. She turned things over to her assistant, and we headed to Chloe's house to fill her in on Dan's underhanded scheme. But when we got there, we found Chloe working in the barn.

Huge double doors were flung open. Overhead fluorescent lighting filled the barn and reflected off the heavy equipment she and Josh had used in their business. Soft country music was coming out of surprisingly nice speakers. We found Chloe in the back of the barn trying to drag a heavy bin out from under a wooden workbench.

"Why isn't Dylan helping you with this?" Maggie asked, her voice and our approach startling Chloe.

She spun to face us, then dusted her gloves off. "You know I have weapons out here."

"Noted." Maggie raised her hands. "We come in peace. Where is your son who should be helping you with this?"

"Ha!" Chloe gave a dismissive flap of her hand. "He was home from college about five minutes before he headed back out the door to hang with his buddies."

"Sounds about right," I said empathetically. "I barely saw my girls when they came home on Christmas break."

"Have they finished up yet?" Chloe asked.

I nodded because I couldn't speak past the lump in my throat. According to Haley they were back from college and settled at home with Dan now.

"What are you wrestling with under there?" Maggie gestured toward the large plastic tub Chloe had been trying to drag out on her own.

"I have an awning in there I thought Kate could use." Chloe looked at me. "It would make a pretty, albeit temporary, outside covered porch for you if you're interested."

The thoughtful consideration and kindness from my friends overwhelmed me again and again, and I wondered how I'd ever repay them. I had so much to make up for. "I would love that, Chloe, but I'm not sure I'll still own the property in a few days." Together, Maggie and I told Chloe about the unpaid taxes and my insurmountable problem.

As Chloe listened, her face got redder and her frown deeper. "Honest to god, Kate, I could hurt that man right now."

"You and me both."

"I hope you're going to force that shithead to pay those taxes."

"He won't do it, Chloe. If I call him, I'll just be giving him the satisfaction of knowing he won."

"He's not going to win," Maggie insisted. "We'll think of something. I promise. Now let's get this awning over to your house."

It took the three of us fifteen minutes to wrestle the tub out and load it into Maggie's SUV, and another two hours to set up the awning beside my house. We attached a string of solar lights that Chloe had used with the awning, then stood back to admire our handiwork.

"This is gorgeous, and deeply appreciated," I said to Chloe.

She eyed the dark bulbs. "The lights should be charged enough to work tomorrow evening."

We moved the chairs under the awning and relocated my little fire pit closer to our sitting area. Then after I fed Sinatra and started a fire, I plopped in the chair beside my friends and accepted the cold beer Chloe offered from her magic cooler. "I owe you about a hundred beers, Chloe."

"You can repay me this winter when we're all camped out in your pretty little house watching the snowfall on the lake."

"Deal," I said, but I couldn't help wondering if I'd still be here then. "I need to take Sinatra to the vet. Any idea how to manage that without a carrier?"

"You can use my pet carrier," she said. "Josh and I got Dylan a dog for his fifth birthday, and she died last year. It was as if she'd known Dylan was heading off to school."

"What a tough year you guys have had," I said, then silently kicked myself for reminding Chloe that they had lost more than a dog.

"Yeah ..." She sighed, took a long drink of her beer, then said, "It's a medium-sized carrier so it'll be perfect for Sinatra. But let me make an appointment at my vet for you, otherwise you'll have to wait weeks or months to get in."

"Gosh, I had no idea." Resting the bottom of my bottle on the arm of my chair, I asked Chloe if she knew what treatments Sinatra would need.

"Considering he's likely a feral cat, I'd suggest he get a full physical, get his claws trimmed, and get all his shots. You should get him dewormed, too. And he could use a bath." She eyed Sinatra who was lounging on the other side of our little campfire. "I'd also suggest a potty patch for that ball of fur."

"A what?" I asked.

"A potty patch." Chloe grinned. "They shave his butt so his poo won't stick to his fur."

"Probably a good idea since Sinatra shares the boathouse with me. I'd rather he didn't carry in any surprises."

"Can we please talk about something else?" Maggie asked. "Y'all are grossing me out."

Chloe laughed. "Try having kids."

"No thanks." Maggie stretched her legs out and settled more deeply into her chair. "I was born devoid of any mothering instincts."

"Nothing wrong with that." Chloe raised her bottle in a mock salute to Maggie. "You've got the awesome aunt gene though."

Maggie tapped her bottle against Chloe's. "I am a badass aunt, aren't I?"

I laughed with them but felt heartbroken that I'd kept my girls from these amazing women. Maggie and Chloe could have both been honorary aunts to my girls. But I'd let Dan convince me that my friends were a bad influence because they didn't believe in or practice his religion. As a young mother I followed Dan blindly, doing everything to make him happy and give our daughters the most loving, stable, and good home possible. In hindsight, it wasn't just me who'd suffered the loss of Maggie and Chloe.

Thinking of Dan riled me up again and sent my thoughts spinning. I told Maggie and Chloe about seeing Sophie. They were immediately excited for me until I shared Sophie's snide comment about taking my money.

Suddenly, as if I'd been slapped upside the head, I gasped aloud. Sinatra jumped to his feet as I leapt from my chair. He scuttled away a few yards. "Sorry, buddy." I turned back to Maggie and Chloe who were looking at me as if uncertain whether to expect an epiphany or psychotic break. "I can sell my ring." I held up my left hand. "I had my ring appraised after Dan gave it to me so we could insure it. It was appraised at twenty-nine thousand dollars."

"Holy mother of ..." Maggie's jaw hung open.

Chloe hooted with laughter. "You're a genius, Kate! And it's the perfect irony."

I grinned. "It is, isn't it? I know you suggested selling it before, Maggie, but I couldn't even consider it then. I'd wanted to save the ring for my girls, but I realize I can give them far more by creating a warm and loving home for them here." Whether they would visit or not was up to them. But this ring meant nothing to me. I'd been keeping it in my purse to protect it from getting damaged while I built my house. I wasn't even sure why I'd worn it today, but I was glad I had. Sophie's comment about the ring must have floated up from my subconscious. It was not only the perfect answer, it was the *only* answer to my dilemma. "Any suggestions on the best place to sell a ring?" I asked.

"Potsdam," Maggie said. "There's a high-end jewelry store there that will be your best bet. But don't expect to get the full value of your ring, Kate. You'll be lucky to get half that and will be more likely to get offered forty percent or less."

My heart sank. "I was hoping to get enough to pay off the taxes and hire an attorney to get my divorce underway. I'll keep my expectations in check, but I need to sell this thing fast. Any chance either of you are going to Potsdam in the next couple of days?"

"I'm not, but you can borrow my truck any time," Chloe said.

"She could, but she shouldn't," Maggie said, then turned back to me, "It's probably best if I go with you, Kate. Not to suggest you're incompetent or can't handle this on your own, but I'm a fearless negotiator. I'm quite a badass if I must say so myself."

"I know," I said. "I've seen you in action. Poor Jeff is still recovering from negotiating my window purchase with you two. I can't thank you enough for your help and for having my back."

"That's what friends do, Kate. We have your back." Maggie stood and set aside her drink. "I'm heading out now. I'll pick you up at nine tomorrow morning."

"I'll head out with you." Chloe got to her feet. She gave me a hug and told me she'd drop the pet carrier off tomorrow afternoon. "Hopefully, I can corral my son long enough to have lunch with him tomorrow, then I'll be over to get some more work done on your place. We are not waiting for a damn building permit. You'll get it."

Chapter Sixteen

Turns out Maggie was right. Getting half the value of my ring wasn't easy. But the jeweler finally offered forty-five percent of the value, and that was only under duress because Maggie verbally beat the man into submission.

We drove straight to the town clerk's office in Dunwith Falls and paid my tax bill. Gladys, our ancient lady clerk, was so thrilled to clear my account she hand-carried the information to Mr. Skives' office and got me an appointment on the spot. Five minutes into the interview I knew I needed Chloe's help explaining our blueprint and materials and installation, so I called her. She walked through the door fifteen minutes later. After an arduous interview we filled out the building permit application and I paid the fees. Then, after Mr. Skives promised to expedite the application, he requested receipts for building materials we'd already used, like the roofing and windows, to ensure they all met code.

Although my brain was mush when we left, I felt like I'd climbed Mount Everest. "I have eighty dollars left from the sale of my ring so I'm treating you ladies to lunch," I announced, feeling elated that I had enough money left to do so. "Oh shoot, Chloe, I forgot you were having lunch with Dylan."

She sighed. "I'm not, actually. He graced me with his presence for a twenty-minute brunch, so that's my allotted time for the day. Lunch with you girls sounds divine!"

We opted for beer and burritos at the Bobcat Brewery at the other end of town. Instead of driving, we took a leisurely one mile walk down South Park Avenue, looking in shop windows as Chloe and Maggie filled me in on the changes that had happened in my absence. The town had come together five years ago in an unprecedented act of unity to create the ultimate tourist destination and provide a luxurious home for its residents. Brick buildings lining both streets had been painted in fun pastels of pink, purple, yellow, and blue. The board and batten wood buildings had been freshly stained in various hues of browns with all of them sporting new rustic signs with charred lettering. I'd never imagined our little town could be so transformed. All businesses had agreed to take on names representing nature and wildlife from the area.

As I walked, I noticed names like the Bear Claw Bakery, Painted Turtle Art Gallery, Purple Finch Bookstore, Lily & Lavender Specialty Shop, Minks Hair Salon, Snowshoe Sports, and Hemlock Hardware, my father's store. I admired their creative window displays and cute names. Sparrows General Store featured two massive windows chock full of temptation. Displays of hiking outfits, jeans, backpacks, and boots resided beside camping equipment and travel mugs. Mannequins were dressed in sharp outfits meant to appeal to any gender. In another window, hand-painted pottery was beautifully displayed on driftwood furniture sitting atop handcrafted rugs and draped with colorful woven throws.

I could envision all of it in my home, but I walked past without a moment's regret. "I'm utterly amazed by the transformation of this place," I said.

Maggie took in the town with a sweeping glance. "Yeah, it's no longer the mishmash of gray colorless buildings it once was. Wait until you see the brewery." She gave me a nudge to get me moving. "You remember Bobbie Jo Kafferty?" When I nodded, Maggie continued. "She converted that dirty old warehouse into a gorgeous bar. They serve delicious food and their own micro brewed beer."

"Sounds wonderful." I followed along for a couple seconds then laughed. "I get it now. Bobbie Jo named the brewery Bobcat Brewery as a play on her name. Smart girl."

Maggie shrugged. "I don't know about that. She's a forty-six-year-old divorcee stalking the young bucks who visit the brewery. She lives above the bar so she should have called it the Cougar's Den."

"Maggie!" Chloe exclaimed with feigned shock. "Don't be catty."

We all laughed at Chloe's play on words.

"Actually, Bobbie Jo's a good friend and still gorgeous enough to turn the heads of those young guys, so I applaud her," Maggie said. "You'll love her, Kate."

"I think I already do."

The Bobcat Brewery, where apparently a cougar lived, sat on a wide patch of gravel with the front door facing the park and the back door facing Dunwith River. The building had been a farm supply and feed store back when I'd lived here. To see so many changes and to be walking into a bar with my best friends felt surreal.

Metal wall art consisting of old beer advertisements covered the brewery walls. Overhead duct pipes snaked across a high ceiling painted black. A long bar took up one end of the brewery, and every stool was occupied with people eating and drinking, some chatting, some sitting alone looking at their phones. Several booths and tables were already filled, but Maggie nabbed a prime booth by a window for us.

We perused the menus, placed our orders, and spent several minutes laughing and joking and enjoying our drinks.

A few minutes after our food was delivered, Bobbie Jo came to our table. She was striking with amethyst-colored eyes and straight silver blonde hair that fell to the middle of her back. The confident way she carried herself exuded power. Her tight jeans were tucked into a pair of white cowboy boots with purple stitching that matched the color of her blouse, all of it emphasizing her youthful figure.

Bobbie Jo welcomed me with such warmth and charm I felt as if I'd known her all my life. I wished I had because she was intriguing and funny and passionate about helping people and taking care of our community.

Several bangle bracelets encircled one of her arms, and her fingers and thumbs were dressed in rings; wide bands of hammered silver, delicate bands of silver and gold, a couple ropey bands bedecked with blue and purple stones, and even an emerald class ring. When she noticed me gawking at her hands, she laughed. "I can never decide which one, so I wear them all."

"I was admiring them and wondering how you could carry that weight around all day."

She laughed, but before she could say anything, Maggie piped in. "Do you have to take all that stuff off before you ... well, you know."

"It builds anticipation," Bobbie Jo said. "I consider disrobing my fingers as foreplay."

We erupted in laughter, but I sat stunned. I couldn't believe we were having this conversation in the middle of a public place or having it at all. I felt like an inexperienced thirteen-year-old hanging out with college girls, pretending I was cool, that the conversation didn't make me uncomfortable, but it did. Not because I didn't get the joke or that I didn't know firsthand about sex and foreplay, but because this sort of conversation hadn't been part of my life since ... well, since my high school days hanging out with Maggie and Chloe.

This was such a different world than I'd been living in with Dan. That world had been gray and restrictive and ... dishonest. We'd always had to be *on*, showing each other only our best, most pleasant self. We didn't air our troubles, share our heartaches, make off-color jokes, or let our guard down. We lived behind our "nice Christian" façade. It was a game of one-upmanship on who could be the most *Christian*. Even at home. Which in hindsight explains why Dan and I rarely exchanged angry words. We would simply bite our tongues and *pray about it*.

I'd revealed more to Maggie and Chloe in a month than I had to Dan over twenty years of living together. As these revelations seeped in, I was slowly beginning to understand why the end of my marriage had been inevitable.

"Are you all right, Kate?" Bobbie Jo asked. "You look a little shell-shocked."

"I am a little, but actually I was wondering if you're wearing colored contacts to make your eyes so purple."

She laughed. "I am. I change my contacts so that my eye color matches my outfits. Brown, blue, purple, green ... so much more fun than wearing glasses." Sliding out of the booth, she stood at the end of our table. "I'll let you gals eat your lunch. But, Chloe, when you finish, would you go to the Eagle's Nest with me? They need some work done that requires heavy equipment."

Chloe shook her head. "Sorry, Bobbie Jo, I'm not doing that work anymore."

"Not even for a good cause?" Bobbie Jo asked. She gave Chloe's shoulder a gentle squeeze. "Just walk over with me and let me show you what needs to be done. If you don't want to do it, maybe you can tell us who to call."

"We'll go with you," Maggie said, sending me a silent message with a nudge in the side. "I want to see how Maria and her kids are doing."

"Sure, I'll go along," I said, hoping I was playing my part correctly.

"All right. You win." Chloe picked up her vegan tuna melt sandwich, then scowled at Bobbie Jo. "Go away now and let me eat in peace."

"Done," Bobbie Jo said, then strolled to the bar.

Chloe turned her scowl on us. "You two were no help at all."

"What are friends for?" Maggie said, then dropped a cheese-covered nacho chip into her grinning mouth.

Unable to determine if Chloe was joking or truly upset, I filled my mouth with salad greens and stayed out of it.

But our lunch progressed without issue and with a discussion about the revitalization of the town and Bobbie Jo's tireless contributions. When our table was cleared and I'd paid the bill, Bobbie Jo met us at the door.

The four of us walked five blocks to what used to be my elementary school and was now called the Eagle's Nest Community Center. A large mural of a soaring eagle covered the brick wall near the front entrance that consisted of several glass doors that opened into a lobby with marble floors. I'd walked through those doors countless times in my school years, but I could barely remember the carefree girl I'd been back then.

"Wow! This place has changed," I said as I looked around the lobby that now resembled a massive living room. The foyer that had once been congested with noisy school kids scurrying between classes was now a serene place with thick carpeting, soft lighting, comfortable furniture broken into several sitting areas, one near bookshelves that formed a reading nook, one positioned around a fireplace for relaxing, and one around a large square coffee table topped with board games. I turned to my friends. "What is this place?"

Before anyone could answer, a petite dark-haired woman dressed in a navy-blue pantsuit and wearing stylish, black-framed glasses approached us. Bobbie Jo welcomed the woman with a hug. "I told you I'd get Chloe over here."

"I owe you my firstborn," the woman joked, then turned and gave Chloe a hug. "Thank you for answering our call for help."

Chloe opened her mouth as if to correct the woman's assumption, then sighed. "What do you need done?"

"I'll show you, but first let me introduce myself to this lovely lady," she said, extending her hand to me. "You look familiar, but I don't believe we've met. I'm Beth Kingsley, the founder and director of the Eagle's Nest."

"Oh, I'm Kate Symmons," I said, shaking her hand. "Nice to meet you."

Bobbie Jo apologized for not introducing us. "I wrongly assumed everyone knew each other."

A look passed between Maggie and Chloe, but I didn't understand what it meant.

"What is this place?" I asked, still uncertain of its purpose.

There was no mistaking the pride in Beth's dark eyes. "It's a place for everyone. It's open to the community and to anyone needing a safe place to stay where they can rebuild their life. Come on, you'll understand better after I show you around." She glanced at Chloe. "Our project is out back, but you might like to see some of the updates we've done since your last visit."

For forty minutes the five of us explored the former elementary school which had been converted into multiple dorm-style rooms where individuals or families in need could take refuge. We met three of the families, one playing board games in the second-floor family room, a woman named Maria and her three children who'd been driven out of their home by her abusive husband, and another family in the gymnasium who'd recently lost their home to a fire. There were other people in residence for various reasons, and volunteer staff members working on premises, along with several members of the community, kids, teens, and adults making use of the gym, pool, and game rooms. Everything had been painted in warm, uplifting colors, and decorated to give the place a homey feel.

"This is incredible," I said, unable to fully take in the transformation of the place. "Who did all of this?"

"Beth started the project nine years ago," Bobbie Jo said. "She was able to get the whole town involved, and now it sort of runs itself."

"So you say," Beth quipped, "but I'm here every day, and I can assure you it doesn't run itself. In all fairness, though, support from the community makes my job easy."

The place baffled me. "Does the town own this then?" I asked.

"No. We're a nonprofit." Beth led us through the cafeteria, which was another mind-bending transformation from cold hard floors and metal tables to a variety of dinner tables topped with vases of flowers, and walls displaying art created by the residents and townspeople. It was a happy place that smelled like oranges and coffee.

"Is this a church facility then?" I asked, thinking about it being a nonprofit. "Is that where you get your funding?"

"No," Beth said. "The two churches in town left Dunwith Falls years ago."

I glanced at Maggie and Chloe, but it was Bobbie Jo who slipped her finger beneath my chin and closed my mouth. "I fear you'll need therapy by the time we're done with you today, Kate."

I nodded because I was genuinely stunned. "That explains the absence of church bells and steeples ..."

Beth shrugged. "The single aim of our town is to be inclusive rather than exclusionary. We simply wanted to bring our community together with our Sunday Fun-days project. While Sunday is often the quietest day in most towns, it's now one of our most active days. Fern Park is the center of the activity with a farmer's market, craft booths, music, games, contests, and picnics happening from morning to late evening. It's also where people come together, and good things happen. Instead of Sunday being a day of repentance, it's a day of celebration. This has nothing to do with anyone's beliefs but rather the simple notion that we, individually and as a community, can be good without a god."

I'd heard that expression before but couldn't recall where.

As we headed outside, Maggie told me how the last local church to leave Dunwith Falls had sent out a press release stating it had donated two thousand dollars to the Eagle's Nest project. But Beth had responded by writing an editorial for the paper thanking the *parishioners* of the church for their generous donation and challenging the church to match the contribution.

"They didn't, of course," Beth said, "but that little revelation opened many eyes here. The pastor who owned and ran the church didn't donate a dime. The parishioners donated all that money."

I thought about the arguments I'd had with Dan over that very subject. I suggested he was overtaxing our parishioners by always putting the burden on them to support special collections. I proposed that Dan could contribute money from his abundant church funds. I lost every time.

We crossed the gymnasium where a group of teens were playing basketball, then followed Beth through a doorway that brought us out behind the Eagle's Nest. The elementary playground was still there, but there were many new additions like a small skatepark for skateboarding and rollerblading. My heart was awash with joy that such a place and town existed, that people like Beth were willing to donate so much of their life to such an admirable pursuit without expecting anything in return or some future reward in an afterlife.

"This is what I wanted to show you," Beth said to Chloe who'd been oddly silent during our tour. "These two trees need to come down. They're so old that limbs break off each time we get a good wind through here. The last one fell and smashed one of the benches. I hate to take them down, but it's too dangerous to leave them standing. As you can see, we have a lot of activity out here." Beth swept her arms out to encompass the people in the park. "Would you consider donating your time to remove the trees for us?"

I could tell Chloe was struggling. I knew she hadn't been able to go back to work without Josh. The first time she'd started one of their pieces of equipment was to brush hog the lake trail for me. But helping me with my projects was apparently different than doing a job she would have once done with Josh.

"I'll help you, Chloe," I said, jumping in and hoping she wouldn't hate me for it. "Whatever you need me to do, with the exception of climbing the tree, I'll do it."

She released a snort of laughter as if my offer were ridiculous.

"Thanks, Kate, but I doubt you'd like hauling limbs and feeding the woodchipper."

"I think I can handle it." I held her gaze, letting her know I was there for her, finally, and I wasn't going anywhere. "We can't do anything at my place without a building permit, so let's do this."

"I'm in," Maggie said, shocking all of us. "What? I can manage a rake when I want to."

"We'll have plenty of volunteers to help you," Beth added.

Releasing a big sigh, Chloe gave a resigned nod. "Okay. Let me check the weather and I'll let you know when we can do it."

"Thank you!" Beth leaned in and gave Chloe a hug. But as she stepped away, she turned toward me with a perplexed expression. "You're Kate Weston."

It was a statement of fact, not a question, and it held no warmth. "I am," I said, a bit unnerved that she knew my maiden name. "Have we met?"

Suddenly the air seemed to crackle with tension. Maggie and Chloe exchanged an *oh shit* look. Bobbie Jo looked on, her expression as confused as I felt.

"I have to admit," Beth said, sizing me up, "I'm not sure whether to thank you or berate you for what you've done."

Everything inside me just dropped to the ground. I didn't know what was happening, but I knew it wasn't good.

"You obviously don't remember me, and I have to admit it took all this time for me to recognize you, but we're stepsisters."

I staggered backward as if she'd punched me. "What?"

"Your father married my mother." *Oh my god …* It dawned on me in that instant that Beth was the child of the woman my father had the affair with and had ultimately married. The woman's last name had been Davis, which is why it hadn't clicked that Beth was one of her children. Beth was apparently married now and using her husband's last name as I was. I'd been using my married name of Symmons to avoid exactly this situation, but it appeared I was bound to face my past whether I wanted to or not.

I didn't know what to say. Should I apologize for breaking their family? Hadn't that been their mother's fault, though? It was her mother who broke my family, but I couldn't condemn Beth for her mother's actions. I groped for words and came up empty.

"Your father is the best thing that ever happened to my family. You were the worst." She shook her head, her eyes drilling into mine. "You have no idea how deeply you hurt my mother and our father."

"*Our* father?" My voice croaked and my mind exploded. This woman considered my father *her* father? Through marriage, he was. But still ...

"Yes, *our* father," she insisted. "But I think this is a conversation for another time."

Only then did I remember that Maggie, Chloe, and Bobbie Jo were listening to all of this. I'd been so caught off guard that everything around me had disappeared. "I agree," I said, "but I can't leave without saying I'm sorry." Because I was sorry. I should have kept my mouth shut and let my father and mother and Beth's parents handle things.

"You don't need to apologize to me," she said. "Save that for your father and my mother." She flashed a forced smile at my friends. "If you'll excuse me now, I need to get back to work. Looking forward to hearing from you, Chloe." With that, she walked away like a woman who'd just taken care of business at a board meeting.

Maggie released a low whistle. "That was intense."

"Why didn't you guys tell me who she was?" I said, feeling betrayed that they'd let me walk into the situation blind.

"I'm sorry, Kate." Chloe reached out and clasped my hand. "The connection didn't dawn on me until Beth introduced herself to you. Then it was too late to give you a heads up."

I blew out my breath. "Well, that felt awful."

"Yeah." Bobbie Jo grimaced. "I think I might be needing therapy after that trauma drama. Anyone else need a beer?"

As we all headed back to the Bobcat Brewery for a much-needed drink, Maggie slung her arm around my shoulders and gave me a little shake. "You know, Kate, you're like a walking earthquake."

Chapter Seventeen

Today was the day we were removing the trees from behind the Eagle's Nest where my stepsister worked. A week had passed since our meeting with Beth. Chloe had scheduled the job for Saturday providing Beth could round up volunteers. She had, and I'd promised to be one of them. "You don't have to do this," Chloe told me as she stood outside the cab of the Dummy dressed in work boots, jeans, and a hoodie. A small tractor with a bucket, a stump grinder, and a scary looking wood chipper sat atop a lowboy trailer attached to the dump truck. In the back of the dump were chainsaws, rakes, gloves, masks, and face shields, along with a bale of straw and a bag of grass seed.

"I'm good to go, Chloe." I wasn't exactly good, but I was going. Living in this town and rebuilding my life here meant I had to work through the mess I'd left behind. And I was standing by my friend no matter how uncomfortable things might be for me. "I really want to contribute," I said, "so quit stalling."

"It's that obvious?" She sagged against the truck door. "This is so hard."

I could see she was struggling, but I knew giving her a hug right now would break her rather than help her. "Is Dylan okay with helping today?"

She nodded. "Yeah. He didn't work with us very often, so his memories with Josh aren't tied in with our business like mine are. This stuff doesn't faze Dylan other than he doesn't like the work," she said, gesturing to the equipment. "His struggle is on football Sundays and that sort of thing because that's where he spent more time with his father."

"Makes sense," I said softly, my heart breaking for them.

"Dylan's going to meet us there. I promised he'd only have to work long enough to show you and the volunteers how to safely feed the chipper. Then he'll be off to his friend's house to spend the day gaming." She shoved away from the truck and opened the door. "If we both survive today, we are having dinner at the lake."

"I'm in." I climbed into the cab and pulled the door shut behind me. "Think Maggie will join us?"

"Count on it." With that Chloe cranked the Dummy to life and pulled her rig onto the road.

It took less than fifteen minutes to get to town and navigate Chloe's long trailer to the backside of the Eagle's Nest. After climbing out of the truck, she spent a few minutes backing the equipment off the trailer, then came to where I stood watching.

"Dylan's here," she said, gesturing toward a young man exiting a car parked along the street.

I didn't plan to fall apart when I met Chloe's son, but I did. He was a handsome young man who resembled his father and had his mother's dark hair, brown eyes, and gorgeous, bronzed skin. But his polite greeting and respectful handshake brought me to tears. We should have met with a hug, like family, like he was my favorite nephew, and I was the honorary aunt I should have been. He was nineteen years old, and I was meeting him for the first time.

"Um ... are you okay?" he asked, casting a helpless look at his mother.

Swiping at my eyes, I murmured an apology and let him slip his hand away from the crazy lady. "Sorry, I just ..." I shook my head. "Doesn't matter. Just a little emotional this morning, I guess. Let's get those trees down."

Empathy filled Chloe's eyes, but she turned and dropped the tailgate on the Dummy while I pulled myself together.

Turns out feeding limbs into a woodchipper isn't so scary if one pays attention and exercises caution. It's noisy as hell though, even with ear protection. Between that and the chainsaws and the loud growl of Chloe's tractor and stump grinder, I was developing a painful headache. I attributed part of it to my stress level. Beth hadn't hidden inside as I'd hoped. She'd arrived dressed in work clothes, then rolled up her sleeves, and helped our crew of five clear the limbs that Chloe cut from the dying hemlocks. Despite Dylan's plan to leave early, he stuck around to run the smaller chainsaw. He cut the thicker limbs into firewood-sized chunks that we tossed into the back of the dump truck. The rest of the debris went through the chipper that spit out yards of wood chips into a heaping pile Beth planned to use for landscaping.

My stepsister was a resourceful and intelligent woman. From what Chloe had said, Beth was seven years younger than us, which explained why I didn't remember her from school. I hadn't really known her family either. All I could remember was the image of her mother kissing my father. At the time, I hadn't been able to see past that transgression to acknowledge the woman in his arms as a mother of children who loved and needed her. All I'd been able to think of was my own mother and how my father was betraying all of us.

Even with so many of us helping Chloe, it took half a day to drop the trees, remove the stumps, clear the debris, and spread grass seed. By the time we'd finished, I was sweaty, covered in sawdust, and had a raging headache. I was glad we were going back to Chloe's house first because I desperately needed to use her shower before going home.

While Chloe loaded her tractor and other equipment on the lowboy trailer, Maggie and the others headed home. I sat on a nearby bench and drank a bottle of water from the stocked cooler that Beth had supplied for the crew.

"Thank you for helping today," Beth said as she sat beside me.

For a moment, she eyed the empty space where the hemlocks had stood this morning. "I'm going to miss those trees."

"They were beautiful," I said, and I meant it. "I have to confess I'm a tree-hugger."

She laughed. "Me too."

We sat in awkward silence for a couple of minutes, watching Chloe navigate the stump grinder onto the lowboy.

"Kate," Beth said, garnering my attention. Her complexion was so light and creamy and her eyebrows so dark, she reminded me of Snow White. "I owe you an apology. I was being judgmental and unkind last week. I suspect the situation with my mother and your father wounded you deeply and I know it hurt your family too. I hope you can overlook my momentary slip and go back to how we were before I misspoke."

For a moment I was speechless, wondering if I'd heard her correctly. She was apologizing to me? She was acknowledging my pain? She wanted to go back to our earlier friendliness?

"I understand if I'm asking too much," she continued, no trace of animosity in her voice.

"No, I ... I would really like to get to know you, Beth."

"Then how about lunch sometime?" she asked. "I'd like to get to know you too. You're not what I expected."

I laughed a little. "I'm not sure how to take that, but I suspect most of what you've heard isn't good but is likely true."

"Actually, I've heard very little about you. You've always been this mysterious person lurking on the periphery of our family in hushed conversations." A smile tipped her lips. "Maybe lunch next week then?"

My heart was hammering. "Sure. Just let me know when and where."

She slipped her phone out of her shirt pocket. "If you don't mind giving me your number, I'll text you as soon as I know my schedule."

I was so intrigued by her that I gave her my old number. "Wait! I have a new phone number," I said, then gave it to her.

She cleared my old number and punched the new one into her phone. "There," she said, "I texted you, so you'll have my number and will know who's messaging or calling you."

Calling me? She thought she might be calling me? Everything about this impromptu meeting felt surreal.

"Hey, Kate, are you ready to head out?" Chloe asked, pulling off her work gloves as she approached us. "I'm beat."

"Me too." As I stood, Beth followed. "Thanks for the water, Beth, and ... well, I guess we'll talk soon." My god, could I be any more awkward?

She laughed and said she was looking forward to it. Then she pulled Chloe into a big hug and thanked her effusively.

When Chloe was finally released there were tears in her eyes. "It feels as if I should be thanking you." Her misty eyes took a sweeping look across the empty space where the old trees had stood. "I hope you'll plant something beautiful there."

"How do Rose of Sharon bushes sound?"

"Get the ones with pink blossoms," Chloe said.

"My thoughts exactly," Beth replied.

"While you two are landscaping the yard, can you give me a couple minutes to run to the corner grocery?" At Chloe's nod, I hurried away and headed to a small grocery store a block away. When I came back carrying a twelve pack, Chloe laughed.

"Good thinking, Kate."

By the time we were back on the road heading home, both Chloe and I had pulled ourselves together.

"You did good today, Kate. You impressed me."

"So did you, Chloe. It was a hard day for both of us."

"So it seems," she said. "What happened between you and Beth? Sounds as if you two found some common ground or at least agreed not to kill each other?"

I laughed. "She apologized."

Chloe's eyebrows shot up and she looked at me. I filled her in on the conversation and admitted that I was both looking forward to, and dreading, having lunch with Beth. But Chloe agreed it would be good for us.

After a couple minutes of riding in silence, she looked over at me. "Kate don't beat yourself up because you missed seeing my son grow up. You had one hell of a roadblock thrown in your path that forced you to take another road. It happens. And it's okay. Life can be hell sometimes and leave us no options but to grip the wheel and hang on for dear life. Believe me, I know."

I slipped my hand over hers. "I know you do."

Hearts aching, we rode the rest of the way in companionable silence. After unloading the equipment and tools, Chloe and I went to the house. Instead of heading straight for the shower, though, we had a beer, talked about our day, and debated on what to make for our supper at the lake. In the end, we called Maggie, asked her to pick up a big-ass pizza. Then I hit the shower. After dressing in the clean clothes I'd brought in my duffle bag, I vacated the bathroom so Chloe could shower.

When she'd finished, we grabbed the twelve-pack, that was now a ten-pack of beer out of the fridge, then filled a plastic bag with ice for the cooler that Chloe had left at my place. Then we climbed back into the Dummy and headed for my house. "This load of firewood is going to come in handy," she said.

"It never crossed my mind that we could take the limbs for firewood."

"Well, we can, and I made sure Dylan cut everything in small enough pieces just for that purpose."

"You are brilliant, my friend."

"And you're just now noticing this?" she asked with a little sass that surprised me.

Before I could make a wisecrack, I noticed a rental car in my driveway. My head nearly exploded. "That better not be Dan or so help me god ..."

"Don't worry about him, Kate. I'll run him over with the Dummy."

I burst out laughing, but I was still seething inside.

It wasn't Dan. It was his minions. Ladies of the church. Three women I'd once considered friends. But with Chloe sitting beside me, I knew they had never been friends. They'd been fellow Christians and pleasant acquaintances.

I climbed out of the truck, so agitated I was trembling. Chloe followed me out and stood beside me in the driveway.

The powerful Trifecta stood outside their vehicle waiting for me, all prayed up and ready to talk me back into their Lord's waiting arms, I'm sure.

They were friendly and pleasant, even when they saw me holding an open twelve pack of beer. I'm not sure why I'd hauled the beer and ice out of the truck with me because Chloe was going to drive us out to the lake. But my brain had short-circuited when I saw the women, so maybe it was my subconscious way of keeping my hands full so I wouldn't choke anyone.

I knew why they were here. Judy was the assistant pastor's wife. Carol was the Outreach leader. And Darlene was head of the Women's Ministry. They were here for an intervention, to witness to me, to lead me back to sanity and Jesus ... and to Dan. But *he'd* sent them. Not Jesus.

"We want you to know, Kate, this visit is just between us," Judy said sweetly. "We're worried about you. And Pastor Dan is just beside himself because he doesn't know how to help you through this time in your life. We're here because we thought we might be able to help. I went through it two years ago."

"Through what?" I asked, then it hit me. "Oh my god, I'm *not* in menopause."

A grimace cut across their faces at my "*god*" expression, but they held their ground like determined soldiers.

Rather than waste their time or mine or let them get me riled enough to be rude, I told them I was fine, my lady parts were fine, and I was content and happy right here.

"I don't believe that, Kate. This isn't you," Judy said, glancing at the beer carton in my hand. "You've been such a beacon of light in our church, and we simply can't stand by and let this happen to you."

"Actually, it's Dan's church, his business, his *job*, and what exactly is supposed to be happening to me?"

Judy cast a helpless look at her backup crew.

Carol released a fake laugh. "You always had the best sense of humor, Kate," she said, taking another direction in their approach to reeling me back in. "We miss that and are just saying we want you back."

Darlene backed her up with gusto. "We do! The girls and I were talking on the way here about you and your funny sermon notes. We're praying you'll come back with us. Service just isn't the same without you."

They were a good tag team, I'd give them that.

"I do believe you were talking about me," I said, "but not because you miss me or my sense of humor or my sermon notes. You were gossiping about my perceived fall from grace and how you'll be superstars if you can bring me back to church. But don't make me your prodigal project because I'm never going back."

I could see I'd shocked and offended them, but I wasn't going to let them think I was buying into their lies. If they wanted to lie to me, I was going to call them on their bullshit. They hadn't missed my sense of humor ... or me. They were doing their job. That's it.

"Um ... Pastor Dan says your girls are home from school now," Judy said, stuttering a bit while taking the lead again. "He's concerned that your absence is having a negative impact on the girls."

Fury ignited in my gut and began to smolder. "Do *not* go there, Judy."

Anxiety flashed in her eyes. "Oh, I'm not judging. I was just mentioning Pastor Dan's concern."

"You *were* judging, but I understand. It's what you're conditioned to do." Their eyes widened. "You've all been brainwashed."

"That's right," Judy said, puffing up with righteous indignation. "We're brainwashed in the blood of—."

"Save your breath," I said, rudely cutting her off because I knew and had spoken all those trite phrases used in battles like this one. "You're just brainwashed in Dan's vitriol." For a moment I looked at them. Really looked at them. "If your family and circle of friends weren't in church, would any of you still be there? Do you like doing this, witnessing and intervening, forsaking your own lives to perceivably save the lives of others? I'm seriously asking because I don't miss it at all. I like waking up each day and living my life as I please, not having to paste on a smile and suppress my emotions, dreams, and desires. It's truly wonderful to be free of all that oppressing nonsense."

Judy's brows knotted. "We are here to serve the Lord, not ourselves. You've apparently forgotten that."

"You're in a cult, Judy. You're serving Dan, not your Savior." My anger flared, and I swallowed hard to rein it in. "Please don't make me be rude. I understand why you're here. I know you mean well. But this is going to end badly if you continue to press me."

"We're here as your friends," she insisted, but there was no light of friendship in her eyes. "You're a lost sheep, Kate, and we're here to take you back home." Judy reached out and latched onto my hand.

Repulsed by her cold fingers circling my hand like a shackle, I ripped free of her grasp. "Don't fucking touch me!"

Their simultaneous gasps and mortified expressions mirrored my own disgust. I'd had it. I simply couldn't tolerate their sanctimonious smiles and lies and ridiculous words another minute. "You ladies need to leave," I demanded. "Right now."

Eyes round as saucers, Judy pressed a hand to her heaving chest. "We're just here to help ... to pray with you and help you find your way again."

For a minute we all stared at each other, then I released a slow breath, trying to get myself under control. "You know, it sickens me to realize that not long ago I was doing the same thing with another couple that you're here doing now. But while I was trying to persuade that couple to return to church, I was silently trying to convince myself too." I met the eyes of the three women who had been in my life for years but whom, I suddenly realized, I barely knew. "Don't you ever doubt or question what you're doing or what you're told to believe?"

"Of course we do," Darlene said, embracing her role as head of the Women's Ministry. "We all question things at some point. But you know our minds are the Devil's playground. Those doubts and questions are put there by him."

"No, they're not. It's your conscience begging you to *wake up*." I shook my head in utter stupefaction. "I can assure you the devil hasn't taken over my mind."

"I respectfully disagree," Judy said, casting a disgusted look at the twelve pack again. Then her eyes shifted to Chloe who was standing beside me. "I imagine you're to blame for our dear Kate backsliding?"

"That's *enough!*" I said, my voice cracking like a whip. "It's one thing to come after me, but you damn well better not talk about my kids or come after my friends. My *real* friends. The one who is standing beside me right now who has never judged me. The one who stepped in to help when I needed it. That's what friends do. That you can think you're here in friendship boggles my mind. But if you really feel you're my friends, then I'm asking you to leave this alone, go home, and let me manage my life and my business with Dan."

Judy drew herself up and opened her mouth as if to ramp up her efforts, but Darlene linked arms with her and said, "Let's give Kate some time to think on things, shall we?"

I could see that Judy was like a dog who didn't want to give up this bone, but Carol stepped in to pry it from her teeth. "Yes, I think that's best." She turned to me. "While you're thinking about things, we'll be praying for you, Kate." With that, the three of them returned to their car and left me to my world of sin and vice.

"Wow, that explains so much," Chloe said, her eyes round as the collection baskets in Dan's church.

I released a derisive snort. "Unfortunately, it does. I tried to keep it together even in the face of their phony façade and jabs at me, but no way in hell was I letting them come after you."

"Honest to god, Kate, I was mesmerized by them," she said. "I could see the collision coming but I couldn't look away." As we headed back to the truck, Chloe burst out laughing. "Damn, I wish Maggie could have seen this."

Chapter Eighteen

"Do I have a drinking problem?" I asked Maggie and Chloe who were at my place sitting around our nightly campfire.

Maggie, who'd just taken a drink of her wine, burst out laughing. Wine flew from her mouth into the fire where it sizzled and popped on the burning logs. "Oh my god, Kate, just when I think we've purged the good-girl virus from your brain, it flares up like a stubborn hemorrhoid."

That set Chloe off in a fit of laughter, but I sat there torn between laughing and honest confusion. "Well, I've been drinking nearly every day since I've gotten here. Isn't that something to be concerned about?"

"Josh and I always had a beer at the end of a hot workday, or an Irish coffee or glass of wine if we'd been working outside in cold weather." Chloe started laughing again as if she couldn't help herself. "It's just a beverage like soda or coffee."

Maggie set her wine glass on the top of the cooler. "Are you getting drunk every day?" she asked as if talking to a five-year-old.

I made a face at her. "Just the one time when I wanted to make a good impression on you and Chloe."

Maggie hooted and threw her arms around me. "Damn, I love you!" she said, her laughter echoing across the lake.

Chloe tapped her foot against mine. "I love you too, Kate."

Tears blurred my eyes because I had the best friends in the world, and I loved them too. But I folded my arms across my chest and gave them a haughty look. "The jury's still out about you two."

"I don't blame you," Maggie said, sliding back into her chair, and reclaiming her wine glass.

After assuring me I didn't have a drinking problem, only a friend problem, and that I should consider hanging out with people who weren't such a bad influence, Chloe told Maggie about my conversation with Beth. And then like a pro commentator at a hockey game, Chloe gave her a play-by-play of my confrontation with Dan's prayed-up Trifecta. By the time she finished, which wasn't easy for her to do amidst her giggles, Maggie was convulsed with laughter.

I drank half of my beer before she pulled herself together enough to speak.

"Oh my god, Kate, of all the things in my life I wished I'd seen, that tops the list." She was out of breath and wiping her eyes. "Seriously, life has gotten so much more interesting since you came home."

"Glad I can provide your entertainment," I said wryly.

"Me too." Her face was lit by the overhead string lights on the canopy. "I've missed these times with you. Just wasn't the same without you."

"That's the truth," Chloe said.

"Well, I'm glad to be back to complete our badass Trifecta," I said, "and I'm really happy to know I don't have a drinking problem."

"Yet," Maggie said, setting us off again.

When we finally settled down, I exhaled a long breath. "It's been one hell of a day."

"Copy that," Chloe said in agreement. As the night settled in, the sound of peepers came from the lake shore and filled the woodlands. "Kate, what the hell are sermon notes?"

I laughed at Chloe's unexpected question. I explained that my job was to create the digital sermon notes that would be displayed on large screens on either side of the platform during Dan's sermons. "The notes always contained bible verses Dan had selected, and also memes I would make that were usually funny and helped keep the congregation engaged."

"That sounds like quite a production."

"It is. Dan has a whole recording studio in our—*his*—home where he records and videos his sermons."

Leaning her head against the chair back, Chloe looked at the night sky for a moment, then turned her head to look at me. "I think we both broke through some barriers today."

"We did." Slipping my hand over hers, I gave it a squeeze. "Wasn't easy for either of us, but we got through it together."

"Yeah," she said softly. "That's why I decided to schedule another job." At our surprised expressions, she shrugged. "It seems that work is the best medicine for me." Her gaze shifted to me. "If you're still interested in a paying job, I happen to know of one. Just a couple of days a week, but the pay is great."

"Maybe I'm drunk," I said, sitting up in my chair to clear my head. "Are you offering me a job working with you?"

Chloe laughed. "Yes, Kate. But I'm only committing to working two days a week. I don't want a full-time commitment. Plus, I love being here helping you build your house. Makes me want to build one for myself."

"Chloe, I'll help you anytime, and you never need to compensate me. It's what friends do."

"This is what friends do," she said, gesturing to my house project. "What I do is a job. I get paid for the work. And I pay my employees. So, if you're interested in that kind of work, the job is yours. I suspect a regular paycheck would make it easier for you to get utilities turned on."

My eyes flooded. "Oh, Chloe ..."

"This isn't just for you, Kate. I need this, too, and I can only manage it if you're with me."

"I'm with you," I croaked. Clearing my throat, I sniffed and blinked the moisture from my eyes. "When do we start?"

"Tomorrow morning at eight."

"What?" I asked, but quickly realized she wasn't kidding. "Oh boy, maybe you should have told me that before I had my third beer."

For a little while, we sat in comfortable silence, our minds wandering where they would.

"Wonder how long it'll take for the building permit to come through," I pondered aloud.

"Hard to say." Chloe took a sip of her beer. "Doesn't mean we have to stop work."

"I'm afraid to continue without it. I really need to live here. If I piss off the code guy, I could be screwed."

"I'm not talking about working on your house," Chloe said. "We need to start salvaging materials from your grandparents' house so they're ready when we need them. I still haven't figured out what's under all that wallpaper."

"Why the hell do people cover everything with wallpaper and carpeting?" Maggie asked. "I don't get it. Especially in old houses. They're covering up the best part of their home."

"They do the same thing with paint," I said. "In the first home Dan and I owned, the doors had three layers of paint on them, each one a different color."

Chloe rocked to her feet. "Come on. I've got to know what's under that fucking wallpaper."

I looked up in surprise. "Right now?"

"Yes, right freaking now."

I glanced toward the dark lake trail. "Let me get my lantern."

"I'll drive us out."

"But I'll be walking back, and we'll need light inside the house, so I'm going to get the lantern."

Sinatra followed me inside. I gave him a bowl of food to keep him safely occupied inside while Chloe took us out to the house in the Dummy.

After she cut the engine, we rolled out of the cab and stumbled to the house using the halo of the lantern. Inside, Chloe grabbed a flashlight and a scraper out of the toolbox she'd left there. A second later, she started scraping the living room wall. Old paper flaked off in sheets and pieces and made a mess on the floor.

"This old paper stinks," she said, and she was right. The paper had absorbed the dampness and musty smell of a vacant house.

"Look at this!" Maggie grabbed hold of a hanging sheaf of paper and tore it off the wall. "There's shiplap under here! They papered right over it." Her gaze did a wide sweep of the deeply shadowed living room. "There's probably enough shiplap in the living room to cover every wall in your house, Kate."

"And that's a good thing, right?"

Maggie grabbed her chest and fell against the wall in mock distress. "Girl, you are killing me."

Chloe laughed at her antics or at my ignorance. "Yeah, it's a good thing, Kate. It will save you having to buy sheetrock which is expensive and takes a crap-ton of work to install."

"Not only that," Maggie said, pushing away from the wall, "It will look gorgeous! You can stain this stuff, paint it, or just do a light wash of color over it to give it a distressed look. You'll see the grain lines in it, and trust me, it's gorgeous."

Elated by good news for a change, I held the lantern high to better illuminate the room. "Do you think there's enough here to do my whole house?"

"Definitely," Chloe said. "These boards are twelve inches wide."

"Kate, this whole place is probably filled with shiplap," Maggie said. "Whatever you don't need for your house, you can sell, or if Jeff does the demo, he'll give you a fair price for anything he can repurpose or resell."

Chloe knelt on one knee, worked her scraper along the edge of the carpet between the living room and kitchen. "Shine that light over here." After a couple of minutes with me holding the lantern and Maggie on flashlight duty, Chloe worked her fingers under the carpet and gave it a hard tug. A small tearing sound encouraged her to keep at it. After several hard tugs, the carpet gave way, and she fell on her ass.

Laughing, Maggie turned the flashlight beam toward the uncovered flooring. "Hardwood!"

Chloe rocked to her knees and began tugging on the carpet again. "Kate, set the lantern down and help me with this."

Together, Chloe and I ripped a two-foot section of carpeting back to reveal more of the floor. As she took a closer look, she said, "You just hit the jackpot, my friend. This is oak flooring, not pine." She glanced over at me and grinned. "I bet we can restore this floor back to its original beauty."

"Really? Am I dreaming right now?"

Maggie pinched my arm.

"Ouch!" I pulled away and tipped over. The room was moving. "Guys, I have an important question. Anyone else feeling buzzed?"

Chloe and Maggie cracked up.

Maggie draped her arm across my shoulders. "Why do you think we're here ripping off wallpaper and tearing up carpeting with flashlights?"

It had been so long since I'd felt this young and lighthearted it made me giggle. "If you guys aren't opposed to sleeping in a canoe, you're welcome to crash at my place."

"Thanks, but I think I'll sleep in my own bed," Chloe said. "But Kate, maybe we should start at nine tomorrow."

"Brilliant idea," I said, heading toward the door. "Now get out of here so I can get some sleep. I start my new job tomorrow."

After my friends left, I walked out the lake trail alone, guided through the dark by the small halo of light from my lantern, and hoping I wasn't being followed by a bear or a bobcat. Settling in beside my campfire, which was now reduced to glowing coals, I noticed Sinatra. He must have jumped out the window after he'd eaten. He was sprawled out in one of the Adirondack chairs watching the coals breathe, flaring from gray to orange and then back to gray as they slowly darkened with the night. For a few minutes Sinatra and I sat beside each other, each of us seeming to enjoy the quiet night.

Then I broke the news to him. "I'm taking you to the vet on Tuesday."

He ignored me.

"That means I'll have to put you in a carrier."

He yawned and stretched his front legs so they stuck out over the edge of the seat.

"Well, if you're not concerned, then I'm not concerned," I said. But I was. I had no idea what to expect from this little guy when he found himself locked inside a carrier. I suspected it wasn't going to be good.

Reaching over, I stroked his back and gently felt the matted fur along his side, knowing he needed care I couldn't give him.

Sinatra licked my hand, a first for him.

I stroked his face with the back of my fingers. "Yeah, you say that now, sweetie, but let's see what you think after we go to the vet."

Chapter Nineteen

Chloe knocked on my door at ten minutes before eight. I was dressed and ready to walk out to the road so I could save her from driving out the lake trail, but she'd decided to come to me.

Looking over her shoulder, I didn't see the Dummy outside. "Are we walking to the job?" I jested, swinging the door wide for her to come inside.

"I didn't feel like negotiating that big ass trailer out here. I parked in the driveway and walked out." She shoved a pile of clothing and a pair of work boots into my arms.

I glanced down. "What's this?"

"You can't work in duct taped sneakers, Kate. You need proper gear for this kind of work." Chloe pointed at the boots. "Those are an old pair of my steel toed boots that should suffice until you can get a pair for yourself. There's also a shirt and pair of pants made from ripstop material that will hold up much better than your jeans and cotton shirt. This is your uniform for your new job."

"Steel toes and ripstop material? Now I'm nervous."

"Well, you'll be running a chainsaw. You'll need safety gear and chainsaw chaps."

I gaped at her.

"We're cutting trees, Kate. Can't do it with a butter knife." She opened the door. "I'll wait outside while you change."

A chainsaw? I'd be running a freaking chainsaw?

She wasn't kidding because when we climbed into the cab of the Dummy fifteen minutes later, she handed me her laptop that had been sitting open on the dash. "Hit play and watch that video while I drive us to the jobsite."

It only took a few seconds to realize I was watching a *how-to* video on the safety of handling, cleaning, and running a chainsaw. While I watched, I sipped the cup of hot coffee she'd brought for me and felt my anxiety increase with each passing mile. When the video ended, I turned to Chloe. "This might not be one of your best ideas ..."

"If I can learn to run a chainsaw, so can you."

"I don't know ..."

"I thought you were a badass, Kate."

Feigning indignation, I arched an eyebrow. "Oh, first day on the job and already my boss is picking a fight with me." The sound of her laughter filling the cab on a day that was surely a struggle for her challenged me to step up too. "I'm beginning to question my decision to take this job, especially when I had so many other opportunities."

For a moment, she looked at me, the humor in her eyes slowly changing to gratitude. "Thank you for doing this."

I lifted my cup. "Thank *you* for the coffee. I think I'll need a few gallons after last night."

"I brought a whole thermos full for us," she said. "I brought lunch too. We'll eat on the job so we can finish today. That way we'll get paid today and won't have to come back to the same job tomorrow. Best way to increase the profit on a job is to do it in one day."

"Yes, Boss."

It was the first time I'd seen Chloe scowl, and I couldn't tell if it was for real or if she was messing with me. "Just to be clear, Kate, we're *partners*. I'm not your boss. If we can't do this together, I don't think I can do it at all."

She wasn't kidding. "I like the sound of *partners*."

"So do I," she said. "I'll have to cover expenses and insurance and worker's comp and crap like that, but after expenses we'll split the jobs fifty-fifty."

"Thank you, but I can't do that, Chloe. Not while you're taking care of all that stuff and scheduling the jobs and providing the equipment and such. Plus you'll be training me. An hourly wage is more than fair as far as I'm concerned."

She considered this for a moment, then gave an affirmative nod. "All right. We'll do that for now while we both get on our feet. But we'll revisit this at some point, okay?"

"Works for me."

"I'll pay you twenty-five dollars an hour while we get things going."

"Wow, that's well above minimum wage for our area."

"The work is more demanding and dangerous than most of those jobs."

"Somehow that's not comforting," I said.

She pointed to a piece of paper lying on the seat between us. "Before you leave tonight, fill out that W-4 so I can get it to my CPA. They handle my payroll checks."

We rode in silence for a moment but my head was full of questions. "Hey Chloe, what the hell are chainsaw chaps?"

She grinned. "They're protective coverings that go over your pants to keep you from cutting your leg."

"Oh boy, I think I'll watch the video again."

"Good idea because we're nearly there."

After gearing up in a hard hat with a face shield and earmuff-style ear protection, I listened as Chloe showed me how to safely start and use the gas-powered saw. But even wearing protective gear, I knew this job was scary business. The morning air was chilly, and Chloe's instructions were slow and clear, but I was sweating like a backslider in Dan's church.

After she'd turned the saw over to me, she began her own work of cutting limbs off the old red maple we would be removing today.

Standing at a safe distance, I remained intensely focused, waiting for her to signal when to clear the limbs from beneath the tree. Limbs small enough for me to drag away I fed into the chipper or cut into firewood. As I worked, the woodchipper spit sweet-scented wood chips into the back of the Dummy. Running a chainsaw scared the bejesus out of me, but after a while I found a rhythm and became so engrossed in my work and the sound of running chainsaws I didn't realize Chloe's saw had gone silent until she was standing a few feet away. In my peripheral vision I saw her doing a slow wave with one hand to get my attention. Releasing the throttle and hitting the off switch, I set aside my saw.

My arms hummed like vibrating rods, and I swear I could still hear chainsaws. Arching my back, I slipped off the ear protectors and hung them around my neck. "Coffee break, I hope?"

Chloe laughed. "Lunch break."

"What?" I looked around the yard and back at her. "What time is it?"

"One-thirty. When we start later, we eat later."

"I totally lost track of time." I smacked my gloves together to knock off the sawdust coating. After slipping them off, I used them to brush the sawdust off my protective jacket. "I'm so going to need a shower after work."

"Why do you think I told you to pack a change of clothes?" A few minutes later as we sat on the tailgate of the Dummy rehy-drating ourselves with glasses of water from her two-gallon water thermos, Chloe said, "I brought turkey sandwiches. But don't worry, it's the plant-based vegan stuff you like. I even bought the vegan cheese and mayo you told me about. It's surprisingly good."

"Isn't it? I don't miss meat at all."

"How long have you been a vegan?" she asked, passing me a thick sandwich on rye topped with fresh greens and a tomato.

"This is delicious," I said around a mouthful of sandwich.

After I swallowed and took a drink, I felt my shoulders begin to relax. "I guess it's been five years now. But I'm only ninety-five percent vegan."

Chloe cracked up. "How does that work?"

"Depending on where I eat, there might be meal choices that contain dairy. You know, like the cheese on the pizzas we eat?"

"Ah, so that little bit of dairy is your five percent *non*-vegan diet then? Well, I'm glad we cleared that up."

As she poked fun at me, I sat on the tailgate, rotated my ankles, and let my feet swing. "Thanks for the boots. I can't imagine trying to do this work in my sneakers."

"Kate, I can't imagine doing any kind of work in those sneakers."

I made a face at her. "You know, you're not very nice today. Those happen to be my favorite pair of shoes."

"That is sadly apparent. You need to take your first paycheck and go shopping."

"I suppose I could use a few things, but I need plumbing more than a new pair of sneakers. Ashe is bringing a plumber by on Friday."

Leaning back on one hand, she crossed her knees and slowly bobbed her foot. "You'll get there, Kate. Just keep doing what you're doing."

"If keeping this life means wearing duct taped sneakers, borrowed boots, and chainsaw chaps, I'm all in."

Sandwich forgotten in her hand, she looked at me with shadows in her eyes. "Seeing you so tough and tenacious in the face of such a shitstorm is really helping me. I couldn't get on my feet after being blindsided by Josh's death." Tears sprang to her eyes. "Jesus, even saying his name tears my heart out. And being here ... doing this work without him ..." She released a shaky breath. "I couldn't do this without you, Kate."

I reached over and pulled her into a side-armed hug. "I was just thinking the same about you." We sat there for a few seconds, then returned to eating our sandwiches and sipping steaming mugs of coffee. "If only Dan and his Trifecta could see me now," I said. "Can you imagine them trying to witness to me while I had a chainsaw in my hands?"

Chloe snorted in her coffee. "Probably less shocking than seeing you with a twelve-pack of beer in your hands."

Our laughter brought a sense of levity back to our lunch, and it carried us through the rest of a long, hard day of work. Chloe dropped the tree then helped me cut up limbs. While I tossed chunks of firewood into a metal bin strapped to the lowboy trailer, Chloe ran the stump grinder. Once she'd finished, she loaded the equipment onto the trailer while I raked out the area where the tree had stood. Together we seeded the bare dirt then covered the grass seed with straw. Chainsaws and rakes and tools got stored in a coffin-size toolbox mounted to the front of the trailer.

Covered in sawdust and sweat, we climbed inside the cab. As Chloe drove her rig out of the rutted driveway, the sound of metal chains and tools clanging against each other followed us. The truck rocked and the trailer groaned as she pulled onto the road. "I'm going to take all this firewood to your place, if that's all right with you," she said.

"Thank you. It's wonderful not to have to scavenge wood for our campfires." Releasing an exhausted sigh, I sank back on the seat with a long groan. "This work is freaking excruciating, Chloe. I would give you my two weeks' notice but I'm too tired to write a resignation letter."

"That's exactly what I said to Josh after my first day, but he wouldn't accept my resignation. I don't accept yours either." She gave my shoulder a nudge. "Before you fall asleep, hand me a bottle of whatever is left in the cooler."

I pulled out two bottles of flavored water and gave one to Chloe. "I don't know if I'll ever get my back unlocked."

"Then I suspect this isn't the best time to tell you we have another job on Thursday."

I groaned like a whiny teenager.

"That gives you two whole days to recover," she said. "Tree work on Thursday. We'll work on your roof on Friday and finish it on Saturday."

"Ugh!" I slipped the earmuffs over my ears to block her out, but I could hear Chloe's laughter roll through the cab.

Chapter Twenty

I f Sinatra's expression was any indication of his thoughts, my trapping him in a pet carrier was a direct betrayal.

"I'm sorry, baby," I said, placing my hand on top of the rocking carrier. Sinatra was banging around inside trying to find a way out. "I know I promised not to cage you, but occasionally I'll need to put you in this thing to take you for your checkups. It's for your own good, so consider this tough love by your mommy. I'll let you out as soon as we get home, I promise."

He clawed at the metal grate door and meowed with attitude.

Chloe, who was taking us to the vet's office for our morning appointment, arched an eyebrow and leaned against her SUV. "I don't think he's buying your promises."

I picked up the carrier. Sinatra wrangled around so much he nearly tumbled the carrier from my hands.

Laughing, Chloe opened the back door for me. "I hope he settles down before his appointment."

"Me too." I put the carrier containing my little wildcat on the back seat of her SUV and climbed into the passenger side. "This is worse than when I used to take the girls for their vaccinations."

"Doctor visits with a toddler were always an adventure," Chloe said, hitting the start button. As the engine came to life, she headed down the lake trail and out onto the road. "Dylan was a child from hell during those visits."

"So were my girls. I'd get so stressed out I wouldn't sleep for a week before their appointments. Now I've got this fur ball to contend with." I glanced in the back seat to check on Sinatra who'd gotten quiet. He crouched in his carrier, mouth open, panting, and glaring at me. "I think Sinatra might look for a new home after this."

"Nah, he'll stick around," Chloe said. "He's found his forever home."

The sound of that sent a flood of warmth through me. "He slept on my bed last night for the first time," I told her.

"See? He's made it his home too. I bet he'll love the loft when we get it in."

"I hadn't thought about that, but you're right. He'll love it." Reaching back, I slipped my finger into Sinatra's carrier, hoping he wouldn't bite me. "I'll put your bed up there for you. Would you like that?"

I could feel Sinatra's wet nose nudging my finger.

"How did you manage to get him in the carrier?" Chloe asked.

"I tricked him." I rubbed my finger along the side of Sinatra's sweet face. "I'm sorry, little guy." Turning around and settling back in my seat, I told Chloe how I'd put his wet food inside the carrier so that he'd have to go inside to eat. Once he started eating, I closed the door behind him. The dish was still in there, his meal unfinished and likely all over him and the inside of the carrier from his immediate revolt. "Seriously, Chloe, I'm still shaking. Being a cat mama is tough business."

She laughed. "Being a mama to any living thing is tough business."

"Can't disagree there."

"Have you heard from your girls?" she asked, a slight hesitation in her voice.

"I've been texting with Haley, and she's supposed to call tonight." Knowing that made me happy. "Haven't heard anything

from Kara even though I've sent texts and left voicemails for her."
And that made me incredibly sad.

Chloe blew out her breath. "As we were saying, kids are tough.
Hopefully, she'll come around soon."

"I hope so." For a few minutes we rode in silence. As we passed
by greening fields populated by lavender bluets and yellow colts-
foot, I thought about my girls. I wondered how they were faring at
home with Dan ... without me. I missed the feeling of being a
family, but I didn't miss Dan or our big house or the stifling life I'd
had to live. I didn't miss the stuff or the events or the people. It had
all been an illusion ... a lie. The only thing that had been real was
my love for my daughters.

Chloe glanced over at me. "Are you falling asleep over
there?"

"Just thinking, which isn't necessarily a good thing." Inhaling
and mentally dragging myself back to the present, I asked her how
she was doing. "You know, if you ever want to talk ..."

She nodded. "I know."

Another silence ensued, then I heard her chuckle. "Did I tell
you what I caught Dylan doing last night?"

"Uh oh, I don't think I want to hear this."

She burst out laughing. "I caught him dancing! In his room."
Her teeth flashed like pearls as she tilted her head back in laughter.
"You should have seen him, Kate. It was like watching Kevin Bacon
in *Footloose*. Dylan had his hair whipped into peaks, and he was
getting down. I mean the full body-hip-shaking-feet-shuffling-
brow-sweating kind of getting down." She pressed one hand to her
chest to catch her breath. "He was awesome, Kate. The kid can
dance."

Convulsed with laughter, I tried to envision Chloe's proper son
busting a move. "I would love to have seen that. Whenever Dan
wasn't around, my girls would crank the stereo and create these
amazing performances of what they called modern dance. My
living room could have been a Broadway stage. We should have a
dance-off at the lake when we finish my house."

Chloe lifted both hands and smacked them against the steering wheel. "Excellent idea! And I intend to participate."

"Me too!"

The carrier rattled in the back seat. I turned around to see Sinatra hunched down, watching me with a guarded expression. "I'm sorry, sweetie. We didn't mean to frighten you." I slipped my finger through the grate door and rubbed his face again. "I'll get you back home soon."

As we drove into town, the fields and woodlands gave way to bricked streets and the Dunwith River. The vet's office was a single-story board-and-batten building three blocks off the main drag. As I gripped the carrier at both ends, Chloe opened the office door for me. After checking in with the front desk staff, Chloe and I took a seat on the cat side of the waiting room. A young couple was sweet talking a calico cat purring in its carrier. On the opposite side of the room a petite gal was petting a huge dog that looked like a wolf.

Protective of my baby, I turned Sinatra's carrier so he couldn't see the big bad wolf on the other side of the room. This trip was already traumatic enough for him.

After about ten minutes, Sinatra's name was called. I carried him into the exam room. Amy, the vet tech and her assistant, Stephanie, asked several questions about Sinatra that I couldn't answer because I had no idea what his history was, although I suspected it wasn't pretty.

"All right let's take a look at this little guy," Amy said. The instant she opened the carrier door, Sinatra shot out like a bullet.

Instinctively, we all stepped back as Sinatra sprang off the table. He hit the tile floor and skidded into the exam room door. In a split second he scrambled to his feet and leapt onto the tech desk, scattering pens and papers and a clipboard in every direction before launching himself off the computer monitor and into the air where he latched onto the upper wall cupboards. Medical instruments crashed to the floor and the computer monitor rocked on the desk so violently I thought it would tip over. While Sinatra hung by his front claws and scrabbled with his hind legs to get purchase on the cupboards, I stood in shock.

Unfazed, the assistant reached up with both hands and pulled him off the cabinets. With an authority I knew I'd never possess, she placed Sinatra back on the exam table and tucked him against her abdomen. With one arm circled around him, she stroked his head with her free hand. "It's okay, little man, we're not going to hurt you."

To my utter disbelief, Sinatra tucked his face against her belly and didn't move.

"I'm so sorry," I whispered, still stunned, my heart pounding. "I had no idea ... I mean, he's a feral cat. This must be the first time he's been caged." I glanced at the mess on the floor. "I'll pick this up and pay for any damage of course."

The vet tech blew out a breath and looked at the mess scattered across the counter and all over the floor. "Don't worry about it. We'll have to sanitize everything anyhow, and nothing appears to be broken." She met my eyes, her own sincere. "I'm glad you care enough to bring him in. Too many of these poor things don't get this lucky."

I released a breathy laugh. "I'm not sure Sinatra would agree that he's lucky. I suspect he'll make me pay for this by running off and never coming back."

"He won't," Amy said, smoothing her palm over Sinatra's back. "He knows you're helping him." After a minute of examining him with her hands, the vet tech sighed. "We've got some work to do today."

Work they did. After a full exam by the doctor, the vet tech and assistant removed several ticks, clipped his claws, carefully shaved the matted fur behind his front legs, a spot on his tummy, and around his bum to give him a potty patch, and then while they gave him a bath followed by a flea and tick treatment, I cleaned the food mess in his carrier. He got his shots and a deworming pill, and finally they returned him to his carrier where he seemed relieved to be.

That's when the vet tech suggested I make an appointment to get Sinatra neutered.

This cat was going to hate me for sure.

When we finally exited the exam room, several people were looking at me with raised eyebrows and a *what-the-hell-went-on-in-there* look. My face heated and I gave them a wobbly smile, but I could tell they were all trying to see what rabid animal I had inside the carrier.

Chloe covered her mouth with her hand, but I could tell she was laughing.

I exhaled a huge, shaky breath of relief that it was over. I hadn't realized this visit would be traumatic for me too.

While the receptionist totaled my bill, I asked the gal with the beautiful wolfdog what breed he was. She claimed he was an Alaskan Malamute. Then she asked what I had in the carrier, as if she didn't want the rabid beast near her dog. The thought of that hit my funny bone and I started to snicker. "It's just my little kitty," I said, then turned back to the counter.

Two hundred and sixty dollars later, we left the vet's office. As we were backing out, I started to tell Chloe about the mayhem in the exam room, but my phone rang. I didn't recognize the number, but I answered.

A minute later, I hung up smiling. "That was Gladys at the clerk's office letting me know my building permit has been approved."

"Perfect timing," she said. "We can swing by and get it now."

As we drove over to the clerk's office, I told Chloe about Sinatra's grand show in the exam room. "Honest to god, Chloe, Sinatra was hanging from the wall cupboards by his front claws. The assistant had to reach above her head to pull him off."

Chloe was laughing so hard she was crying. "Only you, Kate. Seriously, this stuff only happens to you."

I was beginning to believe it. But I laughed anyway and gave silent thanks for my steadfast friend and my cat from hell.

Chapter Twenty-One

It was just over three miles from my grandparents' driveway to downtown. I knew this because I'd made the trip on foot innumerable times as a teenager. I used to walk to Chloe's house, then the two of us would head downtown to meet Maggie. If we weren't spending our days at the lake, we'd hang out downtown or at the river, then we'd head back to my grandparents' place later in the day where we'd make a campfire out at the lake. All summer long our parents took turns keeping track of us and supplying the burgers and hotdogs we'd cook over our evening campfires.

The amount of freedom we'd had back then seemed unimaginable now, but those were the best years of my life. It hurt me deeply to know my girls had never experienced that kind of freedom for even one day.

The rhythmic sound of dirt and gravel crunching beneath my consignment store sneakers created a drumbeat in my head. I was free here. I could breathe again. Walking the roads of my past was liberating and joyful. I'd turned down Chloe's offer to use her SUV today because I'd wanted to walk.

I needed time to think. I wasn't sure what to expect during my lunch with Beth. Although our truce had seemed sincere, I knew there was an underlying anger in her that had been directed at me.

Not that I blamed her. But it made me uncomfortable to think it might flare again and scorch our chance of becoming friends. I knew it was too much to hope that we could one day grow as close as sisters, but I liked the idea of it. Our connection was through marriage, but to have a family again would be so wonderful.

That made me think about my daughters. Haley had called Sunday. Hearing her voice brought tears to my eyes. Assuring me that she and her sister were doing okay, Haley admitted that the house was a cold and lonely place without me which made me feel both better and worse. She said she understood how empty the house must have felt to me with her and Kara away at college. Their father was apparently working hard to win them over, planning to fill their summer break with endless church functions. Haley said Kara hadn't openly defied his plans but she didn't appear happy about them. Knowing Kara was struggling broke my heart, but I knew I had to let her find her way through this difficult time. I'd been reaching out to her twice a week without any response, but she knew I was there if or when she needed me.

Haley wasn't happy either. She intended to hike part of the Appalachian Trail which she hadn't yet divulged to her father. I could have told her how that conversation was going to go, but I'd kept silent. The girls would have to find their own way with him now. It was the only way they would learn to stand up for themselves.

We talked for a long time which had eaten up my prepaid minutes, but I hadn't cared. It was so good to connect with my daughter again. Haley was excited about hiking with her friends and challenging herself with the arduous adventure and the pleasure of immersing herself in nature. I'd told her that her backpack and sleeping bag were at my place with her motorcycle, but she said she could borrow both from a friend. We talked about my progress on my house, and she'd wanted to know every detail of how I was building my new home. I shared every step, but I made sure she knew the most important part of building a home and a new life was building a community of friends to fill it.

The slight downward grade into town made walking the last quarter mile a pleasure. My legs were warmed up, my breathing deep and easy, and my heart light in a way it hadn't felt in years. The temperature was in the mid-sixties with warm sunshine and a light breeze that swept my hair off my face. I'd forgotten the simple pleasure of walking a country road.

The town with its pastel buildings and brick streets and sparkling river in the background looked like a fairytale world. For me to be here connecting with old friends, making new friends, and creating a fulfilling life felt like a dream. One I hoped wouldn't die as I tried to repair the damage I'd done here.

I'd agreed to meet Beth at the White Tail Winery, which was at the opposite end of town from Sophie's café where Beth had originally suggested meeting. I couldn't manage talking with Beth while trying to avoid Sophie's hatred in one day, so I'd suggested grabbing a sandwich at the winery. It was a two-story brick building with a peaked roof and a square bell tower at one end. Once a sprawling mansion for a wealthy industrialist, it sat on a wide stretch of groomed lawn near the river. Purple French doors marking the front entrance of the first floor were thrown open to the beautiful day. A round second-story window, as wide as the double doors below, had been painted in the same grape purple trim as the doors. A sprawling oak tree spread its limbs across a lawn of spring green grass, and a large wooden deck wrapped around two sides of the building. Old wine barrels were used as pub tables on the deck. Half barrels had been filled with yellow daffodils and pink snapdragons and placed strategically around the deck and building.

Inside, it took a moment for my eyes to adjust to the interior lighting of the winery despite the abundance of windows. My nose, however, came instantly awake to the lovely scent of grapes and wine and food. Glancing upward, I spied a wide wrap-around balcony at the second floor, allowing a view from the first floor all the way up to the peaked ceiling two stories overhead. Thick posts and beams stained golden brown and strung with tiny lights supported the balcony and roof, giving the place a storybook feel.

"Over here, Kate," I heard someone call.

Beth was seated at a window table sipping a glass of wine. I made my way over and sat opposite her. I noticed her half-empty glass of wine. "Am I late?" I asked, digging out my phone to check the time.

"Not at all. I finished at the Eagle's Nest a little early today and decided to walk down. Didn't take as long as I expected."

"It's a lovely day for a walk," I said, feeling a little jittery with nerves.

Beth tapped her fingernail against her glass. "I would have ordered a glass of wine for you but wasn't sure what you'd prefer."

"Probably anything they serve." My eyes took in the grapevine decorations twined with tiny white lights, the L-shaped bar, and the old wrought iron lanterns that cast a warm yellow glow across walls of rough-cut planks. "I love what they've done here."

"Me too. It's one of my favorite places." She flagged down a passing server. "Hey, Steve, my um ... my friend would like to order a glass of wine."

Our eyes met, both of us acknowledging our awkward relationship. "I'd like a glass of Merlot, please."

With an affirmative nod, the slightly frumpy but very pleasant young man hurried away.

"He left menus when he brought my wine," Beth said. "We can order whenever you're ready."

"Super," I said a little too brightly, then sighed and admitted, "I think I might need a glass of wine first."

She tilted her glass to indicate it was nearly empty. "Full disclosure. This is my second glass."

Her confession broke the ice, and we spent a couple of minutes talking about the transformation of the winery and the town until Steve returned with my Merlot. After taking a couple sips, I placed it on the table and held the glass between my shaking hands. For a moment we studied each other, not as adversaries but rather with interest. From what I'd learned, Beth was extremely generous and giving, but something told me she was tough as hell.

"Did you know that my father beat my mother?" she asked matter-of-factly. "From what I've been told, that's what started everything between our parents."

A small but audible gasp slipped from my throat at her abrupt entry into what was bound to be an uncomfortable discussion.

"Sorry. I assumed you'd want to know these things."

"I-I do, Beth. I just ... I didn't ... I'm so sorry. I didn't know about your father."

She fingered the edge of one of the menus lying on our table. "For years I thought you'd known about our situation and just hadn't cared why your dad had stepped in. But after meeting you and thinking about everything, I wondered if you hadn't known about it."

"I hadn't," I assured her. "I can't imagine what that must have been like for you."

"It was hell." Moving her hand back to her wine glass, she took another drink. "We lived in a house where we tried not to breathe too loudly, where calling attention to ourselves was dangerous and often painful. My father was a raging alcoholic with a short temper and hard fists. My mother tried to shield me and my three brothers from him, but my father's fists found all of us."

I shook my head in sympathy. I could not imagine that kind of life, how terrifying it must have been for Beth and her siblings.

"I'm only telling you this so you'll understand our situation and why we needed your father's help. Both your parents helped us through that awful time."

"My mother was involved too?"

"Yes. As you know, my mom worked as a clerk at your father's hardware store, so she knew your parents. Your dad and mom both noticed my mother coming in with bruises, but when they asked about them, she lied."

During my years as a pastor's wife, I'd heard a lot of different life stories and had become hyper-alert to noticing signs in those who were trying to cover up ugly truths. "It must have been awful for her to have to deal with that, but worlds worse to know her children were being abused. How old were you at that time?" I asked.

"Twelve."

"My god …" The worst possible time, if there is such a thing as a worst time, in an abuse situation. Beth would have been growing out of childhood into a teen, a time of growing breasts and starting her period, dealing with mean girls at school, unrequited crushes, and agonizing self-esteem issues. I couldn't find words to express my sympathy or how deeply sorry I was she'd had to endure such a traumatic time in her life. "That explains your part in establishing the Eagle's Nest Community Center," I said, my mind opening too many doors at once for me to know which one to step through.

"It's exactly the reason I do this work. I know what it's like to have nowhere to go … when no place is safe. The Eagle's Nest provides that safe place and assistance in building a new life whatever the circumstances." Passion blazed in Beth's voice as she shared that with me.

"Is that how my father helped out?" I asked, trying to understand what had happened. "By donating to the Eagle's Nest or helping there in some manner?"

"Yes, but that wasn't until years later," she answered. "He helped my mother and brothers have a better life by giving my father the beating he deserved."

"What?!" My wine glass tipped and I scrabbled to keep it upright. "My father got in a fight with your dad?"

My response made her smile. "He did. And my dad had it coming. For several months, he'd been getting progressively worse, yelling louder and hitting harder. He went after my mother one night, and he was vicious. There was blood everywhere, Kate …" Her words trailed off and a faraway look filled her eyes. "I really thought he was going to kill her. My brother, Tim, who'd just turned fifteen, decided to step in. It was the first time one of us had dared to cross my father. Tim's intervention saved my mother but nearly got him killed. My father broke four of Tim's ribs and his arm and left him a bloodied mess with a concussion."

I placed my hand over my mouth. I don't know if I did it to stop my gasp of horror, to stop the cry of sympathy that made me want to put my arms around Beth, or to stem the vitriol I wanted to spew at her asshole father. I sat mute, horrified, and heartbroken for her.

"When my mother called your dad to let him know she was at the hospital and couldn't come into work that day, your dad figured out what happened. He said he was putting an end to the nightmare. I was at home when he arrived at our house. My brothers Mark and Kyle and I were hiding out in one of the bedrooms waiting until my father passed out or left the house. But when we heard the kitchen door slam and someone start yelling, we slipped downstairs to see what was happening. Your dad yanked my father off the couch by his shirtfront and slammed him against the wall so hard the whole house shook. When my father put up a fight, your dad beat it out of him, then told him to leave and never bother us again."

I was aghast on so many levels. No matter how I tried I couldn't envision my father striking someone, and certainly not in such a violent manner. "You saw this happen?"

"Yes, I witnessed the whole thing." Beth tilted her head, her eyes beseeching. "You have to understand that to us your dad was a hero. He put an end to my father's abuse. That intervention by your dad allowed us to finally live a normal life." Clasping the back of her neck with one hand, she stretched her neck to the side. "Just talking about this makes me tense. But I meant it when I said your father was the best thing that happened in my life."

I believed her. And I understood why. At one time he'd been the best thing in my life too. But he'd betrayed his own family. "When did your mother and my father ... when did they start seeing each other?"

She shrugged and dropped her hand to the table. "I don't know because they don't know." At my frown, she continued, "Your mom and dad were friends with my mother. But your mom wasn't at the store very often. My mother and your father were there every day. Over the course of working together and going through such a traumatic time your dad and my mother developed a genuine friendship that eventually deepened into romantic feelings for one another. I suspect it was simply a gradual thing they didn't think was more than friendship ... until it wasn't."

I knew those things happened. I understood it wasn't necessarily intentional. But I also understood that at some point the situation would become clear to at least one of the parties involved, and it was then that the situation either crossed lines or reversed direction. Knowingly crossing that line was a decision, and an act of betrayal if one was already committed to someone else. My father had decided to cross that line. He'd chosen another family over his own.

But when I'd shared that betrayal with my mother, she'd told me to mind my own business, that the situation was complicated and between her and my father. I hadn't understood then, and I didn't understand now. My mom had been friendly with Beth's mother and had tried to help her out of a horrible situation. How could that woman have betrayed my mother like that?

And only weeks later my mom had been killed in a car accident. I couldn't stop wondering if it had really been an accident. Had my father's affair made my mother end her own life? Or had the embarrassment I'd caused by publicly revealing my father's affair been too much for my mother to cope with on top of my father's betrayal? Or had it just been an accident?

Even now, as a mature adult, I couldn't fit the pieces together.

For twenty years I'd placed blame and made judgments to support my choice to run away from the mess I'd made. My father was the sinner, or at least that's how I'd seen him at the time. I'd felt justified in revealing his affair even if it had blown up and humiliated two families. The fault belonged to him and Beth's mother. Or so I'd believed.

But it was a position I could no longer defend. There was obviously much to the story and situation I didn't know or understand.

"I wish I'd have known all of this back then," I said to Beth. "I'm so sorry for causing more pain for you and your family at a time when you were already struggling with so much trauma. I feel awful about that."

Sighing, she leaned back and rested her wine glass at the edge of the tabletop. "Until the end of the ordeal with my abusive father, my mother did a good job of hiding our situation, and she made your parents promise not to tell anyone about it. In hindsight, I'm sure you couldn't have known about it. And looking at things from your point of view, Kate, I can understand how devastating it must have been to discover your father cheating on your mom. On behalf of my mother and our family, I'm sorry too."

She was the only one who had ever apologized to me or recognized my pain. My eyes burned with tears that I quickly blinked away. "Thank you," I said, pushing words from my tight throat. I lifted my glass. "Shall we get another round and order lunch?"

A warm smile tilted her lips. "Please. And let's talk about your life. I hear you have two beautiful daughters."

From that point on we kept the conversation light, both of us seeming to enjoy getting to know each other. I learned that Beth was married to a guy named Gary and they had two daughters and a son between the ages of nine and twelve. "How do you do so much at the Eagle's Nest with three young children?" I asked her. "I'm in awe of your seemingly inexhaustible energy."

"I cheat," she said with a laugh. "I do most of my work while they're at school. I nap in my office when I need to. And I've taught my kids the importance of helping others, so they play with the kids at the Eagle's Nest and also do chores at home. We all get one weekend a month to do nothing but play."

"I'm genuinely impressed."

"It's not always easy or without strife, but it works for us."

I nodded. "I hope I can meet your family someday."

After wiping her mouth with her cloth napkin, she laid it on her plate. "Likewise. Your girls sound delightful."

For a moment I pondered how to broach the subject of my

sister, but in the end I knew it was best to be direct. "Do you and my sister have much to do with each other?" I asked.

"With your dad and my mom being married, our families have become blended over the years. Sophie's our stepsister. Our kids think of each other as cousins. In fact, Jessica, Sophie's oldest, babysits for my kids on occasion when she's not working at the café."

Suddenly it dawned on me why the girl at the counter had looked familiar. She was Sophie's daughter Jessica. *My niece*—who I hadn't even recognized.

Choking back tears, a wave of envy rolled through me. Beth had bonded with my sister. She'd probably been at Sophie's wedding. They'd celebrated holidays and raised their kids together. She'd been present for everything I'd missed. Forcing words from my aching throat, I told Beth I was glad they had all become family … and I *was* glad. I had so many questions but none that I could bear hearing the answer to yet.

"I have to stop at the market to pick up a couple of things on my way home, so I should get going."

"Oh dear, I totally lost track of time," she said. "I have a meeting in half an hour."

We paid our bill, and then walked out together. A few blocks later, we stopped to say goodbye.

"Can we do this again sometime?" I asked, still a bit uncertain of our connection and the direction we were taking.

"I'd like that. I'll text you in a couple of weeks, okay?"

"I'm looking forward to it," I replied, and I was. My stepsister was an amazing, strong, and interesting woman. Our intertwined history was something I wanted to understand. With Beth's help I was finally uncovering the complex story surrounding my father's affair, something I might have learned long ago had I not jumped to conclusions, had I not wanted to judge rather than understand, had I been able to comprehend at that time how complicated love and relationships could be.

When Grandma Jean was alive, she'd tried a few times to talk to me about my father and the affair, but I'd angrily shut her down. I cringed now thinking back on how rude I'd been to her, making it clear I wanted to know nothing about him or his affair. I'd told my grandmother that the only people I wanted to hear about were her, Chloe, Maggie, and Sophie. Beyond that I didn't care about anyone from my old life.

What a judgmental ass I'd been.

Chapter Twenty-Two

I had expected Sinatra to hold a grudge, to scorn me, to make me pay for taking him to the vet. But the traumatic episode appeared to have had the opposite effect. For three days he'd twined himself around my legs seeking attention. Now that he was tick-free, bathed, and his matted fur had been removed, he seemed to enjoy curling up on my lap and letting me brush him with the new grooming brush I'd purchased for him. He'd also been sleeping on my bed at night and snoring loud enough to wake me. Today was the first day he'd run off to play or hunt or do whatever he did when he disappeared.

Chloe and I were just setting up our ladders and scaffolding to work on the roof when we heard a vehicle coming down the lake trail.

The sight of Ashe McKensie stepping out of his utility van all long-legged, long-haired, and gorgeous made my stomach somersault. Another man exited the passenger side wearing a tool belt, an old Yankees ball cap, and clothes that looked like they hadn't been washed in months. The round-faced, stocky little man hustled over and introduced himself as Carlos, the guy who was going to install the plumbing in my house provided I could afford him. He greeted me with a toothy grin and an enthusiastic handshake. "Don't let my good looks deceive you, miss. I quit my modeling career to follow my heart and become the best plumber in four counties."

His ability to poke fun at himself and make an introduction in such a playful manner made me fall a little in love with the man. I glanced at Ashe who was chuckling at Carlos, or me, or both of us. "Thank you for making time to come out here today," I said to Carlos. "I'm eager to get the plumbing done so I can start putting up walls."

"What?" An expression of joy lit his round face and dark eyes. "No walls to work around?"

"Not yet."

"This is going to be a good day," he said, hiking up his drooping pants. He introduced himself to Chloe, then he stuck his elbow out as if to escort me inside. "Let's go see what you need."

I ignored his elbow and Ashe's grin and led Carlos inside. Ashe and Chloe followed us.

The first thing Carlos did was turn a slow circle and inspect every facet of the place. "This is going to be one fine house, Miss Kate."

"I think so too," I said, feeling a rush of satisfaction for what we'd accomplished so far and a surge of anticipation for what I envisioned it would become. I could see the same satisfaction in Chloe's eyes.

While Carlos and I talked about the plumbing, Chloe shadowed us, and Ashe worked on whatever electrical work he had to do.

For the better part of an hour, Carlos and Chloe and I discussed the most efficient and inexpensive way to plumb my house while meeting code and protecting the beautiful land around me. In the end, we decided to install a system that would allow me to use the greywater from my shower, sinks, and laundry to water garden plants and such. I had hoped that foregoing a flush toilet would eliminate the need for a septic tank and leach field, but Carlos disagreed. Because my house was so close to the lake, he insisted on a small septic tank with an adequate leach field, located behind my house near the wood line to keep it over one hundred feet from the lake and a good distance from my well, that would filter all waste that wasn't redirected greywater. That meant I would still have to buy a composting toilet or an incinerator toilet so I wouldn't overload the leach field. But until I could afford one, I'd continue using the outhouse.

The only way I could afford to get the plumbing installed was to put in my own leach field, which Chloe assured me we could do. Carlos said he'd take a soil sample and have it tested. He would also provide the materials for the inside plumbing and get the permit needed for the job. After I gave him a five-hundred-dollar down payment, he promised to request the plumbing permit today and return late next week to start the job. "Don't you put up walls on this side of your house, Miss Kate," he said, wagging a thick finger at me.

I laughed. "I'll be too busy putting in a leach field," I said, silently putting my faith in Chloe to help me manage a task I knew nothing about.

Carlos giggled and patted my shoulder. "You wait until we get your soil results back before you start that leach field, Miss Kate."

Outside, he and Chloe dug a hole three feet deep so he could gather a soil sample. Then he climbed into the van, lowered the brim of his ball cap over his eyes, and settled in as if he were going to nap.

In awe of Carlos's relaxed, unhurried manner, I looked at Ashe who'd followed us outside. "I want to live like that man."

"I don't know how he does it, especially when he works so hard," Ashe said. "But he's one of a kind, a superb plumber, and one of the best guys I know."

"And one of the best looking too," I said, making us all laugh. Carlos wasn't a good-looking guy with his gap-toothed grin and jowly face, but it was impossible not to be attracted to the light he radiated. Because of his stained uniform I'd thought he would smell like a walking armpit, but he was clean-shaven and smelled like soap and toothpaste. At that moment I considered my own appearance with my torn and stained work clothes, my duct-taped sneakers, my hair half falling out of its ponytail, and I cringed. I could imagine the first impression I'd made on Carlos, and it made me chuckle.

Ashe lifted his eyebrows, but I dismissed his unasked question with a wave of my hand.

Lifting his ball cap, he raked his hair away from his face, then slipped the cap back on his head. "I have to run Carlos into town and finish up a job, but I can come back around five-thirty to install the breaker panel."

I glanced at Chloe who was standing beside me. "I don't expect you to work late, Ashe, especially on a Friday."

He shrugged. "I don't have any plans for the night. Do you?"

His direct question threw me for a moment. Was he just checking to see if I'd be here so he could do his job? Or could he be asking for a more personal reason?

"I'll be on the roof," Chloe said, grinning as she walked away.

"Well, it's sort of a standing date for Chloe and Maggie to come over on Friday evenings," I told Ashe. "But if you want to work late, you're welcome to do so."

"All right then. I'll see you later." With that, he got into his van and headed out with his buddy, and my new friend, Carlos.

To my surprise, Chloe didn't razz me when I climbed onto the roof with my drill. "Ugh, I'm so sore from yesterday I can barely move."

"You'll get used to the work," she said, referring to my new job with her. "Plus, it'll be easier to do that kind of work when you're not also trying to build a house."

I laughed. "Yeah, it would certainly help to have a day off. Think we can get the roof finished today?"

"No, but I think we can finish it tomorrow."

"I hope so. We need to frame in the kitchen ceiling so Ashe can wire it for overhead lighting. And then he's going to run the wiring up to the loft and out to the living room for overhead lighting there too." He'd already installed the lower-level outlets. I rolled my aching shoulders and sighed. "All this extra electrical work is going to cost me an arm and a leg."

"Or a butt and a breast," Chloe quipped. "Ashe might be happy with that form of payment."

I couldn't help laughing.

Laying her drill on the sheet metal, she flexed her hand. "I have a job for the town scheduled on Monday. When we finish, I thought we could pick up your septic tank and the pipe and gravel we'll need for your leach field. The soil sample test should be done by then. We could put that in on Tuesday and finish the job on Wednesday if needed. That way Carlos should be able to get your plumbing done when he comes later in the week."

"I could kiss you, Chloe."

"I think Ashe is expecting first dibs on your kisses." She wiggled her eyebrows, but I ignored her taunt.

"Actually, I'm saving my lips for Carlos."

Chloe burst out laughing. "His wife might take issue with that."

I mock sighed. "Just my luck to give my heart to a married man." Clamping four roofing screws between my lips, I set to work with my drill, securing the pretty blue sheet metal on the roof that would protect my home.

By the time Ashe returned, Chloe and I had worked our way to the skylights which would require flashing and some special cutting for the surrounding sheet metal. We decided to knock off for the day and try to finish the job tomorrow when we were fresh.

While Ashe installed the breaker panel in the utility room, Chloe and I sank our weary bodies onto the lawn chairs and opened a couple of beers.

"Maggie's coming over around six and bringing a pesto garden pizza with her," Chloe said.

"Just thinking about a veggie pizza is making my mouth water." I glanced over as Chloe settled back in her chair with her legs stretched out in front of her. "Even though my diet has mainly consisted of beer and pizza, I don't think I've ever been in better shape," I said. "My mommy body is becoming a hardbody from all the physical work I've been doing."

"Yep. Don't have to worry about going to exercise class when you do this kind of work."

"I'm surprised at how much I like it. I like feeling strong. I like working with my hands. And I love my independence. I'm not giving that up for any man, even if Carlos promises to leave his wife."

Chloe's bark of laughter brought Ashe out of the house.

"Sounds like I'm missing the party," he said, wiping his hands on a rag.

"Grab a beer." Chloe gestured toward the cooler. "Maggie will be here soon with pizza."

"Sounds great." He retrieved a beer for himself, then sat in a chair on the opposite side of my cold campfire. After taking a long swig from his bottle, he studied the roof. "Looks as if the plate and duct tape will have to come off soon."

His teasing made me laugh. "Yep. Tomorrow's the big day."

"Well, your breaker panel is installed, so I'm free if you need a hand finishing the roof."

"Chloe's helping me," I blurted, then cursed myself for acting like an idiot. "I mean I'm not certain we'll need help."

"Yes, we will," Chloe said. "We'll take all the help we can get. We start at nine."

Ashe grinned. "I'll bring the donuts."

I had mixed emotions about him hanging out with us, but I couldn't very well tell Maggie's brother, who incidentally was doing me a huge favor by giving me a cut rate price on my electrical work and helping with my windows and roof, to leave or that I didn't want his assistance. There was no legitimate reason to exclude him. My awkwardness with him because of an intimate, and admittedly thrilling, night in our past, was immature.

While we waited for Maggie, I asked Ashe if he'd gone into the electrical field right out of high school.

"Sort of." Crossing an ankle over his knee, he rested the beer bottle on his thigh. "I enlisted in the Army, and after Basic Training I did six months of special training as a Power Distribution Specialist."

"Sounds like a big job."

"It could be, but most of the time it was just a normal gig. I was one of the guys who made sure the Army had power wherever, however, and whenever it was needed."

"How long were you enlisted?" I asked, trying to keep the conversation focused on him.

"Four years. I'd have stayed in, but I was married and had a young son. Connie didn't like living in Texas, so after I was discharged, we moved back to Dunwith Falls. That's when I got my electrician's license and started my own business. How about you?" he asked. "What did you do after high school?"

I got pregnant and destroyed my family. I suspected that confession would be a bit abrupt, though, and more than Ashe wanted to know, so I said, "I went to college for a year, got married, and had twins. Then I spent nineteen years being a mom."

"To go from being a full-time mom to a carpenter and part of a tree crew is quite a jump," he said.

"Pretty much like jumping out of a plane without a parachute," I said. "It's terrifying but also exciting."

"Sounds as if you've actually parachuted."

"God, no." Just the thought of jumping out of a plane made my head swoon. "Never have. Never will."

"You might be surprised. It can be addictive."

"You've jumped out of a plane?"

"Five times in Jump School, and a few occasions after that."

I grinned. "Just as I suspected, you're certifiably crazy."

His laugh deepened the lines at the corners of his eyes and revealed white teeth that had never been touched by braces. They weren't crooked, but they weren't precision straight either, which I found refreshing. His smile was all his own as was his charm.

Chloe's bottle thunked down on the arm of her chair. "I think parachuting would be a pretty amazing thing to experience." She turned to me. "We should try it, Kate."

I burst out laughing because there was no way in hell I was ever going to jump out of a plane. I'd already made the biggest leap of my life, and it had nearly killed me. From here on out, I was keeping both feet on the ground and marching my way into my new life like a sane soldier.

It was just after nine, long after Chloe, Maggie, and Ashe had left, when I heard a car engine and the sound of a vehicle creaking as it rolled over small ruts in the lake trail. A moment later the beam of headlights cut across my campfire where I'd been sitting with Sinatra. It was difficult to make out the vehicle in the dark, but I could tell it was an SUV of some sort. But it didn't belong to Chloe, Maggie, or Ashe.

To my surprise, a woman stepped out and slowly closed the door behind her. Although she'd cut the engine and closed her door, she remained standing by the vehicle.

I didn't feel threatened exactly, but I felt vulnerable and at a disadvantage. This person, whoever she was, had come here for a reason, and something told me it wasn't going to be a friendly visit.

"You have a lot of freaking nerve, Kate."

My sister's voice cut through the darkness like a knife, the point sinking deep in my gut and scaring Sinatra away. "Oh, Sophie ..."

Any hesitation she'd initially revealed seemed to be whisked away with my words, because she strode directly toward me. Each footfall drove her anger into the dirt, sending shockwaves through the ground and into my bones. She raised her fist, the firelight revealing a crumpled paper in her hand. "Did you think a note on a piece of paper was going to wipe out everything you've done?" She released a snort of disdain. "You're delusional."

A note? It took me a second to realize she was talking about the note I'd left on the table when I'd first visited her café. It had said *I'm sorry*, and I'd included my phone number. It appeared Sophie was still one who took her time and mulled things over before she acted. Unlike me, who jumped in with both feet, Sophie gnawed at a problem or a question until she got down to the marrow.

Planting her hands on her hips, she glared down at me. "What are you doing back here?"

Stunned by her abrupt appearance and angry question, I groped for words but had no idea where to begin.

She shook the paper at me. "Why are you here, Kate? Why are you having lunch with Beth? What the hell are you trying to do? Break up our family again?"

"N-no. Of course not, Sophie."

"Then why are you here?"

"I'm trying to rebuild my life," I said softly, trying to diffuse her anger. I gestured to an empty chair. "Why don't you sit so we can talk?"

She laughed, the bitter, scoffing sound slicing through my hopes.

"Sophie, I'd like to make amends, if that's possible."

"It's not." She tossed the paper into the fire. "Stay away from me. Stay away from Beth and the rest of my family."

Feeling my blood pressure spike, I rose to my feet, bringing me eye-to-eye with my little sister. "I screwed up, Sophie. I never meant to hurt anyone, and I can't express how sorry I am for the damage I caused. I'm not asking you to forgive me—"

"Good! Because what you did is unforgivable," she said, cutting me off. "You left me, Kate! You just walked away and never looked back. You destroyed our family." Her breath steamed from her nostrils, and she threw her hand out to emphasize her angry statements. "While you were off having babies, I was here grieving our mother's death. Alone. I needed my big sister, but you needed to be right, to be justified in your condemnation of Dad, more than you needed me. Dad was broken. Our house was empty. I had no one, Kate. Because of you."

"I wasn't the one who had an affair, Sophie! Our father started this mess."

"It was only a mess because of you!" Shaking her head, she released an exasperated groan. "You still don't get it, do you? Dad and Mom were dealing with their situation. You should have kept your nose out of their business."

"That's difficult to do when you see your father kissing a woman who isn't his wife."

"Well, if you hadn't blown up our family and stormed off like a righteous ass, maybe he and Mom would have explained the situation to you."

"Maybe he should have called me—"

"He did, Kate! We all did. But you wouldn't answer or return our calls."

I opened my mouth to dispute her statement, but memories of that time flooded in. Dad had called. Mom had called. Sophie had called. The only time I'd responded to any of their messages was when my father had called the guidance counselor at the university and asked her to let me know my mother had died in a car accident. After I'd pulled myself together enough to pack a bag, I'd headed home. Dan drove while I fell apart repeatedly. All I'd wanted to do was hug my mother, but when I'd seen her lifeless body, I simply couldn't touch her.

I attended the funeral without a single word to my father. I'd tried to talk to Sophie, but she was furious with me and had stood steadfastly at my father's side. The only people I talked to were my grandparents who were disgusted with my father over his affair, and brokenhearted over the death of their only child. Our family had completely shattered.

"I'm sorry," I whispered, my throat clogged with regret and heartache.

"Well, that's not good enough, Kate. You missed my graduation, my wedding, the birth of my children, and everything that mattered to me. You weren't here when I really needed you. So, whatever all of this is about ..."—she flung out her hand to encompass the boathouse—"leave me and my family out of it." With that, she stalked back to her SUV, punched the engine to life, and left me standing alone in a place where we'd once spent so many wonderful days together. Our first grown-up sister talk had been here. Our last hug had been here. Now it seemed any hope for saving our relationship had just died here.

Chapter Twenty-Three

A loud crash outside the boathouse startled me awake. Sinatra leapt off the mattress and scurried beneath the bed.

The sound of a fifty-five-gallon metal drum being knocked around made me realize my mistake. I'd stashed my garbage inside the drum thinking it would be safe there until I could take it to the transfer station. I'd thought it would be secure as long as it was covered, but apparently that had been a stupid assumption.

It seemed I'd invited a bear to my door.

Grabbing a pan and metal serving spoon, I opened the window in what would soon be my bathroom and started banging the spoon against the pan. The sound reverberated through my head, making me squint in pain, and making the bear growl in outrage. But I kept wailing on the pan, shouting, and whistling until I saw the black shadowy form of the bear head off toward the woods. I kept banging on the pan for another minute, then closed the window, and apologized to Sinatra who was still cowering under the bed.

The numbers on my phone indicated it was only four-thirty in the morning. I ached to climb back into my warm bed, but I had to clean up the garbage to discourage the bear and other critters from coming around. I did not need anything else threatening me. I already had enough angry threats from Sophie.

After dragging on a pair of jeans and a sweatshirt, I turned on the lantern. I left Sinatra inside and took a couple of garbage bags and the pot and spoon outside with me.

Keeping my noisemaker and lantern close, I cleaned up the mess, then dragged the stinky bags back inside with me. The stuff needed to go to the transfer station, and the only way to get it there was to ask Chloe to borrow her pickup truck. No way would I put this stuff in the back of her SUV. The bear episode made me realize I needed a secure place to store my garbage. I'd already been considering this because I needed a place to store my lawn mower and tools and Haley's bike. The irony of living in a boathouse, but still needing a shed made me laugh, but the thought of another expense and another project wasn't funny at all.

Wide awake, I spent a few minutes calming Sinatra until he was settled in again on the bed, then I pulled out my notebook. I wanted to escape into a fantasy world where I could be a spectator in someone else's adventure.

I'D JUST FINISHED breakfast and gone outside when Chloe arrived in the Dummy. Dressed in a long-sleeved pink T-shirt, blue jeans, work boots, and a bright smile, she looked full of life while I stood by the door feeling drained of energy. After the bear incident and a morning of writing, I felt as if I'd already put in a full day.

When she saw me waiting, coffee cup in hand, she laughed and lifted our morning carafe of dark roast and gave it a jiggle. "Salvation has arrived."

"Thank god," I said, dropping into a chair under the awning.

Sitting next to me, she filled my cup, then topped off her own. "Rough night?"

"You could say that." Cupping the mug between my sore hands, I told Chloe about Sophie's visit last night and the bear's visit this morning.

"You might consider hiring security out here."

"You available?" I asked.

"Sorry, not my skill set. I can take your garbage to the dump, though, if that helps."

"It does, thank you." With a hard sigh, I leaned back in my chair. "I need to get a vehicle. And a coffee maker. And get the electricity turned on so I can use the coffee maker. And I need to get coffee. And I need my plumbing done so I have water to make coffee."

By the time I'd finished, Chloe was laughing. She reached over and stroked my head as if I were a favorite pet. "Hang in there, Kate. You'll get there."

"Aren't you sick of helping me, Chloe? I mean, wouldn't you like a break from being my Uber driver and my contractor and my garbage collector?"

Her smile fell away. "Are you really asking?"

"Yeah, I am. If you need a break, I understand. I can manage things here."

"I've never doubted that. And just so you know, I'm here not just because I want to be but because I *need* to be. But if I'm being intrusive, just say the word and I'll back off."

"Are you kidding me?" I asked, releasing a half-laugh. "Honest to god, Chloe, I'd be utterly lost without you."

Sincerity filled her eyes. "No, you wouldn't. You're one of the strongest, most resourceful people I know. The whole time I'm helping you I'm taking notes on how to rebuild my own life. So, thank you for your friendship, and for giving me a reason to get up each day, and for showing me how to be a badass even when you're getting your ass kicked."

I laughed and teared up at the same time. "What a pair we are."

She shrugged. "I'd like to think we're a team."

"Yeah, we're a badass team," I said, reaching for the carafe. "But I really need a second cup of coffee before we dive into work today."

While we drank our coffee, we planned out our day and the

week ahead. We got so engrossed in our conversation, Ashe's arrival startled both of us. He stepped out of his van with a travel mug in one hand and a bakery box in the other. "The scones and bear claws have arrived."

"Looks like it'll be a three-cup morning," Chloe said, crossing one knee over the other and settling into her chair as if she planned to stay there awhile.

We spent twenty minutes eating and discussing our plan of attack to finish the roof. Since Chloe and Ashe had both done roofing jobs, they suggested I do the measuring and cutting. I argued that I needed to be on the roof so I could learn how to work around the skylights and complete a roofing job. In the end, we decided to cycle our positions to give us each a break from kneeling on the steep roof or standing on ladders and makeshift scaffolding. Then we went to work.

I hadn't been on the roof ten minutes when I received a text from Maggie saying she'd sold the medicine cabinet from my grandparents' house for seventy-five dollars. I texted back saying lunch was on me if she'd pick up subs on her way over. After her confirming text, I got back to work.

Drilling, hammering, and the high-pitched whine of the saw filled the air as we wrangled and cut sheet metal and fixed the custom cut pieces to the roof. With each sheet that went on, my boathouse was closer to looking like a real house. The blue roof was a happy color, like a summer sky, and it filled me with joy.

"I'd love to know what put that beautiful smile on your face," Ashe said, drawing my attention to him. He knelt on the roof, his dark hair sticking out from beneath his ball cap, his gaze focused on me. The two of us were on the roof fitting flashing around the skylights. The tin snips he'd been using seemed forgotten in his gloved hand as his gaze held mine.

Warmth flooded my body, and although my hand tightened around the drill handle, I managed to return his smile. His handsome face and our shared past still flustered me, but I was beginning to enjoy his company. It was liberating to realize I could have male friends. "All right, if you must know, I was just thinking how much I love this blue roof."

"It's the perfect color for your lakeside retreat."

"My retreat?" I considered that for a moment. "Yeah, I like the sound of that."

He smiled.

I stared.

Our eyes locked.

"Hey, you two!" Chloe hollered from the ladder where she was holding a piece of roofing. "Take this damn sheet metal before my arms break."

Ashe winked, then laid aside the tin snips and hauled the long sheet onto the roof. He secured it a couple rows away with one screw to keep it on the roof while we finished the flashing. He walked me through each step as we fit the last piece of flashing around the skylights. Once that was finished, he tapped his tin snips on the roof to get my attention. When I looked up, he gestured to the plastic plate duct taped to the roof. "Would you like to do the honors?"

The plate was faded and cracked from the sun, and the tape was beginning to peel and curl up along the edges. It seemed like a year ago when I had used bedsprings to climb onto the roof and patch the leak with a plate. I'd felt so alone then and had been filled with crushing doubts. To replace that temporary patch with strong metal roofing that would last a lifetime was incredibly empowering. I hadn't quit. I hadn't gone back. I'd used what I had and kept moving forward.

With two hands, I peeled the plate and tape off the roof, then with a triumphant grin, I sent it sailing into the air.

"Hey! Watch it up there," Chloe said, sidestepping the plate.

Ashe and I exchanged smiles, then he retrieved the piece of sheet metal he'd set aside and we got back to work. From that point on, the pieces of metal roofing went on like a dream. Ashe and I would take measurements, call them down to Chloe, and she'd cut the material. My hand began cramping from running the heavy drill, but I was determined to be the one to put the final screw in my roof. We worked through the lunch hour because we were so close to finishing the job. When I finally sank that last roofing screw, I thrust the drill into the air and whooped like a five-year-old. The jubilant act knocked me off balance, and I might have tumbled off the roof had Ashe not grabbed my arm.

"You might want to celebrate after you get off the roof."

"Ya think?" I asked, laughing at my stupidity. "For future reference that should be the first lesson you teach your roofing newbies."

"Cold beer here! Get your cold beer!" Chloe called from below like a beer vendor at a ball game. "Time to celebrate."

After handing down our tools and clearing the roof of debris, Ashe and I climbed down with our remaining tools.

"Congratulations," Chloe said, slipping a chilled beer into my aching hand.

The three of us toasted the completion of the job, then we ambled several yards away to get a good look at my beautiful roof.

"This is going to be quite a place," Ashe said.

I took in the sky-blue roof and French doors and new windows with white trim and the pretty charcoal colored awning strung with lights, and said, "It already is."

Maggie's truck appeared from the lake trail, and she parked behind Ashe's van. Despite her insistence that she didn't do manual labor, she wanted to help us salvage the shiplap material from my grandparents' house. When she got out of her vehicle, she let out a low whistle. "The roof is spectacular."

"It really is," I said, admiring our work. "I can hardly wait to start putting up walls."

"Better not let Carlos hear you talking about walls until after he gets his plumbing work done," Chloe said, making us laugh. "Besides, we have a leach field to put in first."

"Ugh!" I released an exaggerated sigh. "I feel like Cinderella before the ball. So much work to do scrubbing floors, doing dishes, washing clothes, and mending fences, I'll never get to go to the big event."

Maggie propped one hand on her slender hip and gave me the *suck-it-up* stare. "Kate, what are you going to do with yourself when you get all your chores done and are finally at the ball in your fancy dress?"

"I'm going to go back home and sleep for a week."

Although we were all laughing, Maggie pressed me for a real answer. "Seriously, Kate, when you finish building your house and have nothing left to do, what are you going to do with yourself?"

As the smile slid off my face, I said, "I'll file for divorce. And I'll go to work with Chloe two or three days a week. I'll clean my new house. I'll work on my book. And ... um ... well, I'll drink beer with my friends."

"Sounds like a solid plan to me," Chloe said. "Can we eat lunch now? I'm famished."

"Me too," Ashe said, wiping his hands on a rag.

But I was still thinking about my *afterlife* ... that is, my life *after* I was done building my house. Once those expenses were behind me, I would scrounge up the money as quickly as possible to pay the attorney fees and initiate divorce proceedings. Because I'd never be free in my new life until I was legally severed from Dan and my old life.

I grabbed bottles of water from Chloe's cooler and passed them around.

Maggie took subs out of her cloth tote bag, and we ate our lunch. As we sat around talking and joking it reminded me of the picnics my family used to have here by the lake. Maggie and Chloe had been part of my family in those days, the three of us inseparable. Ashe was new to our group now, but somehow he fit.

Maggie wadded her empty sub wrapper and stuffed it into a paper bag. She tore a paper towel off the roll she'd brought, then wiped her mouth and hands. "While my big, strong brother is here to give me a hand, I'm going to pull out all the bathroom fixtures today and take them to my shop."

Ashe looked surprised by her announcement.

"Did you sell them?" I asked hopefully.

She opened her mouth, hesitated, then said, *"Maybe.* I will know next week. But I want to get the pieces to my shop where I can clean them up, and other buyers can see them if the sale doesn't go through."

"Thank you, Maggie. Without your help, all that stuff would have probably ended up in the dump."

She pressed her palms to her ears. "I can't bear to think about such desecration."

I laughed. "I promise not to throw anything away before running it past you."

She dropped her hands to her lap and eyed my beater sneakers. "Okay, but feel free to let those go any time."

"What is with you two and my sneakers?" I cried, feigning indignation. "These shoes and I have traveled a lot of hard roads together."

Although I was jesting with Maggie and Chloe, there was truth in my declaration. It hadn't been just my lawn mowers, Rusty and Gussie, with me all those years. These shoes had been there too. They'd been on my feet when I'd dared to walk away from my old life. They'd been on my feet when I stepped out of the RV knowing I was finally facing my past. And they'd been on my sore, aching feet each day as I laboriously trudged my way into my new life.

After they finished razzing me about my beat-up sneakers, Chloe and Maggie helped me clean up the debris from our lunch. I did not want to invite any more hungry critters to my place. Ashe retrieved the garbage bags from inside and tossed them in the back of the Dummy. Then we all headed out front to my grandparents' house.

We decided to deconstruct the house in the order I would need materials. The first thing I would need is shiplap for my walls. Until Maggie sold the bathroom fixtures, which I hoped would be this week, I didn't have the cash to purchase insulation for my walls, so I wouldn't be able to put up the shiplap until then. My cash was earmarked for Carlos's work, and a septic tank, gravel, and PVC pipe for my leach field.

Although Chloe, Ashe, and I were a bit spent after finishing the roof, we decided to invest a couple of hours stripping wallpaper and pulling shiplap off the walls. But that required us to remove the drop ceiling tiles and framework before we could deconstruct the walls.

After we'd removed a few ceiling tiles, Ashe shone his flashlight into the gaping hole. "Whoa, is that what I think it is," he asked?

Maggie snatched the flashlight from Ashe's hand. She angled the beam across the revealed section and squealed in delight. "There's a tin-plated ceiling under here, Kate, and it's the real deal. The pattern is gorgeous too. This stuff can sell for ten dollars a square foot if you sell it yourself." She glanced around. "I'm guessing this room is about twelve by eighteen or just over two hundred square feet. That means this ceiling could be worth a couple grand if you remove it without damaging it."

I pressed a hand to my thudding chest. "I'm absolutely boggled by all of this. I had no idea there'd be any value in this place."

Maggie and Ashe exchanged a raised-eyebrow look. "Kate, *everything* in this house has value," she said.

Gazing up into the hole in the drop ceiling, I silently thanked my grandparents for giving me their house full of treasures. "How and when should we salvage the tin-plated ceiling?"

"We should leave it safely in place for now," Maggie said. "We need to remove the drop ceiling, though, and then get the shiplap off the walls."

I bowed to her wisdom but wished we could pull the tin plating down and sell it immediately. The money in my envelope was dwindling quickly. I had to pay Ashe for his electrical work when we finished for the day. And I still needed to purchase a pump for my well and put in a leach field and pay Carlos for plumbing services within the next several days. I was broke.

It took an hour to remove the drop ceiling and fully reveal the embossed tin panels covering the ceiling. They'd been painted white and had aged as beautifully as old lace. I longed to keep some of it for my own use.

Once the dropped ceiling was down, we started on the walls. We'd been talking, and prying shiplap off the walls, for about half an hour when Maggie let out a low whistle. "Holy mother lode, my friends, wait 'til you see this."

In tandem, Chloe, Ashe, and I crossed the room to see what had set off Maggie's *oh-my-god* meter.

She'd been working on the wall between the kitchen and living room. From what I could see, she'd removed three lengths of shiplap leaving a thirty-six-inch high by ten-foot-long opening.

"Kate, you have pocket doors hidden in this wall," she said. "Someone just framed around the doors and walled them in."

It took me a moment to see what she was looking at. Then I saw the partially revealed door. "Why would they hide something so beautiful?" I asked, almost offended on behalf of the door.

"I have no idea, but it's quite common in these older homes," she said. "That's why these places are hidden goldmines."

Ashe leaned in and took a closer look. "Hey, Mags, I think that's quarter sawn white oak."

She wiped the panel with her forearm, revealing a gorgeous woodgrain and leaving a smudge of dust on her long-sleeved T-shirt. "You're right, Ashe. And from what I can see the door is in good shape." She stepped back and scanned the whole wall. "There's got to be another door on the other side of that cased opening," she said, gesturing to the entrance between the kitchen and living room.

I'd walked through the wide entrance innumerable times in my young years and never once remembered seeing panel doors there. But according to Maggie, who'd moved to the other side already, there should be another door panel. Chloe and Ashe started working their crowbars to pry the shiplap loose in that section. The squeak of nails being wrenched from the studs tweaked my ears.

As the board they were working on began to bow out at the ends, I stepped in with my crowbar to free up the middle. Together the four of us gently pried three lengths of shiplap off the studs and stacked them on the growing pile at one side of the room.

"I knew it! You have a veritable treasure chest in this house," Maggie said. "Don't you dare discard a single thing. If you're willing to sell these doors, you'll have more than enough money to buy insulation for your house."

The four of us spent a couple of hours stripping every inch of shiplap off that wall, creating a pile of boards four across and thigh-high. "If all of this is from just one wall, I'll definitely have enough shiplap for my house."

My friends exchanged a look with each other. "You'll have enough for two or three houses," Maggie said. "And from what I can see, these doors are worth a bundle." Maggie and Ashe visually inspected the pocket doors that were now fully revealed. "These are incredible, Kate. Being closed in the wall has kept them perfectly preserved. If I had to guess, I'd say you could get two grand for this set."

"Two thousand dollars?" A thrill skittered through my belly, and I felt lightheaded. I'd never dreamed there would be anything of value in this condemned old house, other than my memories. "Will you put them online for me?"

"Of course," Maggie said. "I'll take pictures as soon as I wipe them down. I should be able to get them listed this evening." She arched her back then wiped her hands on the rag she was holding. "These will sell fast."

Ashe smoothed his palm over one of the panels. "All the hardware is here too. Two thousand works for me, if you'll sell them to me, Kate. These are exactly what I've been looking for."

My eyes widened. "Are you serious?"

"Yeah." Lowering his hand, he leaned his shoulder against a bare stud. "I can get the money to you tomorrow."

Cupping my forehead with one hand, I released a laugh of disbelief. "This feels surreal, but okay. Just deduct what I owe you for your electrical work. It'll save me having to pay you when we finish here, which is what I'd planned to do. And give two hundred dollars of that to Maggie. She gets ten percent of every sale."

"No way." Maggie tossed the dusty rag at me. "I didn't do anything for this sale, Kate. No pictures. No social media. Nada. It's all yours."

Removing the rag from my shoulder where it had landed, I faked a scowl. "Maggie, do you want to guess where these doors might have ended up had you guys not been here to tell me what they're worth?"

She scowled back at me. "Don't you dare say the *dump*, Kate. I swear I'll duct tape your mouth shut."

"I won't say it if you take your piece of the sale."

Shaking her head, she stared at me for a moment. "You're getting to be a regular hard ass. How about buying us all dinner tonight at the brewery in lieu of payment?"

"That's a terrible deal for you, but if you're all up for it, I'd love to do that."

"I'm in," Chloe said. "Dylan is off camping with his buddies for the weekend."

"I'm in," Ashe said, "but I need a shower first."

"That goes without saying." Maggie scrunched her face as if he smelled awful.

Ashe laughed and pulled her ponytail. "Watch it or I'll make you pull out all the bathroom fixtures on your own," he said, gesturing with his chin toward the bathroom.

"I'm not doing it now anyhow," she quipped. "I'm going out with my awesome big brother who is going to come back here and help me with that stuff in a few days."

His laugh echoed through the empty house. Their playful brother and sister taunting mesmerized me. It had been so long since I'd done that with Sophie, I'd forgotten what it was like to have a sibling.

"Well, it's five now," Chloe said. "Let's meet at the brewery at seven, okay?"

Our agreement was unanimous as was our desire to stop for the day. As Maggie and Ashe headed out in their vehicles, Chloe drove me back to the boathouse. She relaxed by the lake while I fed Sinatra. After leaving the bathroom window partially open for him to come and go, I filled Haley's backpack with clean clothes, grabbed my purse and left my little house with the pretty new roof, and climbed into the Dummy with my best friend.

Ten minutes later, Chloe parked the dump truck in her driveway, and we headed inside.

"I swear, Chloe, as soon as I can stop living out of this envelope, I'm going to pay your water bill for a year and stock your refrigerator full of beer."

She laughed. "No need, Kate. I have free well water. And I plan to drink a few gallons of beer tonight, so we should be even by midnight." She gave me a nudge toward the bathroom. "You can shower first."

Chapter Twenty-Four

B obbie Jo, who was at her brewery, joined us for dinner. The five of us sat at an outside table on the back deck overlooking the river. The deck canopy was strung with Edison style lights that created a soft glow over the tables and patrons, and at the far end two guys played decades of popular music on their acoustic guitars. In a graveled area just off the deck several people relaxed in colorful Adirondack chairs circled around a crackling fire blazing in a brick fire pit.

Being here in this place where alcohol was served, and the sound of lively music floated across the deck and mingled with my friends' laughter felt ... surreal. As if I'd fallen asleep in the arms of Dan's savior and had woken this morning in a new land, I realized a painful truth—that the arms I'd once believed were sheltering me had been imprisoning me. I'd believed my old life had been one of security. But now I knew I had been an unwitting captive in a cult brainwashed by Dan's brand of Christianity.

"You seem deep in thought tonight," Ashe said from across the table where he sat beside Maggie. The overhead lighting cut gently through the warm night and cast a golden glow across his handsome face.

From beside me, Chloe gave me a gentle nudge. "You okay?"

"Yeah, of course," I said, feeling a bit off balance from my thoughts and from looking into Ashe's dark eyes. "I was just thinking about how odd this feels for me to be here in a bar drinking with my friends. It's just so different from how I used to live."

"Yeah, we probably should have warned you that life with this crew takes some getting used to," Maggie said, cupping her manicured hands around her wineglass. She'd left her hair down this evening and it fell over her shoulders like a chestnut-colored sash. I'd grown accustomed to her ball cap and ponytail, and I couldn't help wondering why she'd primped this evening.

"Well, you're *my* crew," I said, tapping my beer bottle against her wineglass. "Here's to me finally returning to my gang."

Maggie burst out laughing. "You sound as if you've gone *gangstah* with your burner phone and your *gang* talk."

"Well, what should I call you? You're my crew ... my friends ... my ...?" I shrugged, at a loss for words to describe who they were and what they meant to me.

"We're your people, Kate," Chloe said matter-of-factly.

"My *people* ... I love that." I gave Chloe a side-armed hug. "You're all my people."

"You know what that means," Maggie said. "You have to buy your *people* a drink."

I laughed. "I'm buying everything tonight so have as many drinks as you like, Mags."

Maggie's eyebrows lifted. "La-dee-dah, she's using nicknames now that we're her *people*."

In that moment I knew with a bone-deep certainty they were indeed my people. Despite my own marital situation being in limbo, this strong single woman, grieving widow, and two divorcees were my people. And I was rabidly curious about each of them and the choices that had led them to this place in their lives. Had they been forced here? Or had they chosen their own path?

I wasn't sure how to broach the subject so I just dove in. "Do you mind if I ask how long you've been divorced, Bobbie Jo?"

"Of course not," she said, sweeping her long silver-blond hair behind one shoulder, jangling the multiple bracelets on her wrist. "I divorced Craig twelve years ago."

"Did you remain friends like Ashe and his former wife?"

"No," she said, "but we aren't enemies either. We just went our separate ways and didn't look back."

"You're lucky," I said without thinking. But the minute the words left my mouth I wished I could take them back. "Sorry, I didn't mean it that way."

Bobbie Jo flapped a hand to dismiss my apology. "I was fortunate. I didn't have to put up with him hounding me or fighting me for our kids. He was decent. He continued to be a good father to the kids but left me alone to live my life."

"I can't imagine Dan ever leaving me alone," I said, feeling oppressed just mentioning his name.

"Have you filed for divorce yet?" Bobbie Jo asked. When I shook my head, she nodded as if she understood. "Having second thoughts?"

"No, not about him or our marriage or anything I left behind. But I worry about my girls, and that makes me have second thoughts about my decision to leave during their first year of college. Sometimes I wonder if I should have tried to hold on a little longer." I shrugged. "Maybe this would be less upsetting for them if they were older."

"It wouldn't," she said with certainty in her voice that was reaffirmed by Ashe's nod of agreement.

His eyes locked on mine, and I couldn't look away.

"There's no right time to leave, Kate. A decision like that can't be based around anyone but you," he said.

As his words sank in, I gave a slow nod. "I just feel like I'm failing my girls and setting an example that it's okay to quit."

"Is that what you really think?" Bobbie Jo asked in surprise.

"Because leaving doesn't mean quitting. Not if you've truly tried to save or rekindle the relationship. If it's over, then it's over. Leaving at that point is an act of tremendous courage."

"Or maybe cowardice?" I asked, genuinely wanting to know if what I'd done was cowardly.

"I think it depends on why and how you left," she said, then looked at the others. "What do y'all think?"

Ashe took a long draw on his beer bottle then set it on the table. "Sometimes it's staying that's an act of cowardice. It can be downright cruel, especially if staying keeps the other person from being able to move on with their life."

Maggie nodded. "Yep. I'm in complete agreement."

We all looked at Chloe for her to weigh in. Then, as if we realized our error simultaneously, our gazes shot away, clashing with each other, and dropping to our drinks. Josh's death had left Chloe alone. Not his choice, and certainly not hers.

"I think that getting out of bed each day and doing your best to move forward is an act of courage regardless of your marital status," Chloe said. "I watch Dylan leap out of bed each morning and head off into his life with a heart full of grief, a head full of hope, and a gut full of determination. His decision to stay with me during the summer break is an act of courage for him. To be there for me, in my sad place, is much harder for him than if he were crashing at a friend's place and immersing himself in a world with his buddies where he'd prefer to be. And when he goes back to school it'll be an act of courage for him to leave me alone knowing I'm struggling. So, yes, I think the *why* determines the *what* with regard to cowardice and courage. But, Kate, our kids are much stronger than we give them credit for. Your girls will be fine. And you're demonstrating a tremendous amount of courage by rebuilding your life from nothing."

"From *nothing* is the key point here, and exactly why I haven't filed for a divorce yet," I said.

But her words left us sitting in silence as we let them sink in. I realized my staying with Dan for so many years while not believing in him or his work was not an act of honor and support or a good example for our girls. However unintentional, it had been dishonest. In my defense, and in defense of those who try to leave that world of madness, it's like willingly stepping into a vast wilderness alone. If you leave the church, you lose your friends, your family, and your entire community, which often includes your dentist, lawyer, accountant, and even your grocery store because those businesses are all owned by parishioners. The idea of supporting each other's business initially seems benign, kind even, but ultimately it's a way for a cult, religion, or group to create a tightly closed community dependent upon each other—which makes leaving impossible or at the very least terrifying.

It had been easier to convince myself I was happy, or at least okay with the status quo, and that I was doing the right thing by staying for my children's sake. But now that I was out of that tightly controlled world, I was perpetually off balance. My new way of thinking kept tripping over my old patterns and behaviors. I continually struggled to clear my brain of rules that had once governed every facet of my life. And now, like a butterfly emerging from its chrysalis, I had one wing free—but so far to go before I could finally fly.

These thoughts flitted in and out of my mind throughout dinner. Despite our light conversation and joking and laughter, a pervasive sense of heaviness hovered over my shoulder like a black cloud. I needed to settle things with Dan. I couldn't live in limbo forever. The only way I'd ever be free was to be legally severed from him. But the thought of fighting him for a divorce left me exhausted. I had a house to build, and that's where I needed to focus my energy for now.

Bobbie Jo had slipped away from the table for a few minutes and returned with a business card in her hand. She slid the card across the tabletop and left it beside my glass. "If or when you're ready, here's the name of a good attorney right here in town. Paula handled my divorce, and I have no reservation recommending her. And she'll give you a free consultation, so don't delay if you're certain you want a divorce. She'll help you figure out how to get it done."

A surge of hope filled me as I glanced at the card, then back at her. "Thank you, Bobbie Jo," I said, slipping the card into my purse.

"Looks like my date is here," Maggie said, garnering our attention as her gaze locked on an athletic and very sexy blond guy standing at the far end of the deck at the outside bar.

"Ah, that explains the lioness mane and manicured claws," I said, eliciting laughter from our friends.

"You bet." Maggie lowered her dark eyelashes in a seductive flutter. "This little kitty wants to play tonight."

"Well, judging by that man's athletic build, I suspect your little plaything will keep you busy all night," Bobbie Jo said.

"I'm counting on it." Maggie rose to her feet like a goddess. "See y'all tomorrow," she said, then carried herself across the deck with a graceful, long-legged stride as she confidently stalked her man.

"How does she do that?" I asked in awe and utter amazement. "I couldn't imagine being that open about sex or that confident in myself."

Chloe, Ashe, and Bobbie Jo looked back at me wearing confused expressions, but not one of them said a word.

As the realization sank in, they considered Maggie's actions normal, and that my own response was off, my face began to burn. "I suspect my oppressed, messed-up thinking is from living with a religious zealot too long," I said, struggling to explain my surprise over Maggie's nonchalant approach to a playful night of sex. "Guess I need to get out more."

Humor played in Ashe's dark, beautiful eyes as he looked at me. "I agree."

A tight band locked around my chest, and I sent up a prayer that I wasn't having a heart attack. Then I canceled my prayer, a request made from habit, and hoped my friends would call the paramedics if I keeled over.

"How about dinner tomorrow night?" he asked. "I can pick you up at seven."

"Wh-what?" My heart banged around in my chest like a washing machine drum out of balance. Was he asking me out for a platonic meal or was he looking for a smorgasbord with me on the menu? Either option was far too tempting.

"Dinner. With me. Tomorrow night," he reiterated slowly.

"I um ... I can't. I have plans. With Chloe." Beneath the table, I banged my leg against hers.

"Yep! She does," Chloe said, playing her role beautifully.

Ashe grinned, letting me know he was on to me. "Another night then."

Instead of answering, I got to my feet. "I have a lot of work to do tomorrow, so I should go." I turned to Chloe. "That is if you're ready. If not, I'll call an Uber."

"I'm beat and ready for my pajamas," she said, standing up and pushing her chair in. "See you guys soon."

On the way out I flagged down our waiter and paid the bill.

As soon as we climbed into Chloe's SUV, she burst out laughing. "Kate, you should have seen your face when Ashe asked you out. You'd have thought he asked you to have sex on the table."

"After twenty-plus years of living with Dan, that's what it felt like."

Still laughing, Chloe whacked her hands on the steering wheel. "You and Ashe need to take care of whatever's burning between you two before you spontaneously ignite and set the world on fire."

"However tempting that might be, I'm not interested in a relationship. And in case anyone has forgotten, I'm still legally married."

"Give it up, Kate. You know you're getting divorced at some point, and having sex with someone doesn't mean you're in a committed relationship. You're an adult. You don't have to ask permission to do anything. Why not have a little fun?"

Why not indeed? "Because I'm too tired, my body aches, and my mattress sucks."

"Then ask him for a massage and sleep in *his* bed."

I laughed at her prodding. "I'm glad you have all the answers, Chloe."

Her smile faded and she started the vehicle. "Time is short, Kate. Make the most of it. Don't talk yourself out of things you want."

Chapter Twenty-Five

After Chloe and I finished our combination hedge trimming landscaping job in Fern Park, we grabbed an acai bowl from a vegan café two blocks away. It was a small place with four pub style tables, a service counter, one wall full of specialty soaps, handcrafted jewelry, and other unique gifts, and the other wall lined with glass coolers stocked full of chilled beverages, premade sandwiches, and decadent desserts.

"I'm completely in love with this town," I told Chloe as we made our way back to the park where we ate our lunch on a blue metal bench. "It seems to have everything now."

"I don't think you've seen the half of it yet," she said. "There are more small shops and eateries on the side streets that run between the park and the river, and from the other side of the park they sprawl six blocks deep. We're truly committed to being a top-notch tourist destination, and that means giving our visitors a wonderful dining, shopping, and entertainment experience."

"Sounds as if you were on the planning committee," I said.

"Josh and I both were. This is our home, and it was important to us to contribute to its planning and rejuvenation. Not just to make it a tourist destination but to make it a place where we and our neighbors wanted to live."

"Well, you've all done an amazing job of finding and polishing this diamond in the rough."

She laughed. "Funny you should say that. We almost used that as our tagline ... *a diamond in the rough*, but it was too cliché. We just wanted to convey the natural beauty and warmth of the place and make it clear it was a progressive town of free-thinking, nature-loving people."

"You certainly achieved your goal then. I hardly recognize it as my childhood home."

A few minutes passed while we finished our late lunch, then we took our garbage with us, climbed in the Dummy, and headed to a pipe and tank company on the south side of town where we purchased my septic tank, a distribution box, and the plastic drainage pipe for my leach field. Rather than wait for the company to deliver and set the tank for us, Chloe had them load it in the back of the dump truck. She assured me she'd be able to sink the tank herself using her backhoe and some cables which would allow us to do the job when we were ready, not before or after.

"I like the way you think," I told her as we climbed back in the truck. Slowly, I rolled my neck to ease the tension headache that had been growing since I'd climbed out of bed.

"Anything is possible when you have tools and big toys," she said, slipping off her dusty leather work gloves.

"And skills and guts," I added.

"Yeah, those help." With that she cranked the Dummy to life, dropped it into first gear, and we rolled out of the rutted yard like two seasoned pros.

Just over half an hour later we drove out the lake trail and found Carlos walking around the back of my house.

"Missy Kate!" he hollered, hitching up his pants and grinning ear-to-ear as he high-stepped through the grass and headed toward the truck. "I finished my job early so I'm all yours now," he said, still shouting through the open truck window.

Chloe snorted and nudged my side. "You hear that, Kate? You're in luck."

Stifling a laugh, I got out of the truck and shook Carlos's extended hand. He worked my arm like a pump handle, making my nagging headache worse. "What are you pretty girls doing riding around in a big truck like that, 'eh?"

"I suspect the same thing you would be doing with it." I eyed him with a raised eyebrow. "We're hauling in materials for my leach field that we pretty ladies will be installing tomorrow."

Carlos's thick black eyebrows pinched together in a grimace. "Lo siento, Miss Kate. I should know better than to joke about such a thing. My Rosie would box my ears for such a comment. I meant to say it's lovely to see you pretty, *hardworking* ladies."

It was a battle to suppress my grin. "And it's lovely to see your handsome face as well, Carlos."

"Handsome? This face?" Carlos laughed so hard it bent him double. He came up wiping his eyes. "Oh, Miss Kate, we are going to be buenos amigos."

I didn't speak Spanish but I knew enough words to know he was saying we were going to be good friends. "I think we already are, Carlos."

"Then let's go get your plumbing installed," he said, offering his arm to me, elbow out, like a gentleman escort. "Your soil sample was good. You ladies can build your leach field now."

Offering a lady his arm must be one of his quirks or habits, and it cracked me up. I couldn't help it. He was such a funny little guy. Despite his gallant offer, I made it inside without his aid. While he began setting up in the kitchen, Chloe helped me push my bed to the opposite end of the building, away from where he would be installing the plumbing.

"Kate, maybe you'd better opt for a new bed before buying shoes," Chloe said, visibly cringing at the condition of my old mattress.

"I'm going to buy a futon that can double as a bed and a couch, but my money is spoken for at the moment." I gestured toward Carlos who was already at work in the kitchen area, his plumber's crack playing peek-a-boo as he squatted and rummaged through a big toolbox. "My boyfriend gets first dibs on my money."

Chloe laughed quietly. "It seems you two are made for each other."

"Strangely enough, we are — in a platonic he's-funny-as-hell sort of way."

"He really is," Chloe said, a full smile on her face. "As for wanting to buy a futon, I have one I'd give to you, but I know you won't take it, so I'll sell it to you for ten dollars." She held up her hand to stop me. "Before you say anything, it's something I've had in my basement for years. It's in decent shape but doesn't get used. Dylan doesn't hang out at home with his friends anymore. And Josh and I never spent time together down there. I'd have offered it to you before now, but I'd forgotten it was down there. It's yours if you want it."

"Sold," I said. "And thank you. *Again*. For everything."

"Hey, Miss Kate ..." Carlos called from across the room. He was looking at the framework for the utility room walls. "Where you going to put your washing machine?"

I went over the complete layout of my compact utility room and small bathroom with him. As he nodded and made mental notes, I swear I could see a blueprint developing in his eyes.

"Let's see what wiring I have to work around," he said, moving a bucket of tools out of the way. "Eeechee-wah-wah!" he said, jumping back as if he'd grabbed a live wire. "You have a house-guest, Miss Kate."

I looked down to see a dead mouse on the floor. Probably Sinatra's handiwork. It was a tiny little thing, and I felt bad for it. "Come on, little guy, I'll give you a proper burial," I said, picking it up by its tail.

As I headed out the back door, Carlos hollered to my back. "Missy Kate, you make sure you wash your hands after touching that thin'!"

Despite my own giggles, I could hear Chloe's laughter all the way outside. Oh, how I loved that man!

After burying the dead mouse at the end of the leach field and thoroughly scrubbing my hands clean, I checked on Carlos who was already hard at work. He assured me he understood the plan, so I left him to his business.

As the day ended, Chloe and I had managed to finish framing in the kitchen ceiling, which doubled as the floor for the loft above, and Carlos had installed the plumbing for the bathroom shower, sink, hot water on demand unit, and utility room washing machine. That meant we could begin work on the leach field in the morning while Carlos continued his work plumbing the kitchen.

Unfortunately, heavy rain began in the middle of the night, pounding against the roof, streaming rivulets across the skylights, and drenching everything outside. Sinatra and I hunkered down on my bed, the two of us burrowed beneath covers. At some point the downpour leveled off to a soft rain that lulled us both to sleep. I woke a few hours later to a gray, misty morning and Carlos's voice coming from the other side of my French doors. Sinatra and I both leapt from bed. Sinatra shot toward the bathroom where I suspected he was exiting through the open window.

Horrified that I'd overslept, I dragged on my dirty jeans that I'd left on the floor beside my bed, raked my hair back with both hands, and pulled on the ball cap I'd hung on the bedpost. With one big swoop of my arms, I bunched the blankets into a ball and plopped them at the end of the bed. Then I slogged to the door.

Carlos blew in like a hard wind, zipping into the house with his toolbox in one hand and a cup of coffee in the other. "Good morning, Miss Kate!"

Wincing at the loudness of his greeting, I forced a smile. "I'd say you're bright and early, but it's not very bright this morning. You're just early."

Carlos released a gust of laughter. "A gray morning for sure, but your smile lights up your whole house, Miss Kate."

I smiled for real because he was such a lovely man. "Not enough, I'm afraid. I'll start the generator so you can turn on Ashe's work lights." I gestured to the dual lamp tripod standing in the corner of the kitchen.

"No need for that." Carlos squatted and dug something out of his toolbox. A second later he slipped a band of some sort around his head and flicked a button that illuminated a small headlamp that cast an amazing cone of light. "I can see just fine." With that, he set to work.

A few seconds of watching the beam from his headlamp dart around the kitchen made me nauseous, so I turned on my camp lantern. As inconspicuous as possible, I slipped outside to use the outhouse, and then brushed my teeth. After drinking a glass of water, I used what remained in the gallon jug to wash my face. Feeling somewhat restored, I headed back inside to pull on my sweatshirt. The morning was damp and chilly, and all I wanted was to crawl back into bed. But today was the day Chloe and I were digging a leach field.

Thankfully, Chloe showed up minutes later with a steaming carafe of coffee and rain gear for us. I savored two cups while we discussed the job, but I still felt chilled when we set to work. About forty-five minutes into the job, I began to shiver. Making a quick trip into the house, I pulled my jean jacket over my sweatshirt and topped those with the hooded rain jacket Chloe had brought for me. The rain gear had belonged to Josh, so it was huge on me. I had to roll the sleeves to free my hands. Everything felt damp from being outside in the steady mist that continued to descend from the gray sky. Despite the rain jacket, my clothing felt soggy. My forehead felt clammy. And I was tired. Ungodly tired.

Twenty minutes passed before Chloe swung the bucket around, lowered it to rest on the pile of dirt she'd excavated from what would be my leach field, then shut off the machine. Climbing out of the cab, she adjusted the hood of her rain jacket and headed my way.

"Have you been standing out here all this time?" she asked, eyeing the wet brim of my ball cap.

"Yeah, why? I wasn't sure when you might need my help."

"There's nothing you can do until I get the area excavated." Tilting her head, she surveyed me with a critical eye. "No offense, but you look like hell."

"No offense taken. I feel like I look."

"Maybe you should go in and lie down."

I shook my head, flinging a couple of water droplets from my hood. "Carlos's in there working. I don't want to send the wrong message."

Chloe snorted. "Best not to encourage him. You can take my truck and sleep at my house for a while if you like. You really don't look well."

I glanced at the long trailer hooked to the Dummy, and knew I couldn't drive the standard truck with a gazillion gears or negotiate that massive trailer anywhere. "Thanks, Chloe, but I'll be fine. I'm always a little low on gray days, so no need to worry." I glanced at the mucky patch of ground where she'd been digging up earth. "There's got to be something I can do to help."

"Not yet. I need to level out the trenches as best I can with the excavator before we finish leveling with shovels."

"All right. I'll help myself to another cup of coffee while you do your thing out there." I gestured halfheartedly toward the mucky trenches she'd been digging. I huddled over my steaming mug, trying to warm my hands, gulping the hot liquid to warm my insides, but I couldn't warm up. Something told me that putting on more clothing wasn't going to help. And that worried me. I couldn't get sick. I couldn't.

But I did.

My ears rang. My head pounded. My nose ran.

An hour later, eyeing me like a concerned mother, Chloe said, "We're done for the day, and so is Carlos. I'm going to tell him to go home because you need to go to bed." When I opened my mouth to argue, she grabbed my shoulders and spun me around to face my house. "Go. To. Bed." She gave me a hard nudge toward the door and followed at my heels. Inside, she made quick work of explaining to Carlos why he had to quit early.

The fearful look on his face when he realized I was sick, made me snort. Snot shot out of my nose and slapped across my lips.

Horror crossed his face as if I were a tuberculosis patient who'd just hacked up a wad of blood.

I didn't have a tissue, so I tried to hide the mess behind my palm.

On bowed legs, he beat a path to my door as if he were trying to outrun the germs I'd brought inside. "Feel better, Miss Kate!" he shouted as he bolted outside.

I laughed so hard I nearly coughed up a lung. Lightheaded, I sank onto the edge of my bed, wheezing and gasping as I gestured for Chloe, who was in a fit of laughter herself, to bring me a damn paper towel. Once she'd done so, and I'd cleaned up my face, I blew out a breath. "Oh my god, Chloe, he was so grossed out he didn't even gather up his tools."

"I know," she said, hooting as she fell against the wall. "But I can't blame the man. Your display was gross."

We laughed some more, but an onslaught of nausea hit me like a slap across the face. "Uh-oh ..." I glanced at Chloe. "Things are about to get more gross. You'd better leave."

Her smile fled. "Are you going to be sick?"

I nodded because I didn't dare to talk. I toppled over on the bed and dragged my cold feet up onto the mattress.

Chloe scooted outside and was back in seconds with a bucket that she placed beside the bed just seconds before I vomited. "I'm going to take you home with me, Kate. You shouldn't be alone when you're this sick."

"No. You and Dylan will get sick. Plus, I can't move," I whispered. "I'll be fine. Just throw those covers over me, will you?"

She did as I asked. For a moment, she stood looking down at me. "I'll be back shortly." With that, she headed outside. A minute later I heard the Dummy rev to life. I could hear Chloe outside rattling chains, and I suspected she was disconnecting the trailer from the dump truck, but I couldn't have gotten out of bed to check even if my life depended on it. I was too busy hanging over my bucket.

THANKFULLY, I was only sick to my stomach for a couple of hours, but the cold that had lodged in my body lasted for two days ... along with the rain. Chloe had dragged in a couple of the Adirondack chairs from outside, and she'd stayed with me until she was sure my nausea was gone. She fed Sinatra and brought me hot soup and Dylan's old sleeping bag. She went to the store and returned with a plush full-length bathrobe for me and insulated slippers that looked like floppy-eared rabbits. I hadn't been cared for like this since my mother was alive, and it made me cry. And that made my nose run. And that made me cough.

I was such a mess that Chloe threatened to throw me in the lake if I didn't pull myself together and stop being so emotional over a little kindness. Even Sinatra was avoiding me.

She told me she was keeping Carlos informed so he could stay away from my den of disease, and then she broke the news that my gross display of snot had ruined my chances with him. That of course caused another gross display when I burst out laughing and coughing.

What she hadn't done though was ask Ashe to stay away. When he showed up later that morning, I had just slogged back inside after a trip to the outhouse. My hair was a rat's nest. My eyes were bleary, my nose beet red, and my voice sounded like I'd smoked a carton of cigarettes every day of my life. Wrapped in my robe and comforters, I had just sat in one of the chairs when he knocked on the door. I could see him through the glass, which meant he could see me too.

I scooched down in my chair and pulled the blankets over my head. "No one's home!" I croaked, sounding like a hoarse bullfrog.

I heard his laughter through the door. "I have a delivery for the snotty lady who lives here."

I vowed to kill Chloe when I recovered because she'd obviously told Ashe about my snot story. "No one's here but ghosts. Gooooo awaaaay."

The swish of the door swinging open brought in fresh air and Ashe's laughter. "I have a special delivery from Maggie," he said. The sound of his boots thudding across the floor made me sit up and peek from beneath my blanket. He rattled the paper bag he was holding. "Mags sent over sweet potato stew and some crackers, both are vegan." He held up a bottle of whiskey with his other hand. "I brought whiskey, pure maple syrup, and lemon to clear your pipes and hopefully prevent another mishap with your spigot."

"Ha-ha," I said, letting the covers slip a little lower but leaving them bunched around my neck.

Ashe chuckled as he placed the bag of goodies on the floor near my feet that were encased in huge bunny slippers. "Wish I could have seen Carlos's face," he said.

I snickered despite myself. The episode was truly gross and embarrassing, but Carlos's reaction still made me giggle.

Ashe gave me a good looking-over. "Are you hungry?"

"Always."

"Where are your bowls?" he asked, his gaze roving my unconventional storage cupboards, namely a canoe and a workbench.

I flapped a corner of the blanket in the direction of the workbench. "Over there somewhere."

He dug around until he produced a bowl and a spoon. Then he filled the bowl with stew and brought it to me.

I released my grip on the blankets and exposed my disgusting self. I hadn't bathed in three days. I hadn't even brushed my teeth yet today. But I was hungry, and my stomach was a taskmaster when it wanted food. I relieved him of the bowl. Purposely ignoring him, I dipped the spoon and scooped up a mouthful of stew that was, to my absolute delight, still deliciously warm. I groaned with pleasure.

He laughed. "You know, you're pretty cute with that red nose and those bunny slippers."

Spoon poised mid-air, I gaped at him. "Are you really flirting with me while I look like this?"

"God no!" he said with such mock horror it made me laugh.

"Careful, Ashe, you don't want a repeat of my snotty display that horrified Carlos."

"Yeah, I think I can live without seeing that." Lowering his manly body into the other chair, he looked out the window where a family of ducks were gliding along the lake shore. "What a view. I could sit here all day just watching the fish jump."

"But you're not going to, are you?"

"I don't remember you being such a smart-ass."

"I don't remember you at all."

His eyes, so dark and sexy, met mine. "Liar."

No way was I wading any deeper into that conversation. I intentionally filled my mouth with a spoonful of stew. "How long do mother ducks look out for their babies?" I asked.

For a moment he didn't reply. He just let his gaze rove over me. I squirmed knowing I looked like a big lump of misery.

"The babies are called ducklings and they can forage for their own food in as little as a couple of days after they're born," he said. "They usually leave the nest within a month. Would you go out to dinner with me when you're feeling better?"

My spoon plunked back in the bowl. "What?"

"Go to dinner with me."

"We went to dinner the other night. At the brewery. How long before you finish the electrical work?" I asked, turning the tables and spinning the conversation like he just had.

"However long it takes."

I knew he wasn't referring to his electrical work. But I wasn't going down that path again for any man.

"I'm going to meet Maggie out front in a few minutes and help her pull the bathroom fixtures out of your grandparents' house."

"Ugh, I'm glad I can claim that I'm too sick to help you guys."

He rocked out of the chair and headed to the door. "Anything you need before I leave?"

"No, but please tell Maggie thank you for the stew and crackers. And, well, thank you for making the delivery."

"You got it, snotty lady." He winked, then stepped outside and closed the door behind him.

Chapter Twenty-Six

I felt well enough on Friday to wash up and get dressed, and I was able to feed Sinatra without being nauseated by the smell of his cat food, but that was the extent of my ambition. All I could manage after that was to sit outside with Sinatra on my lap and let the sun bake the chill out of my bones. I was still sniffling and coughing, and my nose was still red and sore, but my head didn't swim every time I stood up, so I considered that an improvement.

Chloe and I had agreed we wouldn't resume work again until after the weekend. She'd brought coffee and breakfast this morning, then said she was going to spend the day taking care of a long list of things at her house that had been left undone. Maggie and Ashe were both working, and I wasn't sure if Carlos would ever return.

So, the sound of someone coming down the lake trail surprised me. Sinatra leapt off my lap and scooted around behind the house. It didn't sound like a vehicle coming down the trail. I knew the safest thing was to be on my feet when I met my unexpected visitor, but I didn't have the energy to get up. If someone were here to kill me, they could do it while I was sitting down. Chloe would take care of Sinatra for me.

A young girl on a bicycle rode out of the wooded path, the

chain on her bike clanging against the metal guard as she pedaled across the grassy clearing. She came to a stop a few feet from me, one sandal-covered foot resting on the pedal, the other on the ground to support the bike. She was a blonde-haired beauty, and she looked familiar, but it took me a moment to place her. It was the girl from the café—my *niece*. Sophie's daughter. Oh boy. Her mother was not going to be happy about this.

"You're Kate, right?" the girl asked.

I got to my feet. Not easily or quickly, but I wanted to meet my niece properly. "Yes, I am. And although I didn't recognize you when we first met at the café, I believe you're my niece, Jessica, right?"

She nodded, her blue eyes taking me in from my red nose to my duct taped sneakers. Dismounting, she balanced her bike against one jean clad hip, taking in the yard and house and lake with one sweeping glance. "I heard my mom and Aunt Beth talking about you. Mom wasn't very nice, but Aunt Beth said she really liked you and that my mom should forgive you and ..." Her mouth clicked shut and she grimaced. "Sorry, I probably shouldn't have said all that. It's just that Aunt Beth made me curious about you. I wanted to meet you. I hope it's okay that I came here."

That was a lot to take in, but her youthful exuberance reminded me of my own girls, and it made me smile. "Of course it's okay with me. In fact, I'm really glad to meet you." I gestured to a chair across from mine on the other side of the fire pit. "Would you like to sit for a bit?"

"Sure." She laid her bike on its side in the grass. As she made her way over, she gave me a tentative smile. She was a beautiful girl with her mother's blonde hair and blue eyes, and her daddy's charming smile.

I gestured to the chair farthest from me. "You should sit there. I've been battling a cold and I don't want you to get it." The last thing I needed was to get my niece sick. I could imagine how that would go over with her mother. Knowing Sophie's position on my presence here, I was concerned about even talking with my niece.

"I didn't know you were my aunt when you came in the café," Jessica admitted, lacing her fingers, and shoving them between her knees, a nervous habit Sophie used to have. "My mom hasn't told me much about you, only that you two don't get along."

"We used to," I said. "Has she told you anything about us ... about me?" I asked, wanting to understand what Jessica already knew, what Sophie had left out, for good or bad, and if there was any way for me to talk with my niece without upsetting Sophie. Probably not, but I really wanted to know this beautiful young lady.

"Mom told me that you both spent a lot of time here at the lake with your grandparents when you were girls, but then you went off to college and became someone she didn't like." Jessica's bottom lip tugged down at one corner. "Yikes, I probably shouldn't be sharing that with you either, but after hearing Aunt Beth defend you, it made me wonder if my mom is being a little close-minded about whatever happened between the two of you. Because I've also heard grandpa defend you when Mama has said unkind things about you. It was only a couple of times, though, so it's not like she talks bad about you all the time. In fact, she really hasn't said much about you at all, which is why I'm so curious about you."

For a few seconds I held my breath, waiting to make sure she'd finished speaking, before I released it in one big puff. "That's a lot to absorb."

Jessica laughed, the sound so girlish and sweet it made my eyes water. It seemed all I'd been doing the past three days was blowing my nose and wiping my eyes. I had to get a grip on my emotions or I was going to scare my niece away before I could learn anything about her.

Smiling her beautiful smile, Jessica tucked one side of her long, wavy hair behind her ear. "My mom says my sentences are like one long paragraph and it takes a couple of minutes to unpack it all and understand what I'm saying."

"Well, she sort of has a point," I said, returning her smile. "But I understood what you said. And your mom isn't wrong to feel angry with me. I hurt her. I hadn't meant to, but I did. She was my little sister, and I was supposed to protect her. I didn't do that. And honestly, I didn't like the person I became after I left here either. She's not wrong about that. But, Jessica, this is something you should discuss with your mother. I'm afraid my talking with you about our situation will only make things worse and perhaps cause strife between you and your mom."

Disappointment washed across her face. Her gaze dropped to her hands, and she gave a small nod of acceptance. "I understand."

"I can, however, tell you that your mom and I spent a wonderful childhood here at the lake. Although I'm a bit older than her, we grew up together. We used to swim in the lake every day. We would dive off that dock over there," I said, pointing to the wooden jetty my grandfather had built. "We would float around all day on huge inner tubes that my grandfather would scavenge from old tractor tires. Sometimes we'd haul out the canoes and paddle all around the lake. We played yard games and had picnics right here where we're sitting, although our fire pit was closer to the lake at that time. Back then it seemed like summer was a whole year long," I said, my mind spiraling back to those lazy days. "But then fall would arrive and the trees would drop their leaves. Our grandfather would bring out his tractor and hook a big tarp to the back. Sophie and I would pile armfuls of dried leaves on the tarp, then we'd lie on top of them while Papa Ray pulled us up and down the lake trail."

Jessica's hands were no longer clenched between her knees. They were relaxed on her lap, her eyes sparkling as if she were reliving those moments with me and her mother. "That sounds so fun."

"It was. And your mom was a beautiful girl, like you, Jessica, and she was really funny. That's one of the things I've missed most about her. Even when I would get aggravated with her, she could always make me laugh." I fell silent then because my heart ached too deeply to go on.

"She's still that way." Jessica fiddled with a silver band on her middle finger. "Sometimes she makes me so mad, but it's impossible to stay that way, even when I want to, because she'll do something to make me laugh. I didn't know she was always like that."

"She was." A memory of Sophie surfaced and made me smile. "Does she still spit in her soda so she doesn't have to share it?"

Jessica's sweet laughter floated across the yard like a butterfly flitting through a garden of summer flowers. "My mother did that?" She giggled again. "For real?"

"She did. It used to gross me out, but it was a smart play on her part. She never had to share her drinks."

Jessica pressed her fingertips to her mouth to stifle another giggle. "I can't wait to ask her about that."

Worry streamed through me. I hoped I hadn't said too much, and that these precious moments with my niece wouldn't cause a rift between her and her mother.

"Please tell me more about when you guys were young," Jessica said, her eyes brimming with interest. "This is the first time I've really thought about my mother as a girl. She's always just been my mom, you know?"

I nodded because I understood the surprise and wonder of discovering that parents weren't born as adults, that they had once been curious children and then angsty teenagers, and that they might actually have a clue about the struggle of growing up. It was both intriguing and unsettling. Especially when I thought about my own parents and their journey through life. In my naïve youth, at nineteen years old, I'd believed my father should have been infallible because he was a grown-up. But it suddenly dawned on me that my father had been in his forties, not much older than I am now, when he'd begun his affair. I'd condemned him for it. But now my own life was a mess. I was making decisions that were hurting my girls, even when it was the last thing I wanted to do. I didn't have all the answers that I'd once believed people my age should have—and I wondered if maybe I'd expected too much from my dad. Maybe I'd held him to an unfair standard.

Maybe that's what my mother had understood that I hadn't

been able to comprehend in my young mind and heart. She'd said love was complicated and that life wasn't black and white. I could see that now. Life was lived in the gray area between right and wrong, love and hate, condemnation and forgiveness. But the gray area was messy, a place where only the strong could thrive. With my world in pieces, I'd wanted security. So, I'd taken the easy road with Dan and adopted his beliefs, however messed up, where everything was either right or it was wrong, where rules were black and white, where you were all the way in or all the way out. Unfortunately, that safe road had taken me straight to hell.

"Was my mom a good singer back then?" Jessica asked, snapping my wandering mind back to our conversation. "Cause she has a pretty voice. I told her she should be in a band, but she just laughed and said she's happy singing for me and my brothers."

That Sophie could sing surprised me. "Gosh, I don't know ... Your mom was a constant stream of chatter and noise. Being around her was like having a radio on all the time. After a while you didn't really hear it."

Another soft laugh shook her shoulders. "Do you sing too?"

"Not a note," I readily confessed. "That is one talent I didn't get. My daughter, Kara, has a beautiful voice though."

"My mom said you have two girls."

"Yep, twins." I spent a few minutes telling her about her cousins, and that my girls resembled her, Kara more than Haley, and then I shared some stories about them as little girls and as teenagers. "They just finished their first year of university."

"I wish I knew them," Jessica said. "They sound amazing."

"They are. I wish you girls knew each other too."

"Where are they living?" she asked. "Are they staying at their college for the summer?"

Heartsick, I shook my head. "No, they're back home with their father in North Carolina."

She processed that for a moment. "Does that mean you're divorced?"

"Not yet. But I will be." That was my intention anyhow if I could get Dan to stop being a jerk. "It's complicated."

"Yeah, my mom and dad divorced a couple years ago, and it's been ... complicated for everyone."

"I'm sure it has. And I'm sorry." I wanted to reach over and give her hands, which were crammed between her knees again, a loving squeeze, but I was taking no chance of infecting her. "If it's any consolation, Jess, I'm learning that divorce is just as painful and complicated for the adults as it is for their kids."

Golden hues of sunshine moved over her hair as she gave a small nod. "That's what Mom says. Dad doesn't talk about their divorce though. He says it's best to leave the past in the past."

That surprised me considering her father couldn't seem to leave his glory days as a high school quarterback in the past. "How is your dad?" I asked because I was genuinely curious, and because I believed Mark was a decent guy despite his issues.

"He's doing okay. He works a lot and still coaches high school sports." Her gaze darted away where she focused briefly on the lake, then returned to me. "My younger brothers and I see Dad every other weekend, and we usually do something fun together. My mom and dad both seem happier apart, so it's okay."

Yeah, it was okay but obviously painful for her. This is what I was doing to my daughters.

But *okay* was better than *nothing*. Okay meant you still had a connection. Nothing meant burned bridges and broken hearts. If only things could have been *okay* with my father and my sister and me ...

"Are you going to live here?" Jessica asked, pointing at the boathouse.

"Yep, I'm converting it into a small cottage."

"I'd love a place like this," she said, seemingly enthralled with the idea of having her own little house by a lake. "Mom brought me here once to show me the lake, but she would never bring me back. She said the lake wasn't hers anymore. We always went to the river to swim, or to Tupper Lake or sometimes to Saranac Lake if we wanted to go boating." Jessica leaned back in her chair and crossed one knee over the other. "It's so peaceful here."

"It is, but not so much when a bear is throwing around a big metal barrel."

Her eyebrows raised, and she took a furtive look around us. "You have a bear here?"

"Probably several, along with many other animals you might not want to meet face to face. This is where they live though." I gestured to the lake and surrounding woods and mountains. "I do my best not to bother them or disrupt their lives, and for the most part they give me the same respect."

For a long moment she looked around, her blue eyes taking in the leafy trees and shimmering lake and shadowed mountains. "Other than having a bear as a neighbor, I think this is a beautiful place to live." Her gaze settled back on me. "I bet your house is going to look so cute when it's finished."

"That's the plan, but there's still a lot left to do."

"Are you doing all of this," she asked, gesturing toward the boathouse. "By yourself, I mean?"

"My friends are helping me, but I'm doing everything so I can learn how it's done."

"That's really amazing."

For me, it was, but it was also because I couldn't afford to hire anyone to do it. Suddenly, I was glad I'd had to figure things out for myself. Sure, money would have made things much easier—I would have filed for a divorce long ago—but I'd have learned nothing about myself and what I was capable of.

"I need to head back now so my mom doesn't worry," Jessica said, popping to her feet with a youthful energy I envied. "It was really nice to meet you ... and well, thank you for sharing those stories about my mom as a young girl."

The joy in my niece's eyes sent a warm rush through my chest. I'd given her a piece of her mother she hadn't known. As someone who'd spent the majority of my life without my mother, I understood just how much that meant. "I hope you can come back and visit me again," I said.

"Me too."

"Maybe someday you and your mom can come over together." I smiled to let her know I wasn't expecting it, but that I was hoping for it.

"That would be nice." Jessica returned my smile, then she stood her bike on two wheels, slipped onto the seat, and glanced back at me. "Bye, Aunt Kate."

Tears flooded my eyes and blurred my vision. "Bye sweetie."

With that, my beautiful niece rode away.

And I sat outside and cried.

Chapter Twenty-Seven

I survived my cold.

And Carlos came back.

I watched him hitch up his britches as he approached me, his wide, gap-toothed smile beaming as bright as the sunshine. "*Hola*, Miss Kate. I'm so happy to see you back to your healthy self," he said in his usual boisterous manner that I was growing so fond of.

"And I'm happy to see you came back after my, um ... mishap."

He giggled as he headed toward the house. "I didn't see nothing, Miss Kate." That he didn't offer his elbow to escort me was a surprise, but I think he was playing it safe and not touching the snotty lady who might still be contagious. I wasn't, but he'd made it clear he wanted nothing to do with that mess.

While Carlos worked on installing plumbing in my kitchen, Chloe and I worked outside on the leach field—a task more complicated than I'd imagined.

The trenches Chloe had excavated still had to be painstakingly leveled by hand which required working in the dirt with shovels for three hours. Then the trenches had to be filled with several inches of stone, and several lengths of pipe had to be lain and glued together. By the time we'd finished, my hands were covered in glue, my back screamed in protest, and my stomach growled with hunger.

As I stood and arched my back, Chloe joined me. The two of us hobbled toward the cooler that was sitting near the fire pit where Sinatra was hanging out. "I need to eat something before I pass out," I said.

"Me too." She groaned and flopped down onto a chair. "I don't know how people do this work for a living."

"Now you know how I felt my first day working for you." I dropped onto the chair beside her, then gave Sinatra a good scratching on his head. "If I'd had any idea how hard this work was going to be I'd have waited until I could afford to hire someone."

"It didn't sound that tough when Carlos was explaining how to do it," she said. For a minute we just sat in our chairs, letting our backs unlock while we caught our breath. "I'm sort of proud we're doing it ourselves though."

"Yeah, me too," I said. "But I'll be happy when the job is finished and it can be a proud *memory*."

Laughing, Chloe reached over and opened her cooler. She'd continued to insist on providing our lunches, which were much easier for her to make with the use of a full kitchen, until my own kitchen was functional. I'd accepted her amazing generosity because I was going to repay her somehow, someday, and in a manner she deserved. For now, I was happy to savor the cold pasta salad and fresh pears she'd brought.

Sinatra, who'd lost his shyness around Chloe, snooped in the cooler.

"Yes, little man, I brought something for you too." She pulled out an envelope of tuna, tore it open, and dumped it onto a paper plate. "There you go, sweetie."

Sinatra dove in and began devouring the treat.

"You are spoiling him."

Chloe grinned. "I know. I didn't get to do this with your kids, so I'm doubling down on your cat."

"All to his advantage. If he decides to follow you home and live with you, don't blame me."

"This guy leave you? Not a chance," she said, ruffling his long fur with her fingertips. "You love your mama, don't you."

Sinatra was too engrossed in his meal to love anything but his food.

After we'd drunk a full quart of iced tea, we lounged in our chairs for a few minutes while Sinatra licked his paws and sunned himself.

"What's Maggie been doing?" I asked. "I miss her."

"Me too. She's at an antiques show in Lake Placid. She's going to stop by on her way home tomorrow."

"I'd like to take my girls there when they visit," I said, hoping they would. Haley would go with me. But Kara was still avoiding me, ignoring my texts, and dodging my phone calls.

Yawning, I stretched my aching legs out in front of me. "Think we'll be able to finish the leach field tomorrow?"

"I sure hope so." Chloe leaned her head against the seat back. "I want to get the shiplap on your walls *now*." Rolling her head against the seat back, she looked over at me. "I know you like having Carlos around, but I want your boyfriend to take his toolbox and plumber's crack and go home so we can start on the walls."

I laughed. "You'll miss him as much as I will."

"Yeah, he's pretty awesome."

"I invited Carlos to bring his family to swim at the lake. I don't know if he will, but I'm eager to meet the woman who swept him off his bowed legs and won his big heart."

Chloe burst out laughing. "She's amazing."

Turns out Chloe was right, Rosie was amazing. Chloe and I met her when she dropped Carlos off the next morning. He needed a ride because his work truck was in for service. It was apparent from the first minute of watching the two that Carlos was smitten with his wife. Dark-haired and adorable, she was his height and half his weight but just as lighthearted and with a smile that rivaled his own. Between the two of them and their beaming personalities, I almost needed sunglasses.

"Well, that does it," I said after Rosie left and Chloe and I headed back to the leach field. "It's painfully obvious I have no chance with Carlos."

Chloe laughed. "Yeah, his heart's already spoken for. But Ashe isn't a bad second choice."

"I guess not, but he'll never be Carlos."

"Let it go, Kate. You gotta move on," she said dramatically, giving me a shove from behind that sent me back into the trench. "Work is good medicine for a broken heart."

"You've got that wrong, Chloe. You need good medicine to do this work."

"That too."

Our medicine of choice after we'd finished another long day was cold beer. Maggie showed up shortly after. When Chloe and I stood to give her a hug, she pulled us both into her arms for a three-way squeeze. "I've missed these faces." She sloshed us like towels in a washing machine then released us.

"What? No hot dates to keep you company while you were away?" Chloe asked.

Maggie arched an eyebrow. "I never said that."

While we talked and razzed each other, the forest grew dark and the sky filled with stars. Chloe and I had planned to turn in early, but Maggie wouldn't hear of it. She regaled us with tales of her boy-toy she'd met at the convention and some of her other playful exploits until Chloe and I were bent double with laughter. It felt so good to belly laugh, to howl until tears streamed from our eyes, that we all just let go.

And that's when Chloe broke down and bolted for the beach.

In a full-on crash that had been coming since she'd lost her husband, she collapsed from the weight of her grief. Maggie and I caught up and dropped to our knees beside her, holding her as guttural sobs shook her body. Fragmented phrases burst forth as she wept. She was broken ... So lonely her bones ached ... Josh was her best friend ... Memories of him were everywhere ... Her house ... Her barn ... Their bed ... This beach. They'd had so many plans ... Her son lost his father ... Josh will never see Dylan graduate college ... or see their grandchildren ...

Her pain filled the night, rolling through us like storm-whipped waves. The magnitude of her heartache bowled us over, pulled us under, and left us clinging to each other on the shore.

Her loss was so big I couldn't comprehend it. I could only compare it to my own losses, the closest being my mother's death. But it seemed my never knowing the great love Chloe had shared with Josh was my greatest loss of all.

The storm surge of Chloe's grief left us wilted like seaweed spewed onto the beach.

For several long moments we just sat in silence, sniffling, and wiping our eyes. Then she released a shaky sigh. "I'm sorry," she whispered.

"Oh, Chloe, I expected this months ago," Maggie said, her voice tender and filled with compassion.

Chloe shook her head. "Grief had its claws sunk so deep in me I could barely breathe, much less cry. But your stories about dating reminded me of all the fun Josh and I used to have, and knowing we'd never have that again just ... it just hit me." A small sob shook her shoulders, then she inhaled and wiped her face. "The first time Josh kissed me was right here at the lake," she said. "I've never told anyone this, but we came out here one night after a high school football game. That's the night he told me he was going to marry me, but he made it clear he wasn't asking. He said he would make that moment something I'd never forget." She sniffed. "The thing is, he made every moment something I'll never forget. I think that memory, and too much alcohol—thanks to Maggie—is why I fell apart. Sorry you two had to see that."

"And I'm sorry you had to witness my snot episode," I said.

Releasing a watery laugh, Chloe looked at Maggie. "You missed another Oscar-winning Kate episode. Poor Carlos will never be the same after witnessing that," she said, and proceeded to tell Maggie about my cold and the resulting snot event. By the time she finished, we were all giggling.

"That's it. You two aren't allowed to do anything without me anymore," Maggie said. "I'm missing too much."

Chloe worked up a wobbly smile. "Then maybe you should stop spending all your time with your boy-toys."

My laugh sounded wet and snotty, as if I were underwater.

Maggie wrinkled her nose. "Girl, you need to clean your face."

And so it went while we wiped our eyes, blew our noses, and pulled ourselves together. We walked back to the campfire and opened another bottle of wine, turning our conversation to lighter topics. Maggie told us about all the amazing antiques she'd seen and how she couldn't wait to show us the ones she'd purchased. Chloe was enamored with a handcrafted coffee table Maggie had described to us, and said she wanted it.

"After we finish your place, Kate, I want you and Maggie to help me give my house a facelift," Chloe said, drawing her feet up on the chair. She sat between us with her arms circled around her knees and her empty wine glass held in one hand. "I'm serious. I need to start clearing space and figuring out how I'm going to live the rest of my life without Josh. I'm still breathing. Somehow, someway, I need to start living again."

To see her forcefully straightening her spine after it had been bent beneath the weight of her grief was a transformative moment for me. Friends could help you find the strength to get back up after life flattened you. That's what Chloe and Maggie had done for me—and now we were doing it for Chloe.

Chapter Twenty-Eight

The next day, after I called the attorney's office to schedule a consult, Chloe and I made a trip to a building materials store to pick up dust masks, disposable coveralls, lightweight work gloves, and staples for her staple guns. We placed an online order for the insulation using Chloe's credit card. I didn't have one yet, so I reimbursed her with cash.

The next morning my delivery of rolled insulation arrived. The driver refused to maneuver his big truck out the lake trail, so Chloe and I loaded the insulation into the Dummy. Then we unloaded it and stored it inside where it would be protected from the weather.

Sinatra was in cat-heaven. He climbed on the mountainous rolls of insulation stacked in the middle of my house. I chased him away from an open roll before he could make a mess on the floor and cover himself in fiberglass. But he was inquisitive, exploring the tools and materials piled up in the house, creeping through the dark spaces between the rolls, and eventually climbing onto the top of the stack where he lounged and watched us work. It was hard to believe he was the same cat who'd been too afraid to come within twenty feet of me, even when I was putting food out for him. Seeing him healthy, curious, and content brought me a deep sense of joy. Sinatra had adapted to the constant construction noise and the steady stream of my friends coming and going, making it clear this was his home.

It was *our* home.

And I had friends, one of whom was telling me to quit daydreaming and hold the damn insulation in place. I was guilty of thought-surfing, but Chloe was a taskmaster when it came to work. I'd thought she might want some time alone after her breakdown the other night, but she'd wanted to work. Her goal was to get my walls insulated by the end of the week—two days from now—because she'd decided to take Dylan to Lake George over the long holiday weekend to see Josh's parents whom they hadn't seen since shortly after Josh's funeral. This was the first time she and Dylan would be taking a weekend away without Josh.

"I scheduled tree work for us Wednesday, Thursday, and Friday next week," Chloe said, jarring me from my musings about her emotional state. "We'll be back Tuesday evening. I'll either see you then or pick you up at eight on Wednesday morning."

"Works for me," I said, suspecting she was piling up work and pushing hard to keep herself busy and her mind focused on something other than her heartache. But her upcoming trip to Josh's parents was bound to be an emotional wringer, and one I didn't envy.

My back still had a painful kink from laying the drainage pipe in my leach field, but I managed to keep up with Chloe over the next two days. Since Ashe had finished the electrical work both inside and out, and we'd settled up yesterday, and I'd paid Carlos for the plumbing he'd finished this morning, Chloe and I had the place to ourselves.

The loft area walls were easy to insulate because we were able to stand on planks laid over the floor joists, but the main living area was a trial. Dressed in disposable coveralls, goggles, masks, and gloves, we were soon drenched in sweat. With our ladders placed a couple feet apart, Chloe and I each used one hand to grip a strip of insulation, and our free hand to climb our ladders. At one end of the building, we secured insulation between the wall studs.

Stapling while balancing on metal rungs was tricky work, uncomfortable on the feet, and a bit unnerving at times, but we managed to cover the walls without killing ourselves.

By six-thirty Friday evening, Chloe and I had finished insulating the exterior walls. We pulled off our face masks and gloves and eyed our handiwork. Despite my exhaustion, I did a happy dance across the floor, high-stepping over pieces of insulation, scattered tools, and my paltry belongings.

"I can't believe we did it!" I said, turning a circle, envisioning the walls covered with painted shiplap.

"Yeah, but we still have to do the ceiling, and also the main floor once we frame it in," she said, her eyes roving the place as if mentally calculating the amount of insulating work left to be done.

"Don't be a killjoy, Chloe. Let me savor this small victory for one night."

She winced. "Bad habit, I guess. Josh used to point out how much we'd gotten done on a job, and I'd point out how much we had left to do. Used to drive him crazy, but I couldn't seem to help myself. It's one of my flaws."

"I suspect that's what makes you a good planner. You can see ahead and create a sensible schedule for what needs to be done. Without you, I'd still be trying to clear the lake trail. I'd still have a plate duct taped on my roof. Hell, I'd probably be dead."

"No, you wouldn't, Kate. You'd have figured out a way to build your house without me."

"Maybe, but it wouldn't be nearly as fun, and I'd be drinking alone each night, which would be no fun at all."

She laughed and gave me a friendly shove toward the door. "Not tonight, you won't. Maggie will be here in an hour. Grab your bag and you can shower at my house."

"Deal." I grabbed my duffle bag, already packed in preparation, and followed her out the door. We were back in time to meet Maggie, who pulled in before us.

To my surprise, Maggie hauled a microwave out of her vehicle, and then plugged it into an extension cord that connected to the generator. "It's Friday night and I brought the party. Food and wine for my besties."

"You cooked? For us?" Chloe asked with raised eyebrows.

"I did." Maggie gestured for Chloe to start the generator. She popped three sweet potatoes in the microwave. "I already baked these so we just need to warm them. Wait until you taste this masterpiece."

I couldn't wait. I was starving. But I scooted inside and put food out for Sinatra while Maggie finished prepping our meal.

After she heated a mix of red peppers, onions, black beans, and spices she'd also pre-cooked, we spooned the mixture over our heated potatoes. Then we slathered on vegan sour cream flavored with taco seasoning and topped it all off with chopped scallions and cilantro.

"Oh my god, Maggie, marry me," I said, savoring the explosion of flavor popping across my taste buds. "I'm literally transported right now."

Chloe closed her eyes and groaned. "Damn this is good."

"Wait 'til you taste this wine." Maggie lifted a bottle of pinot blanc and gave it a small shake. "Our dessert."

"Delicious food and my favorite wine? I want to marry you too," Chloe said.

"Well, you're both out of luck. I have no intention of getting married. Not even to you two." Maggie filled three glasses, passed two of them to us, then crossed one knee over the other and leaned back in her chair.

As we ate, evening peepers began their chorus. The conversation was light while we lingered over our meal, then we set aside our empty plates and lounged in our chairs. After a while of quietly sipping our wine and letting our supper settle, I decided to build a fire. Crouched by the fire pit, I fanned the small flame, watching it encase the kindling. I looked up to find Chloe and Maggie talking quietly as if debating something. Then they both glanced at me with concern in their eyes. A twinge of anxiety wormed through me. "What's going on?" I asked.

"Tell her," Chloe said.

Maggie hesitated for a moment, then released her breath. "Your father came by my store late this afternoon. He wanted me to give you a message."

My dad had a message for me? Was he reaching out? Or was he going to warn me away from Beth, and perhaps Jessica, as Sophie had done?

"He knows you're back and would like to talk with you," Maggie said. "He gave me his personal phone number and asked me to give it to you. He said he'd prefer to come here and talk with you in person. Either way, he seemed sincerely eager to connect with you."

I lost my balance, and my butt hit the ground. Speechless, I sat beside the fire pit staring at Maggie. I'd planned to talk with my father at some point, initially to confront him and demand to know why he'd done such a horrible thing to our family. But I realized I no longer felt angry or hateful toward him. I just wanted to understand *why*, and to learn more about the relationship between my parents. I needed to know more about my mother, if she was hurt by his affair, if she'd hated me for going against her wishes. If she'd killed herself. But I wasn't ready for that conversation. I needed to get my life on solid ground and my feet firmly beneath me before I could tread into that emotional swamp.

"What did you tell him?" I asked, my voice strained.

"That I'd pass along his message," Maggie said. "He didn't ask for more, and I didn't offer anything else."

"Good." I sat there for a moment, staring without seeing. My father wanted to talk with me. He was reaching out. But whether that was a good thing or not, I couldn't fathom.

Chloe tapped my foot with the toe of her shoe. "Are you okay?"

I finger-combed my hair, still slightly damp from my earlier shower. "Yeah ... I guess I'm just a bit stunned that my father would visit Maggie's store."

"It's not the first time," Maggie said, surprising me yet again. "He's been in with Sophie and Jessica and with his ... with Sharon.

Usually he wanders out back to the antique shop while the ladies browse up front."

"Oh ..." Somehow that made me feel worse. Had I simply been a second thought for him while he waited for his wife to finish browsing?

"He was alone this time," Maggie said as if reading my mind. "He knows we're hanging out together again, and he knew I could get his message to you."

"You know you're going to have to deal with this at some point," Chloe said softly.

"I know." With a hard sigh, I rocked to my feet and returned to my chair and my glass of wine. "I intend to, but ... I don't know where or how to begin."

Maggie kicked her feet out in front of her and crossed them at the ankles. "A journey of a thousand miles ... and all that stuff."

"Yeah, yeah, but I'm not ready to take that journey." I filled my mouth with wine, savored it for a moment, then swallowed it along with my apprehension. "I don't have the energy or emotional band-width to deal with my father and take care of things here too. He'll just have to wait until I'm ready to talk with him."

"How about Sophie?" Chloe asked. "How do you plan to reconcile with her?"

I closed my eyes and dropped my head against the chairback. "I have no idea." I looked up at the twilight sky where the moon and stars were overtaking the dwindling rays of sunlight. "She won't even talk to me."

"Why not write her a letter?" Chloe suggested. "You're a writer, so write something that'll make her want to talk with you."

"She'd probably burn it without opening it."

"Nah, her curiosity would demand she read it, if nothing else just to see what you would say."

Maggie slapped my knee, startling me. "You need to do that, Kate. Nothing is going to get settled if you don't force Sophie to talk with you or if you keep avoiding your father. Write the letter and go see your dad."

They were right. But I couldn't imagine what to write to Sophie. And I wasn't ready to talk with my father. "You two are a pain in the ass tonight. You need to go home now," I said.

They just laughed and settled deeper into their chairs. I added wood to the fire, then returned to my chair and my annoying friends.

We turned our conversation to other topics and finished the bottle of wine. By the time they left it was after ten o'clock, and I was beat. The fire had burned down to coals, but I made sure it was completely extinguished before heading inside with Sinatra. Fully dressed, I dropped onto my bed, pulled the covers over me, waited for Sinatra to settle himself, then willed my weary body to sleep.

But I didn't sleep. I thought about my father ... and Sophie ... and the hard conversations that were ahead of us.

Chapter Twenty-Nine

I spent the holiday weekend alone pulling beadboard off the bathroom walls in my grandparents' house so I could repurpose it for my kitchen ceiling. I'd hoped to use some of the tin plating from the living room to cover my kitchen ceiling, but I needed the money I could get from selling all of it.

The process of removing the wainscoting was slow, tedious work, but it gave me time to think through what still needed to be done. There was more insulation to hang, then the shiplap needed to go up to finish the walls, then my kitchen ceiling and loft floor had to be finished, and ... ugh, I wanted to weep.

After a few minutes of sitting on the floor feeling sorry for myself, I realized it wasn't the work ahead that made me weepy. I was lonely. I missed my daughters so deeply it was a crushing weight on my chest. I missed Chloe and Maggie too. They were both away for the weekend, Chloe to see Josh's parents, and Maggie to check out an antique desk—and the sexy man who owned it. I considered calling Ashe just for some company, but I didn't want to send the wrong message.

Sinatra nuzzled my elbow then climbed onto my lap. I stroked his soft fur and listened to him purr. After a few minutes, I'd pulled myself together enough to get up. "It's a beautiful day out there, mister, and I'm tired of working. Let's go for a walk."

For an hour I walked deer paths through my property while Sinatra stalked me. He'd trail behind, and I'd pretend I didn't know he was there. Sometimes he'd rush ahead and wait for me, then twine himself around my legs just long enough for me to pet him. Then he'd dart off into the underbrush and begin his playful stalking all over again.

The trails meandered through wooded areas that sloped gently up and down hills and crossed a ravine and a couple small watercourses that wound through the forest. Hobblebush and elderberry shrubs hugged the trails and stream banks. Sophie and I used to pick fiddlehead ferns and leeks out here with my grandparents.

My grandfather had taught us how to identify the red maple, balsam fir, and eastern hemlock that proliferated on the property and towered above my head. Sophie and I might have spent more time with my grandparents than our parents, but it hadn't felt like it at the time because we'd loved being here.

I still did ... and always would. My heart was here in this place.

Pink lady slippers were just beginning to bloom. Grandma Jean had introduced us to many wildflowers during our childhood walks, and being here now with those memories of my grandparents wrung my conscience. I'd promised my grandmother I'd spread her ashes here, but I'd left them behind. I needed to get them, but that meant going back to North Carolina and facing Dan. It had to be done. It *would* be done. But not yet. To my further shame, I had no idea what had happened to my grandfather's ashes.

Just a little more time, Grandma. I promise I'll bring you home. And I'll find you, too, Papa Ray.

As Sinatra and I ambled along a small stream that cut across the property, I realized I'd done more living here in two months than I had in my twenty-plus years with Dan. Thinking about him made me think about my girls. I ached to see them, to snuggle them in my arms and protect them from the pain I was causing them. But they were no longer toddlers who ran to me with their boo-boos, or teenagers who gave me an eye roll one moment and cried on my shoulder the next. They were young women now experiencing the world as adults. They were figuring things out for themselves, and I had to give them time to do that.

Wasn't that what I was doing too? Figuring things out one day at a time?

Closing my eyes, I leaned against the furrowed bark of an old hemlock. For a long time I listened to the sound of the forest, scattered chirping and twittering in the trees, rustling in the undergrowth, the occasional breeze that swept through the forest—and the haunting song of the hermit thrush. My mother used to whistle softly to them *parity-parity-eeh, see-me see-me,* and they'd whistle back as if they'd really understood one another. Maybe it had simply been the plaintive note in their song that connected them.

My father had taught us about wildlife here, but it was my mother who'd taught us about birds. She used to play a game of spotting and identifying them. Sophie and I loved the challenge, and we got good at it. I wished with all my heart I could have walked my girls through this beautiful land and taught them the things I'd learned from my parents and grandparents.

I felt connected to this forest of critters, birds, and deer, one of which was crashing through the underbrush a few feet from me, its white tail flashing as it bounded away. A startled squirrel zipped across a broken tree branch that had fallen to the forest floor.

Seeing Sinatra's avid interest, I said, "No!" But he was already launching himself into the air, his paw swiping a wide arc as the squirrel leapt toward a branch above my head. Sinatra's sharp claws came within a whisker of snagging the poor squirrel, the near miss happening inches from my face. Both the squirrel and I squeaked in alarm. The squirrel landed on the branch.

Sinatra landed at my feet.

I planted my hands on my hips, scowling down at him. "I know this is what cats do. But you do not need to hunt for your food anymore. So holster those claws and leave our critters alone. They live here too."

Eyes locked on the squirrel zipping up the tree, Sinatra completely ignored me.

I scooped him up in my arms and nuzzled his head. "I know dinner options have been slim this past couple of weeks, but I'll go shopping tomorrow and will bring home some of your favorites. How does tuna sound?"

He licked my hand.

I laughed and gave him another nuzzle. He smelled of the forest, like rain and moss and pine needles. "Come on then," I said, setting him back on the ground. "Let's go home and find something for you to eat."

TUESDAY MORNING I CLEANED UP, pulled on a pair of jeans, a long-sleeved shirt, my hooded sweatshirt, and the work boots I was borrowing from Chloe. I fed Sinatra and filled his bowl to the top with dry kibbles. "This is in case I don't make it back in one piece," I told him. "It will keep you fed until Chloe comes by. Don't worry, sweetie, she'll take good care of you if I break my neck."

Sinatra rubbed his face against my leg.

I gave him a good scratching behind the ears. "I'll try not to kill myself."

After hooking my backpack over my shoulders, I gripped the handlebars on Haley's motorcycle and pushed it toward the open doors. It nearly tipped over as the front tire dropped to the ground. Only then did I realize I should have made a ramp out of a plank, but I managed to keep it upright and get it out of the house.

After parking the bike, I went back and closed the doors to my house. It was time to see what I was made of.

I lifted the kickstand, straddled the bike seat, and pulled in the clutch lever. Allowing myself one deep breath, I hit the start button. It stalled out. I adjusted the choke. After a couple of tries

the engine caught with a sputtering rumble. I made another adjust-
ment and the engine evened out. I took a couple of minutes to let
the motor warm up.

I was nervous. The bike felt heavier than I remembered. My
mind spun trying to recall all the safety precautions and details of
operating a bike that I learned at the motorcycle safety course.

Using the toe of my boot, I shifted down to first gear. Slowly, I
eased the clutch out a little and felt the bike begin to move.
Putting along with my legs out to correct my balance when the
bike teetered, I bumped my way out the lake trail. Halfway up I
tried to shift into second but hit neutral instead. The engine
revved, and the loss of momentum rocked me forward, unbal-
ancing the bike. I scrabbled with one foot to lift the shifter lever to
second gear. I made it, but the bike had slowed so much it jerked
and sputtered.

Shifting back to first gear, then increased my speed before
shifting to second. Moving along a little faster now, I dared to put
my feet on the foot pegs but had to keep sticking them out on and
off as the bike bumped along the trail. Finally, I reached the
driveway where I stopped and eyed the road. I really didn't want to
do this.

But Sinatra needed cat food.

Putting along in first gear, I made my way onto the road. The
tires were sliding around on the gravelly dirt road, and I didn't dare
to go faster. When I came to the crossroads by Chloe's house, I
downshifted carefully.

Hoo-wee this was hairy.

I came to a complete stop at the intersection, and that's when I
noticed the pickup truck rolling up behind me.

My heart began pounding. When one is sitting on a small
motorcycle, a truck looks huge in the mirror. I started to make my
turn but stalled the bike. Sweating beneath my helmet and sweatshirt, I tried again and turned right onto the paved road. The truck
followed.

I picked up speed, but the truck was on my tail. My hands

tightened on the grips as I shifted gears and watched the speedometer nudge upward ... forty, forty-five and climbing.

The pickup truck blew by me.

I took a couple slow, deep breaths and settled into the feel of the bike beneath me. The speedometer nudged up to fifty ... then fifty-five! Suddenly, it felt as if the wind were peeling away years of my life, removing the wrinkles of time that had aged me. It pummeled my chest as if saying *wake up!* I remembered how it felt to be young and adventurous and courageous. My spirit soared as if I were standing on the handlebars, stretching my arms wide to embrace the wind ... this moment ... this life ...

A deep, ugly sob burst from my mouth and my eyes flooded with tears. I blinked hard to clear my vision and sucked in a deep breath. I needed to live like this again, untethered, and half-wild. I was done with being scared. I finally understood Haley's love of riding. It was wonderfully liberating.

On the descent into town, I eased the bike into the traffic circle. By the time I pulled off my helmet outside the bank, my hands were shaking, but it wasn't from fear. It was from the exhilaration of stepping outside my comfort zone.

I took a moment to fix my hair, then I went inside to set up a checking account and cash my first paycheck and the other check Chloe had given me. I suspected I'd need to continue paying cash for most things until I'd established my own credit, so I'd kept most of the cash in my worn envelope.

My first stop was at the attorney's office where I paid her retainer fee, which I was only able to do because I'd accepted Chloe's brilliant suggestion and generous offer to give me an advance against my future pay. My attorney reminded me, again, that I was entitled to a lucrative settlement and cautioned me not to be a dumb-ass, but all I wanted was *out*. So, against her strongly-worded advice, I had her draw up the paperwork with my only demands: Dan and I would share joint custody, and he would support the girls through their college years.

Feeling twenty pounds lighter, I left the attorney's office and walked half a block to the power company to see about getting my power connected. Ashe had handled the electrical inspection with the power company, and everything had passed. I'd hoped to have electricity before the end of the week but was disappointed to learn it could be ten to twenty days. The power company needed to install a meter at my house first. I paid my deposit, depleting my money envelope by an additional three hundred dollars, then went back to the bike.

I didn't buy much at the grocery store. I was concerned about overloading the backpack strapped on the bike. Although I'd kept the motorcycle upright and could manage the gears better, I was far from an experienced rider.

"Well, there's a badass lady on a bike," I heard a man say. I turned to see Ashe crossing the grocery store parking lot, all lanky and athletic, his dark eyes and great smile melting me.

I smoothed a hand over my hair, imagining how bad it looked after being crammed under a helmet.

"I had my phone in my hand to call you when I saw you coming out of the store," he said.

"You did? Why?"

"Wondered if I could swing by and get the pocket doors today."

"You're not working?"

"I took today and tomorrow off so I could hang the doors. That's if you don't mind me coming by to get them."

"Of course not."

"You going to be in town long?" he asked.

I shook my head. "I'm heading home now."

"Okay, I have a couple things to take care of here first," he said, "so I'll see you in an hour or so."

"All right," I said, hugely relieved that he wouldn't be following me home. I was nervous enough on the bike without having him judge my performance.

As Ashe headed inside the store, I pulled on my helmet and Haley's riding gloves. A few minutes later I rode out of town and felt my shoulders begin to relax.

As the landscape opened into the countryside, I could hear the whine of the Rebel's engine and the sound of wind buffeting the bike. A sense of utter freedom surged through me. I howled aloud like a she-wolf, breaking the leash that had tethered me to a world foreign to my nature. "I am reclaiming my life!" I shouted to the wind. "I will no longer hide my claws!" My wildish self was meant to roam free, to burn with passion, and to stand and live in my own way.

This was what I wanted to teach my daughters.

Chapter Thirty

The pocket doors were beastly to move, especially when I was the only one helping Ashe haul them out to his van. By the time we'd gotten the second door loaded, my arms felt two inches longer from bearing their ungodly weight. After we'd loaded the hardware, I closed up the old house and walked back to his van.

"Want a ride?" he asked.

"Definitely," I said, climbing in the passenger side. I sat with a weary sigh.

"Want a beer?"

"Of course, but I don't have any."

He laughed. "I picked up a twelve pack before I came out."

"Is that what's in the cooler?" I asked, thumbing toward the back of the van. I'd assumed it was where he kept his lunch and beverages during his workday. To think it was filled with chilled beer made me wonder what he'd had in mind when he bought it.

My mind wandered as he slowly navigated his van down the lake trail. My motorcycle ride had made me less guarded and more daring. I refused to repress my sexuality any longer or even to deny my attraction to Ashe. I wasn't a curious teenager now. We were both adults. Sexual beings. Desire and passion were natural, beautiful things. Maybe one day I'd accept Ashe's invitation to dinner and see where it would lead. That thought led me straight into his bed. The thought of being caressed by him, rocking my hips beneath his hard, athletic body as he kissed me, was so wildly exciting I gasped aloud.

He glanced at me with concern in his eyes. "Something wrong?"

"Just a twinge in my back."

"Did you hurt yourself moving the door?"

"No, I'm just overworking my body I suspect." The tires continued to roll through small divots, and the doors clanked together. "You should put some padding between those doors before you head out," I said, inwardly cringing at the possibility of them being marred.

We came to a stop in my yard, and Ashe put the van in park. "I have a tarp I can put between them." We both stepped out.

"Need a hand?" I asked as he went around back.

"Nah, it'll just take me a minute."

I used the opportunity to cool my burning face and went inside to check on Sinatra. His dish of canned food had been licked clean. Hopefully, he was lazing in the sunshine licking his paws or sleeping rather than causing mayhem with the squirrels.

When I returned outside, Ashe already had two open beer bottles in his hand. He handed one to me. "Thanks for giving me a hand with the doors. I really hope you didn't hurt yourself carrying them."

"I didn't. I just wanted you to feel sorry for me so you'd share your beer with me."

He laughed, the sound so real and warm it wrapped around me like a hug. "I'd planned to share it with you anyhow."

"Wasted effort on my part then," I replied, trying to keep my wits about me in the face of his intoxicating charm.

Instead of sitting, we ambled slowly toward the lake where we watched a pair of mallards motor along the opposite shore.

"Must be their ducklings are off living their own lives now," he said, pressing a palm to his heart, his expression forlorn. "They grow up so fast."

I laughed, but his playful comment was so close to what I was experiencing with my girls, my heart dropped to my feet. My babies had grown up too fast. But it wasn't their growing older that ripped my heart out, it was them not needing me anymore that was killing me. "Do you miss having your son at home?" I asked.

"Yes," he said. "And no." He continued to watch the mallards for a moment, then turned to me. "I miss hanging out with him and being able to give him a hug. But I'm glad he's capable of taking care of himself and is living his own life."

"Yeah, I guess it's our job to help them become self-sufficient then set them free."

"Doesn't make doing it any easier."

"No, it doesn't," I said. "But I'd do it all over again for my girls."

"Me too. But not at this age."

"Just the thought of having a baby at this age is ..." I shook my head. "I can't even find a word for it."

"Horrifying?"

I laughed. "That's one word."

We talked about our kids while we sipped our beer. My gaze drifted between the lake and Ashe like a wave lapping at the shore. His son, Reed, was twenty-one now and had been in the Army since graduating high school. I asked if this was a constant worry for Ashe.

"Sure, but I'll worry about him no matter what he's doing."

"Good point. But I think I'd worry more if my girls chose military service over college."

Ashe shrugged. "Safety and security are an illusion. I'd rather my son risk his life doing something he loves than risk living a life not of his choosing. Daring to chase a dream is always risky, but daring nothing is the biggest risk of all."

I couldn't argue his point. I'd lost far more of myself playing it safe than anything I'd had to sacrifice going after my dream. Considering his words, I watched as fish created small circular ripples on the lake. Sophie and I used to fish here with our dad and Papa Ray. I could still see her sitting on the end of the dock, fishing pole in hand, skinny legs draped over the edge, and her thick braid hanging down her back like a river of gold.

"I know this is all a big risk for you," Ashe said, his quiet voice startling me from a memory I didn't want to release. "But you're not alone. You have friends here. And your girls will come around in time."

I nodded to acknowledge the truth in his statement, and hoped he was right about my girls. Haley seemed okay but this transition was hard on both my girls.

"You okay?" he asked softly.

I looked up and found myself snared by the warmth in his eyes. His head was free of the ball cap he wore during his workday, and a breeze teased a thick strand of hair, lifting it and tapping it against his jaw. I was close enough to lean in and kiss him. For one wild moment, I considered it. The spark in his eyes told me he'd welcome it, but I couldn't bring myself to move in.

"I'd be lost without Maggie and Chloe," I said, purposely keeping my distance. I'd been reeled in by Dan and had spent two decades trying to spit out that hook. I wasn't going to bite again.

But fishermen are smart. They know what bait to use. And hungry fish are vulnerable.

"I hope you consider me your friend too," he said, his voice low and sexy as hell. "Unless our night in the boathouse killed that possibility."

Heat flooded my body. "I'm surprised you remember," I croaked. "It was obvious that I wasn't your first."

"You weren't," he said, "but you're the one I remember."

The sound of a car door closing shattered the moment and snapped me back to sanity.

I spun toward the sound and saw Chloe's SUV parked in the yard. I expected to find her smirking at me for getting caught, but she had her head down texting on her phone. Had she seen us?

Ashe chuckled and winked at me.

I groaned and walked away from him. My life was far too complicated to play games with Ashe.

He stayed and had a beer with us, then headed out. He and Maggie must have passed each other on the lake trail because she pulled in just seconds after he left.

She rolled out of her truck like a woman on a mission, striding directly toward me, her eyes alive with purpose. Before I knew what was happening, she and Chloe took me by the arms and planted me in a chair between them.

"Okay, Kate," Maggie said, "no more evasions or omissions. What is going on between you and my brother?"

I looked at Chloe. "You texted her!"

Chloe nodded. "I did."

"I don't know what you think you saw," I said, trying for a nonchalance I couldn't quite affect. "But it was nothing."

"It was something. You and Ashe were going to kiss," she said.

"We were just talking—"

"Nope!" Maggie threw up her hand to stop my bullshit, her eyes intense. "Seriously, Kate, we'll respect your privacy and leave you alone about this if you prefer. But please stop treating us like idiots."

She was sincere. They would leave me alone and not pester me about my relationship with Ashe if I asked them to. But for me to keep denying there was something between the two of us was insulting to them. "I'm sorry," I said, feeling like a shithead. Releasing a sigh, I made my confession. "Ashe and I had sex in the boathouse the night of our first moon party."

Both Chloe and Maggie hooted with laughter.

Maggie slapped her thigh. "I knew it! I knew there was something going on with you two."

"Nothing's going on now," I said, but knew that wasn't quite true. Nothing had happened but there was definitely something going on.

"I don't buy it," Chloe said. "The heat between you two could roast hotdogs."

"There's still a little chemistry there." I gave a one-shoulder shrug. "Doesn't mean anything."

Maggie wiggled her eyebrows. "It could mean something if you wanted it to. It's obvious my brother would like to scratch your itch."

Chloe burst out laughing, and I couldn't help grinning. "I can take care of my own itch, thank you. But frankly, I'm too exhausted these days for anything to itch."

And so it went for the next ten minutes as Chloe and Maggie razzed me about my lady parts needing to be scratched. I told them that the only thing between my legs today was Haley's motorcycle seat. I shared my experience of riding to town, and said it's where I'd seen Ashe, and that he'd wanted the pocket doors which is why he'd been at the lake today. That brought us right back to the "almost kiss" incident. In the moment I'd not only wanted his mouth on mine ... I'd ached for it. It had been a long time since my body had burned with passion. But despite my primal urges, I was glad I hadn't succumbed to his heat. I needed to find my own way in my own time and on my own terms.

Chapter Thirty-One

Chloe and I spent the rest of the week doing tree work and landscaping. The days were long. The work was hard. And by Friday evening, I was bone weary. Chloe offered me the use of her shower as she did each night after work, but I wanted to cool my sweaty body with a swim in the lake.

The water in early June was still chilly, but it felt good on my aching muscles. Making quick work of rinsing off and cleaning my hair without soap, something I wouldn't use in the lake, I headed back to shore. Feeling somewhat rejuvenated, I strode onto the shore of my private sanctuary in all my naked glory. Water streamed down my body in rivulets, peaking my nipples and raising gooseflesh on my exposed skin in the cool evening air.

"Oops! Sorry ..."

The sound of a male voice startled me so badly I screeched in alarm and tried to shield myself with my arms. I looked up and locked eyes with Ashe.

"I probably should have honked the horn on my way in," he said, wincing in apology.

Sweeping my towel off the beach, I whipped it around me and glared at him. "I swear to god I'm going to hang a gate out front to keep you people from sneaking up on me."

"I can do that for you," he said. A slow smile tilted his lips as he took in my dripping outraged self. "A camera might be more effective. That way you could see who is out there."

"Are we really having this discussion? While I'm naked? And shivering?"

"You can get one with a battery backup so it'll work without electricity. It would work for now, and I could wire it in once your power is turned on. It's pretty simple really. You just download the camera app to your phone. Then you'll be able to open the app and look out front any time you like."

"Are you for real right now?" I asked, half agitated and half-laughing.

"Considering the fact I just caught you in a very vulnerable moment, yeah, I'm for real. You should get at least one camera out there, Kate. I'd add one on the lake trail too. And maybe consider getting a gun."

"Trust me, I am considering it."

His laugh was so intoxicating I wanted to kick him ... and kiss him.

Shivering, I swiped water off my face and sniffed. "I can't afford a camera," I said, and stalked toward the house. "I'm going to get dressed now, and I'd appreciate it if you wouldn't look in my windows. I don't have curtains yet."

Despite my rude exit, he laughed. "Wouldn't think of it."

Wrenching the door open, I turned back. "Why are you here?"

"To see you naked, of course."

Of all the things I'd expected him to say, his comment was so extreme and unexpected I laughed.

"I'm sorry, Kate. I hadn't meant to invade your privacy," he said sincerely. "I think I left one of my tools here that I'll need for a job next week."

"Next time, call first. Let me get dressed, then we can look for it."

"Okay, thanks. And if you put on your good sneakers, I'll take you out for dinner," he said.

I laughed despite my agitation with him. "And if I choose to wear my old beaters?"

He feigned an apologetic expression. "Sorry but I can't be seen in public with them." As I searched for a suitable retort, his grin faded and his gaze swept over my body. "Please get dressed, Kate, before I come over there."

A hard twist of desire curled in my belly. It would be so easy to drop my towel and slip into his arms.

He started walking toward me, his eyes smoldering.

To save myself from succumbing to Ashe's charm and my own desires, I stepped inside and slammed the door behind me. *No way was I crossing that bridge. Not even going to consider it.*

But I did.

I threw on my clothes, then found the only tool in my house that didn't belong to me or Chloe. When I carried the socket-wrench thingy out to Ashe, and he saw me wearing my duct taped shoes, he chuckled.

"So, that's a 'no' to dinner?"

I gave him the wrench. "Sorry, you just can't compete with a tomato and cheese sandwich and a cuddly cat for a dinner date."

For a moment he looked at me as if he wanted to say something, then whacked the tool against one palm. "Okay then, you and Sinatra have a good night."

"You too." As soon as his van disappeared down the lake trail, I slithered down the door frame and sat on the step. Holy moly that man was trouble—and my raging teenage hormones were back in full swing.

For three weeks Chloe and I worked two days a week doing tree work, and nearly every other waking moment on my house. Dylan and Maggie gave us a hand loading and transporting the harvested shiplap planks out to the boathouse where we stacked huge piles of them beneath the awning. Dylan stuck around and helped us hang some shiplap in the loft, but he'd lost interest by the end of the day. From that point on it was just Chloe and me.

The building inspector had stopped by to inspect the wiring and plumbing, both of which met code, and gave me the go-ahead to finish my walls—something I was already in the process of doing much to his dismay.

By the end of the third week, we'd completely covered the walls and ceiling with shiplap and laid my main floor. Although I'd originally planned to repurpose the oak hardwood flooring from my grandparents' place, I traded it to Jeff for a half pallet of five-inch-wide dark chocolate colored hardwood flooring. He'd even delivered it for me, but I suspect he used it as an excuse to see Maggie.

The work was grueling, and every part of my body hurt. My arms and hands trembled from hours of working a heavy nail gun. My neck and shoulders ached so badly I'd had to inch my way out of bed each morning. But after Chloe and I finally nailed the last piece of hardwood in place just after lunch, I stood and dragged the back of my gloved hand across my sweaty forehead. "I refuse to do another lick of work the rest of the weekend."

"Same here," Chloe said, setting her heavy nail gun on the floor. "I'm beat."

Together, we unplugged all the power tools and battery chargers from the extension cords leading to the generator. The noisy machine, once so loud outside the back door, was now muffled by insulated walls. Our voices sounded different here, too. They no longer echoed. The framed shell that had once made the place feel so lonely had been transformed into a cozy nest of wood and insulation. Looking up at the loft that now had a finished floor, I could envision two small beds on either side of the dressing table my grandfather had built.

"It's awesome, isn't it?" Chloe said as she surveyed the loft with me. "That round window really sets off the space."

"It does. I can't wait to put beds up there."

"You'll need stairs first," she said.

"Yeah, I'm eager to see how much storage we can incorporate under the stairs. I'll need every inch possible."

"We can brainstorm with Maggie. I don't suppose I need to warn you, but Maggie isn't going to be able to control herself when it comes time to decorate your place."

"I'm counting on it. I'll welcome all the help I can get." I released a weary sigh. "I'm so tired I don't think I have the energy to shower tonight. I can't imagine lifting my arms long enough to wash my hair."

"Same here." For a moment we stood quietly, both of us surveying our work and how different the place looked with walls. "This old wood is going to be beautiful once it's stained or painted. It'll change the entire look of the place." She hooked my elbow and pulled me outside where we collapsed on chairs. "We are officially off duty for the next two days. All we're going to do is eat and sleep."

"I hurt too much to sleep."

She reached into her cooler and retrieved two bottles. "Think you can lift your arm to drink a beer?"

"It's the only thing that could entice me to do so."

A cold beer at the end of a hot, sweaty workday is therapeutic. Something about the effervescent brew arouses the taste buds, cools the throat, and is incredibly soothing.

While we cooled off, we watched the guy from the power company install a meter for my house. By the time we'd opened our second beer, Maggie had joined our party.

She stopped, tilted her head, and gave us a thorough inspection. "You two look awful."

"Thank you," I said. "You look gorgeous as always."

Helping herself to a beer, she opened it and took a sip. "What's he doing?" she asked, gesturing to the meter guy who was on the phone.

"Hopefully hooking up my power," I replied.

After he'd finished his call and did whatever was required to "energize the line" according to him, he announced that I now had power.

Chloe, Maggie, and I whooped and raised our beer bottles in a toast to a man who will forever be my hero. "Thank you, Mr. Meter Man," I said.

He laughed and bowed, his tool belt jangling, but his eyes were riveted on Maggie.

"I don't think my house is the only thing that guy wants to energize," I whispered, which set us all off.

But the meter guy just picked up his remaining tools, then casually made his way to his van. Giving us a final wave, and Maggie a final looking over, he drove away.

Maggie braced one hand on the back of a chair and gazed at my house as if she'd already forgotten about the meter guy. "Jeez, Kate, you'll be able to turn on lights tonight."

I released a dreamy sigh. "I could if I had any lamps or light bulbs."

"I can help with those things," Chloe said. "I've got some in the basement I don't need."

"Chloe, between your barn full of equipment and your basement full of used furniture, you've saved me literally thousands of dollars. I truly can't accept any more. You've helped too much already. But thank you." I clicked my bottle against hers then Maggie's. "Here's to you, my beautiful, generous, amazing friends."

"I've got your first housewarming gift in my truck," Maggie said.

My eyebrows lifted, the only part of me that was still able to move without pain. "I don't recall housewarming gifts being part of my building plan."

"Well, it's part of mine. I brought paint, trays, rollers, and brushes. Guess what we're doing tomorrow?"

"Argh! Maggie, I could kiss you and kill you right now, but I'm too tired to do either."

"You'll feel better tomorrow." She nudged my chair with her leg. "Show me what you guys got done this week."

I looked to Chloe for help. "Tell her I'm too tired to get up. Tell her we're taking the weekend off. Tell her to go away."

"We're taking the weekend off. Go away," Choe said in a monotone that made Maggie laugh.

"Get-up-get-up-get-up!" she said, rocking my chair with a hip bump. "Come on, I'm dying to see what you've done."

With a low groan, Chloe and I pushed ourselves to our feet and slogged inside with Maggie leading the way.

She squealed with delight. "This looks amazing, you guys." Turning slowly, she inspected every inch of the place. By the time her gaze returned to mine, her eyes were alive with excitement. "I'm begging you to let me help decorate this place."

"No begging necessary," I said, leaning my aching back against the wall. "Consider the place yours."

"What colors are you going to use in here?" she asked. "I brought white paint because that will work as a good first coat no matter what color you want to finish with. But I'd go with something light to contrast with that gorgeous hardwood floor and the overhead beams."

"I have no idea what to use."

"Once the walls are painted white, you'll know what's going to work."

"That might not be for a week or so," I said. "I'm too sore and exhausted to work for a couple of days."

"Well, I'm not. If you don't mind, I'll come over tomorrow and start painting."

Thunderstruck, I stared at her. "I thought you didn't do this sort of work."

"Painting walls is a lot different than building them. I'm a badass when it comes to painting."

"Then by all means the house is yours. Just please don't start before nine tomorrow."

Laughing, she hooked her arms around Chloe and me and guided us back to our chairs. We'd seen each other on and off over the last three weeks, but we'd all been busy with projects and hadn't really had an evening of just hanging out.

"I'm a little surprised Ashe hasn't been around to help," Maggie said, settling into her chair, her legs stretched out and crossed at the ankles.

"I probably scared him off when he saw me naked."

Maggie's eyes rounded and she exchanged a look with Chloe.

Chloe lifted a hand to block Maggie's accusatory stare. "It's the first I've heard about this," she said, "but I definitely want to know the story."

Intentionally keeping them in suspense, I put my empty bottle in the cardboard container with the other empties and opened my second beer. "I'd just finished taking a bath in the lake when Ashe came rolling in. To say we were both shocked is an understatement."

Maggie slapped the arm of her chair. "These things aren't supposed to happen unless I'm around to witness them."

"Yeah, having Ashe's sister there would have surely made things less awkward," I said drolly.

Chloe's laughter bubbled up and out like a foaming beer bottle. "I can imagine Ashe's face when he saw you."

Maggie shook her head and eyed me with affection. "Kate, life is so much more fun with you around."

Chloe reached over and pulled my lopsided ponytail. "I couldn't agree more. You're the best, Katie-poo."

"How did I live without you two?" I asked. They might have thought I was kidding but I wasn't. Life before I'd reunited with them seemed so ... gray and oppressive. "You should know I'm going to ask your brother to come back," I told Maggie. "I need someone to hook up my lights and ceiling fan. I'm going to have him install a camera out front too so people can't sneak up on me."

"That's probably a good idea," Maggie said.

"Believe it or not, it was Ashe's idea."

SINCE ASHE HAD SUGGESTED the camera, I texted and asked him to purchase the unit and charge me for the whole job because I had no idea what to buy. He agreed and arrived on Wednesday afternoon with an outdoor camera. He didn't seem to feel at all awkward about our previous encounter at the lake, so I couldn't help teasing him a little.

"I've been wondering if you'd recovered from your shock of seeing me skinny-dipping," I said, trying to break the ice. "I hope you didn't need therapy after that because I don't have homeowners insurance yet."

I was rewarded with his grin. "I was ... pleasantly surprised, not shocked." Resting his elbow on the stone pylon, his smile faded. "Kate, I thought you might be upset with me for intruding on your privacy, so I've stayed away. Can't say I've enjoyed it though."

"Then don't stay away." I gestured for him to follow me. "Come out and see what Chloe and I have done in the house while you've been off gallivanting."

"Let me finish this first."

I waited for him to mount the camera on top of one pylon and angle it so I'd be able to see both vehicle and driver should anyone pull in. After helping me download the app to my phone and showing me how to navigate the app, he tested it by walking between the pylons, causing the app on my phone to beep. I could see his image clearly on my phone and even hear him talking.

"This is definitely worth whatever you're charging me."

"No charge," he said. "It's the least I can do to apologize for intruding on you."

"That's not necessary. It was just a ... a thing."

"So is this," he said, dismissing my argument about paying him. "Come on and show me what you've done in your house."

"We'll argue about your payment later," I said, heading toward his vehicle.

We drove out in his van, talking easily as we'd done before the *incident*. Sinatra was curled up in a chair under the awning when we pulled up. He lifted his head, saw it was me, then tucked his nose under one paw and went back to sleep.

I opened the door and gestured for Ashe to go in before me.

He stopped just inside the door, his gaze slowly circling the house as he took in the shiplap walls, hardwood floor, and finished loft. "You and Chloe have been busy." As he walked around, he looked deep in thought.

"Did we miss something or mess up somewhere?" I asked, growing apprehensive.

"Not at all," he said. "You did a great job here. I was just thinking about your light fixtures. You said you wanted recessed lights in the kitchen, right?"

I nodded. "I'd planned to use some of the tin plating from the old house for my ceiling, but I've decided to sell it all and just use beadboard."

"That'll look great and be easier to install." He turned and eyed the cathedral ceiling in the living room. "Do you have a ceiling fan picked out yet?"

"Not one I can afford," I said. "I suspect I'll be using lamps in my living room for a long time. I need other things like a kitchen and bathroom and stairs to the loft."

"But you don't need walls or a floor or a roof now," he said, reminding me how far I'd come. "You'll get there, Kate, and when you do this place is going to be spectacular." He returned to the kitchen and spent a couple minutes checking the overhead wiring. "The beadboard is going to have to be cut around the recessed lights, so why not let me put it up for you? I can do it all in two or three hours."

"That's music to my ears, but I can't afford the added expense."

"No charge." He must have seen the suspicion in my eyes because he said, "Really, Kate. It's a small area to cover. It'll be just as easy and efficient for me to do it while installing the light canisters."

If he put up the ceiling, I could help Maggie with the painting.

"All right," I said, "but I plan to compensate you somehow for all of this. Especially if you'd be willing to do the utility room and bath-room ceilings too."

He laughed and eyed me as if I'd intentionally manipulated him. "Not a problem."

Chapter Thirty-Two

W hile Ashe installed the kitchen ceiling and lighting, I inspected the appliances in the camper again and decided I didn't want them. A small cooktop was all I'd need for cooking, at least short term. And the sink in the camper was so small it wasn't worth the effort to repurpose it.

But the deep laundry tub in my grandmother's shed would give me a place to wash dishes, launder my clothes, and wash up until I could afford a shower. Although a cast iron washtub would be worth some money, they were ungodly heavy, so I was vastly relieved to see that the tub was plastic. The faucet was old and corroded, but the knobs turned, so I assumed it worked. I spent the morning disassembling the tub and plumbing, then headed out the lake trail to see if Ashe would help me cart the tub out to my place.

I found him lying on his back with his legs dangling over the edge of the dock.

"You aren't dead, are you?" I asked, giving him a nudge with the toe of my ratty sneaker.

A warm chuckle rumbled in his chest. "I'm sleeping. Go away."

"This is prime real estate and docking rates are expensive here. Move out, sailor."

"Your prime real estate is in need of repair."

"Are you serious?"

"Yep. Some of these planks need replacing." He rapped the knuckles of one hand against a weathered deck board.

Exhausted, I flopped down and sat beside him. "I'll be a hundred years old before I can finish my house and repair everything here. I don't know how my grandfather managed all of this."

Jackknifing to a sitting position, Ashe gestured to a warped section of the dock. "It's just a few boards, Kate. The rest of the dock looks good. I've finished installing your kitchen ceiling and lighting, so I can fix the dock if you like. I'm not doing anything this weekend."

"Hmm ... is finding more work here your way of angling for a dinner date?"

"Is it working?"

"Only because I'm hungry and we'll be in public. Chloe and I are meeting Maggie at the park later. You're welcome to join us."

"Then it's a date," he said. "I'll pick you up at seven."

"No, Ashe, it's just a few friends getting together for a night out. And I'll ride with Chloe."

For a moment he looked at me, then a slow grin climbed his cheek. "Are you saying we're friends?"

"If you'll help me haul the laundry tub from my grandmother's house and carry it inside, then yes, we're friends."

"All right, but you'd better wear your dancing shoes tonight."

I glanced down at my tissue thin, duct taped, mud-covered sneakers. "These are my dancing shoes."

His laughter skipped across the lake, then he hauled me into his muscular arms and gave me a kiss so hot it scorched the dock beneath me.

FOUR HOURS after Ashe helped me transport the laundry tub and hook it up in the bathroom, I still felt jittery. It was just a kiss, I kept telling myself. He hadn't even lingered over it. He'd just laid one on me, gotten to his feet, and gone about his business as if nothing had happened. But the thrill of that kiss was still thrumming through me as if I'd been plugged into Chloe's generator.

She was going to be here soon, and I was still dithering over what to wear. There would be music and dancing in the park tonight. I hadn't danced since college. And I certainly hadn't worn anything as revealing as my consignment store sundress since my college days.

I tugged at the hem, wishing I had a mirror. The dress felt too short. Looking down at my naked legs exposed to mid-thigh, I waffled. My logical brain tried to convince me I was just as exposed in shorts. But my body felt safer when zipped and buttoned in my ratty jean shorts. As I hurried to the bathroom to brush my teeth in the laundry tub sink that now had running water, thanks to Ashe, I felt the soft fabric of my dress swish across my thighs. Maybe I should change ...

I dithered. I brushed. I spit. Bending over the sink to rinse my mouth, and feeling cool air circle my thighs, is when I decided to wear my jeans.

I wore the boots though.

When Chloe arrived, she nearly whooped with joy when she saw me wearing a shirt with rolled sleeves and tied at the waist, and my best jeans tucked into stylish cowboy boots. "You look amazing. Ashe is going to love seeing your hair down. There's hope for you yet," she said, giving me a thorough looking over.

Her unexpected quip caught me off guard. That she was trying to joke when facing one of the hardest transitions of her widowhood left me speechless with admiration. A night out for dinner and drinks with close friends was one thing. A night out at a town festival with music and dancing, without her partner, was quite another.

"Well, thank you for the backhanded compliment, Chloe, but I didn't dress for Ashe or anyone else tonight. I dressed for comfort and to please myself. And that's how I intend to roll, as my girls would say. Now quit stalling." I slipped my arm around her and turned her toward the door. "Let's get this over with, shall we?"

As we rode into town in Chloe's SUV, we could hear the band playing in the park. Surprised to hear popular music from my generation, I asked, "Are the oldies bands playing first?"

"I think it's just two bands playing tonight, and I believe they both play hits from several decades. At least that's how it worked last year."

Last year. When Josh was alive. When they'd likely danced in the park together.

"We can turn around, Chloe," I said softly. "If this is going to be too painful for you, we can go back to my place."

For a moment, she said nothing. Then she inhaled hard and shook her head. "I have to do this. I promised Dylan a dance tonight."

"He's going to be there?" I leaned forward a bit, forcing her to look at me. "You are one courageous woman. Truly, Chloe, I'm in awe of you."

"It's not courage that's bringing me here. It's love for my son. Dylan needs to see that I'm moving forward with life so he can feel free to do the same. I can't let my grief hold him back or make him feel responsible for me." I thought about that while Chloe parked the SUV, but before we got out, she laid her hand on my forearm. "Thank you for coming with me tonight. I'm not sure I could actually do this without you, and it would kill me to not be here for Dylan."

"Of course," I said, as if I were sure of myself and my ability to be her rock or her crutch or whatever she needed me to be. But the truth was I felt intimidated. I hadn't been to an event like this, or any sort of festival, nor had I danced since before the girls were born. Because, according to the brand of faith Dan practiced and preached, and I'd passively ascribed to, dancing could lead to sinful thoughts or sinful deeds. Well, so could a glance between two people sitting in church. Such nonsense.

"I suppose we should get out," Chloe said, breaking into my anguished thoughts.

I exited the vehicle, but she stopped in the middle of the street, as if her feet wouldn't move. For a moment, she took in the crowd, the park filled with string lights, and the sounds and smells of a festival in full swing. "Doing this without Josh sure gives Independence Day a new meaning."

There wasn't one thing I could say to that, so I simply waited for her to decide whether we were going in or going back.

To her credit, she got herself moving again. It took several minutes to navigate through the milling crowd and make our way to where we were to meet Maggie. Person after person greeted Chloe and told her how lovely it was to see her out and about again. It had happened when we were out for lunch or dinner too, but on those occasions it had been one or two people. Now, I cringed every time a well-meaning acquaintance approached her one after another. Although she thanked them and did her best to offer a smile, I could see she was dying inside.

Like an offensive lineman protecting his quarterback, I intercepted and diverted everyone heading our way wearing a smile on their face and zeroing in on Chloe. Wrangling her through the crowd to the relative safety of our friends, we both sighed with relief when we saw Maggie waving at us.

She and Ashe and Bobbie Jo had already claimed an octagon-shaped picnic table for us near the bandstand. As we approached, a curious expression crossed their faces. I glanced around wondering what they were looking at, then Chloe nudged me in the ribs. "They're looking at you, Kate."

"Why?" I asked, afraid that my zipper was open.

"Because you look different, and frankly amazing, with your hair down."

I hadn't thought much about it, but the truth was I felt different with it down. In my former life, I'd styled my hair in a straight long bob. But I no longer had a blow dryer or a flat iron. I didn't even have a mirror. I'd let my hair dry in the Adirondack air, then finger-combed the waves, hoping it didn't look too messy. I hadn't had a hair cut in nearly five months, and it now fell just below my shoulder blades.

Maggie caught my hand, pumping it in a hearty handshake. "Hi, I'm Chloe's friend Maggie. Pleased to meet you."

"Ha-ha," I said, making a face at her, hoping my cheeks weren't as blazing red as they felt. But Ashe's appreciative wink raised my temperature another few degrees, and I began to sweat.

"I'll grab you ladies a drink. Beer? Wine?" he asked, unfolding his athletic body as he stepped away from the table.

My stomach flipped as if I'd just traversed a peak on a roller coaster track.

"Beer," we both said.

As he started to pass by me, he leaned close to my ear and said, "You owe me a dance, gorgeous."

I did. But I didn't trust myself to get that close to him. "Sorry, my dance card is full."

He just laughed and walked away.

So began my night. Feeling like a fish out of water, I tried to keep my balance for Chloe's sake. As much as I wanted to, I couldn't rush back to the SUV and head home. She needed to be here for her son. And I needed to be here for her.

Bobbie Jo and Maggie hit the dance floor before Chloe and I sat down. Bobbie Jo with her silver blonde hair swinging around her waist, jewelry flashing in the lights strung across the park and those that lit the stage, and Maggie with her coppery mane and stunning smile were riveting. The crowd loved them. But the thing about my friends that anchored my attention was how free they seemed to be. I could see them talking and laughing and dancing with each other, and how easily they included those around them, and all of it seemed as natural to them as breathing.

How could I have let Dan convince me, and tell our girls, that dancing was sinful? The only time and place my girls had been free to physically express their joy and youthful exuberance in such a manner had been when Dan wasn't home. Now, I felt so ashamed that I'd participated in squelching something so natural and joyous in my beautiful girls, I had to fight back tears.

"We all used to be like that," Chloe said, noticing me watching Bobbie Jo and Maggie.

"Do you think it's possible to get back to that place?" I asked. "It feels like another lifetime to me."

"I don't know," she said, and after a moment, she shrugged. "Right now, I can't imagine it."

I nodded because I understood. And I didn't want to go back. I did, however, want to move forward to a place where I could breathe again without the weight of my past riding on my shoulders.

All I could think about were my daughters trapped in Dan's oppressive world. I wanted to rush back and rescue them, to show them there was another way of living life, of spreading love and kindness and helping others. I'd always been there for my family, but I'd given more of myself, more freely and wholeheartedly, in the short time I'd been here than I'd given to others in all the years I'd been a pastor's wife. I wanted my girls to know the kind of freedom that Bobbie Jo and Maggie knew, but I feared my daughters were too indoctrinated by now to diverge from the path Dan and I had set them on. Perhaps not Haley. But Kara was following the strict code of cutting ties with those who were luked-out or a lost cause. I was a lost cause. And her silence made it clear on which side her allegiance fell.

Ashe returned with our drinks and took a seat on the opposite side of the table. Maggie and Bobbie Jo returned a couple minutes later, and we sank into easy conversation. Bobbie Jo told us about her plan to expand the back deck of the brewery so she could close it in and still offer outside seating during the winter months and open it back up during the warm weather. She asked how my house was coming along, and the four of us filled her in on what we'd been doing. Our conversation wound like a river through a valley, carrying us along as we bounded through a myriad of topics and lost track of time.

The sound of Neil Diamond's "Sweet Caroline" caught everyone's attention. It boomed from the stage and swept across the park like a wave, the happy melody lifting every person in its wake like boats on a river. Those who couldn't get to their feet danced in their chairs. Chloe's son stepped up behind her, swept his arms around her, and swung her onto the lawn as if he were Kevin Bacon in "Footloose." It was so dramatic and funny, and Chloe's reaction was so surprised as she landed on her feet, I couldn't help laughing.

That's when I felt myself being swept from my seat and into a mad crush of happy, dancing, singing people. As I tried to gain my balance, Ashe gave me a twirl that made me teeter on my boot heels. I grabbed his shoulders to steady myself—and he circled his strong arms around my waist.

"You just stole a dance from one of my suitors," I said loudly, trying to talk above hundreds of joyfully singing people. The volume rivaled Dan's Sunday evening service.

"Might as well rip up your dance card because I intend to steal them all," Ashe said, giving me a spin that sent me out two steps before he reeled me right back into his arms.

I wanted to be as graceful and skilled as the hundreds of people around me, all of whom seemed to not only know the swing-line-whatever-it-was dance but also every word to the song. But I felt awkward and stiff, my body still clenched in its Christian crouch. Flushing with embarrassment—and burning from the feel of Ashe's body brushing against mine—I considered bailing out of the crush and taking refuge at the picnic table. But I saw Chloe toughing it out, keeping her chin up, pasting on a smile, as she danced with her son. She was doing what it took to set him free.

I needed to do whatever it took to stand by my friend.

Drawing me against him, Ashe said, "No copping out or trying to duck away during our dance."

I tried to relax, accepting that I'd be finishing the dance, but there was no relaxing in Ashe's arms. "I guess I do owe you a dance ... and at least one beer."

His smile faded, and he pulled me close. "Kate, you owe *yourself* this dance."

The fact that he knew this about me made me feel as exposed as I'd felt standing naked on the beach. I didn't want him to know these things. His observation was too personal. Despite my hormonal reaction to him, all I wanted was friendship. It's all I could handle. It's all I could allow.

As if he knew I was teetering on bolting, he kept his embrace loose and his mouth closed.

Surrounded by a crush of dancing, singing people shouting, *So good! So good! So good!* I tried to embrace the moment, the energy of the crowd, the feeling of my body moving in a way it hadn't moved in decades. I felt as if my joints had rusted and needed to be oiled and broken free.

"Relax, Kate."

As I tried to keep time with the music, I did my best to ease the tension in my body and avoid locking eyes with Ashe. I looked everywhere but at his gorgeous face.

That's when I saw my sister.

My steps faltered, and Ashe steadied me.

A short distance away, Sophie was laughing and dancing, her beautiful hair bouncing around her shoulders, her eyes sparkling ... I saw flashes of my little sister in the woman she'd become ... I wanted to walk over and pull her into my arms and just hug her forever, but I'd ruined enough of Sophie's life. I wasn't going to ruin this night for her when she seemed so happy.

As the song ended, Ashe relaxed his arms, and I slipped from his embrace.

As if seeking a buoy to hold onto, Chloe appeared at my side. "Are you going to go over and say hello?" she asked, gesturing toward Sophie.

Every cell in my body longed to go to my little sister, but I squashed down the longing like dirty clothes in a hamper. This wasn't the time or place. I wanted Sophie to enjoy her night with her friends and her family. *Our* family, I reminded myself. If I ever hoped to be a part of it again, I knew I'd have to write that letter. The one I'd been putting off writing to Sophie because I had no idea how to begin to apologize or to explain or to justify my choices that had hurt her so deeply.

"Actually, Chloe, if you don't mind, I'm ready to go home."

She seemed to deflate with relief. "I was hoping you'd say that."

We told Ashe and Dylan, who were still standing with us, we were leaving, then we slipped through the crowd without saying goodbye to anyone else. Neither of us wanted to risk getting waylaid when all we wanted to do was escape the crush and noise and the pressure of trying to keep a smile on our faces while we were slowly dying inside.

Chapter Thirty-Three

F or three weeks, Maggie, Chloe, and I worked on my house. Maggie and I got the painting done. The white walls and ceiling made the place a bright, beautiful space and was a perfect contrast to the dark wood beams and posts.

Ashe built the stairs and created a hidden clothes closet underneath. He'd also ingeniously created three concealed drawers in the three lowest steps. Then he helped me cart my old iron bed up to the loft.

Despite my protest, Chloe had brought over two table lamps she'd retrieved from her basement, and had Dylan help her deliver the futon. With those items, and a couple cobbled together boards to make end tables and a coffee table, I was able to set up a cozy living room.

"It's beginning to look like a real home," Chloe said at the end of a long day. We'd worked three days that week doing excavating and landscaping work, all of it backbreaking but financially rewarding, and the other two days working on my house.

Chloe and I hadn't talked about the night of the festival because, well, we didn't need to. We knew the only thing either of us could do was to continue putting one foot in front of the other. Rebuilding our lives was like hiking the forty-six peaks of the Adirondacks. Sometimes it was a day hike. At other times it was like summiting Mount Marcy. But every day was like walking a deer path through the wilderness with no trail markers.

I'd been using my early morning hours to work on my book—and Sophie's letter. I'd finished the letter this morning and needed to mail it. But just thinking about sending the letter made my stomach queasy.

"All you need now are kitchen appliances," Chloe said, wiping her hands on the bottom of an old T-shirt she was wearing.

"Yep. And cupboards and countertop, and bathroom fixtures, and a washer and dryer, and ..." I let my sentence trail off with a light laugh. "I think I've saved enough to buy a kitchen sink, faucets, and a hot plate."

Leaning one shoulder against the painted shiplap wall, Chloe took a long look around. "It's amazing how much you've gotten done on a shoestring. You should write a book about it."

"Yeah, I'll do that right after I finish the book I'm working on. And don't forget, I still haven't paid you for my roofing materials, so ..."

Chloe flapped her hand at me. "I wish you'd forget about that, Kate. You did me a favor getting all that stuff out of my barn."

"I can't do that, and you know it. But thanks."

She scrunched her nose but didn't argue with me. "Think I'll head home for the night. Need anything else before I go?" she asked.

It was Friday night, when Maggie and Chloe usually came over, but Maggie had other plans, and Chloe and I were worn out from a week of hard work. "I'm good," I said, giving her a hug. "Enjoy a night of loafing on your sofa."

She returned my hug and stepped back. "And you enjoy your night of loafing on your futon."

"I fully intend to," I said. But I didn't.

I sat outside by the fire and brushed Sinatra. It was a warm evening, and I just wanted to enjoy the breeze and the sound of evening peepers. The house still smelled a little like fresh paint, so I had the windows open to air it out before I headed to bed.

I thought about the letter I'd written to Sophie, and the more I thought about it, the more I worried about it. The last thing I wanted was to make matters worse. But could they get worse?

After a couple minutes of mulling and dithering, I went inside and retrieved the letter from my briefcase. Carrying it back outside, I sat beneath the solar lights strung along the awning and read it for the tenth time.

Dear Sophie,

Do you remember that time the two of us got lost at the southern edge of Papa and Grandma's property? How scared we were, tromping around for hours trying to find the path home, certain each time we saw a landmark it would be the one to guide us back to safety only to find ourselves more lost?

It feels as if I've been wandering for twenty-three years trying to find my way back home—to you. I'd never imagined living my life without you in it. Nor had I imagined getting so turned around I'd lose all compass.

You need to know, Soph, I never planned to stay away. I was just so shell-shocked and lost and in need of a safe place to land after discovering Dad's affair that I sought refuge in the one place I thought I'd be safe. Looking back, I wonder how I'd let myself get sucked in, but I was so broken, Soph. I'd just miscarried my first baby. Did you know I'd gotten pregnant near the end of my freshman year of college? To lose my baby boy in my seventh month was ... well, I was inconsolable. Living a life with Jesus as my comfort and my guide seemed safe, benign, and I was too numb to direct my own life or even question what I believed. I hadn't known that Dan's religion would invade and take over every aspect of my life, that it would systematically shrink my world and cut me off from everyone I loved.

This isn't meant to be an excuse. I just wanted you to know this about me. I feel like someone who has finally escaped a cult. I know many people would take issue with this, but living in Christendom, at least the brand I fell into, was a mind-fuck every minute of every day.

I have been as lost as a person can be, Sophie. I told you the day we were wandering in the woods that I'd keep you safe, that I'd even fight a bear to protect you, but I left you out there alone. I can see that now.

I've finally found my way home—and so much has changed. What hasn't changed, though, is my love for you and how deeply, desperately sorry I am to have deserted you.

Sophie, if you give me another chance to be your big sister, I'll do a better job. I'll do whatever it takes to protect our relationship—even if that means fighting a bear for you.

I have never stopped loving you—and I never will ...

Kate

I folded the letter and slipped it back into the stamped envelope Chloe had given me. All I needed was to pop it in the mail. But I still felt torn about sending it. Had I shared too much? Had I said enough? Would Sophie even read it?

Like the ball in Sinatra's toy that he batted around and around a circular track, my thoughts spun until I leaned my aching head back and closed my eyes. I felt Sinatra land on my lap where he settled in for our nightly snuggle. Eyes still closed, I stroked his neck and back feeling how clean and soft his fur was now. He no longer scratched and gnawed at his body. The ticks and fleas were gone as were the matted sections of fur. Now he soaked up every bit of grooming and attention I gave him.

At some point the two of us must have drifted off, because the ding on my phone surprised me and startled Sinatra. He leapt off my lap and headed out back where he was probably climbing through an open window to hide inside. It was time for me to go inside too, but someone was out front at my gate.

Scooping up my phone, I tapped on my camera app but I'd missed whoever had triggered the camera. I scrolled back a minute and replayed the grainy video. I replayed it twice before I rocketed out of my chair.

Swiping the flashlight app on my phone to life, I headed for the lake trail where I saw my daughter jogging toward me, her own phone flashlight leading the way.

"Kara?" I asked, hardly daring to believe my angry daughter was here.

"Mom!" She threw herself into my arms and burst into tears.

"Sweetie, what's wrong? Is everyone okay? Did something happen?" I asked in a half-panic, but she was sobbing too hard to talk. We stood there, both of us gripping the other, the joy of holding my daughter in my arms again bringing tears to my eyes. But I was terrified that something had happened to her sister. "Is Haley okay?"

Kara nodded.

"Is your father okay?"

She nodded again, but she was tense and shaking, so I simply held her. As she settled down, I slipped my arm around her waist and turned her toward the house. "How did you get here?"

"Uber," she said, sniffing.

I was dumbfounded. "Are you saying you took an Uber all the way here?"

"No," she said, releasing a watery half-laugh. "Just from the airport."

"Well, that makes more sense." I opened the door and guided her toward the futon, feeling proud I could offer her a place to sit. But she stopped just inside, her mouth hanging open.

"Wow ..." Shaking her head, she looked around with bloodshot eyes, her beautiful face soaked with tears. "This is amazing, Mom." Her eyes welled up again and tears rolled down her cheeks. "I'm so sorry I was such a brat about you being here."

"It's all right."

"No, it's not," she said, swiping her fingertips across her cheeks.

"I was only thinking of myself then. I never once considered why you were here."

"Oh, honey, come sit down and tell me what's going on," I said, guiding her the rest of the way to my couch.

"I got a tattoo."

It felt as if I'd shifted dimensions and found myself in another conversation.

"And it got infected."

"Oh my gosh, are you all right?" I knew how bad infections could get—bad enough to kill a person.

"Yeah, I just needed antibiotics for ten days."

"Oookay ..." I said, doing my best to follow my daughter's odd conversation so I could make sense of it. "I'm sorry, baby, but I'm not following why you're so upset."

"Dad found out about the tattoo because I had to go to the doctor for antibiotics."

"Ohhh ..." Things were beginning to fall into place. "I presume he wasn't happy about you getting a tattoo?"

"Not at all." Her lips compressed, and I could tell she was fighting back emotion. "He was livid. Especially when he saw it."

"Why? Is it that big? Or that bad?"

"It's just a floral sprig underlining a name. *Jamie*."

I wanted to ask, but I let Kara continue without interrupting her.

"Dad told me to cover it up until I could get it removed because he didn't want Jonathan or his parents to see it, or anyone else for that matter."

Jonathan was Kara's friend and the young man Dan had taken under his wing and was grooming to become his right hand at some point, but I was still having a difficult time understanding Kara's level of upset.

"I told Dad I didn't have romantic feelings for Jonathan, that we're just friends, but Dad didn't want to hear it. He insists we're perfect for each other and wants us to marry when we graduate so

Jonathan can take over running the church when Dad's ready to retire."

"What?!" I gaped in disbelief.

Kara nodded. "He almost insisted on it. So, I told him I'm in love with Jamie, and that we met in Springfield, and that I plan to go back to Missouri but not to the university." Her gaze dropped to her clenched hands. "Dad told me I'd be staying home if I didn't want to go back to school, and that I'd be marrying a good young man from our church and not some boy I met in Springfield."

"Oh boy ..."

"Yeah," she whispered. "That's when I told him Jamie isn't a boy."

For a moment it didn't register what she was saying. Her eyes met mine, her face filled with trepidation. Then it clicked, and all Kara's anxiety issues over the last several years began to make sense.

"Please don't hate me, Mom."

"Hate you?" I asked, utterly bewildered. "Kara, I could never feel anything but love for you. And I'm truly thrilled that you've followed your heart, sweetheart. That takes tremendous courage. Especially coming from the home you were raised in."

"It feels more like a betrayal," she whispered.

"But it shouldn't," I responded, stroking my palm over her back, feeling her long, soft hair under my work-roughened hands.

She leaned over and hugged me hard for a moment, then sat back. "Dad wants to send me to conversion therapy." She shook her head as if her father were being ridiculous—and he was. "I told Dad you can't convert people from their sexual orientation; that you can only get them to comply with an expected behavior, but I'll never comply with something so inhumane. That's when he exploded." I watched my daughter's face crumple in grief. "He hates me, Mom." During her sobs, she tried to tell me the rest. "He's disgusted with me. He told me I'm perverted, and that I'm an embarrassment to him."

I wanted to kill him.

"Dad says I'm cut off unless I go to conversion therapy. If I don't, he said he'll no longer pay for anything or even recognize me as his daughter."

Rage rolled through me like an earthquake, shaking me to my core as I rocked my daughter in my arms. This was the last straw. I was done with Dan and his abusive beliefs. The time had come for me to return and finalize things—and to make Dan pay for his sins against his daughter.

"I finally understand why you left," Kara said, her voice muffled against my shoulder.

And I finally understood why I was going back.

Chapter Thirty-Four

S tanding in my hotel room near the Charlotte airport, I listened to the distant roar of plane engines and sound of traffic as I adjusted the straps on my sundress. Now that I had access to a full-length mirror in which to see myself for the first time in months, I was looking at a different woman.

A younger, stronger, pissed off woman with surprisingly nice legs.

I arrived last night, checked into my suite, and ordered a five-course meal, all of it being charged to Kara's credit card, which Dan paid each month. Unbeknownst to him, he would also be paying for my flight here and for Kara's flight to Missouri. I refused to let my heartbroken daughter live with a man who had completely lost his humanity. I'd sent her to Missouri to stay with her girlfriend, Jamie, something they'd both wanted. I could hardly wait to share the news with Dan.

In my rage over his treatment of our daughter, I'd mindlessly tossed things in a backpack without much thought. But my subconscious must have been on the job because I was dressed for battle. I pulled on my boots, grabbed my backpack, and headed to the lobby to meet my Uber driver. As the miles ticked by, he remained quiet and left me to my thoughts. I felt my resolve building with each rotation of the tires, and by the time we pulled up in front of Dan's church campus, I was laser focused on my mission.

I entered the large foyer where two ushers stood guard, ready to welcome and assist parishioners or to turn away troublemakers like me. I knew both men who were high ranking members in the church, and they knew me, but their expressions of utter surprise suggested they barely recognized me. They'd obviously been warned about me because they seemed awkward and indecisive about how to handle me. I couldn't let them put me out before I'd done what I'd come here to do. I greeted them warmly, wearing a big smile to disarm them.

It worked. I sailed by with a friendly wave and continued through the lobby.

As I made my way toward the auditorium where I knew Dan would be holding Sunday morning service, the most attended service of the week, I passed the bookstore where he sold Bibles and other merchandise like T-shirts, mugs, and Bible covers with his logo stamped prominently on everything. The aroma of coffee beckoned me toward the café as I passed, but I'd timed my arrival to the minute, and I wasn't going to miss my cue. Not even for a cup of the city's best coffee.

The auditorium was a huge place with multiple entrance doors that ushers with headsets were now quietly closing. I could hear the Praise Team whipping the congregation into a frenzy. I knew Dan would now be taking the platform at a brisk stride, reveling in the attention like an actor taking the stage. In my mind's eye, I could see his wide, practiced smile, one hand raised as he acknowledged the congregation with a nod and a wave. He oozed charisma, and all eyes would be riveted on him. This was his theater, and he was their star actor.

With my backpack hooked over one bare shoulder, I positioned myself at the center door. Inhaling a deep breath, I thought about Kara's tearstained face and broken heart, and how Dan had made his little girl feel perverted for something as natural as loving another human being. I wanted to hurt him, to kick him in the balls and slam his fucking Bible over his head to wake him up.

As the music ended, I grabbed hold of the metal handle and yanked on the large door, flinging it open with all the force I could manage. It banged against the wall, rattling the crash bar, and startling the ushers who were standing just inside the entrance. Every head in the congregation turned to see what happened. Dan stopped mid-sentence, a scowl on his face as he squinted to see who had dared to interrupt his act.

I counted three seconds before he recognized me. Then his jaw dropped.

The congregation seemed to gasp in unison, and whispers rolled across the auditorium like a growing wave.

Their reaction was exactly what I'd hoped for. Releasing a hard breath, I unleashed my inner demon and headed down the main aisle as if the Devil himself were escorting me. The heels of my stylish cowboy boots thudded with each determined step, and I felt my sundress slap the back of my thighs just shy of my ass. I was tanned and toned from all the hard work I'd been doing, and my hair was unbound and bouncing around my bare shoulders. I felt the lustful looks from the men and the scathing looks from the ladies, and I smiled and let them look.

Dan stumbled over his words, something I'd never witnessed before. His camera crew didn't seem to know where to aim their cameras. Since the pandemic, Dan had been streaming his services to the local television station, his You-Tube channel, and Facebook to monetize the service. With attendance down during that time, he'd even had an app set up for tithing. It had been so successful he continued to stream every service. But today, he was groping for words. He faked a laugh and tried to excuse my revealing sundress by saying I'd just returned from a sunny vacation visiting family.

Ignoring his disapproval, I turned a full circle to wave to everyone as if I were thrilled to be back. I swear Dan moaned, as if he'd forgotten his mic was on. Good, I wanted to bring the whole damn place down on his head.

But like a seasoned actor, he started his sermon, desperately trying to regain the attention of several thousand congregants while I finished my red-carpet strut and took a seat in the front row. The auditorium seats were richly upholstered padded chairs, connected in long rows. This was where I'd sat with our girls when we were all a family. But my girls weren't here. According to Kara, Haley had witnessed the blowup with their father, and she was disgusted with him. She'd dropped Kara at the airport, then headed out to meet up with friends at a trailhead so she could hike the Appalachian Trail with them as she'd wanted to do.

I sat alone now because I'd chosen to leave this life. And Dan was alone because he'd chosen his bogus faith instead of his family. He'd better hope his god had his back today because I was crouched and ready to fight tooth and claw for my daughter.

The Trifecta, Judy, Carol, and Darlene were huddled up whispering, each of them wearing an appalled expression and casting disapproving glances in my direction. Then, as one unit, they rose and scurried out a side door together, probably to team up with their husbands, two of whom were the ushers in the lobby. I knew what they were doing. They were strategizing how to build a hedge of protection around Dan. But I wondered why Dan's god couldn't handle things on his own. There would be no doubt in their minds that the Devil had taken hold of me, which meant the Devil was in their house, and they would call upon every prayer-warrior here to pray me out of church.

From the pulpit, Dan was doing his best to oust me. "As I'm seeking the Lord's guidance and direction this morning," he began, his voice booming through the auditorium as loud and powerful as if he were a god himself. "I'm being led by the Holy Spirit that someone in this room needs to hear this message today about the dangers of being unequally yoked."

And there it was. I saw Dan's slight hand signal to the tech crew, and a second later the theater-sized screens on both sides of the stage went dark. Another soft gasp swept through the room at this unexpected event. Dan was changing up his sermon, and that meant the sermon notes he'd prepared were no longer relevant. This sermon was directed at me.

Several high-ranking congregants cast side-eyed glances in my direction, all of them looking apprehensive and uncomfortable, as if uncertain what to expect from Dan—or from me.

Dan stood behind the glass lectern, droning on about the dangers of couples who are unequally yoked. If they don't share the same beliefs, then they are unequally yoked. And it's the responsibility of the one who believes to guide the other one back to the righteous path or to part ways with the sinner.

Dan was laying the foundation for excommunicating me from the church. A wasted effort on his part because I'd chosen to leave. He was building a justifiable reason for divorcing me. Did that mean he was preparing to sign the divorce papers? Was that why he was in front of the congregation, a righteous believer standing in the light of his god, figuratively pointing the accusing finger at me, laying the blame for everything at my feet? As he whipped the congregation into a righteous fury, he conducted an altar call. He called for all wayward souls to heed the call back to salvation, to march their sinful selves to the altar and repent and ask forgiveness.

He was talking to me.

But I wasn't answering his fucking call.

For the first time since I'd entered the auditorium, Dan's gaze didn't skitter away from mine. Instead, he looked down his arrogant nose at me, as if the power of his faith could protect him, and he proclaimed it was his responsibility to call out us sinners by name if we refused to answer the call.

I looked back at him without flinching—and I smiled. *If you really want to do this, Dan ...*

He shrank like a balloon losing air, then swept his gaze across the congregation. To my shock and outrage, he called out a woman who'd continued dating a non-believer after being warned it was an unsanctioned union because they were not equally yoked.

I heard the poor woman's horrified gasp two sections away,

then witnessed her stumble toward a side door in tears, her sobs echoing in the deafening silence as she left. The door banged closed behind her, the ushers too shocked to catch the door. But Dan had succeeded in expelling her from his church. According to him, they had prayed her out. He'd stated it with immense pride, as if they'd accomplished something amazing instead of the vile act it was.

My heart banged in my chest. This wasn't the first time I'd seen someone bullied and prayed out of church or witnessed this appalling side of my husband.

Dan had done it to his own brother.

Although I wanted to follow the ostracized woman out of the auditorium, I forced myself to remain the final five minutes while Dan finished the service. I refused to give him a reprieve for a single second.

As soon as he'd bid everyone a good day, the band lit up the room with an uplifting song to send the congregants out into the world where they could spread the Good Word—all of it lies and bullshit. Dan popped off the stage, hurried over to where I stood waiting, and pretended to place a chaste kiss on my cheek. But it was a cover for his fierce whisper warning me not to make any more of a scene.

"Then I suggest you get me out of here now. We need to get some things straight about your treatment of our daughter, and I intend to get some things from the house."

"You're not taking anything from the house," he hissed, "and my relationship with our girls is not your business."

"You're wrong on both counts, Dan, but if you prefer to do this here, I'm sure the council members would be interested to hear about your disgusting scene with our daughter."

Eyes flashing with anger, he pasted on a fake smile, slung one arm around my shoulders and rushed me out a side door. Once in the hall, he released me with a disgusted grunt. We walked to an exit door and went outside to where he parked his car. He was so pissed, and I was so sick at heart over what had just happened to the poor woman in church—and to our daughter—that neither of us spoke a word during the five minutes it took to reach the house.

When we pulled in, I felt an immediate aversion, as if someone were pressing a pillow over my face.

Dan got out, slammed the door, and headed inside without a word to me.

I followed, but when I got inside, he'd already disappeared into the bowels of the house. I knew where I'd find him though. I stalked into his studio to find him pacing.

He wheeled around to face me, eyes flashing with rage. "All right. Let's get this over with. What do you want?" he asked, ice coating his voice.

"I want a divorce and for you to stop being an asshole to our daughters."

His eyebrows raised. "You abandon them and have the nerve to tell me how to treat our daughters?"

His comment pierced my heart, but I couldn't allow him to flip or redirect the conversation. I was here for a purpose, and I wanted to get it accomplished as quickly as possible. "I hardly think I abandoned our nineteen-year-old daughters while they were safely living in dorm rooms at college. I left *you*, Dan, not our girls."

"Semantics." He flicked his hand dismissively and dropped into his chair. He leaned back as if he were bored with me and my theatrics. "They came home, and you were gone. What else were they to think?"

I planted both palms on his massive desk and leaned in so he could see the rage in my eyes. "*You* were the one who hurt our babies. *You* were the one who used them and tried to turn them against me. *You* were the one who made our sweet, beautiful daughter feel perverted and disgusting—and I could *fucking* kill you for that. I mean it, Dan, my hands are on your desk right now to keep them off your throat. How could you say those things to Kara?"

"Because she's a mess, Kate! She thinks she likes girls."

"She does! So what?"

"Well, it's not natural."

"Do you really believe that?" I asked. "Seriously. In your heart, if you still have one, do you really believe that there's something wrong with Kara because of who she loves?"

His mouth opened but he hesitated for a moment. "It doesn't matter what I think. *His* thoughts are above mine."

I laughed. "Don't quote that Bronze age scripture crap to me, Dan. That makes as much sense as me saying Harry Potter's thoughts are above mine."

Dan rocked forward in his chair as if to back me off. "*His* thoughts, *God's* thoughts, take priority, always, and it's something you'd do well to remember."

"Is that so?" I asked, noting how Dan's gaze kept dropping to my cleavage. "From the way you're checking out my breasts, I'd say *your* thoughts are taking priority at the moment."

Nostrils flaring, jaw clenched, he glared at me but didn't dispute my statement.

"How could you put your business before our daughter?" I asked quietly, my heart breaking all over again for Kara.

"I have a ministry, not a business, and that means I have a responsibility to my congregants. I can't preach against perverse acts while my daughter claims she's in love with another girl."

"Of course not," I said. "So, you believe it's your duty to put your *business* before your daughter." I snorted in disgust. "I'm not surprised."

"I put my ministry before *everything*, Kate. And, lest you forget, it's that ministry that has provided a good life for our daughters."

"It's a great paying gig, I'll admit, and you've been a good provider for our family. I won't dispute that. But I will not stand by and let you put *anything*, including your job or *your* messed-up beliefs, before the welfare of our beautiful daughters."

"That's not your choice," he said, rising to his feet.

My fingers curled until fists formed and my knuckles turned white. I had to back away. I swear, I could have joyfully choked him at that moment. I knew there'd be no reasoning with him. He was a lost cause, buried so deep in his illusion there was no getting him to see it for what it was. A lie. A story created for the sole purpose of controlling people and their money.

Now on his feet, he stalked toward the door. "Get what you came for and get out."

"I came for my grandmother's ashes." He seemed confused for a moment until I gestured toward his wall safe that was hidden behind a tall bookshelf.

He half scoffed, as if my attachment to her remains was as ridiculous as my attachment to my lawn mower. He believed in an afterlife, and that my grandmother's choice of cremation exempted her from that salvation. I stood mute in the face of his contempt for her ashes, for my feelings, battling a fierce desire to kick him for being so disrespectful and heartless. With a flourish, he slid the bookshelf aside, then blocked my view with one broad shoulder while he punched in a password. When he swung open the door to the safe, I was thunderstruck.

There were stacks of cash filling the safe. He began pulling them out and stacking them on top of the bookcase. "What the hell, Dan? How do you have all that cash?" I asked, truly stupefied as to why he'd hide cash in his personal safe.

"Not your business," he said, continuing to move stacks of twenty, fifty, and one-hundred-dollar bills.

"I suspect you didn't pay taxes on that money—like I had to pay on my property."

He glanced at me over one shoulder, a mix of guilt and pleasure brimming in his eyes.

"That's right, Dan. I paid the delinquent taxes, so I still own the property. I sold the ring you gave me for our twentieth anniversary," I said, deriving a bit of pleasure in revealing that news. "While you've got your safe open, I'd like that money back. In fact, I'll take everything you have there."

"The devil you will," he said, spinning to face me.

"Would you rather I share this information in court while we battle over *all* your assets, since you can't be bothered to sign the divorce papers?"

"There's a hundred grand here!" He raked his hair back, a sign he was highly agitated ... and worried. "I'll give you the property tax money, but that's it."

I cocked my head and pretended to be mentally calculating. "Let's see, I worked about thirty hours a week for at least sixteen years. Even at minimum wage that puts it over three hundred grand. And since you took the RV and are keeping the cars and house and furnishings and your business, and I haven't yet asked for alimony, and then there's the fact of where this cash in your safe came from, I'd say I'm being more than fair," I said, repeating my attorney's words when she'd summarized what I would be entitled to and cautioned me not to be a dumb-ass.

"Kate, I'm warning you ..." Dan clamped his lips together as if to stop himself from spewing a geyser of vitriol at me, but his face was so red I thought he might burst a blood vessel.

I lifted my hands, palms up, and pretended they were a balance scale. "Let's see," I said in a singsong voice, "on this hand, you sacrifice the cash in your safe." I dipped my hand a bit to show the weight of his loss. "But on this hand, I come after half of everything you have plus alimony." I dropped that hand like a lead weight had been added. My other hand responded by popping up as if it held a feather. "Your choice, Dan. One hundred thousand dollars for me and you sign the divorce papers my attorney sent to you. You keep everything else, and I go away."

I must admit, I was a bit unnerved by the venom in his eyes.

Turning back to his safe, he reached to the back and pulled out a package. He thrust the box of ashes at me. "Take this and the money and get out of my life."

"Well, on second thought, how will I explain where all that cash came from?" I asked. "Unlike you, I have to pay taxes on my income, so ..." I shrugged. "I'll take half now and a certified check for the rest."

He began stalking toward me. "Honest to god, Kate, I'm literally fighting the urge to throttle you."

For Dan to use such a sacrilegious expression was so out of character, I knew he was losing his shit—and I was treading a fine line. "Watch it, Dan, you know your outrage is just the Devil causing havoc in your mind."

"It's *you*, Kate!" He backed me against the wall and planted his hands on either side of my head. "Go ahead and push one more button. I dare you."

Oh boy ... I'd found his tipping point. And now that I had him where I wanted him, I ducked beneath his arm and went to his desk.

Plucking a pen from the expensive pewter pen stand on his desk, I tore a couple pieces of paper from a tablet inside his leather binder and began to write. A couple of minutes later, I handed the papers to him. "Since it's obvious by your sermon this morning that we are unequally yoked, and you want to be the one to sue for a divorce so you can justify it to your board and congregation, these bullet points are non-negotiable and had better be included in any divorce paperwork you send to me," I said. "You provide financial support for our daughters through their college years and for future events like their weddings—whether you agree with their choices or not. You advance me fifty thousand dollars against a settlement of one hundred thousand, pocket change for you, and sign this receipt stating I received fifty thousand dollars in *cash* from you."

His cheek was ticking, a sign he was about to blow, but I wasn't finished.

"And finally, Dan, you need to have those divorce papers with every one of these terms included sent to my attorney by the end of next week. I'll leave her card on the table on my way out."

Some people might call me crazy or stupid for walking away from what could surely amount to a large divorce settlement, but I didn't want Dan's money, especially knowing how he'd earned it. But I did want my girls to be able to stay with me without having to cook our meals over a campfire or bathe in the lake or relieve themselves in an outhouse. And I wanted to pay Chloe for the roofing material I'd needed because Dan had taken the RV. And I was damn sure demanding to be reimbursed for the tax monies he hadn't paid. I was going to accept money so I could take care of my girls and my friends. Beyond that, I wanted nothing to do with Dan and his messed-up world.

I wanted my girls.

I wanted my friends.

I wanted my freedom.

That was enough for me.

I CARRIED the money and my grandmother's ashes upstairs to the bedroom I'd shared with Dan only a short time ago. Surprisingly, nothing had been changed in the room, and yet it felt as if I'd never lived here. I suppose I hadn't lived here. I'd existed here as a wife and mother, not as a woman in possession of her life. I'd given my hours and my heart to my family—and my power to my husband and his god.

Still, I was shocked to find everything as I'd left it. I'd assumed Dan would have ripped my clothes from my closet and tossed them in the trash. But they were still there, my skirts, blouses, and dresses hanging in orderly rows, my sweaters stacked in neat piles on the shelves, and my dress shoes displayed neatly in racks. Standing here in my sundress and cowboy boots, it felt as though I were looking through someone else's closet. I took two pairs of jeans, my favorite heavy sweater my daughters had bought for me, and all my jewelry because I could sell it and use the cash to do things for my girls, then placed it all in a suitcase along with the money Dan had reluctantly given me. But everything else here was no longer me. Not the suits or dress shoes, and definitely not the mommy underwear.

At that moment it struck me that I'd once been an old person. I hadn't known it was a real thing until my epiphany in the closet.

But standing here looking at my former life, I knew I'd wound the clock back twenty years by daring to walk away.

I retrieved our old photo albums that we'd accumulated before digital photos and online storage were the norm. I would scan the pics and send the images to Dan so we both had copies. I didn't trust him to do the same, so the albums went into the suitcase.

With a last look around the bedroom, I walked out and closed the door to that part of my life. Leaving my suitcase and the box of ashes in the hall, I went to Kara's room to retrieve the items she'd asked me to get for her.

The instant I opened the door I was torn between laughing and weeping. My messy child had left her bedroom in shambles of course. Discarded clothes were strung across the room. She hadn't made her bed, and the lilac-colored spread hung over the footboard and spilled onto the hardwood floor. The thick area rug beside her bed was littered with lint and books and shoes. Sunlight streamed through the lacy curtains and splashed across her vanity and the desk in the corner of the room, both of which were buried under ... stuff. Lots of it.

The scent of buttered popcorn lingered in the room. I found the empty bowl on her desk where Kara preferred to spend her time working on her computer. Graphic design was her passion, and that's what she wanted to pursue in college, which is why she wanted to switch universities. I hoped my earlier battle with Dan had made it clear he was to support her in that choice.

As I gathered the items she'd asked for, some clothing, a notebook, a couple of flash drives, and the keys and title to her vehicle, memories rolled by like passing cars on a train. At two-and-a-half years old, she'd been thrilled about her first "big girl" bed with a pink lacy canopy and matching bedspread. She'd slept with a stuffed tiger she'd called Kitty. Her world was filled with toys and baby dolls and bedtime stories, and later Barbie dolls and pillow fights, and then slumber parties and long nights of giggling with her friends, then the slow descent into anxiety and spending her time alone in her room. I finally understood that this room had been

Kara's safe place where she could close out the world and be herself.

Being here without her was agony for me. I'd only been able to spend a few short hours with her and Haley in far too long. But as soon as I finished my house, I was going to ask them, or beg them, to come for a visit. This mama needed some time with her babies.

Haley's room was the utter antithesis of Kara's room. Haley liked cooler tones and heavier fabrics, and she was organized to a fault. Her closet was filled with jeans and sweatshirts and worn hiking boots. Instead of smelling popcorn, I smelled sage and ... boot oil. The pictures on Haley's walls were images she'd captured of wildlife and serene landscapes. Remembering the night she'd stayed with me in my lumpy bed, and how her hair had smelled like coconut, made me want to curl up on her bed and bury my face in her pillow.

But I left her room before memories buried *me*.

Dan wasn't around when I went downstairs, and I had no desire to see him. I left my attorney's business card on the table, then went outside and loaded my bulging suitcase in the trunk of Kara's car. With Grandma Jean's ashes strapped securely in the passenger seat, I left the house where I'd raised my girls, and I didn't look back.

The next part of our journey would be on the land where I'd spent my childhood ... in a home I'd built with my own hands ... in a place where I was reclaiming my wild, authentic self. There I would teach my daughters the truly important things in life.

Chapter Thirty-Five

As I drove through the night, I thought about the first time I'd left North Carolina. I'd been running away then. I'd had four dollars in my purse, a head full of doubts, and I'd second-guessed myself with every passing mile. This time I wasn't running away from anything. I'd closed the door to my past and was embracing my future with confidence. I'd finally spoken my truth, faced down Dan, and reclaimed my power. I only wish it hadn't taken something as heartbreaking as Dan wounding our daughter for me to stand up and fight.

But now that my claws were out, I refused to tolerate anyone else's bullshit, especially if it involved my girls.

Just after four in the morning, I drove down the lake trail and parked Kara's car on a level stretch of worn grass that doubled as my driveway. Weary to the bone after driving all night, I dragged myself out of the car and slogged inside.

Sinatra, who'd been curled up on the futon, popped up on all fours as if preparing to bolt.

"Hi baby ..." I said, quietly closing the door behind me. "I missed you."

Apparently, he'd missed me too because he leapt off the futon and trotted over to me. I picked him up and buried my face in his fur. He smelled like fall, like browning leaves and crisp air. He rubbed his head against my cheek, and I kissed his sweet face. I'd been gone for less than forty-eight hours but it felt like a month since I'd held him. The weight and warmth of his warm body nestled against my chest brought tears to my eyes. His paws opened and closed, kneading my shoulder, his purr a low rumble of contentment as we snuggled each other.

I kicked off my shoes and carried him to the futon. The cushion he'd been lying on was still warm and felt good on my aching backside. Stretching out my legs, I put my feet up on my makeshift coffee table, a cobbled together wooden box, then pulled the quilt off the back of the futon and draped it over us. Sinatra settled in with his head lying on my chest while I gave him all the petting and attention he'd missed out on while I was away. Although I was certain Chloe had spoiled him rotten in my absence, I needed to cuddle with him. I fell asleep to the soothing sound of his purring, and didn't wake until almost nine—when Sinatra was calling, very loudly, for his long-overdue breakfast. I had texted Chloe on my way home to let her know I'd be back during the night so she wouldn't need to feed or check on Sinatra this morning.

Stretching my arms toward the cathedral ceiling, I smiled. It was good to be home. "Okay, mister, I'm on it," I said, pushing to my feet, tired but eager to talk with Chloe. I needed to tell her about my trip and thank her for taking care of Sinatra. And I wanted to ask her to go shopping with me. I had a house to finish and finally had the cash to get it done.

The thought of having a finished bathroom, especially now when my body longed for the soothing heat and pounding spray of a hot shower, made me impatient. I'd enjoyed learning how to do things like wire an outlet, set a window, and cover a roof with sheet metal, but I was tired and didn't want to do all the work myself now that I could afford to hire someone to do it. I didn't want to wait to have a bathroom or kitchen. I wanted to relax and enjoy my home. I wanted to wake up in the morning and have nothing to do but enjoy my coffee—and feed Sinatra, of course.

I wanted to have my girls come to a place they could be comfortable in and call home.

I wanted a life that consisted of more than work.

Today, I was going shopping. But first I called my attorney's office, shared the details of my encounter with Dan, and told them I'd given him a deadline to sign our agreement or send his own.

After that, I texted Ashe to see if he'd be willing to do the work for me, and if so, to put me on his schedule as soon as he could fit me in.

I received an immediate reply. *Call me,* it said. And after a lengthy call explaining what I wanted and that I planned to purchase the items and materials today, Ashe told me to meet him at the supply store where he could get a contractor discount and save me a few bucks. Depending on what I picked up today, it could save me two thousand dollars or more, so I was all in. I was really beginning to appreciate this guy.

I called Chloe, who was elated to hear my news and was as eager as I to finish my house. An hour later, I met her out at the road where she was waiting in the Dummy with the lowboy trailer attached. I climbed in and gave her a big hug. "Girl, I missed you!"

Laughing, she hugged me back. "I missed you too, and I'm dying to hear all about your visit with Dan."

Settling back in my seat, I told her about my grand entrance into the auditorium, and how the Trifecta had scurried out in search of reinforcements, and how Dan had tried to pray me out of church. She was laughing so hard, I had to give her a few minutes to gather herself before I could continue. When I told her what Dan had done to that poor woman who'd left the service in tears, Chloe gasped.

"What a fucking asshole!" she said.

"Yep, just another word for a zealot," I replied. I told her about my fight with Dan in his studio, and about his safe full of cash, and how I'd wanted to throat-punch him for being such a judgmental jerk to our daughter.

"You should have punched him," she said, scowling.

"Taking his money hurt him more," I said.

As we drove into town, I told her about backing Dan into a corner, pressing him to meet my demands for the girls and a quick divorce for me, and that I'd taken a good chunk of the cash from his safe.

Chloe thumped the steering wheel and cheered me on. But when I shared my heartache of walking through my daughters' bedrooms, and the realizations I'd had about my former life while looking through my closet, she reached over and squeezed my hand. "Life transitions are hard as shit," she said, a deep sorrow in her voice.

I nodded. "That they are."

During the rest of the ride to the supply store, we discussed cabinets, hardware, fixtures, and layout, and were still talking about the composting toilet when we walked in.

Ashe was hanging out at the end of an aisle of lumber, using a stylus to write something on his phone. When he saw us, he tucked his phone in his back pocket and met us in the main aisle. "What's your plan of attack?" he asked, his gaze roving my face as if I'd changed in a way that he couldn't put his finger on.

I shrugged. "My plan is to let you and Chloe get me through this massive undertaking without losing my mind."

"Let's take it one room at a time," Ashe suggested, exchanging a look with Chloe.

"My thoughts exactly. Bathroom first. This girl needs an indoor toilet," she said.

"All right then." He gestured to a long row of industrial carts used for moving big items like lumber, appliances, and cabinets through the store. "You'd better each grab a cart. We're going to need them."

And we did. Many of them. We spent three hours debating, inspecting, and selecting items for my house. Between the three of us, we'd come up with the most efficient layout and the best options for each room. Cart after cart stacked high with kitchen cabinets, an apartment-sized stove and fridge, a bathroom vanity and medicine cabinet set, a shower stall, a composting toilet, a washer-dryer unit, a kitchen sink, a countertop, faucets with hardware, as well as a tankless hot water heater were hauled to the parking lot and loaded onto Chloe's lowboy trailer.

The only thing I couldn't get at the store was an electric heating furnace for my house. Ashe said he'd order it for me and install it when it came in. In the end, he had saved me almost two thousand dollars by using his contractor discount, so I insisted on buying them lunch. A small token of my appreciation, but one meant from the bottom of my heart.

We sat outside on a large deck and enjoyed Indian cuisine under a beautiful blue sky. I couldn't believe this was my life now. Being here with friends—and I did consider Ashe my friend, even if my body vibrated each time he was near me—who were all helping me rebuild my life, was so fulfilling. The fact that I could afford to finish my house, or even afford to pay for lunch, was such a relief I couldn't stop smiling.

"Care to let us in on whatever is putting that beautiful smile on your face?" Ashe asked.

"Just thinking about how awesome my house will look when it's finished ... and how to ask you to cancel all your other jobs and work on mine right now. Today. As soon as we get back to my place."

By the time I'd finished, Ashe and Chloe were both laughing. "Sorry, Kate, I can't cancel my jobs this week," he said, "but I can work a couple of hours each evening, if that helps. You're on my schedule for late next week, then I'll be all yours until your rooms are finished."

"Sounds great. What are you doing after work tonight?" I asked like a smart-ass.

The warmth of his chuckle, and Chloe's hoot, was oddly rewarding. I'd nearly forgotten how to joke and play with friends, and to be doing so now brought a lightness to my heart that stayed with me throughout our meal. When we finished, and we parted ways with Ashe, I climbed into the Dummy with ease. I was getting stronger and fitter each day.

After Chloe got us on the road, I placed a thick envelope on the seat beside her. "This is for the roofing," I said, reminding her I'd promised to reimburse her. "If six thousand isn't enough—"

"Holy crap, Kate!" she said, cutting me off. "There's no way I'm taking money for something I would have sold off at a yard sale or just given away. Put it back in your purse."

"I can't do that, Chloe." Our eyes met. "I really can't."

For a moment, she said nothing, then she sighed. "We've talked about becoming partners at some point. Let's consider this your investment in our partnership. I'll accept the money, but you have to accept a fifty-fifty split on our net income from now on."

I sagged against the seat. "How did Josh ever win an argument with you?"

"He didn't." A sad smile tilted her mouth. "Because we never argued."

"Well, after spending fourteen hours on the road and getting about four hours of sleep before Sinatra woke me up, I'm too tired to argue with you."

"Good. But you'd better get some sleep tonight because we have a job first thing tomorrow morning."

"You're killing me, Chloe."

EVERY DAY I thought about the letter in my purse that I'd written to Sophie. I'd made a hundred excuses for not doing so. I was too busy working on jobs with Chloe or on my house. I was trying to carve out hours to write each morning, which wasn't easy after tossing all night on a lumpy mattress. The futon was just as uncomfortable as my bed, so night after night I wandered between the two, then spent the first hour each morning working on my book, bleary-eyed and tired.

I'd been talking almost every evening with Kara about the new life she was embarking upon, and Haley had checked in once to let me know she was having the time of her life hiking with her friends. She said it had changed her mind about a lot of things—things she wanted to talk with me about when she finished her hike. The weight of all of this felt too heavy to risk sending the letter to Sophie and adding one more brick to my aching back—perhaps that final brick would break me. And so the letter had sat at the bottom of my purse waiting for me to get up the nerve to send it. But the longer I waited the longer Sophie and I remained estranged, and I knew I needed to quit stalling.

Chloe hadn't taken on any landscaping jobs this week so we could dedicate ourselves to finishing my kitchen. We'd gotten my composting toilet installed a week ago. It felt so good to have an indoor toilet, to not have to go outside at night, sometimes dashing through the rain with a flashlight, to use the outhouse. I'd never known what critters might be hiding in there or skulking around behind my house. Now the only critter in my bathroom was Sinatra who had decided he liked sleeping in the sink.

Ashe had finished installing my shower three days ago. That evening I'd spent the first two minutes in the shower crying over the simple pleasure of feeling warm water raining over my aching shoulders and having a real bathroom in my home.

Ashe had been working full time here for a week now. After long, sweaty days of work, he would hang out for a half hour or so and have a cold beverage with Chloe and me, and sometimes Maggie when she stopped by as she had tonight. In some ways it felt natural having him around. He was funny and smart and incredibly helpful with building my house. But he was too damn sexy for me to stay focused on my work or ignore my attraction to him.

He flirted openly with me, but I parried like an Olympic fencer. I cut off his playful advances with deft blocks and counter strikes, keeping him at a distance when he tried to move in. Our fencing matches entertained Chloe and Maggie, and Ashe seemed to enjoy the game. The truth is, I did too, but I refused to succumb to his charm and take any action that would change our relationship.

"We should be able to finish the kitchen in a couple of days," he said to all of us in general, but his eyes cut to me. "What are you going to do when your house is finished?"

"Read the magazines I bought months ago while I soak in my bathtub and pretend there aren't a dozen other projects I need to do."

"More projects? If you're looking for a way to keep me around, you can just ask," he said. "You know I'll be happy to help out."

"Good. Would you do me a favor then?" I asked to distract him from his playful pursuit that had Maggie and Chloe smiling behind their wine glasses.

"If it's not illegal."

"Nah, I handle that stuff myself," I said, getting to my feet. Placing a hand on my sore lower back, I stretched and groaned. "I do want to report a crime though. My mattress is killing me."

"You need a new bed," Chloe insisted, not for the first time.

"I know, but I don't want to take time away from working on my house to go to the store." I continued to massage my back. "I plan to put Sophie's old bed in the loft so I'll need to buy two mattresses and box springs. And I'll need bedding and other things that I don't have time to mess with right now. Kitchen first. Then the loft bedroom."

She lifted her hands in defeat. "Then don't expect us to feel sorry for you."

"You can stay at my place," Ashe offered with a wink. "I have a new mattress."

I laughed. I couldn't help myself. I knew despite his light flirtation he wouldn't pressure me to do anything I didn't want to do. Somehow he'd become a true friend—one I'd needed and deeply appreciated. "I'll pass on that chivalrous offer but take you up on the favor," I said. "Would you drop a letter in the mail for me on your way home?"

"Sure, and I can take a hint," he said, getting to his feet. "I'll leave you ladies to your lady-talk."

"It's a girl-gab," Maggie said with fake exasperation. "There's a world of difference between a girl-gab and lady-talk."

"A difference I'm sure I don't want to know." Reaching over, he smooshed Maggie's ball cap down over her eyes. "See ya later, sis."

"You're a pain in the ass," she said, swatting at him, but she was laughing, and so were Chloe and I.

I went inside to retrieve the letter, but as I carried it back outside and handed it to Ashe, my heart started pounding so hard it made me lightheaded. For a moment, I wanted to snatch it back, to rethink what I'd written, but he tucked it in his shirt pocket and headed to his van. As he drove away, I sank onto my chair, knowing there was no turning back now.

The next move was Sophie's.

Chapter Thirty-Six

I hadn't expected Sophie to make her move so soon. Nor had I expected her to show up with a bottle of wine.

"What?" she said, scowling at me as I stood there dumbfounded. "Are you judging me for bringing alcohol or do you think I'm going to hit you with the bottle?"

"I ... I honestly don't know what to think," I said, feeling a little breathless from surprise.

Her scowl deepened. "I suppose you still don't touch alcohol?"

That she believed me to be my former holier-than-thou-judgmental self was evident. "I drink," I said, defending myself.

She eyed me with an arched eyebrow as if she didn't quite believe me. Then she wiggled the bottle. "Any chance you have glasses?"

"Um, yeah. Sure." It felt as if I were sleepwalking through sludge. I stumbled inside to get the glasses Maggie had brought over. My hands were shaking, and my mouth was dry. I wanted a glass of water or a cold beer rather than wine, but I wasn't going to turn down a chance to have a drink with my sister.

When I went back outside, Sophie was standing near the old dock. Without speaking, she opened the bottle and filled our glasses. The awkward silence between us swelled like an incoming wave, and I knew if I didn't say something it might bowl us over and drag us into water so deep we could never recover.

"Where do we start?" I asked quietly.

Her eyes, filled with anger, cut to mine. I felt as if I were approaching a wounded animal. I wanted to help and comfort it, but it was all teeth and claws just waiting for me to make a wrong move.

"Where the hell have you been? Let's start there," she snapped.

I could see she had no intention of making this an easy conversation. I didn't know where to begin, so I started with when I married Dan, and then began to recap my life with him and our girls.

Sophie groaned. "Don't give me that glossed over summary. I want to know why you would dive so deep into something as fucked up as Dan's religion—and to walk away from a family who loved you."

"For starters, Sophie, I'd seen our father kissing another woman. Our mother had died. I lost a baby. And I had no one to talk to. Not one fucking person, Sophie. I was alone and heart-broken and ..." I released a hard breath, frustrated and emotional. "I was lost. I'm sorry I hurt you. Believe me, Soph, it's the last thing I ever wanted to do."

For a long moment, the two of us stood in silence, our gazes clashing then skittering away to the safety of the lake where we'd spent so much of our childhood.

Finally, after what seemed an eternity, she looked at me. "I'm sorry about your baby," she said, her voice soft and filled with empathy. "I can't even imagine ..." Her voice trailed off as if she couldn't find the words to finish. There were no words, and we both knew it.

In the ensuing silence, it seemed natural for the two of us to walk out onto the dock. Sophie kicked off her sandals and sat at the end of the wooden pier. She refilled her glass then placed the wine bottle on the weathered planks. Feeling I had nothing left to lose, I slipped off my flip-flops, sat beside her, then helped myself to another glass of wine. With our legs dangling over the edge and our feet submerged to our ankles, it felt like old times. But it wasn't old times. The sister who used to drive me crazy with her constant chatter could barely speak to me now.

"Your daughter is beautiful," I said softly. "She reminds me of you around that age."

"You mean she's a chatterbox."

"No. I mean she's beautiful, sweet and caring."

It was the first time in years I'd seen any softness in Sophie's eyes, and I didn't know if it was because of my comment or because she was thinking of her daughter.

"That girl can certainly string together a lot of sentences," I added.

A wry grin tipped Sophie's mouth. "Yeah, she might be a little like her mother in that regard."

I didn't comment. Sophie had made it clear we were doing this on her terms. I was treading carefully and waiting for her to lead the way.

She was in no hurry it seemed, for we sat there for long minutes just watching nature. Fish swam past our submerged feet and leapt from the water to snap up hovering insects, then dropped back in with a blip or splash. It seemed time was winding backwards, carrying us along with it. I noticed the small scar on Sophie's ankle where she'd slipped off the dock when she was seven and slashed it open. I was only eleven at the time, but I'd given her a piggyback ride all the way to my grandparents' house where Grandma Jean was preparing a picnic lunch for us. After she patched up Sophie's ankle, we all headed back to the lake, Grandma Jean carrying the picnic basket, me carrying Sophie.

"Did you find our old inner tubes in the boathouse?" Sophie asked, her voice sounding as far away as my memories.

"Yeah, the rubber was dried and rotted so I tossed them out. But I still have the canoes."

She gave a slight nod but said nothing.

"I did find our old Frisbee," I said. For a few minutes I told her about the things I'd unearthed in the boathouse and our grandparents' house. Then I thanked her for giving some of the furnishings a good home.

"I assume you want them back?" she asked.

"Of course not," I said. "Seriously, Sophie, I was so happy to see those things in your gorgeous café. That's where they belong."

"Not according to our grandparents," she said, matter-of-factly, but I could hear the pain and condemnation in her voice.

They'd left everything to me, and I was beginning to understand why. "Soph, I think Grandma Jean left the house and property to me hoping I'd come home. I think she knew my situation with Dan, that he owned and controlled everything, and she wanted to make sure I always had a place to come back to."

Sophie mulled this over for a moment. "Then I don't understand why she wouldn't let Dad and me help her keep her house from rotting away."

"You tried to help?" I asked.

"Of course we did!" she replied, obviously offended that I'd even need to ask.

"Sorry, I just wasn't sure how connected you were with her."

"I visited her almost every week, but she felt I was being unfair to you, and she refused to speak to Dad, so I think that's why she wouldn't take any help from him."

Because she believed he'd hurt her daughter. I'd feel the same way about anyone who hurt my girls.

"The condition of her house wasn't because I didn't want to help her, Kate. Mark even offered to help or pay for repairs. But Grandma said she didn't want the noise or the charity. That's why you got stuck with a house you can't live in."

"I have everything I need here," I said. "Converting Papa Ray's boathouse into my home, however difficult it's been, is unbelievably rewarding." My eyes swept the area around us, lush with greenery and woodlands and mountains ... and our beautiful lake and my perfect home. "I can't express how deeply I've missed this place—and you, Sophie. Thank you for looking after Grandma."

When Sophie didn't respond, I knew I'd have to push us through this hard conversation. It seemed my little sister had lost her steam.

"There's something that's been gnawing at me, and there's no easy way to ask, so I'm just going to say it. Do you think Mom killed herself?"

A gasp burst from Sophie, and she gaped at me. "Jesus, Kate! Of course not." Shaking her head, she said, "How could you think she'd do something so selfish or stupid?"

"Because I broke her heart when I told her I saw our father kissing another woman."

Sophie groaned. "Kate, there's so much you don't know about that situation, and it's not for me to share. But I will tell you this. Mom did *not* kill herself."

I wanted to believe my sister, but the question still lingered like a wound that wouldn't heal. I don't know if it's because I kept picking at the scab, or if I needed the right medication to take care of the problem.

"If you want answers, Kate, you need to talk to Dad, like you should have done twenty-four years ago," she said, setting her wine glass beside the bottle. Then she added, "And if you want any chance of being in my life, that's a conversation that has to happen."

"I want that more than anything, Soph, but so much time has passed, I have no idea how to talk to our father."

And it seemed she didn't know how to talk to me because she merely shrugged and didn't comment. I was on my own then. The growing silence between us felt endless. She wasn't making this easy on me. "Sophie, how do I build a bridge that will connect us again?"

She leaned back on her hands, her blonde hair as long and beautiful as her daughter's. As she looked at the mountains we'd once roamed together, she said, "I don't know if you can."

"Why not?" I asked with my heart in my throat. "If we just talk things through, and maybe give each other a little grace, you can learn to forgive me, and I can learn how to become part of our family again."

"I don't know if that'll ever be possible," she said, getting to her feet. "Because I don't trust you. I think you'll go back to your husband ... and your church, and your judgmental idiotic self. And I want nothing to do with that person."

I followed her up. "I'm not like that anymore," I insisted. "I'm never going back, Sophie. I mean it. I'm done with that life."

"We'll see," she said, doubt thick in her voice as she began to walk away.

"Please don't leave, Soph. You haven't told me anything about your life. All I know is you own the café and that you're divorced now. I'm so sorry about that. Can we grab coffee together or something ... sometime?" I asked, not wanting her to leave. "We still have so much to talk about."

She shrugged and cast a final look across the lake. "I don't know. So much time has passed ... So much has been lost."

With that, she walked away, got in her car, and left me standing on the dock with her wet footprints staining the wood and her final words staining my heart.

Chapter Thirty-Seven

hloe, Ashe, and I had finished installing my kitchen. My little house was complete—almost. To know I finally had a real home, a place of my own made me long to celebrate.

"I'm taking you all out tonight," I said. "If you're available."

Chloe dragged the back of her hand across her sweaty forehead. "Free food? I'm in."

Ashe looked at me with flirtatious eyes. "It's about time you asked me out."

I tossed one of my gloves at him. "Not a date. Just a thank-you meal. Meet us at seven. And bring Maggie." I didn't have to tell him where to meet us. The Bobcat Brewery was our favorite place, our default unless specifically told otherwise.

After picking up our tools and stashing them out of the way, Chloe and Ashe headed out, and I made a beeline to the shower. It had been a scorching hot workday. I lathered, rinsed, and lingered, enjoying several minutes beneath a cool, soothing spray. My heating and air conditioning units were supposed to arrive next week, and Ashe promised he'd install them as soon as they were delivered. I intended to hold him to that promise. Sleeping without fans or air conditioning in our humid summer heat was impossible.

Sinatra wouldn't even cuddle with me until the early morning hours.

I still felt overheated after my shower. My two pairs of shorts were dirty from working in them. The thought of wearing jeans and sitting outside at the brewery convinced me to wear my sundress. If it was suitable for Dan's church, it was suitable for a night out.

Twenty minutes before seven, I pulled into Chloe's driveway. Although I was still using Kara's car, it felt good to be able to give Chloe a break from carting me everywhere. Before I could get out, she popped outside dressed in jean shorts, a blue tank top, and sandals. I wished I had her ability to throw on something as simple as shorts and a tank and look that beautiful. Chloe was a little lighter and brighter these days, but there was still a deep sadness in her eyes that made me want to hug her.

"Hope you brought your wallet," she said, getting in the car. "I'm famished. And thirsty."

"Ditto, and yes." Backing out of the driveway, I noticed her eyeing my dress. "What? It's freaking hot outside and my shorts are dirty."

She just smiled. "I think I'm about to win a bet."

"What are you talking about?" I asked, heading toward town. "What bet?"

"Never mind. Have you heard anything from Sophie?" she asked, spinning the conversation in another direction.

"Nope. It's been two days since Sophie came by to talk, or to punish me, and I'm still uncertain of her motives. I don't know if she'll ever come back or talk with me again."

"She will," Chloe said with a confidence I didn't feel.

"From your lips," I said, then smacked my forehead. "Argh!"

Chloe burst out laughing. "Still got some of that old code in there, huh?"

"How freaking long is this deprogramming going to take?" I asked in exasperation. "I want to scrub those stupid sayings out of my brain. I used to want to punch Dan when someone would ask him how he was doing, and he'd say, 'I'm blessed beyond measure' or 'my cup runneth over' every fucking time."

Still laughing, she reached over and patted my shoulder. "You need to do something to eradicate that virus."

"Ya think?" I huffed out a breath. "Don't ever join a cult, Chloe. It really fucks with your head."

"I'll keep that in mind if I'm ever approached by one."

"It happens every day, and people have no idea what they're signing up for or that they're giving up every facet of their freedom." I glanced over to see her nodding in agreement. "It's like a fucking cancer, insidious and frankly terrifying."

She patted my arm as if to calm me down. "We should probably talk about something else," she said.

I laughed. "Might be a good idea."

And so we talked about our kids while I drove us to the brewery. Dylan was getting ready to head back to college, something Chloe was both anticipating and dreading. I told her Kara seemed to be doing well with her new partner Jamie and sounded happier than she'd been in years. Haley's last text said she'd be heading back to her father's house in a few days, then she planned to visit me.

"I'm so excited, Chloe. The last time Haley was here we slept in a building. Now she'll be staying in my gorgeous little house."

Chloe nodded in agreement. "It really is beautiful."

"Thanks to you. Can you believe we built a freaking house together? If we can do that, we can do anything, Chloe—even rebuild our lives."

A sad smile tipped her mouth. "I think that's what we've been doing all along."

WHEN CHLOE and I walked into the brewery, someone called our names. We turned to find Beth having dinner with a broad-shouldered man wearing a ball cap, the two of them scrunched into a booth with three kids, a boy and two girls, I assumed to be their kids.

Beth stood to give us both a hug then presented me to her husband and kids. "This is my stepsister Kate," she said as if genuinely pleased to introduce me to her family. "The one I've been telling you about."

Smiles bloomed on their faces and their eyes lit up as if they were meeting someone important. But I stood in stunned surprise. I had no idea Beth had told her family about me. Her husband, Gary, a rugged-looking guy with kind eyes, extended his hand. "I'm glad to finally meet you. Beth is really excited about connecting with you."

It felt as if I were having an out-of-body experience. I shook his large, callused hand, and told him it was good to meet him and that I was incredibly happy about my blossoming relationship with Beth. As I was introduced to each of their children: twelve-year-old Abby, ten-year-old Ethan, and nine-year-old Kaylee, they each said, "Hi, Aunt Kate." I was so taken aback I almost couldn't respond. Before coming back to Dunwith Falls and meeting Sophie's daughter, Jessica, I had never been called Aunt Kate. Now here were three more adorable children I would add to my growing treasure trove of nieces and nephews.

I met Beth's eyes. *Thank you,* I mouthed silently, hoping she could see the joy and gratitude warming my heart.

"We're just finishing up, but you're welcome to join us," her husband said, beginning to slide over and make room for Chloe and me.

"Thank you but we're meeting some people for dinner," I said. "Perhaps we can all meet for a meal sometime? I'd love to get to know each of you."

"We'll definitely set up something," Beth said. "Why don't you and Chloe meet me for lunch next week and we'll make a date for a family night for all of us? I'll text you about scheduling lunch."

"Sounds wonderful," I said, meaning it sincerely, but my attention was diverted to Ashe who was standing across the room, leaning his tall, sexy body against the bar. He smiled and lifted his beer glass as though asking if Chloe and I wanted one. Instead of responding, I beamed a smile at Beth and her beautiful family and told them I was looking forward to getting to know them. "We'll let you get back to those yummy looking desserts now," I said, then we exchanged our final goodbye and Chloe and I headed to the bar.

Ashe had two frosted mugs of ale waiting for us. I arched an eyebrow and considered razzing him about being presumptuous. "What?" he said defensively, giving me a head-to-toe glance. "You look hot. Thought you might want a cold beer."

Chloe laughed and tapped her mug against Ashe's glass. "I said the same thing on the way here. She claims her shorts were dirty, but I think this girl is ready for a real night out."

"Hey!" I gaped at Chloe. "Whose side are you on?"

She ignored me and took a long sip of her beer. "Ah ... nothing like a cold beer after a long hot day." She glanced at me. "Or during a long, hot night."

"Seriously! What is going on with you?" I asked, surprised by her teasing but glad she was growing more comfortable being out with her friends.

Instead of replying, she glanced around the bar. "Is Maggie coming?"

"She's already outside on the deck," Ashe said. "I was just grabbing a beer before heading out."

We found Maggie outside on the massive deck talking with Bobbie Jo and a small group of people. Just as we approached them Carlos burst from the group like an Olympic sprinter. "Missy Kate!" he said, grabbing my hand and pumping it with both of his. "It's so good to see you. How is your plumbing?"

I arched an eyebrow in mock offense. "My plumbing is fine, thank you very much."

He giggled like a boy. "I mean the plumbing in your house."

I couldn't help laughing. I'd missed this boisterous little man. He was dressed for a night out in a short-sleeved, button-down shirt and tan polyester pants, his black hair combed back and his face freshly shaved.

"Everything is absolutely perfect, thanks to you," I said. "You'll have to come by and see what we've accomplished since you were there last. I have a working bathroom and kitchen now."

"No!" His eyes widened in disbelief. "That's so fast. Is this true, Miss Kate?"

"It is. Come by with your lovely wife and kids, and I'll show you around. We can have a cookout at the lake if you like. The kids can swim and canoe, and you can fish, and Rosie can ... well, she can just relax for a change."

His smile widened and he turned to his wife who was standing beside Maggie. "You hear that, Rosie? Miss Kate has invited us to picnic at her house."

Rosie laughed. "She will regret it five minutes after we arrive."

"Nah, Miss Kate is good people."

I don't know why that small compliment made me feel so good, but it did.

Giving me a wink, he said, "Save me a dance." There was a band playing on the lower deck that doubled as a dance floor where several people were already dancing.

"It's too hot to dance."

"Never!" he exclaimed. "You must always dance, Miss Kate." With that, he leapfrogged into conversation with Ashe.

Maggie sauntered over, all slender and gorgeous in her white capris and mint green sleeveless top. She made a show of eyeing me up and down. "I knew you'd rock that sundress. Glad to see you've finally screwed up the courage to wear it."

"This is the *second* time I've worn it," I reminded her. The first time, when I'd strutted into Dan's church, I'd been angry and feral. Tonight, I felt empowered and genuinely happy. "Thanks for making me buy it."

"You bought it because you wouldn't let me give it to you." She tapped her bottle against mine. "Congratulations on finishing your house. I'm thrilled for you."

"I couldn't have done it without you and Chloe," I said sincerely. "I'll never be able to thank you guys."

"It's what friends do," she said. "You're still going to let me help you decorate, right?"

"Yes," I said with a laugh, "but I need your talent with a paint-brush first, if you're willing. I have to stain the outside of my house."

Grimacing, she seemed to think about it for a moment, then said, "When are you doing it?"

"The weather looks good through next week, so I'm thinking about doing it Tuesday since Chloe hasn't scheduled anything else for that day. That'll give me time to buy the stain and power wash outside so the walls have time to dry."

"Okay, if that's the only way to get some time with my gal-pals, I'm in."

"Thank you. I promise we'll have plenty of time for hanging out."

For several minutes Chloe and I talked with Maggie, then we grabbed Ashe and headed to our table to eat dinner. At various points throughout our meal, friends popped in and out. Carlos and Rosie visited while we looked at the menus and placed our orders, then they headed to the dance floor. Bobbie Jo sat with us while we ate our salads, then she joined a group of people lingering at the outside bar. Others, some I knew, some I didn't, popped over briefly to say hello. The meal was delicious, our conversation lively and full of laughter as we chatted about music we loved, and movies we wanted to see, and vacation destinations on our bucket lists. We finished eating and ordered another round of drinks just as the band brought the crowd to its feet. I hadn't realized I was tapping my foot until Ashe slipped his arm around my waist and asked me to dance.

Feeling lighthearted and emboldened I said, "Sure," and pushed away from the table.

"Atta girl," he said near my ear as we headed toward the mass of writhing bodies. He turned me in his arms and smiled down at me. "You are stunning tonight."

So was he. His dark, wavy hair shone beneath the lights strung across the bandstand, and his eyes sparkled with mischief. He pulled me close, and I lost my breath a little—but I couldn't look away. I didn't want to look away. I wanted to drown in his eyes, bask in his touch, and spend the night in his arms. This thing between us had been a slow burn from the moment we met, smoldering and flaring, and the flames were building fast and throwing off scorching heat.

"You'd better stop looking at me like that," he said, his voice husky.

"What if I don't want to?" I was playing with fire, and I knew it and didn't care.

His mouth parted a bit and he seemed at a momentary loss for words. Then a seductive grin tipped his mouth. "Look all you like, Kate. Just know I'm looking back."

I smiled. "Good."

He leaned back a little and gawked at me. "Who is this woman in my arms?"

A woman who needed to set herself free.

Carlos and Rosie swept past, the two of them laughing and twirling and so in love they were mesmerizing. They seemed full of life, simply happy in the moment, their smiles wide as they gazed at each other.

Ashe and I exchanged a look, our gazes tangling, our bodies brushing, the fire building ...

"Miss Kate," Carlos exclaimed as he swooped in and captured my wrist. "I'm stealing you away for a dance!"

I had no choice when his wife tugged Ashe in the opposite direction. Carlos extended his arm, elbow out, and for the first time I slipped my hand into the crook of his elbow and let him escort me deeper into the crowd of dancers. The next thing I knew, he nearly lifted me off my feet with a wild spin that gave me a moment of vertigo. Around we went with Carlos grinning his gap-toothed smile and tossing me like a yoyo, spinning me out then reeling me right back. I could feel my dress lifting with each turn, but I couldn't brush it down because I was too busy trying to stay on my feet. For a small man, he was insanely strong, casting me out again and again until I thought I might lose my supper.

Just when I was about to beg for release, Ashe cut in and told Carlos to get his own girl. With a hoot of laughter Carlos swept Rosie back into his arms and off they went.

I leaned against Ashe's chest, trying to catch my breath. "That was worse than those hellish rides at the county fair."

His shoulders shook from laughter. "I know. I felt as if I'd been dumped into a washing machine."

And so went our night, flirting and dancing with each other, visiting with our friends, me dancing with Maggie and Chloe and Bobbie Jo and a couple other gals whose guys were more interested in hanging out at the bar talking sports. Ashe joined those guys a couple of times, but his eyes seemed to track back to me—just as mine seemed to gravitate to him.

Chloe slipped away for a moment, then returned. "I hope you won't mind, Kate, but I'm going to catch a ride home with Carlos and Rosie."

I knew these nights weren't easy for her, and I felt guilty that I hadn't once asked if she was all right or if she wanted to go home. "I'm sorry, Chloe. I lost track of time. I can take you home," I said, willing to do anything for this woman who'd done so much for me. But a small selfish part of me was disappointed to have to leave when I was having the best night of my life.

"No way!" she said forcefully. "Not a chance, Kate. You're going to stay here and enjoy yourself as you *deserve* to do. Carlos will be driving right past my house so it's no imposition for them to drop me off. And just because I'm tired and ready to call it a night is no reason for you to do so." She caught my hand and gave it a squeeze. "You're celebrating a huge accomplishment. This is your night." She gave me a hug. "Enjoy every minute of it."

Maggie's slight nod assured me I was doing the right thing by letting Chloe leave without me. Still, I felt guilty. After Chloe disappeared inside with Carlos and his wife, Maggie told me that Chloe needed to know her grief wasn't holding us back.

"She needs to know she can come and go at her own pace without disrupting ours." Maggie's gaze cut to where Ashe stood at the outside bar talking with friends. "Judging by your pace tonight, I suspect you're heading straight into a long, hot night."

Maybe I'd grown used to Maggie's outrageous comments, or perhaps I was simply succeeding at scrubbing the prudishness from my brain. I no longer cared what it was that allowed me to feel so bold and carefree tonight; I only cared that I did.

"Well, Mags, I guess hanging out with you has ruined my morals."

"You're welcome."

I laughed and nudged her toward the bar. "Let's get a drink. I've been so busy dancing I've only had a beer and one glass of wine all night. I'm thirsty."

"You're not the only one," she said, gesturing with her chin toward a group of guys who were checking us out as we approached the bar. "Told you you'd be a knockout in that dress."

"That she is," Ashe said, stepping aside to widen the circle of the people he'd been talking with. Maggie stepped in beside Bobbie Jo and they fell into conversation. I stood by Ashe, but the heat of the night and crush of bodies and sound of the band began to grow smothering. "Would you like a drink?" he asked.

"Actually, I'd like some air ... and a walk maybe. Care to join me?"

He placed his bottle on the bar with a light thunk, his gaze never leaving my face. "Thought you'd never ask."

As his hand slipped over mine, a thrill zipped through my abdomen. We wove our way through the crowded deck then cut across the parking lot. Then we crossed the street and entered the park that was softly lit with lamp posts. We just ambled along holding hands and drinking in the night air. I tried to think of things to say but everything sounded trite and I had no interest in talking about projects.

We were a few blocks down when Ashe drew me to a stop beneath a sprawling tree and kissed me. Slowly. Sensually. Thrilling me. I'd never been kissed like this, as if we had all night, as if the walk were as important as the destination.

Nuzzling my cheek, he asked, "Would you like a cup of coffee?"

His question threw me.

"At my place," he continued.

I wanted more than coffee. I wanted *so* much more. "Sounds lovely."

We crossed the street and continued down a block to his flat above the sports store. He guided me up a wide staircase to a large landing that looked like a sitting nook in a high-end hotel. He punched in a security code, then opened the door to his flat. A soft light came on, illuminating a spacious loft, handsomely decorated in gray and white with touches of blue and sand-colored accents. The pocket doors he'd purchased from my grandparents' house were mounted like barn doors and drawn back to either side of a large, cased opening that revealed a bedroom. *His* bedroom. And a large king bed.

From behind, he slipped his arms around my waist and kissed my neck. "Would you really like a cup of coffee?"

I turned and pulled him into a long, lingering kiss, wanting to leave no doubt about what I wanted. He groaned and tightened his embrace. Our bodies melded together as the heat between us that had been building for months burst into flames of hot desire. He slipped his hand beneath my skirt and slid his warm palm up my naked thigh. Then he moved higher, cupping my butt, driving me wild. I arched my back and rubbed my body against his, aching to scratch my itch.

"Bedroom," I whispered between kisses that were driving us both wild.

Continuing to kiss me, he walked me backward all the way to the bed.

We kicked off our shoes and pulled off our clothes and tumbled onto the bed.

The feel of the mattress against my back was so sublime I lost focus for a moment. Ashe noticed my slight hesitation.

"Are we okay?" he asked, his voice husky with passion.

"More than okay," I said, sitting up and pushing him to his back. I could not lie on that mattress and ignore how damn good it felt. Nor could I ignore the hard desire coiling in my body.

Like a bobcat exploring the wilderness, I moved with purpose along the ridges and valleys of Ashe's muscled body. After years of being caged, I was wild and hungry. As we stalked each other, I prowled and pounced and growled with animalistic desire. Claws unsheathed, teeth bared, we took each other to the top of the mountain—then we leapt, thrashing wildly in our free fall.

Chapter Thirty-Eight

I felt Sinatra nuzzle my neck as he did each morning. "Hey, baby," I said, drifting between sleeping and waking.

"Good morning, wildcat."

My eyes sprang open, and I rolled over to find myself looking at a ridiculously gorgeous Ashe McKensie. His wavy hair was mussed and his torso was bare, revealing a muscled chest and a scar that slashed across his side.

A smile tipped his lips. "Forget where you were?"

"Until you woke me up, I thought I was in nirvana sleeping on a cloud," I said, intentionally avoiding his question.

A chuckle rumbled deep in his chest. "I knew you'd like my mattress."

That wasn't all I liked about being in Ashe's bed. The night came flooding back; the laughing and flirting, dancing, and touching ... and the most amazing sex I'd ever had. I didn't regret a moment of it. In fact, I wanted more. I finally understood the appeal of a friends-with-benefits relationship. But this thing with Ashe had to be on my terms.

"I thought I was sleeping with Sinatra, who I sometimes call *baby*," I said. "I wasn't referring to you."

"You sure about that?"

I laughed because he was so damn playful and charming. "Positive," I said, snuggling deeper into the mattress and soaking up the last few seconds of bliss. "It was simply a case of mistaken identity."

He slipped one hand into my hair as he leaned over and kissed my forehead. "How about some coffee and breakfast?"

My body began to purr, and I knew I had to get out of his bed before we were making love instead of toast. "I've got too much to do to lie abed and eat toast. But thanks anyway."

"I can make an omelet to go with the toast."

"Sinatra isn't happy when he has to eat dry kibbles for breakfast, so I'll have to pass on the omelet. Plus, I don't eat eggs."

"Well, thanks for staying the night," he said, his fingers still in my hair, his gaze roving my face. "It was ... nice."

It was more than nice. It was spectacularly, erotically, wildly fabulous. But I wouldn't admit that to him. Instead, I gave a nonchalant shrug. "Figured I might as well take advantage of a good mattress."

Another rumble of laughter rolled through his chest. "That's the only reason you stayed?"

I grinned. "Of course."

His laughter filled the bedroom. "You're welcome to stay again tonight but I can't guarantee how much sleep you'll get."

I would like nothing better than to climb that mountain with him again and rest my weary bones on a luxurious mattress, but I was not falling into anyone else's life. I had my own life. My own bed. And I intended to keep it that way.

IT WAS JUST after seven in the morning when I stepped onto the sidewalk outside Ashe's flat. A few people were out, but it was a man down the street approaching the hardware store who caught my attention. He was an older man with graying hair, and there was something hauntingly familiar about him. I wondered if he was one of my dad's regular customers, someone I'd met in my childhood. Then it struck me like a punch in the chest. The man was my father. He was opening his store as he'd done nearly every day for the past thirty plus years. As he fiddled with the door, he cast a brief glance in my direction.

Ducking my head so he wouldn't recognize me, I turned away and walked the opposite direction toward the brewery where I'd left Kara's car last night. But before I'd gone one block, I knew I had to turn around. It was time to face my biggest nightmare. I was as ready as I'd ever be to talk with my father and learn what really happened all those years ago. I just hoped he was ready to talk to me.

Sucking in a deep breath, I squared my shoulders and walked back to the hardware store. But the door was locked. My father had gone inside and locked the door behind him, indicating the store wasn't open yet. The *closed* sign on the door confirmed it. For a moment, I peered through the full-length window of the door, but all I saw were shadowed aisles filled with parts, tools, and equipment. Halfway back and to one side of the store was the counter for cashing out. My father wasn't there either. As I scanned the store, I began to feel a sense of panic. I needed to see him today. Right *now*. While I felt strong enough to handle the conversation. While I might have a moment alone with him. While I still had a chance to get my sister back in my life. She'd made it clear that wasn't going to happen until I talked with our father.

I knocked on the door, then did so more forcefully when he didn't answer. If my father was still the man he used to be, he wouldn't keep anyone out even though the store was closed. I knocked again and was relieved to see him cutting down a center aisle toward the door. When he arrived, I stepped back and waited for him to unlatch the deadbolt.

Rather than scowling and telling me he wasn't yet open, my father greeted me with a smile. "Good morning," he said, opening the door as if to welcome me inside. But when he saw my face and realized his daughter was standing in front of him, his smile dissolved. Surprise and shock and heartache filled his eyes. "Katie ..." he said in a graveled whisper.

I'd expected our meeting to be emotional, but I wasn't prepared for the sadness, anger, and regret that flooded me. "Hi, Dad."

For a moment it seemed as though neither of us knew what to do or say. While my father's eyes drank me in, my own marked the changes in him. His hair was mostly white now, but his back and shoulders that used to carry me so easily still appeared straight and strong. Was he marking the changes in me too? Could he see the lines of my life etched in my face, see how I'd been shattered, and how I'd glued myself back together the best I could?

The business hours sign on the door indicated the store opened at eight. That would give us just under an hour to talk if he were willing. It would be a start. "Can I come in?" I asked.

He stepped back and welcomed me inside. "My door is always open to you, Katie."

I crossed the threshold, and he locked up behind me. "Let's talk in the back where we won't be bothered," he suggested.

As I crossed the store and entered the back room, a wave of memories washed through me. There was still a lounge area on one side of the large back section of the store, and a small office and kitchenette on the other side. I'd spent so many hours here as a child, roller skating on the hardwood floor, playing with my dolls on the area rug, sleeping on the sofa, and in my teens helping my father with paperwork.

"Would you like something to drink?" he asked, gesturing toward the kitchen. "The coffee just finished brewing."

"Coffee sounds great." I needed a jolt of caffeine to snap me out of my memory haze. While he filled our cups, I looked around. The dollhouse in the corner had been replaced with a coat tree where a ladies' windbreaker and my dad's hat and coat hung. The overstuffed, beat-up furniture I'd played on as a child had been replaced with a couple of recliners. The small boxy television had been moved out in favor of a large flat screen television mounted on the wall. I could tell it had been positioned so it could also be seen from the front of the store, likely so my dad, a lover of sports, and his like-minded customers could watch the games that were so important to them.

"Cream or sugar?" he asked, placing two cups on a small table.

"Just black, thanks." I joined him at the table, but we both took refuge in our coffee, sipping quietly for a moment. Cupping my hands around my mug, I struggled to begin. He waited in silence, but I had no idea how to talk with him or how to ask the questions I needed answered. It dawned on me that I'd never had an adult relationship with my dad. I knew the man he used to be, or the man I'd believed him to be, but not this man.

As if taking pity on me, he slipped his hand over my fist. "I'm sorry, Katie. For everything."

Damn it. My eyes burned but I refused to fall apart.

After a hard swallow and a deep inhale, I said, "I need to know what happened, Dad. Why did you ... do what you did? Sophie says I don't understand what happened. So, I'm here to find out the truth."

Sorrow filled his eyes and he gave a small nod. "The truth might hurt more than help, Katie. I want you to know that before I begin."

"Our family was shattered over this situation. I can't imagine anything more hurtful than that."

"Fair enough," he acknowledged. For a moment we sat in silence, his gaze looking inward as if organizing his thoughts. "Your mother and I were in college when we met at a party. We spent one night together and then went our separate ways. About three months later, your mother tracked me down and told me we were expecting a child. *You*."

My coffee was forgotten as he wove his way into the story of how two strangers decided to get married and have the baby they'd made during one careless night.

"We moved back here and rented a small apartment. I got a job at the hardware store which, as you know, I eventually bought. I also took a part-time night job to support you and your mother. About a year after you were born, we bought a small house and settled in as a family. During that time, your mother and I grew to love each other. But Katie, it was a love between friends, not the romantic kind of love between married couples."

I nodded to acknowledge I knew the difference between friends and lovers and that it was a significantly different kind of love.

"We tried though. We dedicated ourselves completely to you and to being a family. After three years, we knew our relationship would never become more than a deep and loving friendship. But because we had such a wonderful friendship, we agreed to stay together until you were through school, then separate and build the lives we wanted."

"That's a pretty contemporary mindset," I said, thinking of how archaic my marriage to Dan had been.

A slight smile tipped his mouth. "It was your mother's idea. She started taking college courses so she could have her degree when the time came for us to dissolve our marriage, but then Sophie came along. Two small children didn't leave time for much of anything else, so your mother dropped out of school. She didn't start back until Sophie was fourteen."

A year before everything blew up.

"When did you start seeing Sharon?" I asked, both needing and dreading the answer.

"Around that same time." Disapproval must have shown on my face, because my father leaned back in his chair with a sigh. "Your mother encouraged my relationship with Sharon."

I snorted. "I seriously doubt that." There was only so much I was willing to believe.

"She wanted me to be happy. And your mother had plans of her own. She intended to finish college while Sophie finished high school, then your mom was going to move to San Francisco."

"What?" I was stunned. My mother grew up in Dunwith Falls.

In my memory she'd never once indicated we, or she, would live anywhere else.

"Your mom always talked about living on the West Coast near the ocean. But I wanted to stay here and raise you girls. She agreed because she always put you and Sophie first, plus she needed to finish school because she wanted to work for an engineering firm when she moved to California."

"Wait." I rubbed my temples. "Are you saying Mom was working on an engineering degree?"

"Yes, and she was top of her class," he said, pride evident in his voice.

This was something about my mother I hadn't known. Suddenly, it wasn't only my father who felt like a stranger. I'd never once considered my mother might want something more than a family. I'd never asked. She was just Mom, the person who was always there to provide a warm nest for Sophie and me. How oblivious I'd been. How heart wrenching to have missed knowing that side of my mother.

"Katie," my father said softly, drawing me back to our conversation. "Your mother and I were friends who loved each other very much. We knew happiness meant different things to each of us. She was so excited about finishing school and starting the next phase of her life in a place dripping with sunshine and ocean breezes. We talked about every decision, including my decision to embrace a relationship with Sharon. Your mother insisted it would be stupid to let something special slip away. She liked Sharon and wanted me to be happy. Her only concern was for you girls, so we agreed to keep everything private until after Sophie graduated and your mother and I were divorced."

"But I opened my big mouth and blew up the world and destroyed two families," I said regretfully.

"No, Katie, I did that." His eyes shimmered with emotion. "It was my fault, and I'm truly sorry."

All this time I'd carried that burden on my shoulders, but I could see now it wasn't entirely my fault. My father and I were equal partners in the destruction we'd caused. The difference was my father had stayed and rebuilt those injured families. I'd run away and left them bleeding in the rubble.

I dropped my forehead into my hand, thinking about all the time we'd wasted. "Why didn't you try to explain all of this to me?" I asked.

"I did, honey. I called you. I wrote you three letters saying I wanted to explain what happened. But they went unanswered."

"Because I'd thrown them in the trash without opening them."

"I went to your college campus to see you, Kate, but you refused to talk to me. I didn't know what else to do or how to reach you."

I lifted my head to glare at him. "You should have locked me in a room and forced me to listen. You were my father. You could have saved us all a lot of heartache if you'd have just forced me to listen to you."

"It would have only made you hate me more." He sighed and rubbed his thumb around the rim of his cup. "Sometimes you have to let your children stomp off into the world with a chip on their shoulder. Sometimes they can only understand the complexity of life and relationships by experiencing them firsthand."

And sometimes they have to get thoroughly lost before they desperately want to find the path that leads them back home.

"Why didn't Mom try to tell me this before she ... before she died?"

"Because you were mad at her for telling you to mind your own business, and you wouldn't talk to her either. And then, unfortunately, it was too late."

Regret had a foul taste, so bitter it wrenched my gut. Breathing became impossible with the wad of grief lodged in my throat. To think I'd lost those few precious weeks with my mother, and so many years with my sister and father because I'd wanted to judge them rather than understand them was ... shattering. My coffee cup blurred but I couldn't blink away the moisture beading up in my eyes. My mother hadn't killed herself. My father hadn't cheated. I cupped my hand over my mouth to stop a sob.

"Come here, Katie." My father wrapped his arms around me and drew me to his chest.

I burst into tears. Huge ugly sobs rolled up from my chest as I clung to him. It had been twenty-four years since my father had hugged me, since I'd felt the comfort and safety of his arms. His voice rumbled in his chest as he apologized. But I was the one who was sorry. I was so damn sorry.

Chapter Thirty-Nine

After I gained some control over my emotions, however tenuous, I told my father I had to leave. I didn't have the emotional bandwidth to answer his questions about my daughters or my shithead husband or why I'd come back to Dunwith Falls without them. But seeing the shimmer of tears in my father's eyes made me promise I'd come back to talk with him when we both had more time.

He gave me a hard hug then let me go.

Not in the mood to talk to anyone, I escaped out the back door of his store and stayed on the side street that ran behind the buildings lining South Park Avenue. When I reached the Bobcat Brewery, I hurried across the parking lot to where I'd left Kara's car, then headed to the nearest equipment rental and paint store.

An hour later, I drove out the lake trail to find Sinatra waiting for me by the front door. He leapt up and wrapped himself around my legs, purring and swishing his bushy tail.

"I'm sorry to keep you waiting, sweetie," I said, giving him a good scratch behind the ears. I plucked a twig out of his fur. "You need to be brushed, little man." He stuck his nose into my palm, making me laugh. "Yes, I know. Breakfast first."

Once I'd given him his wet food and topped off his dry kibbles and water bowl, I unloaded the power washer and paint from the trunk of Kara's car. I needed to power wash my house today so it would be dry and ready for painting on Wednesday when Maggie and Chloe planned to help me.

There's something about spraying down the exterior walls of a building that gives one time to reflect—or obsess—over every detail of life. For long moments at a time I'd find myself zoning out, my thoughts streaming through my head like the dirty water sluicing down the walls of my house. I thought about my parents and their unusual relationship and how they'd been so good at lying to their daughters. Never once had I considered they were planning to divorce. There had been no arguments, no battles or unkind words exchanged between them, not one fucking clue that would have made me question the strength of their marriage. That's why my father's affair—could it even be called an affair now?—was so earth-shattering for me. Like the ultimate sucker-punch, I'd never seen it coming. Just blam! And my world exploded.

Wounded animals don't stick around to ask why you shot them. They run like hell. And they hide from the one who hurt them. That's what I'd done.

But I was tired of running and hiding and licking my wounds. I didn't want to blame my father—or myself—any longer. In Papa Ray's words, "What's done is done." I still had things to discuss with my father, but I didn't want to think about those conversations today. I wanted to think about the amazing night I'd had with Ashe.

Despite the exhaustion in my arms and being soaked by the blowback spray from the power washer, my body hummed. The memory of being kissed and caressed and pressed between the soft mattress and Ashe's hard body made me tremble.

I wanted more. I ached for more. And I couldn't help craving another night of sleeping on a real mattress. But I refused to allow Ashe and his hard body and soft mattress to become my addiction. Besides, I already had the perfect male sharing my house, and I had no intention of replacing him.

As I washed years of weather and accumulated dust off the walls, I let my mind wander. At times, I slogged through family memories that made me melancholy. Moments lingered like small eddies along the shore. Then at odd moments, I'd find myself thinking about decorating my house. I made a mental note to create a list of items I needed to buy, like a new mattress and bedding.

I spent the rest of the day and Sunday alone, making lists in my head and power washing my house. Sunday evening, I made supper in my own kitchen for the first time. It's surprising how delicious a packet of Ramen noodles and canned green beans can be. Eating alone in my little house with Sinatra lying on my lap was a moment of utter bliss.

Later, with Sinatra snoozing beside me on the futon, I pulled out my notebook and stepped back into the fantasy world I'd been creating word-by-word for so many years.

Chapter Forty

I 'd written for hours and fell asleep on the futon. After a wretched night of tossing and turning, I woke up determined to rectify my sleeping situation. Late Monday morning, I borrowed Chloe's pickup truck and went shopping. I returned home hours later with two mattresses and box springs, converter rails for both beds, bedding, and a closet bar I'd needed for my closet. I'd also purchased a set of pots and pans and three baking sheets. The first thing I did after returning home was toss the new bed sheets in the washer—another thrilling moment. I had a washer and dryer!

While they washed and dried, I got rid of the old mattresses. They were so beat, I folded them like hotdog rolls and pushed them out the loft window, then went outside and loaded them in the back of the truck. Moving the old bedsprings out was a challenge, but I managed to haul them out and slide them into the pickup bed with the junk mattresses.

When I returned inside, I spent a good deal of time installing the converter rails on the beds to support the new box springs. Then I hauled in the new mattresses and popped them on the beds.

Once that was finished, I installed the new bar in my closet under the stairs. I hung my clothes and stashed my boots and sneakers on the floor beneath them. Then I spent a couple of hours moving my dishes and food from the workbench and canoe to the kitchen cupboards. The canoe was empty! I could finally move it outside along with the workbench. But I couldn't do it without help, so I spent the rest of the day doing laundry, making the beds, and finally taking the old mattresses to the transfer station before returning Chloe's truck.

To my surprise, she wasn't home, so I tucked the keys under the seat and headed home on foot. I made a light supper then took my journal outside where Sinatra was lounging in an Adirondack chair.

"Hey, sweet boy," I said, sitting beside him. He opened one eye, curled himself into a tight ball of fur, and began purring. "I'm worn out too, little man." After a minute of petting him and stroking his adorable face, I opened my journal and returned to my story.

I'D FALLEN asleep in my chair, and upon waking to a star-filled sky, I dragged myself inside with Sinatra tucked in one arm, my journal in the other. Sinatra opted for the futon while I slogged upstairs to my new bed.

I slept like the dead and woke to the feel of kitty paws kneading my head.

"Get-up-get-up-get-up!" Sinatra seemed to be saying, apparently ready for his breakfast.

Birdsong and bright sunshine streamed through my windows as I slipped out of bed. After feeding my persistent cat, I made a pot of coffee in my new coffee maker, then made a bowl of cereal for myself. I wanted to linger over the first cup of coffee I'd made in my own house, but I had to get cleaned up. Today Chloe and Maggie were going to help me stain the outside of my house.

Although my house was small, I'd expected it to take two days to finish. But Maggie wasn't kidding about being a badass painter. She showed up with two spray painters, which Chloe and I used while Maggie knocked out the white trim work. We finished up just before six o'clock. We were tired and thirsty and covered in gray stain by the time we'd finished. Other than wrapping our brushes in plastic, soaking the spray painters in two deep buckets of water, and tucking our supplies beneath a tarp under my awning, we didn't spend another ounce of energy cleaning ourselves up.

I went inside, drank a huge glass of water, fresh from my faucet, then pulled out the casserole I'd made last night and popped it in my new microwave to heat. For the first time ever, I was able to make a meal for my friends in my own kitchen. We had made sandwiches for lunch, chowed them down, and had returned to painting, intent on finishing the job today. And we'd done it. Now it was time to rest our backs and celebrate our accomplishment.

We flopped onto our chairs, drank beer, and ate the Mexican tortilla casserole I'd made.

My feet hurt, so I kicked off my ratty shoes and slid them out of the way with my foot.

"When are you going to throw those sad things away?" Maggie asked. "It's time to put them out of their misery."

Looking down at the heap of tape and broken strings I'd been wearing on my feet for years, I realized she was right. It was time. I'd walked with them to their end, just as I'd done with Rusty. "Okay, you guys have a point. But you'll have to toss them out. I can't bring myself to do it," I said, only half kidding.

"Done!" Maggie leaned over and snatched up my shoes. She walked over to Chloe's truck and tossed them in the back.

I pressed my palm to my heart. "I already feel lost without them."

Chloe laughed but Maggie just handed me a beer. "This will help you get over it."

It was nearly seven o'clock, and two beers later, when we heard a vehicle coming down the lake trail. A minute later, Sophie pulled up, cut the engine, and stepped out wearing a grin. I was so stunned not only by her appearance but by the smile on her face, I sat mute.

"It appears you really have changed," she said to me, sauntering over as if she had a secret she was dying to share. "Hey, Chloe. Hi, Maggie," she said, acknowledging each of them in turn as they said hello. "Have you seen this?" she asked me, turning her phone so I could see the screen. "You're trending on social media."

"What?" Dumbfounded, my gaze bounced between her phone and her face.

"Your video went viral." She laughed. My sister actually *laughed*.

"What video?" I asked, wondering what was happening.

"Your little church walk has over a million views." Before I could ask what she was talking about, she tapped her screen. The sound of church music blared from her phone then screeched to a halt like tires on pavement, followed by metal crashing and glass smashing, as a video of me bursting into Dan's church filled her screen. Then a bass guitar began a deep, soulful, sexy groove as I strutted down the aisle in my boots and short swinging dress.

"This is awesome!" Maggie exclaimed as she burst out laughing.

I sat with my jaw on my knees, watching the video someone had creatively put together. It was surreal to be watching this, to get an outside perspective of my bold sashay into a world that now seemed ridiculous to me. I looked windblown and half wild. The camera kept flashing to my ass and my flapping skirt then to Dan's face filled with a mix of horror and terror. The camera panned from my boots up my bare thighs, then to me smiling and waving to the congregation—but the expression on my face suggested I was mentally flipping them the bird. Slow motion body shots of me, my hair bouncing across my bare shoulders, my hips swaying with each strutting step, played out over a sexy groove. Interjected throughout the video was Dan's fearful face and his voice saying *Devil's in the house*, sending the girls into fits of laughter.

Maggie and Chloe were howling and cheering me on with fist pumps in the air.

Sophie was smiling as if immensely proud of me. "I can't imagine you being welcomed back after that shit show."

That set us all off again, but as soon as I caught my breath, I said, "I'm never going back, Soph."

"I believe you," she said, her voice free of anger and disdain.

I asked her how she got the video.

A flicker of guilt crossed her face. "I've been creeping on you."

"Creeping?" I asked, utterly lost as to what that meant.

"I've been searching online for your name and Dan's church since you came back. The video popped up in my social media feed, probably because of my previous searches, but it's been out long enough to hit a million views and start trending."

Oh my god. "Who made it?" I asked.

She shrugged. "I have no idea. There aren't any credits listed."

The original recording had to have come from Dan's film crew. But who would have manipulated it with such mastery and with such a humorous, albeit irreverent, slant? I had been royally pissed off, and on a mission, when I'd burst into Dan's church, but the video made me look bold and sassy and ... powerful.

I wondered if Dan knew about it, then worried my girls might have seen it. I didn't care how the video affected Dan, but I didn't want my girls to be publicly embarrassed by me.

"Want a beer?" Chloe asked, holding one out to Sophie.

"I'd love one, but I have to head back to work and help Jessica close for the night. I just popped over to show Kate the video."

"How about Friday night?" I asked before Sophie could leave. "We're usually here on Friday evenings. Come by if you like."

Sophie seemed to think about it for a moment, then tucked her phone in the back pocket of her jeans. "Maybe. If I can get someone to cover for me."

Not a commitment, but also not a *no*. "Well, thanks for telling me about the video."

She grinned. "My pleasure. Walk me to my car, will you?"

It wasn't really a question, nor a demand, but more a request. My body ached and longed to stay collapsed in my chair, but I pushed myself to my feet. "Of course."

Once we neared Sophie's SUV, she said, "Dad told me you stopped by."

I nodded, but this was such a touchy topic I didn't dare to comment.

"Good," was all she said. She opened her door, then faced me. "It's a start, Kate." With that, she slid onto her seat, closed the door behind her, then drove out the lake trail.

Once I'd slogged back to my chair, Maggie said, "Now that you're a video star, I sort of want to ask for your autograph."

"Ha-ha," I said, stretching my aching legs out in front of me.

Maggie thumped her fist on the arm of her chair. "You looked freaking amazing, Kate!"

I couldn't stop my grin. "I did, didn't I?"

For several minutes we joked about the video. Then I sobered. "I hope my girls don't see it."

Chloe flapped a hand as if to dismiss my concern. "Your girls will know it's just a prank."

"I just don't want them to look at their dad in a different light. He looked like a scared wimp."

"I think you'll be the one they see differently," Maggie said.

"I'm sure! They'll see their mother as a crazy lady wearing a too-short skirt and causing a scene they'll never live down."

"Or they'll see you as a gorgeous, powerful woman, instead of a submissive sheep, taking a stand for her daughters," Chloe countered.

That made me pause, and after a moment, I sighed and raised my beer in a toast. "To powerful women. Thank you both for helping me today." My gaze roved over my beautiful little house with the sky-blue roof, the exterior walls stained a light driftwood gray, the windows and doors trimmed in white, and I felt a deep sense of gratitude for my wonderful friends and my beautiful new life.

Maggie's voice broke into my thoughts. "You chose the perfect colors for your lake house."

"Chloe chose the color when she ordered her blue roof," I said. "All I had to do was select a wall color that wouldn't clash."

"Nah, you could have totally screwed up the color scheme, but you nailed it." Maggie reached over and rubbed my head. "I'm proud of you."

"Gee thanks," I said with a laugh. "When will you be available to help me finish the interior? I need furniture. And I need to know if we're sticking with the white walls."

"Definitely keeping the white," she said, "and I have ideas for outfitting your living space."

The three of us spent an hour discussing options before they helped clean up, then headed home.

Alone in my quiet kitchen, I washed, dried, and put away our supper dishes, then went to the bathroom to shower off a day's worth of grime. After pulling on my robe, I headed up to bed with Sinatra tucked in my arms. As he settled in beside me, I thought about the video and Dan and the storm that was sure to come when he saw it. He would blame me of course—but perhaps the video would prompt him to get the damn divorce paperwork done so he could tell everyone he'd cut ties with me. He was supposed to have sent the papers by now, but as usual, he was playing his passive-aggressive game. If I didn't have papers in hand by Monday, my visit to his church was going to seem like a mere prank compared to my next move.

Chapter Forty-One

A few days had passed when Kara called me. She'd heard from her father who was irate over the video.

He'd finally seen it.

Dan had accused Kara of helping whoever made the video because she was angry with him over their previous argument. Kara hadn't known anything about the video, and his unjust accusation had upset her so much she'd hung up on him.

I could only imagine how her rebellious act had infuriated Dan. Until recently, our girls did not argue or disobey their father. Ever.

But Kara was justifiably insulted and angry with him. "I haven't a clue what he's talking about, Mom. Jamie is searching for the video right now."

"It might be best if you don't see it," I said, feeling my gut coil into a knot. "It's not a flattering moment for either of your parents."

"I've got to see it," she said. "I need to know why Dad was so rabid over it." I heard Jamie say something in the background. "Hang on a sec, Mom. Jamie just found the video."

To my disappointment, I heard the soul popping bass line from the video playing in the background.

Kara gasped, then the sound of snickers and giggles came

through the phone. Then an "Oh my!" from Kara, and a "Wow, she's gorgeous ..." from Jamie. I was both flattered and horrified.

"Honey, I'm sorry," I said, as the music faded, indicating the video was ending. "I just couldn't tolerate your father's ill treatment of you, so I paid him a visit to tell him to knock it off."

"Mom, it's really funny. I mean, it's a little shocking to see this new you, but you look amazing. And Dad's been a ... well, not very nice lately. So, thank you for always protecting and supporting me, even when I haven't deserved it."

For a moment I couldn't say anything.

I heard her mumble something to Jamie, then she was back. "Jamie and I are thinking of flying in to visit you next weekend if that's okay with you. We can stay for a week if you have the room."

My heart filled to bursting. "I'd love that, sweetie!"

"Me too," she said, sincerity in her voice. "If it's okay with you, we'd like to fly in, then drive my car back. But I don't have to take it. I can leave it with you if you still need it."

"Of course you can take your car, honey. With fall and winter coming, I'll need a four-wheel drive vehicle to navigate the lake trail. I'd planned to go vehicle shopping next week, so your timing is perfect. Just let me know when you'll need to be picked up at the airport."

"I will, Mom. Thank you. I can't wait for you and Jamie to meet each other," she said, warmth and excitement in her voice. "I think you'll love each other."

"I think so too, honey."

"See you next weekend," she said cheerily. "Love you, Mom!"

"You too, sweetie," I whispered back, choked with emotion as we ended the call. It had been such a painful separation from my beautiful daughter during her angry period with me, and such a sweet reunion to hear the warmth and love in her voice again.

Chloe and I spent all day Friday trimming a massive row of overgrown hedges. By the time we'd finished, my arms and shoulders ached from working the beastly hedge trimmers, raking the debris, and feeding it all into the chipper. The two of us had taken turns doing each job, but they were all physically demanding.

After work, Chloe drove the Dummy out the lake trail, pulled off to the side, and cut the engine. I fed Sinatra, put a vegan lasagna I'd thrown together the night before into the oven to heat, then returned outside where Chloe sprawled in a chair drinking a bottle of water.

I'd just joined her when Maggie rolled up. The three of us quenched our thirst with water, then enjoyed a glass of wine as we assuaged our hunger with lasagna.

"What's in this?" Maggie asked, poking her fork into the wide noodles and sauce. "It's delicious."

"It is," Chloe said in agreement. "Is this really vegan?"

"Yeah. It's full of veggies, and cheese made from cashew nuts and nutritional yeast. I used store-bought tomato sauce because I didn't have any of my own canned sauce. I like this better than the traditional Italian recipe."

"Me too," they said in unison.

"Can I just say how much I love having a kitchen and being able to feed you guys for a change?"

"We do too," Maggie said, setting aside her empty plate, then leaning back in her chair. She stretched her arms overhead and yawned. "Feel free to cook for us any time."

A few minutes later Chloe looked over at me. "You seem a little quiet this evening. Is everything all right?"

"I'd hoped Sophie would stop by this evening, but I haven't heard from her, so I assume it won't happen. I'm disappointed but not surprised. In good news, though, I talked with Kara last night, and she's coming for a visit next weekend. I feel almost giddy inside that you'll all finally get to meet each other."

"I can't wait," Chloe said with Maggie chiming in her agreement.

I proceeded to tell them about the conversation I'd had with Kara and how her father had been a raging ass on the phone as he accused her of helping make the video. "Kara hung up on him."

Maggie released a belt of laughter. "Good for her! Sounds as if she's got a bit of her mama's backbone."

"I hope so because with a religious zealot for a father, she'll need it."

"Is Haley coming in too?" Chloe asked, switching her empty beer bottle for a bottle of sparkling water.

I shrugged. "She's supposed to call when she gets to a trailhead early next week. She'll know then if she's going to continue her hike or head home, and hopefully come here shortly after."

"I miss those days. Remember when we used to hike the trails?" Maggie asked, referring to the overnight hikes the three of us used to take in our late teens. We would lie to our parents about spending the night at one of the other's houses, then we would sneak off to whatever trail led to the party for that night. It was a high school thing. We'd loved those parties in the woods, but we hadn't realized how vulnerable we'd been. Not from the animals but from the college guys who would crash those events.

"How did we manage to survive our teens?" I asked. "We did some pretty dumb things."

Chloe released a belt of laughter and sat up in her chair. "Remember that grapevine we used to swing on and drop into the gorge? It had to be a twenty-foot drop. We could have broken our ... well, we could have broken anything! What stupid kids we were."

"Or maybe we were adventurous and brave kids," Maggie countered. "Seriously, why do dangerous things have to be considered stupid? We were bold and daring and a little naive, but we had guts and grit. Safety is just an illusion anyway. I could die of heart failure sitting right here in this chair. But if my heart is going to fail, I'd rather it be while I'm doing something wildly fun and exciting."

"That's a valid point," I said. "But I'm too damn tired at the end of the day to do anything more exciting than to crash on the futon with Sinatra."

Maggie wiggled her eyebrows. "I suspect my brother would disagree."

Chloe laughed but didn't comment.

I made a face at Maggie. "That damn dress you made me buy has caused nothing but trouble each time I've worn it."

The sound of a vehicle thundering down the lake trail interrupted our laughter. A couple seconds later a car I didn't recognize skidded to a stop just feet from us. The door was flung open, and Dan stepped out dressed as if he'd just stepped away from the lectern. He was wearing expensive Italian shoes, a crisp white shirt beneath what I estimated was a four-thousand-dollar suit, his hair combed to perfection, and a scowl as deep as the Grand Canyon.

"We need to talk," he said, stalking toward me as if he intended to mow me down like dried weeds beneath a brush hog.

I pushed to my feet and met his glare with my own. "You're damn right we do. Where are my divorce papers?"

"Be warned, Kate, I'm in no mood for your nonsense." He strode past me, completely ignoring Maggie and Chloe as he headed toward the dock.

"This ought to be good," Maggie said, making Chloe snicker.

I glanced at my friends. "I'd like to live in my house rather than a prison cell, so don't let me kill him." I said, then followed Dan.

He paced near the dock, clenching his fists. When I approached, he turned on me with fury in his eyes. "If you had anything to do with that video, Kate, I'll sue you for everything you have. I'll make you rue the day you met me. I'll have this place bulldozed and turned into a parking lot. I'll—"

"What do you want?" I asked, cutting him off.

"I want to know if you made that video!" he said, his angry voice lashing over the water like the crack of a whip.

"Of course I didn't. And neither did Kara!" I planted my hands on my waist to keep from punching him. "If you ever speak to her like that again, or tell her she's anything less than perfect, I will beat you with a fucking shovel." We glared at each other. "I'm serious, Dan. You've gone too far. You're losing your shit and crossing lines that can't be uncrossed. You'd better get it together before you lose your daughters."

He jabbed his finger an inch from my face. "You're the cause of this mess! From the minute you left, our family has been in chaos. Every bit of this mess rests on your shoulders."

I slapped his hand away. "Get the hell off my property."

"I'm not leaving until you tell me who made the video."

"I haven't a fucking clue, but if I ever find out, I'm going to thank them. I looked pretty damn good strutting into your bullshit church, didn't I?"

His eyes flashed and his cheek ticked. For a moment I thought he'd strike me. "You looked like a tramp. My mother saw the video, which did not help her condition one bit, Kate. She's on her deathbed because of you," he said, a hitch in his voice prompting him to clear his throat.

For a moment, I felt bad. Dan's mother was a decent lady, and she was the only person Dan had truly made sacrifices for. He was a mama's boy, and that's one of the things that had reeled me in after suffering the loss of my own mother. That he'd continued to be dedicated to his mother through her bouts with cancer, I'd had to support him, even as I questioned everything I saw in his cynical ministry.

"I assume you didn't tell her that your mistreatment of our daughter prompted my visit?"

Scoffing aloud, Dan cast scathing eyes over me, condemning me head to toe. "It's one thing for you to go astray, Kate, but to draw our daughters into this sin-filled life of yours is criminal. How pathetic you've become."

Shaking with anger and loathing, I knew I had to walk away before I gave in to the urge to kick him in the crotch of his expensive suit. I made it halfway down the dock when I felt my wrist grabbed and was forcefully yanked around to face Dan.

My reaction to being accosted was so spontaneous, I twisted

my wrist and hit him in the chest with my other hand before I realized I'd done it.

He stumbled back a step, his eyes flashing and arms flailing as he teetered on the edge of the dock, suspended for a humorously long second before falling backward into the lake. Water shot up like a geyser and splashed over the dock. I stood in shock as he surfaced with a howl of outrage.

I saw Maggie and Chloe leap to their feet as if ready to step in should Dan come after me.

In two angry strokes, he brought himself back to the edge of the dock, clamped both hands on the weathered planks, and tried to pull himself up.

Twice. Three times he tried, and he couldn't muster enough strength or leverage to haul his sopping ass out of the lake.

I started to giggle, which infuriated him.

"Damn it!" he shouted, eyes blazing like hot coals.

He was so angry he couldn't form a coherent sentence as he spit and sputtered at me. With a hard grunt, he shoved away from the dock and propelled his arms in a sloppy, water-slapping crawl toward the shore. When he could finally stand, he swept his arms wide to move himself inland through the chest deep water. Finally, after much flailing and sputtering, he'd made it to the shallow edge where the water was knee deep. He kicked and stomped his way through the water as if his rage would put the fear of his god in me.

What he hadn't realized yet was that he was about to hit ankle-deep mud. That's why we'd usually enter and exit the lake from the dock, using the built-in ladder near the end of the dock that Dan hadn't noticed—and I hadn't pointed out.

In his tantrum, he lost his balance. Hopping once, he fell forward, catching himself by planting one hand in the water. Pushing himself upright again, he shook thick mud off his hand and scanned the water. After a couple seconds, he shouted, "Screw it!" then sloshed out of the water with a limp.

It took me a moment to realize he wasn't limping because he'd gotten hurt. He'd lost his thousand-dollar shoe! And likely a good bit of his pride.

He spun to face me, water streaming from his hair and clothing, his expression as wild-eyed and half-crazed as the most dedicated zealot. "This isn't over," he ground out between clenched teeth.

"Yes, it is, Dan. I want those divorce papers in hand by next Friday, exactly as I'd outlined, or your shoe won't be the only thing you lose. I'll come after everything. And I'll make your life a living hell."

"You already have!" With that, he whipped around and stalked to his rental car. The door slammed, the engine caught and revved, the tires spun, and the car whipped around, spraying grass and dirt behind it. What Dan had failed to notice during his immature tantrum was the other car emerging from the lake trail. At the last second, he swerved to avoid the incoming vehicle—and sideswiped the iron bumper on the Dummy.

The sound of metal crunching and a long *schreeeeech* mingled with our gasps of shock. The side mirror snapped off and banged against the passenger window, but Dan didn't stop. He just barreled past Sophie's SUV and stormed out the lake trail, that poor mirror bouncing and banging against the side of his wrecked car.

I stood on the dock, stock still and speechless for a few seconds, wondering if this had really happened. Maggie's howl of laughter cutting through the evening air assured me it had. Chloe's laughter rolled across the lake in waves as I made my way toward them.

"What the hell was that about?" Sophie asked, wide-eyed as she made her way over.

"Oh my god, I have to show you," Maggie said between gasps of laughter. "I recorded the whole thing!"

The anger and outrage that had been coursing through my body moments before was draining away and leaving a tremor behind. I dropped into my chair beside Maggie who could barely contain herself. Sophie pulled a chair over, and we all huddled around Maggie's phone. Watching the scene play out from an outsider point of view was far more humorous than being a character in that shit show. By the time the video showed Dan crashing past the Dummy and out the lake trail, we were all bent double with laughter.

Swiping tears away with my forearm, I tried to apologize to Chloe for my asshole ex hitting her truck. "I'll pay for any damage."

Flopping back in her chair, trying to catch her breath, Chloe flapped a hand at me. "That little rental car wouldn't have left a scratch on the Dummy."

"That's right! He was driving a rental car!" I pressed a palm to my aching belly, still convulsed with laughter. "I wish I could see him explain the damage to the rental company."

That set us off again and had us reaching into the cooler for beer. As I handed one to Sophie, our eyes met. "I'm so glad you made it, Soph."

"Me too," she said, twisting off the cap and raising her bottle as if making a toast. "Nice to finally be old enough to drink with you guys."

Chapter Forty-Two

B right the next morning, I visited my attorney to update her on my situation with Dan. Although she saw the humor in his unexpected plunge in the lake, she saw none whatsoever in his passive-aggressive behavior. She strenuously suggested we update my divorce paperwork stipulating significantly higher and more painful-to-Dan terms. And then she sent it with a strongly worded cover letter for him to sign and return by our deadline or we'd seek a forensic audit and come after everything I was entitled to under spousal law. I finally agreed with my attorney, not because I wanted more but because I wanted *out*.

Afterward, I made the rounds to several dealerships and found a used Trailblazer on a car lot just outside of town. It was love at first sight, just as it had been when I'd seen Gussie on the sidewalk outside the big box store. But I knew next to nothing about vehicles and engines and such, and I didn't know if I could trust the salesman, so I called the one person I considered an expert. My father. For several minutes, I'd hesitated and dithered over making the call but eventually realized this presented an opportunity for us to begin rebuilding our relationship. I called him.

He'd said he'd have his clerk tend the store and be over in a few minutes. Ten minutes later, he pulled in and parked his old, black pickup truck in the lot. His stride was steady and confident as he crossed the lot. The smile on his face and warmth in his eyes when he spotted me whisked me back to my childhood when he would come home from work. He would kneel on one knee and open his arms. "How's my Katie-girl?" he'd ask, and I'd launch myself into his embrace. Sometimes he'd have a treat for me, and I'd have to guess in which hand he held the toy or coloring book or piece of candy. Other times, he'd just pop me onto his shoulders and carry me inside to the kitchen where my mother would be cooking supper. As I moved into my teen years, I felt too old and far too cool to be getting hugs from my father—but he didn't care a whit. He'd ignore my laughing protests and would wrestle me into his arms for a hug. I would pretend to be exasperated, but I secretly loved the attention and his hugs.

A breeze ruffled his hair as he approached. Without a preamble that might have made our meeting uncomfortable, he scanned the lot.

"Which one are you looking at?" he asked.

"Whichever one runs the best and costs the least," I said, relieved that he wasn't making this awkward by giving me a hug.

I hadn't heard my father laugh in so many years, I'd forgotten how the sound rolled through his chest and tumbled out in a joyful chortle.

"Okay then," he said, "let's take a look around."

"Actually, I'm a little in love with that silver Trailblazer over there," I said, pointing several cars away. "The salesman said it came in yesterday afternoon, and that's why they haven't had time to detail it. But he told me it would move fast."

With one hand shading his eyes from the morning sun, my father squinted into the distance. "Ah, I see it. I'll take a look under the hood. If it looks good, I'll have Clark put her up on the lift so I can check the undercarriage."

A sense of relief washed over me to have my dad here. He'd helped me buy my first car three months before I'd gone off to college—and only a few weeks before our world had blown apart.

I'd worked part time at the hardware store during my junior and senior years of high school, so I'd saved up enough for a used car. My father added another thousand dollars to upgrade me to a more reliable vehicle.

We crossed the lot and stopped beside the SUV where he looked it over with his keen eye. "I know this vehicle," he said, walking around it.

It seemed such an odd thing to say it made me laugh.

His mouth quirked in a half-smile. "I know who owned it."

"Is that a good thing?"

"It belonged to Tuck and Laura, so they'll have taken good care of it."

"Then I hope it belonged to them." Eyeing the vehicle, I asked, "How will you know?"

"We can ask Clark. But I don't think we'll have to." My dad pointed to a bumper sticker of Jesus riding a dinosaur.

I burst out laughing. If ever there was a sign the Trailblazer was meant to be mine, this was it. "I presume the sticker means it was theirs?"

"Definitely, but I'll check her over just to make sure everything looks good."

After he looked under the hood and listened to the engine, we took it for a test drive. It was surreal driving around town with my father riding shotgun. We experienced a few awkward moments but managed to keep conversation going with discussions about vehicles and all the bells and whistles my dad felt were unnecessary and frequently a damn nuisance.

"A man can't even work on his own truck these days," he said. "Everything's computerized and the engine compartment is so cramped you couldn't get a screwdriver in there if your life depended on it."

I glanced over at him. "Is that why you're driving that old pickup?" I wasn't sure if it was his choice or if it might be a lack of funds driving that decision.

"Darn right," he said, a sense of pride in his voice. "Used to be you could pop the hood, change your air filter, and replace the spark plugs or monkey with the carburetor and whatnot. I like being able to take care of some of those things on my own."

"But if you had a newer vehicle, you might not have to mess with any of it."

"Bah," he said with a wave of his hand. "My old girl will outlive me." He leaned over and peeked at the dash instruments. "Low mileage. That's a plus."

"What do you think?" I asked as we pulled back into the car lot. "Should I buy it?"

"Let's get her on the lift first."

Twenty minutes later, my father was satisfied that the SUV was in great shape and worth what they were asking. After negotiating a deal to include four new tires, new wipers, and six free oil changes, I bought the Trailblazer. I had Kara's car, so I texted Chloe, and she agreed to run me back to the lot in the afternoon to pick up my new SUV. Clark agreed to clean the vehicle and have it ready for me, but I made it clear that under no circumstances were they to remove the bumper sticker.

Back outside, I walked with my dad to his truck. We stopped and faced each other for an awkward moment as if neither of us knew what to do next. Were we supposed to hug goodbye? Just say goodbye and walk away?

I hooked my fingers over the tailgate and eased back a step. "Thanks, Dad. I really appreciate you doing this for me."

He smiled. "I'd do anything for you, Katie-girl."

If he would have said anything else I'd have been able to say goodbye and walk away. But hearing him use his pet name for me and remembering all those hugs and how he'd made me feel like the most special girl in the world, had my eyes swimming.

I didn't want our time together to end. Not yet.

"Do you think you could ... go for an early lunch with me?" I asked, longing for him to say yes but fearing he wouldn't have the time. "And maybe you could bring your wife too?"

Without answering, he just pulled me into his arms and gave me a hard, rocking hug. "Where do you want to go, sweetheart?"

I swallowed hard to release the emotion that had a stranglehold on my throat. "Um, how about Sophie's place?"

As I DROVE out the lake trail in my new-to-me Trailblazer, which I'd already named *The Duchess*, I surveyed my beautiful property. The leaves on the trees had dulled with the approach of fall, but the forest was alive with the twitter and buzzing sounds of nature. The lake shimmered in the afternoon sunshine. Sinatra crouched at the shoreline peering intently at something in the water. My lakeside cottage with its sky-blue roof and driftwood-colored walls blended into the landscape as if it had been grown from nature. Long blades of grass fluttered in the breeze and reminded me it was finally time to mow my lawn.

Gussie's battery was fully charged and waiting for me in my utility room. After I changed into shorts and my work shoes, I grabbed a quick glass of water, then went outside. My yard had been filled with ladders and materials and machines for so long it had been impossible to mow. And I'd been so busy building my house and working with Chloe, I hadn't the time to do so anyhow.

Finally hearing Gussie's motor purr again made me smile. It was the first time I'd heard her sweet song since the day I'd left my old life behind. Now I was mowing my own yard in my new life that included my sister and my father—and a stepmother I admired.

My father's wife hadn't tried to win me over or impress me during our lunch visit. She'd simply taken my hand in hers and said she was sorry. She hadn't needed to elaborate because the story of our intertwined lives was in her eyes. Life was full of hard choices and painful mistakes and roads not taken. There was an inherent understanding between us that we would both have done things differently if there were do-overs, and that our lives were no longer about the past but about this moment and the next and the next.

Sophie had joined us while we ate dessert, and I knew I would make the most of every moment like that for the rest of my life.

Even something as simple and mundane as mowing my yard was a moment I cherished.

I spent the rest of the day outside cleaning up around the yard, gathering up a few things I planned to store in the shed by my grandparents' home. I wanted to move the shed out here, but it was filled with my grandfather's stuff and the heavy workbench I'd moved out of my house. For now it would stay put. When I'd finished loading a pile of scrap pieces of shiplap into the back of the Duchess, I realized I had one more piece of debris to pick up. For several minutes, I waded through the mucky shore before I found Dan's lost shoe. When I pulled it out of the sucking mud, I burst out laughing. What a shit show that had been. I would never understand what drove him to be such a dumb-ass.

I swished his shoe through the water to detach the mud, then whacked it on the grass to remove some of the water. After tossing it onto the pile of shiplap, I hauled everything out to the shed. The whole time I was unloading the shiplap and stacking it inside the shed, I thought about Dan and his bizarre behavior and his idiotic beliefs and his despicable treatment of his own child. I was beyond fed up with his crazy-ass world and his threats and his endless attacks on me. I threw his shoe and hit an old wooden sign that toppled over. I wanted a damn divorce, not just from Dan but from all that shit. And until I had legal documents severing me from that life, I'd never feel truly free.

Plopping my behind on an overturned bucket, I sat in the corner hoping I wouldn't have to go to court to force him to give me a divorce. I felt as trapped as the dead fly stuck in the spiderweb under the workbench.

Sighing in frustration, I dragged my forearm across my sweaty forehead and gazed at the floor as if I'd find the answer written there. All I saw was the old wooden sign for my grandfather's septic cleaning business. It said *Dunwith Septic Service* in bold white letters across the top of the sign. This sign had stood out front for so many years it had become part of the landscape. Seeing it here made me sad. It hurt that my grandparents were gone. And it hurt that I hadn't yet found Papa Ray's ashes.

It took a good bit of muscling to haul the heavy wood sign outside, then a quick trip to my father's hardware store for paint, brushes, and two bags of fast-setting concrete mix, before I began my project. Two hours later, I'd brushed white paint over the whole sign. After the white paint had dried, I used black paint and a small brush to paint my declaration on the face of the sign. Then I dug two holes for the posts beside one of the stone pylons and poured in the concrete mix. But I had one last thing to do before I could set the sign.

Returning to the shed, I found the coffee can with screws and nails. The spike was still in there where I'd put it months ago when I'd cleaned off the workbench in the boathouse. Now I had a use for it. On the way out, I grabbed a hammer, and Dan's wet shoe off the floor, and headed outside. Kneeling by the sign, I raised the hammer and drove the spike through Dan's expensive shoe, nailing it to the wood as I declared my independence.

After I'd set the sign in place, I stood back to view my handiwork.

I smiled the whole time I put away my tools and while I drove out the lake trail to my little *Done With* world.

After cleaning my paintbrush and feeding Sinatra, I made a tomato and cheese sandwich and took it outside to enjoy my supper by the lake. Sinatra joined me on the dock where we lounged a good long time before my phone pinged, indicating someone had just come through the gate. I didn't bother looking. Whoever or whatever was heading my way no longer threatened me. Sinatra and I were watching a mallard pedal through the cattails a short distance down shore.

The sound of a door closing drew our attention. "Love the sign out front," Ashe said as he strode to the dock.

He looked so damned gorgeous all dark-eyed and smiling, I immediately wondered how he'd feel about having sex in a single bed.

"Hey, buddy," he said, stooping down to give Sinatra's head a frisky rub. "Your mama is one crazy lady, you know that?"

I arched an eyebrow in mock offense. "Sanity is overrated."

"Agreed. Got time for a drink?"

"Got all night," I replied but remained sitting with Sinatra on my lap.

"Be right back." With that, he walked back to his van, then returned with a couple bottles of iced tea. "Has Maggie seen your sign yet?" he asked, beginning to chuckle.

"No, she won't be over until tomorrow afternoon. Chloe and I are meeting her in town to go furniture shopping for my place."

"Hard to believe you're ready to furnish your home. Seems like we just put the roof on."

"I know. It's nice to be this far along, but it's just not the same place without the plate and duct tape on the roof."

"No, it's not," he said, wearing such a devastated expression I burst out laughing.

"That sure is a nice sound," he said, his gaze holding mine. "I've missed you."

"I've been busy."

"I heard. I saw Sophie at the café this afternoon. She said you were in for lunch with your dad ... and your stepmother. And she said your daughter is coming for a visit this weekend. That's quite a day, Kate. You must be thrilled."

"I'm beyond excited."

"Good for you," he said. "I've got another surprise for you. Your heating stove finally came in."

"It did?" I asked, thrilled to know I'd have heat in my home before cold weather set in.

"Thought I might install it for you this evening."

"That would be fantastic. I'll even make supper for you. Peanut butter and jelly sound okay?"

A wry grin tipped his mouth. "Sounds great." He tucked a flyaway strand of my hair behind my ear. Water lapped against the dock and mingled with Sinatra's purring as Ashe's thumb caressed my cheek. I felt the familiar lift and spin in my belly as he leaned close. "I need to ask you something," he said, his gaze holding mine. "Is that Dan's shoe nailed to the sign?"

Chapter Forty-Three

S pending the day with Chloe and Maggie was a treat. Dressed in shorts, T-shirts, and flip flops, we had gone back to Potsdam where we'd visited several consignment shops and used furniture stores. I had already told Maggie I wanted to repurpose as many items as possible to furnish my house, but with one exception. I wanted a new top-of-the-line sofa sleeper with a kickass mattress. I fell in love with a queen size sleeper sofa in a graphite gray linen fabric with a memory foam topped mattress. Other than a sheet set for the foldout bed, it was the only new item I purchased.

We loaded the couch into the pickup bed of Chloe's truck and slid it in beside the outdoor furniture and other items I'd purchased. Everything I'd needed to furnish my home was now loaded in Chloe's truck and covered up to keep it protected during our ride home.

After pulling around the corner and parking in front of a café with outdoor seating, we snagged a table outside and settled in to enjoy a leisurely lunch.

"I can't wait to see that couch in my living room," I said, already envisioning how it would look, and more importantly how it would *feel* to sit on those dreamy cushions.

"It's going to look amazing." Maggie took a drink of her tea, then proceeded to share her vision of how we could lay out the space to give it a more open feel. With her thick braid draped over one shoulder like a red sash, she sketched out her plan on the back of a placemat. "Sofa goes here," she said, moving her pen across the paper, "and we'll put that pretty carpet in front of it, then place a chair at each end with the coffee table in the center. That'll create a comfy sitting area without filling every inch of your living room."

"Ah, so that's why you insisted I purchase the outdoor furniture set."

"Exactly," she said, giving the placemat a tap with her pen. "The chairs have a smaller footprint but are comfy enough to lounge in. And you can use the loveseat outside."

"You are brilliant, Maggie. Thank you both for doing this with me. It's much more fun shopping and decorating with you two."

Maggie leaned back in her chair. "Well, thank you for buying lunch and for letting me play in your house. I can't wait to get this stuff in there and start creating magic."

Chloe drained her glass of lemonade and plunked it on the table. "Neither can I, so let's go."

"Shotgun!" I said, standing up.

Maggie wrinkled her nose. "Damn it."

We left the café laughing. But when we got to the truck, I climbed in ahead of Maggie. She stood at the door wearing a confused expression. "Um, Kate, I don't think you understand the meaning of *shotgun*."

I feigned a haughty look. "I know what it means, but look at you," I said with mock disdain. "Where are you going to put those long legs if you sit in the middle?"

"Good point," she said, making a scene climbing into the truck, nudging me with her knee and kicking the dash as she pretended to wrangle her long legs into the cab.

I gave her a hard shoulder nudge. "Knock it off."

"Both of you knock it off," Chloe said, but her laughter ruined her attempt to scold us.

A few minutes into our ride, Maggie released a huge sigh. "I'm disappointed," she said gazing out the window. "I was hoping to see Nature Boy today."

The naked nature boy we'd seen on our last trip to Potsdam wasn't anything I'd soon forget. "You should track him down, Maggie. He looked like your ideal playmate."

"Would if I could," she quipped. "Haven't been able to scrub that vision from my brain."

"Yeah, it's one of those things you can't unsee," Chloe said.

"Why the hell would you want to?" Maggie asked, making us all laugh.

Our conversation wandered like the winding road, taking us from sexy men on horseback to our jobs and kids. I'd told them about Kara coming in, and how my dad had helped me when I bought my Trailblazer. They were thrilled to hear I'd had lunch with him and Sharon, and that Sophie had joined us for dessert.

Maggie patted my knee. "Sounds as if the dust is finally settling."

"I hope so."

"Dylan will be heading back to school soon," Chloe said. "Let's not take any jobs next week so we can spend the whole week with our kids."

I was so relieved and happy to be able to spend the whole week with Kara, I gave Chloe a side-armed hug. "Thank you! And if it doesn't mess with your plans, I want you and Dylan to come over on Sunday to meet Kara and Jamie."

"I'd love that," she said, casting a warm glance at me.

I turned to Maggie. "Will you come too?"

She gave me a gentle nudge with her shoulder. "Of course."

"You're welcome to bring Nature Boy with you," I said. "But tell him clothing is required."

She laughed. "Believe me, if I could find him, I'd invite him."

And so it went until we hit my driveway. Chloe stomped on the brake, and the truck came to a rocking stop between the stone pylons. "What the hell is that?" she asked, pointing to my sign.

Maggie slapped her palm on the dash and released a hoot of

laughter. "Oh my god, that's Dan's shoe!" She looked at Chloe, and they both burst out laughing. "She nailed the damn thing to the sign!"

The two of them rolled out of the truck cab and went to investigate my handiwork.

I'd been agitated when I'd painted the sign, but now, viewing it from their point of view, I could see the humor in it. "Yeah, I might have been feeling a little vindictive that day," I said, following along. "But I've really had enough of his ridiculous nonsense."

"That's wildly apparent," Chloe said, still giggling.

Trying to catch her breath, Maggie stood with her palm pressed to her abdomen. "How the hell did you find his shoe?"

I snickered a little as a vision of Dan wobbling and falling over in the muck filled my mind. "Let's just say it was a scene I'll never forget, so I knew where he'd lost his shoe. Took a little fishing around, but I found the stupid thing. I just wanted to leave it where he could find it should he ever want it back."

Chloe shook her head as if she didn't know what to make of me. "How thoughtful of you." She turned to Maggie. "Remind me to never piss her off."

"All right, you guys, quit razzing me and get in the truck. I can't wait another minute to start decorating my house."

We all piled back into the cab, but Maggie and Chloe snickered and giggled all the way to my house.

"What's my brother doing here?" Maggie asked, gesturing to Ashe's van parked next to my Trailblazer. "Something you want to tell us?"

I lifted my chin and feigned a haughty expression. "Not really."

"Then I'll just ask him," she said, sliding out of the cab. With that, she marched into my house, presumably to demand answers from her brother, but both doors swung open a moment later. Sinatra shot outside and retreated to the dock where he settled on the sunbaked planks. Ashe and Maggie followed him out of the house carrying the futon I'd bought from Chloe. After parking it out of the way under the awning, they came over to where Chloe and I were watching.

"I hear you ladies have a truck full of furniture that needs to be hauled in," he said, giving me a little wink as if to say *good for you*.

"Sofa goes in first," Maggie said.

The four of us carried in the heavy sofa and did our best to position it per Maggie's instructions, but we weren't achieving the precise angle she wanted.

Chloe groaned aloud. "Come on, Mags, we're oozing spinal fluid here."

Maggie snickered. "Ashe do not move," she instructed. "You guys move your end six inches to your left. Another inch ... There!"

We lowered the beastly sofa to the floor with a hard thump. Maggie immediately dropped onto the cushions. Flapping a hand at us, she said, "Get out of my way. I need to see out the windows." Following orders, we all stepped aside, arching our backs and flexing our strained fingers while Maggie moved from one end to the other and then back to the middle of the sofa. Then she got up, crossed the room, and spent a minute eyeballing everything. "Nope. It's got to be moved."

"Noooo ..." I whined like a lazy teenager.

"Suck it up, Kate." She waved us over and instructed us to move the sofa precisely four inches back and two inches to the left.

She was so anal about it, I began to laugh. Then I couldn't stop.

She propped her hands on her hips. "What's so funny?"

"Just thinking how much I love you."

"Sure you were." Slinging her arm around my neck, she pulled me toward the open door. "Let's get the rest of your stuff."

During our shopping trip, Maggie had found a waist-high narrow dresser she insisted I purchase. She'd tried to explain why I needed it, but until we'd hauled the thing up to the loft, a strenuous chore even with Ashe's assistance, and set it in place, I hadn't been able to visualize just how perfect it would be. By placing the unit at the front of the loft it created a half-wall and provided a bit of privacy while still allowing light from the loft window to illuminate the rest of the house. It also provided me with six drawers, which meant I wouldn't have to store some of my clothing in plastic bins under my bed. Now I had a closet downstairs and a dresser upstairs.

For the next forty minutes, we carried in my new-to-me furnishings a piece at a time and placed them exactly where Maggie indicated. I became so caught up in watching her work, I didn't see her vision come to life until the last lamp was placed on an end table. While Ashe returned to his work connecting the propane fireplace that would keep my home cozy during the cold months, Chloe and I helped Maggie hang a few things on my bare walls.

Then Maggie carried in a couple of items I knew I hadn't purchased. "Where did you get those things?" I asked.

"Out of Ashe's van. I had him bring them over for me."

"You little sneak! You knew all along he'd be here!" I said with a laugh.

She shrugged. "Guilty."

"Did you make those pieces?"

"Yep, now quit hassling me and help me hang them."

She had created frames from weathered gray barn-wood and black iron hardware. The largest rectangular frame was a piece of wall art. Three maple trees cut from sheet metal, attached to the frame by their trunks and branches, were hand-painted with fall colors of rust and gold.

"That is absolutely gorgeous!" I said, in utter awe of her talent. "Did you make this?"

"Mostly. I had a friend laser cut the metal. I did the rest."

"It's breathtaking, Maggie. I can't imagine how you made this."

"It's the kind of thing I like to dabble with in the evenings, if I don't have anything more interesting to do."

Chloe rolled her eyes. "Like that ever happens."

Maggie ignored us. "I thought you might like to frame a couple pictures of your girls," she said to me, holding up two smaller barn-wood style frames that coordinated with the piece of wall art we'd just hung. She held them up against the opposite wall. "I thought they'd look good over here."

I knew exactly which pictures I'd put in the frames. "They're perfect, Maggie. Really. I can't thank you enough for these gorgeous gifts and, well, for the million ways you've helped me." I glanced at Chloe and Ashe. "I mean that for you guys too. I appreciate all of you more than I can say."

"You might change your mind after you see our last surprise," Maggie said. "Chloe and I have one more finishing touch to add before your home is complete. We'll be back in a minute." With that, she and Chloe scooted outside. A minute later, they carried in a reusable shopping bag containing contents I couldn't see.

"Hey, Kate, can you come over here for a minute?" Ashe asked from where he'd been working on my heater. "I want to show you how to operate this thing."

I looked at Maggie to see if she needed my help. "Go ahead." She dismissed me with a flap of her hand. "We've got this."

Ashe had mounted the small propane fireplace on the living room wall toward the center of the house. "This should do a good job of heating the main area of your house," he said. "But I'd still like to mount a small electric baseboard heater in your bathroom. You'll want it in the winter months, plus having a dedicated heat source back there will keep your utility room heated and prevent any issues with frozen water lines."

"I agree. I've just been waiting for you to do it."

There was something utterly mesmerizing watching the slow grin tilt his lips and flood his eyes—and me—with warmth. "Sounds like an after-hours project to me," he said.

I fanned my hot face. "That thing really puts out the heat." I gestured toward the heater. Flames danced behind a glass panel, and I imagined cuddling with Sinatra on a cold winter night watching the mini fireplace together. Then I imagined being in the dark with Ashe, but it was at his place on his big bed watching each other and doing far more than cuddling.

"Earth to Kate," he said with a laugh. "Do I need to repeat the instructions for operating this thing?"

"Um, yeah." I warned myself to snap out of it. "But shut it off. I'm burning up."

His lips compressed as if he were fighting a smile. After making sure I was mentally present and listening, he walked through the operating instructions.

"Got it," I said, relieved at the ease of operating the unit. "Thanks for installing it for me. Don't leave without letting me pay you."

"You can reimburse me for the unit, and a beer will cover the install."

"That's not enough. I don't expect you to do this stuff free of charge."

He gave me a just-between-us wink. "Can't a guy help out a friend?"

Before I could reply, Chloe and Maggie called me over to where they'd been hanging something on my wall. It took a moment before it dawned on me what I was looking at. They'd repurposed a section of an old mantelpiece and mounted it to the wall with black iron brackets to make it a shelf. A dark brown vase filled with colorful wildflowers sat on the shelf, and beside it sat my grungy old sneakers with melted soles, duct taped sides and knotted together shoelaces. Above the dirt-stained shoes, they had stenciled a quote on the wall: "A journey of a thousand miles begins with a single step."

"My shoes," I whispered, both laughing and fighting back tears. "I thought you guys had thrown them away."

"We considered it," Chloe said.

"It took enormous willpower to resist," Maggie added, "but we knew what they symbolized to you."

I'd clung to my old beaters for several reasons, but mainly because of the hard journey they represented. "You guys are too much," I blubbered, trying and failing to blink back tears.

"Just so you don't get any ideas, Kate, we've glued the damn things to the shelf so you can't wear them." Maggie's warning look dared me to try to remove them.

"Well, that's just cruel."

She slung her arm around my shoulders and gave me a hard shake. "Come on, girl, there's only so much you can ask of them. They're old and tired. You've got to let 'em go."

Ashe and Chloe were laughing at Maggie's mock dramatics, and I was trying to hold it together while I stood in my newly furnished home with my best friends and an old pair of sneakers that had walked with me all this way.

Dragging in a big breath, I said, "Anyone else need a drink?"

"For future reference, the answer to that question is always Yes," Maggie quipped as she sank onto a chair.

Chloe and Ashe followed me to the kitchen.

"I hope wine is okay with everyone," I said, retrieving wine glasses from the cupboard, and filling them with a Mondavi Riesling. Chloe took two glasses and carried one into Maggie, then sat in the chair opposite Maggie. I handed one to Ashe, and he leaned against the counter beside me.

For a moment, I simply sipped my wine and took in my stunning home. Somehow, Maggie had created a spacious sitting area atop a slightly worn but beautiful area carpet of smoky blue and charcoal gray. She'd placed the sofa and two chairs around a wooden flat-top trunk that doubled as a coffee table and extra storage. The end tables were antique wooden crates stood on end and topped with matching lamps. Everything except the sofa had been used and was now being repurposed for my home. Somehow Maggie had tied all those old things together in a dreamy magazine-quality presentation.

"I suppose my new mattress is no longer an enticement for you to come to my place," Ashe said quietly, drawing my attention to his handsome face.

Trying to maintain a neutral expression and suppress the laughter I felt bubbling up, I sighed as if I felt sorry for him. "Yeah,

I can't think of a single reason I'd need to sleep anywhere but here."

His eyes drank me in. "Who said anything about sleeping?"

"Are you two going to join us or flirt in the kitchen all night?" Maggie asked, kicking her feet up and propping them on the coffee table.

"We're going to flirt in the kitchen," Ashe replied.

"I don't have the energy to flirt with anyone," I said. "I'm going to sit my weary bones on my new sofa." With that, I left temptation, and Ashe, in the kitchen. The instant my body sank onto the thick couch cushions, I groaned aloud. "I'm never leaving this spot."

Ashe came over and sat at the other end of the couch. "What a difference, Kate. Your futon cushions were so thin you might as well have been sitting on the crossbars."

"Well, it beats sitting on the floor or sleeping in a canoe," I said.

Chapter Forty-Four

Early Saturday morning, I fed Sinatra, cleaned my house, then showered and headed to the airport to pick up Kara and Jamie. They were waiting outside when I pulled into the arrivals pick up area.

I spotted Kara right away. Her sunshine-colored hair and bright smile were hard to miss. A girl about her age with gorgeous mocha skin, long braided hair, and almond-shaped eyes was laughing at something Kara was saying. When I pulled up to the curb, they both angled their heads to see inside the vehicle.

I waved and got out to open the hatch.

Kara met me at the back of the vehicle where we exchanged a big hug. "It's so good to see you, Mom!"

"And you, little bit," I said, using her pet name from her toddler years.

"Really, Mom?" she said with a laugh. Stepping back, she gestured to the girl standing beside her. "This is Jamie."

Jamie was so adorable I wanted to hug her, but I fought the urge. "It's nice to finally meet you," I said. "I'm so thrilled you girls are here."

Jamie met my eyes with a confidence rarely seen in people her age. "I've been looking forward to this. Kara has told me so many wonderful things about you."

Warmth flooded my chest. "Same here. Are you two hungry?" I asked, opening the SUV's back gate so the girls could load their bags.

"We're starving," Kara said, tossing her bag into the back.

Within minutes we'd made our way to a pizza place—their choice—and the girls told me about their long day. They'd gotten up before dawn to catch their first flight and were relieved to finally be here. Excitement oozed from Kara as she told Jamie about *our lake* and the house I'd built, and how she couldn't wait for me to show them around the property and take them into town.

I'd witnessed Kara's excitement numerous times during her childhood, less so during her teen years, but had never seen such a sense of lightness in her.

During our lunch and the long ride home, Jamie had shared that she was a year older than Kara, was one of six children, was in love with her area of study in animation and hoped to work for a studio when she graduated in two years.

Kara planned to take this semester off and return in January, but she worried her father wouldn't support her changing to another university.

"When did you last talk to him?" I asked, hoping Dan had called and apologized to her.

"Not since he accused me of making the video of you barging into church."

I cringed. "I'm sorry about that."

"You didn't do anything wrong, Mom, and Dad sort of deserved it after the way he's treated you."

Surprised by the venom in her voice, I looked over to see her scowling. "Sweetie, it was the way he treated *you* that drove me through those doors."

She leaned her forehead against the side window and sighed. "I wish he would lighten up a little and not be so ..." she let her sentence trail off on another sigh.

Judgmental? Narrow-minded? A complete ass? I thought to myself as I finally turned the corner by Chloe's house and headed toward my own. "Oh, I need to mention something before we get to the house," I said. "There's a sign out front that you or Jamie might find offensive. I admit to being a little angry when I made it, but I stand by my convictions, so the sign stays."

Kara's eyebrows knit in confusion, or apprehension. "Okay, um, thanks for the heads-up I guess."

A couple minutes later, I watched her reaction to the sign. Her mouth formed an O, then she pressed her fingers to her mouth to hide a grin.

I glanced in the mirror to see Jamie reading the words I'd written, then give a slow nod as if to acknowledge them as truth. "My father would love this," she said. "He's always on his soapbox about the injustice and unfairness of religious tax breaks." Her eyes met mine in the rearview mirror. "He's a cardiologist who works long hours and pays an obscene amount of taxes. I really need to send him a pic of your sign."

Before I could suggest it might not be a good idea, she'd lifted her phone and taken the shot.

"Mom," Kara asked wide-eyed, "is that Dad's shoe?"

For the first time since driving a spike through Dan's expensive loafer, I questioned the wisdom of my defiant act. But it's how I felt about his asinine behavior and beliefs, and my grown-up children were going to have to understand that their mother was entitled to her own opinion.

"Is that the one he lost in the lake?" Kara asked.

"Yeah." I pulled away from the gate. That's all I was going to say on the matter, but I heard Kara's quiet snickers. When I dared to glance over, she had her face turned to the window as if trying to hide her laughter.

After I parked, we retrieved their baggage and headed inside. Kara stopped just inside the door and looked around. "Wow ... Mom, this is really pretty." For a full minute she took in every detail as if utterly stunned by the transformation of an old gambrel-roofed building that had been converted into a gorgeous lakeside cottage.

"This is so cute, Mrs. Symmons—or Ms. Weston." Jamie wrinkled her cute nose. "I'm not sure how to address you."

"Kate works just fine," I said.

"All right, thank you. I was just going to say this is my dream home." Her pretty brown eyes took in everything in a long sweeping glance. "It's the perfect size, and I love the way you furnished it."

"Thank you. My friends helped with everything. You'll get to meet them on Sunday."

Kara turned with a surprised expression on her face. "Is it Maggie and Chloe you've told me about?"

"Yep. And Chloe's son, Dylan," I said. Since Kara had begun talking with me again, I'd been telling her about Maggie and Chloe and our long friendship. "We'll have a cookout in the afternoon."

"Sounds nice, Mom." She glanced around again. "I can't believe three women did all of this."

"Well, we didn't do quite everything. I hired a plumber and an electrician for that type of work, and Ashe helped us with a lot of other work too."

"Who's Ashe?" she asked.

Oh boy ... "He's an electrician, and Maggie's brother. And my friend," I said, not about to elaborate the friends-with-benefits side of my relationship with him.

"Well, you all made this place look amazing. I could have never imagined this." Looking down at her suitcase, she asked, "Where should we put our bags?"

"You girls can sleep in the loft."

I'd barely gotten the words out of my mouth before she grabbed her bag and headed up the stairs. A second later, she called down, "Whoa, Mom! It's so pretty up here."

Before I could reply, Sinatra shot down the stairs, into the utility room, and a second later I heard the metallic click of the cat door I'd recently installed snapping closed behind him.

"Sorry! I forgot you had a cat," Kara said over the half-wall.

After the girls had stashed their bags and settled in, we headed outside to take a walk along the lake. Watching them was like looking through a window to my past when Sophie and I had spent our days here. Memories unspooled as we ambled out to the dock.

"Does this thing float?" Kara asked when she saw my canoe lying bottom-up on the dock. Her eyes lit up. "Can we take it out?"

"Yes, and yes," I said with a laugh. It took a bit of muscling and heaving to tip the canoe into the lake. After the girls climbed down the dock ladder and settled themselves in the rocking canoe, I passed them the paddles. "Jamie, I trust you know how to swim? I don't have life jackets yet." I knew Kara was a good swimmer, but I needed to be certain Jamie could swim.

"I was on the swim team in high school," Jamie volunteered. "Didn't have time for it in college though." Her dark eyes looked longingly at the lake. "I am so in love with this place."

Jamie was sweet and polite and a deep thinker—and I liked the way she and Kara balanced each other.

"All right, then, be careful and pay attention. Don't get hung up in the reeds along the shore." I gave the canoe a shove to send them on their way. "And don't fall out!"

They didn't fall out, but they did spend part of the afternoon paddling around and exploring my childhood playground. Sinatra had made his way back and spent an hour snoozing on my lap while I made some notes in my journal for my next writing session.

THE GIRLS and I had finished supper and were relaxing outside by the fire pit when my phone pinged that someone or something was at the front gate. I swiped on the app and rolled the video back a few seconds.

"What the ..." I glanced over at Kara. "Does your father know you're here?" I asked, having just seen Big Bart roll in between the stone pylons. I hadn't been able to see who was driving, but if Dan was coming to cause more trouble, I'd be at a huge disadvantage because I wouldn't fight him with our daughter here.

"I don't know how he could. Why?" Kara asked, but the flicker of headlights cutting through the shadowed trees caught our attention.

Big Bart emerged from the wooded lake trail and came to a stop. The driver cut the engine, and I felt my tension mount. Kara and I stood at the same time, but she headed straight for the RV wearing a big smile. A second later, the door opened, and Haley stepped out.

"Surprise!" she shouted, spreading her arms wide. Dressed in jean shorts, a T-shirt, and hiking boots, she strode forward to meet Kara. "Did we pull it off?" she asked, hugging her sister.

Laughing, Kara said, "We sure did. Mom had no idea you were coming."

I stood in open-mouthed surprise as my daughters sauntered over, obviously proud of themselves for pulling off such a wonderful surprise.

"Hi, Mom." Haley gave me a warm hug then turned to introduce herself to Jamie.

Barely able to contain myself, I pulled Haley back in for another hug, then reached out and pulled Kara in too. "You little rascals."

"Be right back," Haley said. While she ran back to the RV to get her bottle of tea, I added more wood to the fire. Then she returned and settled in beside me. Stretching her legs out and rolling her ankles, she groaned. "That is a *long* drive. I left at five this morning and only stopped for gas and to grab a quick bite to eat."

"How were you able to persuade your father to let you take the RV?" I asked, boggled that she'd been able to do so.

"I told him I needed it so I could pick up my motorcycle."

"Oh, is that why you're here?" I hoped she'd also come to see me.

"Not exactly. Kara and I wanted to surprise you with a visit.

It's been a while since we've all been together. Plus, I really wanted to meet Jamie."

To be sitting here with my girls, after the shit show we'd been through when I'd left their father, was the best feeling in the world.

"But would you mind if I take my motorcycle back with me?" Haley asked. "I sort of need to since I told Dad it's why I had to take Big Bart."

"Of course you can," I said with a laugh. "I've had my fun on it."

"You rode it?" she asked in shock.

I didn't tell them about my first ride where I'd nearly run down their father, but I shared my one and only ride to town.

"Wow, I'm proud of you, Mom. Were you scared?"

"At first," I said, "but then I really loved it."

A dreamy smile crossed Haley's face. "Yeah, it's a great feeling to ride without doors."

It's a great way to live, too, I wanted to say, but I didn't want my opinions to influence my girls any longer. Dan and I had already shoved nineteen years of it down their throats. It was now up to them how they wanted to live their lives. I just hoped they would each choose their own authentic path and not one of obligation.

"Tell us about your hike." Kara leaned forward in her chair as if eager to hear every detail of her sister's recent trek along the Appalachian trail.

"Yes, please," Jamie added. "We've been dying to hear all about it. Did you see any bears or snakes?"

Haley kicked her shoes off and rested her feet on the edge of her chair. With her arms circled around her up-drawn knees, she told us about her days of walking, climbing, and sweating on the trail. She talked about the breathtaking, indescribable views from mountain vistas, getting soaked in the rain, painful blisters that had nagged her and many of her fellow hikers each step of the journey, nights sleeping outside under a blanket of stars that seemed so close she could touch them, and the friendships she'd made with other hikers that she and her group of friends had met on the trail or at the shelters.

As the three of us sat enthralled, Haley talked about the enormous moose she'd seen and how surprisingly graceful it was as it moved through the forest, and a snake on the path that startled her so badly she'd nearly wet herself. She explained how morning dew and fog made the rocks slippery, and what a gift it was to come upon a box or cooler of food and beverages that had been placed there by Trail Angels who wanted to help and support hikers.

A moment of silence ensued while her gaze seemed to linger on some faraway trail. "I can't describe what it's like to be out there co-existing in the wild with nature. It changed me," she said quietly. As her gaze cleared, she turned to me. "I don't want to go back to college, Mom."

I was shocked by her announcement, but not surprised. She'd mentioned that she wanted to talk with me when she finished her hike. This must be what she'd had on her mind.

"I'm not going back until next semester," Kara said. "What are you going to do if you don't go back?"

That was my question too, but I let the girls talk.

Haley shrugged. "I don't know. I just can't tolerate being caged in a classroom all day learning stuff I don't care about." She glanced at me. "Sorry, Mom, but I just can't go back."

"Sweetie, you need to live *your* life, not the one you were pushed into." I glanced at Kara. "I thought sending you off to college was the right thing to do, that I was helping you girls get a foothold in your future. But I want to make it abundantly clear right now that your lives are your own. You don't need to ask permission to choose your own path and chase your own dreams."

Haley slid her feet off the chair and looked at me as if uncertain she'd heard correctly. "Then you're okay with me not going to college?"

"Honey, if there's one thing I've learned in the last few months it's that life should be joyful and fulfilling, not obligatory and stifling. Whatever path you take will present challenges. That's just a fact of life. But if that path is *your* path, it can be as beautiful and moving as your hike through the wilderness."

She pushed from her chair and wrapped her arms around me. "Thank you," she whispered.

Over her shoulder, I met Kara's eyes. "I support both of you in your life choices. I want you girls to be free to create whatever kind of life makes you happy. But there is one thing I ask."

Haley released me and sat back on her chair.

"Find a way to contribute," I said. "I'm not talking about giving money to organizations. Reach out to people who need a helping hand, and don't just pray for them. Actually *do* something. Do what you can to protect nature and take care of our planet. And just to be clear, I'm not talking about becoming an activist or taking up causes. Just be willing to give a bit of your time for the things that matter."

"That's all I could think about during my hike," Haley said ardently. "I want to do something to help preserve places like that. I'm considering joining a volunteer trail crew. They clean and groom the trail. And they do other things like roping off sections of greenery that need to be protected and that type of stuff. Each crew works and camps trailside a few weeks at a time. It's such a fascinating job, and I think I'd like it."

"That would be amazing," Jamie said, joining our conversation. "Do you have to take courses to be on a trail crew?"

"I don't know," Haley replied, her expression dulling with concern. "I've got a lot to look into before I know what I'm going to do. Then I have to persuade Dad to go along with it."

Reaching over, I tweaked her lopsided ponytail. "Don't worry about your father. When it's time to talk to him, we can do it together." I had a few words of my own to say to him. He still hadn't sent the divorce paperwork, and his deadline was approaching fast.

"After Mom's visit to church, I don't think Dad will mess with her," Kara said with a little smirk.

Haley glanced at me, her brows drawn together in confusion. "You went to church?"

"Maybe we should change the subject," I suggested strongly.

But true to her age, my teenage daughter ignored my suggestion. With a quick swipe and tap on her phone, Kara started the video. She passed it to Haley who watched with her eyes getting wider by the second and ending with her jaw on her lap. Finally, she turned to me as if I were a stranger. "Where did you get those boots?" she asked.

"W-what?" I asked, completely dumbstruck that she'd just witnessed my wild strut into church and all she wanted to know was where I'd gotten my boots.

"I'm kidding!" she said, releasing a belly laugh that bent her forward. "That was epic, Mom!"

That sent Kara and Jamie into a fit of laughter.

My reaction wobbled all over the place. A dribble of laughter. A moment of intense embarrassment. A stunning realization that my babies were adults, that our relationship was transitioning to a different level where we could share grown-up jokes and have mature conversations, and they could see humor in something that would have mortified them just a few months ago.

It seemed we were all on a new journey now, uncaged, and testing our wings.

Chapter Forty-Five

At ten o'clock Sunday morning, after lingering over breakfast and rushing through showers, I took the girls into town. I'd parked near the winery at the north end of town so we could do a complete circuit on foot and end up back at my vehicle.

"What a neat building," Kara said, eyeing the unique brick structure and bell tower that now housed the winery.

"They converted an old church into a winery," I said, then gave them a quick tour inside. I watched as the three of them gazed up to the mezzanine and beyond to the vaulted ceiling. While we were there, I purchased four bottles of wine.

"What river is that?" Jamie asked, shading her eyes as she squinted toward the river cutting a path behind the winery. "It's so pretty."

"It's the Dunwith River, and it skirts the whole town. You'll see it again when we get to the brewery at the other end of town." I guided them back to my SUV where I stashed the wine I'd purchased.

The girls peppered me with questions as we walked up to South Park Avenue and began our trek through the center of town.

"Mom, this place looks like a centerfold feature in a resort magazine," Haley said, her gaze taking in everything around us.

The girls were agog at the beauty of the town and delighted by the names of the businesses. When I told them the names were to remind people to protect nature and wildlife, Jamie said it was very forward-thinking of the town.

"More places should do this sort of thing," Haley said.

I agreed with her and adjusted my pace to give the girls time to window shop or pop inside if something caught their eye. It took us an hour to wander three blocks, and I loved every minute of it. We passed the grocery store, and I made a mental note to pick up a few groceries on the way out of town.

When we finally approached my dad's hardware store, I asked the girls to stop. As we lingered outside the large display windows, I told them I wanted them to meet their grandfather. Their eyes widened and my girls seemed speechless. Jamie glanced at me as if she didn't know what was happening.

"Could one of you please open the door?" I asked, indicating they were congregating in front of it.

Jamie reacted first and held it open for us as we entered a place that I would always consider synonymous with my father. The smell of wood and oils and antiquity lingered in the building, and the sound of our footfalls across the hardwood floor whisked me back to the years I spent walking or running across them. It struck me at that moment that I no longer associated the place with my father's affair or the implosion of my family.

"Look at all this great stuff," Haley said, taking in the long rows of shelving loaded with a wide variety of parts and tools and other items. "Is that a camp seat?" she asked, gesturing to a canvas foldout chair.

"I think it's a gardening stool." I slipped my arm around her shoulder. "Come on. Your grandfather is probably in the back." Butterflies flitted through my belly with each step we took toward a meeting that was nineteen long years overdue.

"Can I help you with something?" my dad asked, coming out of the back room. The instant his gaze landed on Kara, his lips compressed, and he didn't, or couldn't, speak. He glanced at me, then back to Kara, then just opened his arms to welcome his granddaughter with a hug.

I could see that Kara was a little taken aback and uncomfortable, but there was also a spark of joy in her eyes. She was meeting her grandfather for the first time in her life, and he greeted her with a hug and all the love his heart could hold.

Holding her at arm's length, he said, "You look just like your mother did at your age." He extended one arm to Haley who moved into his warm, welcoming hug. He tugged Kara back in and held them both for a brief second as his eyes met mine. "Meeting you girls is one of the happiest moments of my life." Releasing them, he turned to Jamie. "And who is this beautiful young lady?"

"She's my girlfriend," Kara said, with warmth and pride in her voice. That she felt free to openly declare her wonderful relationship was a pivotal moment for her and a proud moment for me. My baby was getting stronger and braver.

"Come greet your honorary grandfather," he said, giving Jamie a playful hug that made us all laugh. When he turned her loose, he pulled me into a hard hug and whispered, "Thank you, Katie. *Thank you.*"

My emotions were wobbling like a runaway tire. I told him we were spending the day in town and planned to have lunch at Sophie's café. "I know you're working today and can't join us, but we'd love for you and Sharon to come for dinner tomorrow evening. Say six o'clock?"

He accepted with great joy, then the girls and I headed back out into the September sunshine so they could explore the rest of the town.

"That was ... it was really nice," Kara said. "I've never been able to imagine what he would be like."

To realize my daughter had thought about her grandfather, who was absent in her life because of me, shamed me deeply. But I refused to dwell on it and darken our day with my emotional baggage. I pointed to the store we were approaching. "This place makes the best maple popcorn and chocolates I've ever had. Want to go in?"

"Absolutely," Jamie said, already opening the door.

Haley playfully nudged Kara aside. "Definitely!"

I followed my group of energetic teenagers inside where I spent almost seventy dollars on flavored popcorn and decadent chocolates. "We are definitely having a late lunch, girls."

Happily munching on popcorn, we ambled along as the girls chatted and pointed out things to one another, asking me questions so often I barely ate a handful of popcorn. "Yes, that used to be a church," I said to Kara who seemed a little surprised to see it painted purple, "but it's been converted to a local theater. They host lectures and do improv events and put on full-fledged performances using local actors. Anyone in the community can try out."

"That would be so much fun," she said to Jamie. "Can you imagine being in a play? On stage? In front of a crowd? I'd love it— if I didn't faint from nerves."

Jamie laughed. "You could do it."

"They give acting lessons there," I chimed in to encourage Kara to try anything that interested her.

"It seems odd to see businesses open on a Sunday. Not that I'm complaining," she said, shoveling a handful of popcorn—purchased at one of those open businesses—into her mouth. "Can we cross over to the park?"

This child and her penchant for switching topics in the same breath was about to give my brain a concussion.

We crossed the street and meandered through the park. People of all ages filled the green space, playing lawn shuffleboard, tossing beanbags at boards with holes in them, or throwing Frisbees and balls and engaging in other games. Crowds gathered in multiple areas throughout the park.

"Is there a special event going on today?" Haley asked, taking in the crowds and activities happening around us. The mix of people was so culturally diverse and so intermingled, there were no minorities, no differences, no identity issues here. They were simply people enjoying the day with other people.

"I don't think so," I said. "Seems to be a normal Sunday."

I could see my girls taking in everything around them, from the thriving farmers' market, bins piled high with fresh fruits and veggies, the scent of homemade breads and baked goods wafting through the air, to the craft booths selling everything from hand-crafted jewelry and quilts to clothing and furniture. Art exhibits and artists painting or sketching lined the edge of the park, and a bit farther down was the bandstand where a band was playing.

Jamie popped her arm around Kara's shoulders. "If this is a normal Sunday, I think we should move here."

"Me too," Kara mumbled, still munching popcorn.

"Please do," I said from behind them, giving them both a squeeze because they were so adorable.

A large group of people wearing matching T-shirts that said *Because it's the right thing to do* were standing nearby. Haley asked one of them about their shirts. The young man, who seemed as interested in Haley as she was in his shirt, told her they weren't really a group but more of a response team that helped with things as small as building a wheelchair ramp for someone in need, or as big as traveling across the country to assist with major disasters.

I could see he'd garnered Haley's interest in the response team, and perhaps in him, so I stepped away and took a moment to breathe. It felt as if I hadn't taken a full breath since I'd picked Kara and Jamie up at the airport. I'd forgotten what it was like being in the midst of all that youthful energy. I loved it and I'd missed my girls, but moments like this gave me a deep appreciation for the peaceful solitude of my lakeside home.

After a few minutes, I joined Kara and Jamie at the craft booth and bought them each a bracelet they had been admiring. I knew Haley wouldn't be interested in jewelry but would likely be eager for what was becoming a very late lunch. We would need to grab groceries and head home after we ate because Maggie and Chloe would be coming over in a couple of hours.

As we crossed the street to Sophie's café, Haley shook her head as if utterly bewildered. "This is one unusual and totally amazing town."

Chapter Forty-Six

Neither Sophie nor Jessica had been at the café, so I'd called Sophie on our way home and invited her and the kids to dinner tomorrow night. There was a brief hesitation at her end, so I quickly added that our father and Sharon would be coming over too—and that my girls were here visiting and would like to meet her.

She said she'd be over with Jessica, but the boys would be with their father. I felt a little crestfallen that she hadn't yet introduced me to my nephews but reminded myself we were making progress, even if it was only in baby steps.

I'd just finished putting the groceries away and had gone outside to sit on the loveseat and relax with the girls when Chloe pulled in. Dylan followed her out of the vehicle, and the two of them walked over. Like a gentleman, Dylan expressed his pleasure at meeting the girls as he shook their hands, and Chloe nearly hugged the life out of them, including Jamie who was quickly learning to expect the same treatment.

Standing beneath the awning, we chatted for a couple minutes before Haley asked if anyone wanted to walk around the lake. Dylan and the girls readily agreed, and off they went. Left alone,

Chloe and I watched them head to the shore, then she sank onto a chair and released a big breath.

"Now I understand how you felt when you met Dylan for the first time. Wow ..." She swallowed hard. "It was tough to hold it together, but I didn't want to scare them off by blubbering on their shoulders."

I laughed. "Why not? That's what I did with Dylan."

"And he survived it just fine. I think I've desensitized him to women weeping on his shoulder." She glanced toward the lake where Dylan and the girls were peering into a cluster of reeds. "Your daughters are so lovely, Kate. To see our kids spending time together here at the lake is ... wonderful."

It was beyond wonderful, but words fall short when feelings are so big.

For a few minutes we watched our kids goofing around by the lake as they got to know each other. Dylan, who'd acted a bit uncomfortable about meeting the girls, seemed to be enjoying himself now, talking and gesturing to something in the water.

Leaving them to their youthful curiosity and conversation, Chloe and I settled in to wait for Maggie. I poured each of us a glass of wine and brought the bottle and an extra glass back outdoors with me.

"Did you get your divorce papers yet?" she asked.

I shook my head because there was nothing else to say.

"What will you do if he doesn't grant you a divorce."

"The only thing I *can* do ... take him to court." But the thought of an expensive, drawn-out court battle filled me with dread. Releasing a tired sigh, I dropped my forehead into my hand. "Why can't he just give me a freaking divorce?"

"You wouldn't need one if you shot him."

I snorted and looked at Chloe. "Now that's something I'd expect Maggie to say."

She shrugged. "What can I say? She's a bad influence on both of us."

The bad influence made her appearance ten minutes later,

looking around as if she'd lost something. "Where are my nieces?" she asked.

"With your nephew and Kara's girlfriend." I pointed to the far side of the lake where the kids were milling about, stepping over fallen tree trunks and kicking through the tall grass. My grandfather had only ever groomed this side of the lake, saying the other side was for wildlife, not us. And so that's how I intended to leave it.

"How's everything going?" she asked as she sat across from me.

I poured a glass of wine for her and topped off my and Chloe's glasses. I told them about my conversations with my girls, and how bittersweet it had been to witness them meeting their grandfather for the first time, and how the girls had fallen in love with our town.

"Sounds like a wonderful, productive couple of days," Maggie said. "Are you divorced yet?"

"Ugh! I can't go there right now."

"She really can't," Chloe said.

"Okay then, how do you like your sleeper sofa?" she asked, making me laugh.

"Maggie, if I didn't know better, I'd say Kara was your kid. The way you two topic hop makes my brain feel like a marble in a pinball machine. Zing! Zing! Zing!" I took a sip of wine, taking a few seconds to gather my thoughts. "To answer your question, the mattress is divine."

She wiggled her eyebrows. "Is it as nice as my brother's mattress?"

My heart thumped, and I looked around to see if my girls were within earshot. They were making their way around the west edge of the lake.

Maggie's laughter rang out. "I've been watching them the whole time we've been talking," she said. "You know I wouldn't drop a bomb like that in front of your girls."

I looked at Chloe. "Punch her."

And so it went until the kids returned and introductions were made. "These two crazy women are your honorary aunts," I told my girls. "Try to like them, because it appears we're stuck with them."

The kids laughed and settled in for an evening of joking and talking with the old people.

Monday evening wasn't as relaxed with my father and Sophie, but we'd made our way through supper as gently as possible, navigating around the landmines as best we could.

Despite Sophie's genuinely warm welcome to my girls and Jamie, and her pleasantness throughout the evening, there was an undercurrent of unease.

Jessica had been a little enamored with her older cousins. But my girls, who'd been encapsulated in the bubble of Christendom, were just as taken with Jessica who'd lived her whole life out in the world. Jamie seemed the most balanced and mature of all of them not only because of her age but because she was extremely bright and had been raised in a home with intelligent, empathetic parents who'd encouraged her to explore the world around her with curiosity and an open mind.

As soon as we'd finished our meal, the four girls had quickly taken themselves down to the dock to presumably escape the tension inside and have a girl-gab.

Left alone with Sophie and our father and stepmother, I'd taken a moment to thank them for coming over and for being so kind to the girls. They'd acknowledge my thanks with *of course* and *we wouldn't miss it,* but I'd needed to let them know how much their presence and their kindness to my daughters meant to me.

Baby steps. Acknowledgments. Thank you. And maybe someday, I love you.

As much as I'd relished having my family together again and seeing my girls hanging out with my niece, I was relieved when Sophie and my dad left.

After the girls and I cleaned up dishes, we pulled on sweatshirts and sat outside around a campfire. The nights were growing cool, foreshadowing the change of season. In some ways it seemed I'd been here forever, that I'd left my spirit sleeping on shore, and it hadn't woken up until my body returned all these years later.

"Hey, Mom? Can I ask you something?"

I looked over at Haley who'd spoken to me. She was nested down in her chair with one foot parked on the edge of her seat and one arm draped over her up-drawn knee.

"Of course, you can ask me anything," I said.

"What happened to you and your family?"

It felt as if I'd just flown over a speed bump and landed with a jarring thump in my chair. It's not that I hadn't expected my girls to ask the question; I just hadn't expected it to throw me so off center.

"How honest do you want me to be?" I asked, trying to get my wheels under me again. "It's not a pretty story, and certainly not a good reflection on me."

Kara wrinkled her nose as if offended. "Mom, in case you haven't noticed, we're not ten years old. I think we can handle it."

In my mind, where memories of my daughters lived, they would always be babies and toddlers and adolescents and these beautiful nineteen-year-old girls who continued to amaze me. Kara was right though. They were intelligent young adults now who could handle the subject matter. And this was an opportunity for me to share my story and hopefully teach them something important about life.

"Before I begin, I need you girls to really listen and withhold judgment until you've heard the whole story. It took me more than two decades and years of heartache to learn that judgment closes doors, ends discussions, and destroys relationships."

They all nodded their agreement as if afraid to interrupt me.

"Okay," I said, puffing out a breath to steady myself. "The first thing you need to know is it was mostly my fault."

Surprise, and a bit of disappointment, crossed their fire-lit faces.

I didn't know how to wade in gracefully, so I dove in and took them with me. Deeper and deeper we went as I took them into the depths of my family's troubles. We slogged through swamps filled with tears and regret, and wiped our eyes over losing my mom and their grandmother who would have adored them. They gasped in shock over harsh words exchanged in anger by me ... and with resentment by Sophie. In the shadowed depths, I shared my journey through Christendom and how what I'd thought would save me had only caged me behind church doors. Like moving through seagrass, I took them gently through the demise of my relationship with their father so they could understand that paths sometimes diverge, and a person must go their own way. I held their hands and told them about returning to my childhood home and learning the truth about my father and mother. I admitted that reconciliation was a slow process of forgiving and healing and moving forward—that it could be arduous and painful, but if you just kept going, one discussion at a time, it was a deeply rewarding journey.

Finally, I dragged in a hard breath and sagged in my chair, completely wrung out. Tears sparkled on Kara's lashes. Jamie's expression was filled with empathy as she slipped her hand over Kara's. But Haley looked deep in thought. For a moment no one spoke, and I worried I said too much, that I'd overestimated their emotional maturity and ability to understand the mistakes, decisions, and nuances that had made up my life.

"Mom, do you think we could meet our step-aunt and uncles? And cousins?" Haley asked softly. "It's kind of amazing to discover we have this whole other side to our family."

I sure hadn't expected that to be the first comment from any of them, but it hit me right in the heart. Pushing to my feet, I pulled my daughters from their chairs and held them tight. "How about a big family party before you girls leave?" I asked, easing back so I could see their faces.

"That would be really nice," Haley said while Kara answered with a happy nod.

"I want to walk you around the property tomorrow and show you where your aunt Sophie and I grew up. And I want to take you to Lake Placid and White Face Mountain the day after tomorrow." I knew my nature girl would love hiking the property and exploring White Face, but to appeal to Kara and Jamie, I added, "There are lots of great shops in Lake Placid you girls will love. Sound good?"

Smiles blossomed on my girls' faces, similar like twins and yet so individually their own.

"This is turning out to be a perfect vacation," Haley said with enthusiasm.

"We're in." Kara cast a glance at Jamie and received a happy nod.

I expected the questions to begin after we sat again, but all I could hear were the night peepers and crackling fire and the lake lapping at the shoreline.

Finally, Kara looked over at me. "Do you have any marsh-mallows?"

Chapter Forty-Seven

The girls and I packed a picnic lunch and set out for a day of exploring my childhood home. As we walked the trails that wound through the forest and along stream banks, I told them about my parents and grandparents and the lessons they'd each taught me about the land and wildlife that lived here.

As the path widened, I circled my arms around my daughters' shoulders, Kara's strong and slender, Haley's muscled and toned. "I'm sorry for not giving you girls the opportunity to grow up here."

"That would have been amazing," Haley said as I released them at a narrow juncture in the trail. "I've already fallen in love with what I've seen of the Adirondacks, and I feel at home on these trails."

"Is this what your hike was like?" Kara asked, stepping over a small limb that crossed her path.

"Kind of. It depends on what part of the trail you hike. Grasslands are level and easy to hike through. Mountain inclines are another thing altogether. Especially if the terrain is rocky or heavily wooded. Then you'd better put on your big girl boots."

"How far did you hike?" Jamie asked, her hair pulled back in a long braid that nested between her shoulder blades. She was slender like Kara but more athletic and seemed to be enjoying our hike.

"Just over three hundred and fifty miles," Haley said nonchalantly.

We exchanged incredulous looks with each other as she continued to take in the scenery with a keen eye.

"I literally can't imagine that," Kara said, taking the words out of my mouth. "Didn't you get tired?"

Haley grinned at her sister. "Yes, but you're allowed to take breaks."

"Did you get bored just walking every day?"

Haley stopped and looked at Kara as if she'd just said the dumbest thing in the world. "Look around you." Haley swept her arm out to encompass the towering conifers and the innumerable creatures scampering and twittering around us. "Everywhere you look there's something to see. It was incredible to be out there day after day in the middle of nowhere with all of this"—again she gestured around us—"and to just listen and take it all in. It was ... majestic."

"It does sound beautiful," Kara said softly as if a little hypnotized by Haley's description. "But I absolutely could not sleep outside under the stars with all those wild animals roving the forest and snakes looking for a warm place to nest." She shuddered. "Nope. I'm pretty sure you're crazy."

"You're hopeless." Haley palmed Kara's face and pushed her to get her moving again. "Come on. I want to get to the picnic area. I'm starving."

Laughing, we made our way to a clearing near a wide section of the stream that snaked across my property. After spreading a blanket on the grass, we opened Haley's backpack and devoured our sandwiches.

As the girls talked about school and the things that were important to them at this point in their lives, I leaned back on my hands and listened with a warm sense of pride. They were all smart young women engrossed in meaningful conversation about life and their futures. Their conversation was thought-provoking as they deeply considered their options and their passions as they stepped fully into the world of adulthood. The sun peeped in and out of puffy white clouds, casting light and shadows over us as we lingered in a place I loved. The girls' youthful laughter tumbled over the stream bank and burbled over rocks as it floated downstream. I imagined Sophie and I had sounded like that when we were girls. And now my girls were here adding their voices to nature's song.

As their conversation wound down and we finished eating, the girls were ready to move on. We deposited our empty bottles into Haley's backpack, and finished our hike, exiting the forest on the east side of the lake.

"It's going to be hard to leave this place," Haley said as we approached my house.

My first instinct was to tell her to stay, but I swallowed my words. She needed to experience the world, not stay tucked under my wing. And I needed to continue my own journey.

But Haley continued to fall in love with the Adirondacks as we explored Lake Placid and White Face Mountain the following day.

We ambled along the sidewalks all morning browsing in shops selling Adirondack memorabilia. I bought the girls hoodies and a big lunch, then we explored White Face Mountain where Haley met a small group of people wearing orange vests crouched in ditches doing something we couldn't see. By the end of the day I was exhausted but filled to the brim with joy. The girls wanted to go back the following day, but I bowed out. As much as I was enjoying their visit, I was glad they were eager to explore on their own. I needed a couple of hours to handle some things in town.

AFTER A LATE BREAKFAST, the girls headed out. I spent a few minutes brushing and cuddling Sinatra, then I drove to town to do the one thing I should have done long ago.

Ninety minutes later, as I was coming out of my attorney's office, I saw Ashe tucking a note under the windshield wiper of my vehicle.

"Vandalism is a crime, you know," I said, coming up behind him.

He turned with a smile on his face. "Guilty and willing to pay the fine."

"It could be a big bill," I said, wondering how he could look that good in work clothes and a ball cap. But he did. *Really* good.

Plucking the note from under the wiper, he handed it to me. "I wrote it in code in case your daughters found it."

"What?" Glancing at the folded paper, I wondered what could be so risqué he'd have to write it in code. "Will I need a cypher to decode this?"

"Nope, just a sense of humor."

Intrigued, I opened the paper. He'd sketched a pair of cowboy boots, a guitar, two hands with their fingers interlaced, and had written the words *Friday with A*. Laughing at his boyish code and surprisingly nice sketching, I asked, "Is this an invitation to go dancing with you Friday night?"

A lazy grin lingered on his lips as his gaze tangled with mine. "I knew you'd get it."

His offer of a night of dancing, and more, was tempting, but I had to pass. "Thanks for the creative invitation, but my girls aren't leaving until Sunday."

"Ah, didn't know that." He braced one hand on the hood of my vehicle and hooked the thumb of his other hand in his front pocket. "Does that mean you'll be free Sunday night?"

"Even if I am, I'm sure I'll be too exhausted to even pull on my slippers, much less my cowboy boots."

"I'd make an exception this one time and take you out in your sneakers."

"Wow," I said with a laugh. "As tempting as that is, I have to pass. But just so you don't feel rejected, I'm having a picnic on

Saturday so my girls can spend some time with everybody before they leave. You're welcome to come."

His expression sobered a little. "I appreciate the invite, but if it's a family thing I'm not going to intrude."

"It's not just for family." Maggie and Chloe are coming. They're my friends, and as it turns out, so are you."

"Wow, I finally made the friends list," he said, pretending to be deeply honored.

I gave his boot a nudge with my shoe. "Stop hassling me. I already told you we're friends. Are you coming to the picnic or not?"

"Sure," he said, "but I have to say your invitation was a lot less creative than mine."

I mimed eating off a plate, pointed at him, and gestured for him to come over. "Are you happy now?"

"You need to work on that, but yeah, I'll be there. What do you want me to bring?"

Just your gorgeous self, I thought, but told him I had everything covered. "You can bring swim shorts and a towel if you want to go swimming. Otherwise, nothing."

"Got it." His warm gaze held me captive. "So, what are you doing in town other than harassing men on the street?"

"Harassing men via the mail, courtesy of my attorney," I replied, feeling a huge sense of relief that my attorney would overnight a final notice to Dan stating *sign it or your wife is coming after every-thing she's entitled to under spousal law*. She'd also reminded him *again* that we would be digging deep into his finances should he choose to ignore the deadline or fight the agreement.

"Good for you," Ashe said, but he didn't pry. "Got time for a cup of coffee?"

"Considering the last time you offered me coffee, and we defi-nitely did *not* have coffee, I'll have to take a raincheck."

His eyebrows lifted. "Rain check? As in you might have coffee with me again?"

Count on it, my body said, but I merely smiled. "I need to go grocery shopping if you'll ever let me get in my vehicle."

AT HOME, I was just putting the last of my groceries away when Sophie knocked on my door. I'd heard the ping on my phone alerting me that someone had passed through the gate, but I'd thought it was just the girls coming home and hadn't bothered to check.

"Got a minute?" she asked, waiting for me to invite her in.

"Of course." I swung the door wide for her to come inside. "I was actually about to call you."

Her eyebrows lifted in surprise. "You were?"

"Yes," I said, moving a loaf of bread from my small kitchen island to the counter. "I'm having a picnic on Saturday so the girls can spend some time with our family. Dad and Sharon are coming. Beth and Gary will be here with their kids. Chloe and Maggie are coming. And I'm hoping you and the kids will come too." Releasing a sigh, I leaned against the counter. "Soph, please come. I'd really like to meet my nephews."

"That's actually why I stopped by," she said, sitting on one of the kitchen stools. She was dressed in jeans and a white shirt, with her hair pulled up and clipped in the back. "I'd intended to bring the boys to supper the other night," she said, sincerity in her eyes, "but it was their night with their father, and he was being obstinate about letting me have them. I offered to pick them up and drop them back off after supper, but Mark said he had other plans for them."

"Thanks for telling me, Soph. I thought you didn't want them to meet me."

"At first, I didn't. We were struggling to work through our stuff, I wanted to make sure you were going to stay here before I let them meet you. You'd already met Jessica, and she's old enough to understand things, so I didn't worry about her. But the boys are only eleven and thirteen and they don't need more drama. They get enough of that from their father."

"I understand."

"Kate, I wanted you to know this so you don't think I'm being a resentful ass. Not that I haven't been," she said with a wry grin.

"You were justified," I said.

She didn't acknowledge my comment. "Anyway, that's why I wasn't the best company the other night. I was pissed at Mark, not at you."

"Does that mean you're not pissed at me anymore?"

She released a soft laugh. "I still am a little bit. Depends on where my mind goes, but for the most part, we're good."

My heart skipped and filled with hope. "Good? As in, we can go back to being sisters again?"

Her smile faded. "We can't go back, Kate. It's not possible. But we're good."

"Good is the first step to better," I said. "Got time for a cup of coffee?"

"I have to get back to the café," she said, standing up. Glancing around, she said, "Papa Ray would be proud of what you've done to his old boathouse." Before I could comment, she peered through the windows. "Where are the girls?"

"Exploring Lake Placid. I took them yesterday, and they enjoyed it so much they went back today."

She seemed a little disappointed to have missed them. "They are sweet girls, Kate. It hurts to have missed watching them grow up, and that's the part of me that's still a little pissed at you," she said. "But I'm glad they're here now."

"Me too," I said quietly, not wanting to ruin the moment. "I'd really like to meet your boys, Soph, while the girls are here. Any chance you could stop back tonight?"

"I can't," she said. "I have to close the café." A moment of silence hung between us as she walked to the door. Then she stopped with her hand on the door handle. "Have you taken your girls to the Wild Center?"

"Not yet. I thought we might go on Friday. I've never been because—" I didn't finish the sentence because we both knew the answer. Because the Wild Center had been established during the years I'd been away.

"I can't go Friday," she said, "but if you can go tomorrow afternoon around three o'clock, after I pick up the boys, we could meet you there."

My knees got a little wobbly. "Really?"

"Order your tickets online, and we'll see you tomorrow," she said, then slipped outside and was gone.

Chapter Forty-Eight

We were waiting in the parking lot at the Wild Center when Sophie's SUV pulled in. Anticipation and excitement made me shaky. Sophie was extending a good bit of trust in me, and I didn't want to make a misstep of any kind. I warned myself not to be a weepy basket case. *Don't smother them. Take your cues from Sophie.*

As warnings swirled in my head, Sophie and her kids climbed out of her vehicle and headed our way. Jessica led the way with a big smile. "Hi, Aunt Kate," she said, giving me a hug, then exchanging hugs with Jamie and my girls, all of them having become fast friends.

The boys approached with their mom. Nicolas, her thirteen-year-old who was nearly Sophie's height, was the image of his father with his dark hair and dark eyes, and I knew he would become a handsome man when he passed through the awkward stage of puberty. Chris, her eleven-year-old, was still every bit a boy and cute as a button with Sophie's blonde hair and blue eyes.

"Say hello to your Aunt Kate," Sophie said, gesturing toward me as she spoke to her boys.

Nicolas extended his hand as if to shake mine, but I simply could not greet my nephew with an impersonal handshake. I pulled him into a warm hug and told him how happy I was to finally meet him. When I released him, his face was flaming red. I'd forgotten how emasculating things like this were to boys his age. But he got no mercy from my girls or Jamie who smothered him with welcoming hugs. Although he continued to flush, he didn't seem to mind those hugs at all. Sophie and I exchanged a knowing smile.

"Hi, Aunt Kate," Christopher said, having no qualms about hugging a woman and three girls he didn't know. "Can we go in now?" he asked, gazing up at his mother with eager eyes.

The eight of us made our way to the entrance path and walked to the Hall of the Adirondacks where we spent nearly two hours looking in giant tanks of water filled with a myriad of fish and gazing through glass display windows at turtles and innumerable species of amphibians, reptiles, insects, and birds that made their home in this part of the world.

The thing we were most taken with was the Otter Falls exhibit. Otters were the absolute cutest creatures on earth. Two of the otters put on a hilarious display, sliding down rocks and landing in a large pool of water with a big splash, then chasing each other back up and around the rock feature to do their slippery slide into the pool again. They swam up to the window, pressing their wide noses and whiskered chins against the glass, making us laugh.

"I want one of those, Mom!" Christopher said. "Can we get one?"

Sophie moaned and we all laughed, but I silently vowed to make a nice yearly donation and help support this amazing animal refuge. "Let's head outside," she said, guiding him out the main door.

We all followed along and found ourselves on a wide path covered in pine needles and mulch. Slowly, we wandered through a forest of towering trees beginning to turn shades of red and gold. We spent a few minutes looking for fish in a trout-filled pond topped with fading water lilies, then continued into a forested area where the world seemed to disappear. The sound of kettle drums boomed around us and held us still and silent. A hollow boom sounded in front of us ... then to our left ... then from behind, the vibrations moving through our bodies and anchoring us in a place of enchantment. Soft strains of a violin and another string instrument I didn't recognize mingled with the kettle drums, the music drifting through the trees as if the forest were releasing a breath, saying, *ahh ... relax ... you're safe here.*

"Mom," Haley whispered, "this place reminds me of the story you started writing when we were little. You should finish writing that book. It was really good."

Sophie, who was standing close enough to hear Haley, looked at me in surprise. "You're writing a book?" she asked, appearing genuinely intrigued.

I started to say I was trying to write one, but I was *doing* it, and I intended to finish it. "Yes, but I've got a long way to go. I haven't finished a full draft, yet, and I'm not published so ..." I shrugged. "Not sure that qualifies me as a writer."

"You're writing and working on a project. I'd say that's the definition of a writer."

"Perhaps," I said with a smile. "Your café is a work of art, Sophie, but what do you do with your off hours? Do you still sing?" At her surprised look, I said, "Jessica mentioned it."

A melancholy smile tipped her lips. "Only in the shower. Between the café and kids, the only thing I want to do when I have a minute to myself is sleep or read a good book in the bathtub."

"I remember those days well. If you ever want a break, I'm available. I think the boys would love hanging out at the lake."

Her gaze shifted to the kids who were walking some distance ahead of us.

"Jessica said you took her to the lake once before I came back," I said.

Sophie's expression darkened. "It was the day I finished cleaning out the stuff at Grandma Jean's house. I'm sorry I didn't ask what you wanted to do with Grandma's stuff. I was too angry to try to track you down. And I didn't want all that stuff sitting in an empty house just waiting to be vandalized, so I moved some of her furniture and things to the café, and I donated the rest to the Eagle's Nest. Beth made good use of the linens, dishes, pans, and such. But Kate, if you want anything back, just let me know."

"What I want is to kick myself for being such a self-centered ass and leaving all that on your shoulders. I'm sorry, Soph ... really, truly sorry about everything."

She nodded and gazed out across the forest treetops.

"Soph, when you were cleaning things out, did you by chance come across Papa Ray's ashes? I promised Grandma Jean I'd mix their ashes and spread them around the lake, but I don't know what happened to his urn."

She cringed a little. "I found the urn when I cleaned out the house. I considered sprinkling his ashes in the lake, but it didn't feel right without having Grandma's ashes too. I put the urn aside and forgot about it until just now."

"Maybe we could do it together," I said softly.

She said nothing, just stared into the distance as if she were seeing into the past, perhaps seeing them as they used to be.

My phone rang, startling us. When I glanced at the screen and saw it was my attorney's number, my belly swirled with hope, then clenched with dread. "I have to take this," I said, then took a deep breath and answered.

By the time my attorney finished talking, I could not breathe. My hands shook so badly I had to swipe the screen three times to end the call.

Sophie's forehead creased with concern. "Is everything okay?"

My heart pounded so hard I was lightheaded. I teetered on my feet, and Sophie caught my arm to steady me.

"Did something happen?" she asked.

A surge of emotion clogged my throat, and tears blurred my vision. I clapped a hand over my mouth to stop a sob, but it broke through like a storm-filled river bursting through a dam.

"What the hell's happening?" Sophie asked, jiggling my elbow.

For a moment, all I could do was weep. Deep, gulping sobs

wracked my shoulders, embarrassing me, but I could not hold them back.

Cupping my shoulders, Sophie turned my back to the beach where our children were exploring. "Kate, you're scaring me. What's wrong?"

"Dan signed the p-papers," I blubbered.

Her brows creased, and she asked, "Are you talking about your divorce papers?"

Nodding, I wiped my cheeks, but tears continued to stream over my fingers.

"I thought that would be a good thing," she said.

"It is ... it's just ... I'm relieved and overwhelmed." I sniffed and dragged my arm across my eyes. "I've felt like an escapee being hunted and hounded since leaving Dan. But I'm finally free, Soph."

"Jesus, Kate, I'm so sorry."

"So am I, Soph." I dried my eyes and wiped my cheeks. "Will you please bring the kids to my picnic on Saturday," I said, my voice wobbling, my eyes still watering.

Her gaze shifted toward the river where our kids were watching a tour guide dock a canoe. Any awkwardness our kids had felt upon meeting each other seemed to have disappeared during our walk, and they were talking and gesturing and hanging out as if they'd known each other forever.

"Okay," she said softly. "Other than Papa Ray's ashes, what would you like me to bring?"

Chapter Forty-Nine

S ophie had texted that she would come over early so we could spread our grandparents' ashes before the picnic. She showed up with three fruit pies, four lifejackets, and Papa Ray's ashes. "Ready to do this?" she asked.

I was. This day had been a long time coming—and was painfully overdue.

We didn't mix the ashes, and we didn't go alone. We walked around the lake as a family, each of us scooping ashes into our hands and letting them sift through our fingers to fall along the shoreline where our grandparents were finally laid to rest on the land they loved.

"I thought the kids might not want to touch the ashes, but it seems to be their way to connect with their grandparents," Sophie said, a tenderness in her voice I hadn't heard since our teens. "Do you remember all those walks we took with them?"

"Those were great walks," I said with fondness. "I'll never forget them."

"What'd you guys do on your walks?" Christopher asked, squatting down to rinse his hands in the lake.

"Well, we climbed trees and made forts out of fallen pine

branches," Sophie said. "We made a raft once out of balloons and sticks—"

"Did it work?" Christopher asked, his eyes wide with interest.

"No, and don't ever try something that stupid," Sophie cautioned. "We did some dumb things, but that doesn't mean you should do them."

"We did," I said in agreement. "We spent hours one day sneaking through the woods, trying to catch a deer so we could ride on its back."

Christopher released a boyish giggle, and I heard the girls laugh. Nicolas rolled his eyes because he was at the age where his parents were dumb.

"Did ya ever catch one?" Christopher asked, wiping his wet hands on his jeans.

"Our grandpa almost did," Sophie said with a wink to the girls. Then, to my surprise, she told the kids about our grandparents and the wonderful life they gave us and how much they would have loved taking walks like this with their great-grandchildren. "Thank you for helping us spread your grandparents' ashes," she said to all of them. "It would have meant the world to them, and it means a lot to me."

"Me too," I added as I stepped over a thick clump of mud and grass. We had made a complete circuit around the lake, so I released the last handful of ashes into the weave of grass and earth along the shore. "That's it," I said. We all stopped to rinse our hands in the lake. "Soph, should we say something? Like a eulogy?"

A relaxed smile tipped her lips. "I think we just did."

She was right. We'd told our children about their grandparents, and had spread their ashes as a family, and had celebrated the moment with love and stories rather than grief. Had I tried to do this years ago, it would have been alone with an ocean of tears and bone-deep regret.

As we turned toward the house, a dreamy look crossed Christopher's face. "It would be awesome to ride a deer."

"Sure would," I said, pulling him in for a hug because I simply could not help myself.

***

"GRANDPA'S HERE." Kara pointed toward the lake trail where his vehicle was coming out of the wooded path.

"Will you kids go help him unload and set up the tables please?"

As a group, they headed to my father's parked truck where they were met with his hearty laugh and warm hugs. Sophie and I received our own from him and Sharon.

"How's the SUV running?" he asked me as the kids began pulling tables from his pickup bed.

"Great. I love it."

"That's quite the sign you have out front," he said with an amused grin on his face.

"Yeah, I was having a moment." I pointed toward a shaded spot in the yard. "You can put the tables over there."

From that point on, my house and yard buzzed with activity. Beth and Gary and their children rolled in next, then Chloe and Dylan, then Maggie and Ashe who had come together. I introduced my girls and Jamie to their Grandma Sharon, and their Aunt Beth and Uncle Gary and their cousins Abby, Ethan, and Ava, then left them to visit and get to know one another.

I found Ashe talking with my dad, the two of them leaning against his truck.

The instant Ashe's dark eyes met mine, I felt the familiar swirl of heat in my belly. "If you have a minute, Ashe, I'd like to introduce you to my daughters," I said.

He pushed off the truck. "Of course. Looking forward to it."

I wanted my girls to meet Ashe in the midst of the many introductions they were making, so they didn't focus on him. But they did. They smiled and shook his hand and said it was a pleasure to meet him, while giving me side-eyed glances that said *Wow*!

"And you girls already know everyone else," I said with relief, "so I'm going to start bringing the food out."

"I'll give you a hand," Ashe said, and several others chimed in with offers to cart food out of my kitchen.

By the time I'd reached the door, I felt like a mama duck with twelve chicks on her tail. "Two or three helping hands will be more than enough," I said with a laugh. "Maggie and Ashe can help. The rest of you go enjoy yourselves."

Inside, I collapsed back against my kitchen counter, wishing I could be like Sinatra and hide in the loft or scoot out the back door and take refuge in the woods. "I need a drink."

Ashe grinned as if he enjoyed seeing me flustered. "I brought beer."

"I brought wine," Maggie added. "Pick your poison."

"Wine. I don't trust myself with beer."

She poked Ashe in the ribs. "I don't think I ever told you about our first girl gab with Kate—"

"And you're not going to," I said, shoving a veggie tray in her hands. "Take this out and don't come back."

She laughed all the way out the door.

"Told you she was a pain in the ass," Ashe said, standing staunchly behind his sister like any good brother would do.

Laughter and chatter came from outside, but we were alone in the kitchen. "I have something for you." I slipped my hand into the front pocket of my jeans and pulled out a folded piece of paper.

He unfolded it and his eyes widened. He glanced between me and the note twice before he spoke. "Is this what I think it is?"

"It is if you think it's an invitation."

A slow grin climbed his cheek. "And a very creative one," he said, glancing back at the note where I'd drawn a pair of cowboy boots, a coffee cup, and the word *Monday?*

"Does this mean coffee? Or *coffee?*"

"Depends on how the evening goes."

He blew out his breath. "Damn, this is all I'll be able to think about for the rest of the day."

"That's why I gave it to you now," I said, passing him a fruit tray. "Take this out, and please don't come back in."

He laughed and leaned in, putting his lips close to mine. "You know the saying, Kate. *If you can't take the heat ...*"

"Out," I said, shooing him with my hand. "Send my girls in to help."

I thought it would be a good idea to have my girls helping while I regained my equilibrium, but they just added fuel to my fire.

"Ashe is a very handsome man," Kara said.

"And you're a beautiful girl." I tweaked her cheek to shut her up. "Take this casserole outside."

As I passed a large bowl of tortellini salad to Haley, she gave me a knowing look. "For a mild day, it's pretty hot in this kitchen. Maybe you should open a window."

"And maybe you should close your mouth," I said, kissing her on the forehead and nudging her toward the door.

After we ate, the activities began in earnest. The kids threw Frisbee and paddled around the lake in the canoes, then came back and devoured a table full of desserts. I visited with my family and my friends, our topics of conversation bouncing between us like a volleyball. Seeing Sophie in this setting where she was completely at ease with everyone and seemed to be enjoying herself was wonderful. As the afternoon leaned toward evening, our laughter grew more robust.

Someone turned the music up, and I thought the kids were messing around with the tablet Dylan had paired with his Bluetooth speaker. But it was Chloe who stood by the tablet. With a smile on her face, she said, "Let the dance-off begin." She wiggled her eyebrows at me. "Are you game?"

Laughter bubbled up in my chest, and I rose to my feet. "Absolutely."

"On your feet people," Chloe said. "The rules state that everybody has to dance."

Moans and groans and laughter rolled through the yard. But to see Chloe, a woman who could barely get out of bed a few months ago, standing strong with half her heart missing was so damn admirable, every one of us stood to support her.

As the music kicked in and the volume went up, the younger kids got silly and made us laugh, then the older kids joined the mix. The adults were standing but not fully engaged, so the girls and Dylan pulled them into what was becoming a crush of people dancing across the grass. Soon we were all singing *Sweet Caroline*.

As if time suddenly slowed to a crawl, I took a moment to absorb everything ... the beautiful home I'd built using duct tape and shoelaces and the helping hands of my friends, the beloved and growing family I'd reconnected with, the joy my daughters were exhibiting as they danced and embraced their first moments of real freedom, the sound of laughter and music floating across the lake as it had during my youth when my family had been whole, Chloe and Maggie who were in my life again, strong, steady, and inseparable, and Ashe, a man who could be my friend and lover while respecting and supporting my freedom, and my sweet Sinatra, who had befriended me in my darkest, loneliest hours, who was safe and loved and had a forever home.

And there was Sophie, my beautiful little sister who was dancing beside me. As I looked at the amazing woman she had become, I pulled her into a hard hug.

For the first time since I was nineteen years old, my sister hugged me back. My heart soared into the blue sky above, spreading its wings to glide over the land and people I loved so deeply. Sophie and I were *good*—and getting better.

And I was finally, truly home.

Also by Wendy Lindstrom

Captured by Your Love

Until I Found You

About Wendy Lindstrom

Wendy Lindstrom is the RITA award-winning and *New York Times* bestselling author of the Grayson family saga, a captivating series of feel-good, emotionally powerful novels. Her books are unforgettable, heartwarming stories about enduring friendships, family bonds, and romantic relationships between strong, complex characters living in a charming small town in America.

Fans of uplifting, binge-worthy historical romance will love Miss Lindstrom's popular Grayson family series, a #1 storewide best-seller on Barnes and Noble, and a *New York Times* and *USA Today* bestselling series. Romantic Times has dubbed her "one of romance's finest writers," and readers rave about her enthralling characters and the "awesome underlying emotional power" of her work. The Grayson Brothers series is a must-read for those who love stories that uplift and warm the heart.

For more information about the author, her books, and to get the behind-the-scenes scoop at her Rustic Studio—a world much like the Grayson world—visit her website and also subscribe to her engaging newsletter where she shares personal stories about the magnificent wildlife at her Rustic Studio, her insights on writing, her tiny house obsession, landscaping her beautiful water-garden, her passion for great books, her love of martial arts, and other fun subjects.

You can also follow her on BookBub.

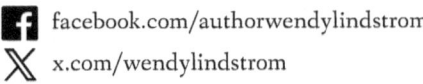

facebook.com/authorwendylindstrom

x.com/wendylindstrom